DESPERATE

<u>BOOKS BY MILLIE CRISWELL</u>

Flowers of the West Trilogy
Wild Heather
Sweet Laurel
Prim Rose

PUBLISHED BY
WARNER BOOKS

MILLIE CRISWELL

DESPERATE

WARNER BOOKS

A Time Warner Company

To my wonderful, wise, and witty agent, Meg Ruley, who
inspires, encourages, and makes me laugh.
Thanks for everything.

WARNER BOOKS EDITION

Copyright © 1997 by Millie Criswell
All rights reserved.

Cover design by Diane Luger
Hand lettering by Carl Dellacroce
Cover art by Ron Broda

Warner Books, Inc.
1271 Avenue of the Americas
New York, NY 10020

Visit our Web site at
http://pathfinder.com/twep

Ⓦ A Time Warner Company

Printed in the United States of America

First Printing: July, 1997

10 9 8 7 6 5 4 3 2 1

Chapter One

THE GNAWING IN RAFE BODINE'S BELLY AND THE position of the setting sun told the ex-Ranger that suppertime was at hand. It took a lot of food to fill his six-foot, three-inch frame, and the considerable improvement in his wife's cooking over the past three months made him eager to reach their small house.

Ellie had made the cabin a real home—a welcome retreat. Sweet-scented wildflowers graced the center of the rough-hewn kitchen table, and blue gingham curtains hung crisply at the windows. She had even fashioned a handsome starburst-pattern quilt for their bed.

Rafe's impulsive decision to marry his best friend and neighbor was working out after all. Despite niggling doubts about quitting the Rangers, and his brother Ethan's repeated warnings that marrying Ellie would be like marrying his own sister, Rafe felt confident that he'd made the right decision.

He loved Ellie in his own special way. It wasn't an all-consuming, hearts-on-fire, romantic kind of love that young girls were prone to dream about, but a genuine, caring, dependable kind of love—one that promised contentment and friendship. That was more than most couples shared in their lifetime.

And now there would be a baby to cement their relationship, to bring them even closer together.

He'd been stunned last night when Ellie had revealed the news of her pregnancy. But now that he'd had time to ponder things, the idea of becoming a father wasn't nearly as frightening. In fact, he was growing downright comfortable with the notion.

"Guess we'll be adding another room onto the cabin now, Buck," he told his horse, gently nudging the stallion's flanks to quicken his pace. "With the baby coming, we're going to need another bedroom for a nursery." The thought made him grin.

As Rafe drew closer to the cabin, an uneasy feeling took hold of him. Things didn't seem quite right. The smoke that usually belched from the stone chimney was absent, as was the sound of Ellie's sweet singing, which he could always hear when he approached.

Tying the horse to the porch rail, he moved cautiously to the front door. Years of sneaking up on hombres and Indians had made Rafe careful by nature, and his hand went to the butt of the Colt revolver slung at his hip.

"Ellie," he called out, noting that the cabin door stood ajar. He drew his weapon, entered, and called out again for his wife, but no warm, familiar greeting answered him. The house appeared empty.

He looked about. The cabin was neat and tidy, as was

always Ellie's practice to leave it. An apple pie was cooling on the table, and everything appeared to be in order. Chiding himself for starting to worry like an old woman, he holstered his gun.

Most likely Ellie had gone out back to fetch more firewood, which was probably not such a good idea, considering her present condition. He would have to put a stop to her strenuous activities until after the baby was born.

A sudden gust of wind slammed the door shut, and Rafe spun toward it. It was then that he noticed the small pool of blood on the floor, and he wondered if Ellie had cut herself while paring the apples for the pie. He didn't want to think about the other possibility: that she might be having female trouble because of the baby. "Complications," Doc Leahy would call it. Ellie was of an age when having babies could prove difficult.

Fear gripped his innards at the possibility of her losing their child. What just a short while ago had seemed so remote and unreal had now become an important element in their lives and their marriage. A child could forge their union just as Ethan's birth had melded Ben and Patsy Bodine's.

His parents' arranged marriage had started off on shaky ground. The two had come together as virtual strangers, but the birth of their first son had been the catalyst to ignite a love that had burned brighter and grown stronger than any other union Rafe had witnessed, until his mother's untimely death from pneumonia eight years ago.

It was Rafe's hope that the child Ellie carried in her womb would have a similar effect on their marriage.

He pushed those thoughts aside and headed outside. The sun dipped slowly to the horizon, making it more difficult to follow the trail of blood that shone dull red against the pale sandy soil. It led across the yard toward the barn, and he thought it strange that Ellie would have cause to visit the barn at that time of evening. Unless something had happened to one of the animals—that could explain the blood, he reassured himself.

One of Ellie's lambs might have gotten hurt, cut itself on that damned barbed wire he was forced to string to keep his herd from straying, or maybe the new colt had gotten into something he wasn't supposed to. Ellie had a soft heart for animals and helpless creatures, and she was always bringing them back to the house to tend them. Perhaps she had done so today.

The eerie silence surrounding him as he drew nearer to the barn made the hairs on the back of his neck stand on end. His sixth sense—the one that had saved him countless times from gunslingers and cattle thieves—told him that something wasn't right. He pulled the .45 from his holster once again and approached cautiously.

The barn doors were closed, but the latch that fastened them was not in its fixed position. Grasping the edge of the heavy door, he pulled it open; it creaked loudly in protest. Still, there was no sound from the animals.

He searched for the lantern that hung on the wall to the right of the door and, finding it, struck a match.

Flies buzzed around his head, and the cloying, familiar odor of blood rose up to torment his senses. A fear he'd never known before gripped his belly, twisting it into a tight knot.

"Ellie!" he called, holding the lantern out in front of him as he walked farther into the barn. It was then that he saw the two slaughtered lambs. They'd been gutted, their lifeless heads severed from their bodies.

Disgusted at such wanton violence and alarmed for his wife's safety, he rushed forward, shouting her name again and again. Then he stopped dead in his tracks at the gruesome sight he encountered.

Ellie's lifeless body lay before him in a mound of hay colored red by blood. She'd been knifed viciously, thoroughly, almost ritualistically, and tears of grief filled his eyes.

Screaming out her name, Rafe dropped to his knees beside his dead wife, his mind refusing to believe what his eyes beheld.

Why, God? Why did you allow this to happen? She was such an innocent, so kind. . . .

Ellie and his child, like his hopes for a new beginning, were dead.

He'd seen men murdered countless times, some who'd been butchered by the Comanche, others by Mexicans out for retribution, but he'd never before seen a woman so viciously slaughtered and violated, never in all his years of rangering and Indian fighting.

Rafe shut his eyes to wipe out the hideous sight, though he knew that his wife's lifeless visage would haunt him the rest of his days. Then he fetched a horse blanket and wrapped it about her, and as he lifted her tenderly in his arms, he saw that whoever the murdering bastard was, he'd secured himself a trophy. Ellie's long blond braid had been severed.

A killing rage, unlike anything Rafe had ever felt before, consumed him, and he shook from the force of it. "I'll kill you, you murdering bastard. I'll kill you if it's the last thing I do."

Guilt rode heavy on Rafe's shoulders, thick and cold as a slab of marble. In the short time it had taken him to clean Ellie's body and wrap it in linens for transport to her parents' home, he had done a lot of thinking about her murder, and her murderer.

In a cold, calculated, detached manner he had tried to fathom the reason for her killing, and the only conclusion he had drawn was that Ellie had been killed because of him, because of the profession he'd chosen. His creed that justice must be served at all costs—the Rangers' creed—had ultimately destroyed his own wife.

In his heart he knew who the murderer was, who had vowed to get even, and had threatened to "cut Rafe to ribbons" if he ever got the chance.

Hank Slaughter was a man capable of such mayhem and torture. The sick, twisted bastard, whom he and Ethan had sent to prison five years before for robbing the Misery Bank and Trust, was no doubt on the loose again and on a mission of revenge.

There'd be no place for Slaughter to hide. Rafe would hunt him down and exact his pound of flesh. He had pledged as much on his dead wife's body, and he would keep his promise to the dead woman, whose only crime had been loving him too much.

Later there would be time for self-recriminations and sorrow that he hadn't loved Ellie as much as he should have. Now he had to inform the Masters that their only daughter was dead. They would be devastated by the news, but would draw comfort in the knowledge that Ellie would have a proper Christian burial. Then he would set out on his mission.

Hank Slaughter was feeling good, and it wasn't just the half bottle of rye whiskey he'd drunk. Killing made him feel good, made him feel powerful, and right now he felt as if he could conquer the whole goddamn world and Texas to boot.

The lamplight glinted through his red hair and beard, both sprinkled with generous amounts of gray. He looked much older than his forty years, but then, he'd lived a harder life than most, and prison had never been conducive to keeping a man young.

"Well, boys," he said, leaning back in his chair as if he didn't have a care in the world, and grinning at his compatriots, "we got our revenge on Bodine. And sweet it was."

Bobby leaned over the card table and whispered to his older brother, so the other patrons of Sweetwater's only saloon couldn't overhear him, "You shouldn't'ta killed the woman, Hank. It wasn't right. She didn't have nothing to do with Bodine putting you in jail."

"She was his wife. That makes her guilty by association. Besides, the deed's done. What the hell you acting so jumpy about? Once we've had a few whiskeys, we'll hightail it outta here and ride to the hideout. We'll lay low for a while. No one will find us there."

The two brothers, Roy Lee and Luther, cast their cousin a skeptical look but kept silent. They had no intention of bucking Hank Slaughter. Arguing with him wasn't a real healthy thing to do, and Bobby was just plain foolish for questioning his brother's actions.

Bobby snorted, then downed his glass of whiskey. "You're a fool if you think that. Bodine's a Ranger. He's going to come looking for us, and when he finds us he's going to kill us all."

The bearded man's eyes, silver like the skin of a snake, narrowed into reptilian slits, and he grasped his brother's arm, knocking the glass from his hand. "Don't ever call me a fool, you lily-livered coward. I ain't the one peeing my pants over Bodine. Let him come if he's got a hankerin' to die. I'd still like to carve his ass into little pieces. It wasn't nearly as satisfying carving his wife's."

Bobby didn't bother to hide his disgust. "I think we should split up. It'll be harder for Bodine to find us if we're not riding together."

Luther belched, then wiped his mouth on his dirty shirt sleeve. "There's safety in numbers, Bobby. We should stick together like always. Ain't that right, boss?"

Hank nodded. "Luther's right."

"Well, I'm splitting off," Bobby declared, unwilling to look his brother in the eye for fear of what he'd see there.

He knew he was a big disappointment to Hank. But not every man could live up to Hank's twisted values.

"Judy'll put me up, and I'd just as soon take my chances in a whore's bed than in a saddle, waiting to be picked off by a bullet from a rifle."

Roy Lee didn't look quite as convinced as Luther of the need to remain together. "You gonna stay at Madam DeBerry's whorehouse, Bobby? 'Cause if you are, maybe I should go to Justiceburg with you. Judy's got herself some real nice whores, and the biggest tits I ever seen on a woman."

Bobby shook his head. In his opinion, Roy Lee and Luther were liabilities and should never have been included in the first place. But Hank was big on family ties, and he liked the fact that the two brothers were so easy to lead around. "You go with Hank and Luther, Roy Lee. I don't want to be responsible for your hide."

The skinny man looked offended at first, then disappointed that he wouldn't be getting a poke.

Hank pushed himself to his feet and the other two men followed suit. "We'll wait for you at the hideout. If you don't show, say in a month's time, I'm gonna assume you're dead." Hank's laugh was sinister. "That'd be a real crying shame, me losing a baby brother."

Bobby figured that the only thing Hank was sorry about was the fact that he wouldn't get to kill him himself. Hank surely was a sick son of a bitch.

Rafe had just finished hitching the team to the wagon

when the sound of hoofbeats caught his attention. He recognized Ethan approaching and wasn't glad to see him. Once the Texas Ranger found out what had happened, he would be adamant in his desire to hunt down Ellie's killers. But this was one time, Rafe decided, he'd be going it alone.

"Hey, little brother," Ethan called out before dismounting. "Where you off to? I come out here for a meal and some companionship, and I find you running off to who knows where. Anybody with a lick of sense would know it's too goddamn late to be traveling." He grinned, winking suggestively. "Guess I'll just have to keep that little wife of yours company, until you . . ."

"Ellie's dead." Rafe didn't flinch as he said the words, didn't let on to his brother that grief consumed him. He couldn't afford the weakness of letting it show.

Ethan's face paled, and he removed his hat, hitting the dust off his pant leg with it. "Dead? Did she have an accident or something? Did she—"

"Ellie was murdered. I found her in the barn a little while ago. Her throat's been slashed, and she's been . . ." He swallowed with difficulty, trying to block the hideous sight from his memory as he said the word: "Violated."

"Jesus!" Ethan stepped forward to put a comforting hand on his brother's shoulder. "Rafe, I'm sorry. I don't know what to say. Who'd do something so terrible to a sweet little thing like Ellie? She never harmed a fly." He looked into the back of the wagon and saw the shrouded body.

Rafe saw the grief in his brother's eyes and said,

"There's only one man I can think of capable of such evil. One man who'd have the motive to revenge himself on me."

"Hank Slaughter?" Ethan's lips flattened into a grim line as he asked the question, then he nodded to himself. "It's possible. Slaughter and his brother were seen in town a couple of days ago. They had a drink at the saloon and left. I didn't see 'em myself, or I might have hauled them in for questioning."

Rafe masked his anger and hostility behind a cold facade, unwilling to let Ethan know the hatred he felt for the Slaughters. "I'm taking Ellie to her parents' home for burial. I was just leaving when you rode up."

"I'll come with you. I can deputize you as a Ranger, and we can hunt for the Slaughters together, just like we used to. But first there's some business I need to attend to in Fort Worth. It should only take about a week, two at the most, then we can hunt the Slaughters down."

It wasn't hard for Rafe to figure out his brother's motive. It wasn't out of disrespect for Ellie—the Ranger had thought the world of her—but because of his hard-edged, unfaltering opinion that Rafe should never have left the Texas Rangers to begin with.

The bitter irony surrounding Ellie's death was that Rafe had never wanted to be a lawman. It was Ethan, whom Rafe had looked up to and admired, who had the hankering for rangering. And it was Ethan, those many years ago, who had persuaded him to join the Texas Rangers, with promises of adventure and glory and reminders of duty and allegiance to the glorious state of Texas. Rafe had wanted to be a rancher, build a herd of black Aberdeen Angus, and follow in his father's footsteps.

Maybe if he had been his own man back then, none of this would have happened, Rafe thought, listening to the mournful howl of a coyote, which seemed somehow fitting.

"What do you say?" Ethan prodded.

Rafe nodded in agreement, though he knew he wouldn't take Ethan up on his offer. He was through with the Rangers, with civilized justice and the law. There was only one kind of justice left for killers like the Slaughters—vigilante justice—and he aimed to mete it out.

Ethan was too much a lawman ever to agree to that kind of retribution. Captain Bodine liked doing things by the book, all legal and proper. In the past, Rafe had, too. But not this time. Not after the way his wife had been butchered. He wasn't waiting for any judge and jury who might make the wrong decision. And he wasn't waiting for Ethan to get back from Fort Worth and allow the trail to get cold. So he lied.

"Sounds good, Ethan. I've got to get Ellie settled with her parents first, then there's the matter of the funeral. Most likely it'll take a few days. I think the Masters are going to need some time to adjust to Ellie's death." And there was the matter of the grandchild, which they didn't yet know about.

But he wouldn't tell Ethan of that now. It was too soon, too painful, the wound too raw to probe.

Ethan cast Rafe a searching look. "And what about

you, little brother? How much time are you going to need?"

"Only as long as it takes to bury my wife." The words were said with cold finality, and Ethan seemed to accept them.

Rafe knew he had no time for such civilized matters as funerals. He intended to go after the Slaughter gang before their trail grew cold. He would grieve for Ellie and the unborn child in his own way, in his own time—grieve for everything that might have been and now would not because of Hank Slaughter.

Chapter Two

IT WAS SAID THAT TO BE A TEXAS RANGER A MAN had to "ride like a Mexican, track like a Comanche, shoot like a Tennessean, and fight like the devil."

Rafe Bodine was no exception. Rangering had taught him all those things. Revenge pushed him past the limits of a normal man's endurance.

For two days and nights he rode, dozing in the saddle, living on beef jerky and stale biscuits, the thought of killing Hank Slaughter and his men never far from his mind.

He had only to remember the Masterses' grief-stricken, ashen faces when he'd told them about Ellie's murder to know that he was doing the right thing. Though they had asked a multitude of questions, he had given them only evasive answers, for he couldn't afford to let Ethan know of his plan for revenge. And if there was one thing in this world he could count on, it was that Ethan would be coming after him.

The Slaughter gang's tracks had been easy enough to pick up. There were four of them, by Rafe's estimation— Hank and his brother, Bobby, and most likely their cousins, Roy Lee and Luther.

The four Slaughters were notorious for the crimes they committed and the gruesome way they dealt with their victims. It had taken Rafe and Ethan two years to capture them and bring them to trial after the Misery bank robbery. But only Hank had been convicted of that crime. The charges against the others had been dropped for lack of evidence—witnesses had suddenly disappeared—and Rafe wished now that he had executed the rest of the gang on the spot. Ellie would still be alive if he had.

Rafe stopped briefly in the Texas town of Sweetwater. Having confirmed with some of the locals that the Slaughters had ridden through the day before, he remained only long enough to purchase additional provisions, then rode out again, following the trail of the lone rider.

Three of the horses' tracks led northwest toward New Mexico Territory, while the other rider headed west. Since Rafe knew that Roy Lee and Luther didn't have the intelligence to go it alone, he figured that either Hank or his brother had split off from the gang to make his escape. It was an evasive move that wouldn't work. Rafe had no intention of allowing any of the Slaughters to sneak away. Or to live.

Madam DeBerry's Pleasure Palace was smoky, crowded, and noisy when Rafe entered later that evening. The roulette wheel in the far corner whirred and clicked, chairs scraped against the wide pine-plank floor as restless cowboys adjusted irritably to their poker losses, and the raucous laughter of whores and their eager customers rang as loud as the clanking of coins dropping into the till.

With a practiced eye, Rafe observed the crowd as he leaned casually against the bar and sipped a whiskey. His eyes swept the room, searching each man's face, searching for Hank or Bobby Slaughter.

"Care for another drink, stranger?" The bartender wiped away the beer foam overflowing its container before setting it before the travel-weary cowboy standing next to Rafe.

Rafe held out his glass for another shot of whiskey. "You know a man named Slaughter?"

Suddenly, the man's affable expression soured into one of suspicion. "I tend bar and mind my own business. Seems to me you should do the same, stranger."

"I got business with Slaughter. He said to meet him here."

"Yeah? Well, Judy never mentioned a thing to me. And she would know, seeing as how she's Bobby's woman and all."

Rafe shrugged nonchalantly as Slaughter's identity was confirmed. He should have realized that Hank would never split off from his gang, never relinquish control. That wasn't his style.

"Bobby don't like his personal business spread about. Maybe he knows Judy has a loose tongue."

The barrel-chested barkeep snickered, and his long mustache twitched. "Judy's got a loose tongue, all right. It's how she makes her living." He laughed at his ribald jest, and Rafe forced a smile.

"Maybe I'll go on up and find out for myself how loose this whore's tongue really is. I ain't had me a woman in a while," Rafe said, noting the apprehension on the bartender's face.

"Judy's with someone. And she don't like being disturbed when she's servicing one of her regulars."

"That so? Guess I'll just have to bide my time with a game of chance till she's done." Rafe headed in the direction of the roulette wheel, but when the bartender turned to fetch another bottle of whiskey, he slipped up the stairs unnoticed.

Judy DeBerry was proud to be a businesswoman with a thriving clientele, and she had boldly stated that fact on the brass plate on her bedroom door: JUDY DEBERRY, PROPRIETRESS. Not "whore," "madam," or "prostitute," but *proprietress*.

Rafe had to give the woman her due. She did have a successful business, even if she wasn't too particular about whom she bedded.

Pushing open the whore's door, Rafe stood in the threshold and observed a plump, feminine butt aimed at the ceiling. Madam DeBerry was servicing her regular.

The frenzied pumping motion, accompanied by excessive grunting noises, told him that Bobby Slaughter was aware of nothing but being screwed good and proper. Rafe slammed the door loudly, finally catching the lovers' attention.

Bobby's face whitened as he gazed into the steel-blue eyes of the man who had come to kill him. "I knew you'd come." He pushed the whore off of him.

Realizing that the tall man was Rafe Bodine, Judy's face paled. Though he wasn't wearing the badge of a Texas Ranger, she knew him to be one. The Bodine brothers had come through Justiceburg several years ago in pursuit of outlaws. They might not have taken notice of her, but she wasn't likely to forget their masculine forms.

It had been rumored that the Bodine brothers could love longer and shoot straighter than any two men on the face of the earth. They'd left a trail of dead men and smiling whores in their wake as testimony to those facts.

"What'd you do, Bobby? Why's the Ranger here?"

Rafe's eyes hardened and the grooves around his mouth deepened. "Tell her, Slaughter. Tell her how you and the others butchered my wife and unborn child."

The whore gasped and covered her mouth, gazing at her lover in disbelief and horror.

Bobby shook his head in denial. "It weren't me. I wasn't part of it. I told Hank not to touch the woman, but he wouldn't listen. You know what a crazy son of a bitch he is, Bodine. I just couldn't make him listen."

Rafe took a menacing step forward, and Bobby plastered himself against the brass headboard. The scent of his fear permeated the room, overpowering the odors of sex and stale perfume. "Did you rape my wife, Slaughter? Did you help cut her throat afterward?"

"No!" The man's voice shook as he declared his innocence. "I swear it weren't me. I don't harm women. It was Hank and the others. I'd never do such a thing." But even as he protested, his hand reached for the gun hidden beneath the pillow, and he brought it forward and fired.

Rafe answered the challenge in the space of a heartbeat, pumping a .45 straight between Bobby Slaughter's wide, desperate eyes.

Judy's screams reverberated around the room until Rafe's harsh voice silenced her. "You'd better shut up and start talking, unless you want some of the same."

"You killed Bobby . . . you killed Bobby . . ." she chanted over and over again, staring at his lifeless body.

"That's right. The murdering bastard had it coming. Now tell me where the Slaughters are headed. And don't try to pretend you don't know. Bobby was a cowardly animal, the kind who would need to unburden himself."

Easing herself away from the dead body of her lover, the whore reached for a red silk wrapper to cover her nakedness, then rose unsteadily to her feet. "I don't hold with murdering women, but I know Bobby would have taken no part in it. It wasn't in him to murder a woman."

"Maybe that's true," Rafe said, though he seriously doubted it. All the Slaughters were capable of murder, *had* murdered men, women, and children. It made no difference to them who their victims were.

"It *is* true, I tell you."

"But he was there, didn't stop it from happening, and in my mind that makes him as guilty as the rest. Now tell me where the other bastards are heading, and make it quick." Rafe knew that the town's sheriff, Elmo Scruggs, wasn't much of a lawman, but he also knew that eventually he would come to investigate the shooting, and Rafe intended to be long gone from Justiceburg by then.

"They're heading north to their hideout in Wyoming,"

the whore confessed, her eyes fixed on the smoking gun the ex-Ranger held. "Bobby said that the others planned to hole up there until things cooled off."

Rafe dropped the Colt back into his holster, and his gaze flicked over the dead man. "Things never cool off in hell. Bobby should have been smart enough to realize that."

Texas Ranger Ethan Bodine stared at his father's grief-stricken face across the fresh mound of dirt that was Ellie's grave and cursed inwardly at his stupidity and Rafe's. Rafe had left the day of Ellie's murder, never intending to wait for Ethan, who'd been gone nearly two weeks and was well aware of the substantial lead his brother had on him.

Why did I trust that conniving brother of mine? Why didn't I realize that Rafe would go out for revenge? He was still unable to believe that Rafe had played him for a fool. And won.

For years Rafe and Ethan had ridden together as Texas Rangers. They'd been inseparable, until Rafe had gotten it in his head to quit the Rangers and settle down to a life of normalcy, as he called it.

Ethan had been devastated by Rafe's decision to quit rangering and disappointed that his brother had chosen Ellie Masters to spend the rest of his life with. Ellie was a sweet girl, but she and Rafe had been more like brother and sister than husband and wife, and Ethan had thought the pairing unnatural. And unnecessary.

Rafe hadn't needed a wife any more than Ethan needed or wanted one. It wasn't normal for a man to go against his natural inclination, and Rafe was born to rangering, the same as Ethan. A woman, no matter how pretty or sweet, couldn't provide the same feeling of camaraderie as a camp full of men bent on the same mission.

Ethan planned to remain a bachelor for the remainder of his days.

He glanced at his younger brother, Travis, who now stood next to their stepmother, and thought of how close the foolish young man had come to marrying that strong-willed daughter of Judge Barkley's. Thank God the boy had come to his senses in time, Ethan thought, wishing that Rafe had done the same and spared them all this grief and concern.

"What do you intend to do, Ethan?" Ben Bodine's voice was thick with emotion as he questioned his oldest son.

Ethan liked playing his cards close to his chest, and his face gave no clue as to his intention. Clasping his father's arm, he led him out of earshot of his stepmother and brother, whose heads were bowed in prayer.

"I'm going after Rafe. I've got no other choice."

"But he left many days ago. How will you find him now? He could be anywhere."

Rafe was a good tracker, but Ethan was a damn sight better. He would find his brother eventually. "Rafe's not just anywhere. He's following the Slaughters. I'd bet my last dollar on it. It shouldn't be hard to pick up his trail."

"And when you find him, what then?"

Ethan shrugged, hating to answer the question that had been uppermost on his mind, hating to acknowledge the fear evident in his father's voice. Ben Bodine had never been afraid of anything in his life.

The Ranger knew that having a family involved changed things, and that notion gave him pause to think before answering. "That depends on how foolish Rafe's been. I've been sworn to uphold the law, and that's what I intend to do." And if he could prevent his brother from breaking that law—protect Rafe from himself—he would.

Ben's eyes widened in disbelief as he stared at his son, unwilling to believe that Ethan would arrest his own brother. "Rafe has just cause to avenge his wife's murder, and he's your brother."

Ethan stiffened. Not much had changed in the fifteen years since he'd left the ranch to join the Rangers to lessen the animosity between him and his father, and not much ever would. "No one knows that better'n me, Pa. But if Rafe gets the chance, he's going to kill the Slaughters, and I can't allow that to happen. It's my duty to stop him. No one can take the law into their own hands and get away with it. Not even Rafe."

Sadness deepened the age lines around Ben's eyes and mouth, and in a rare display of affection he encircled his son's shoulders with his arm, and his voice grew heavy with despair. "You are your brother's keeper, Ethan."

"I intend to remember that, Pa. Truly, I do."

* * *

I am stranded. That was Emmaline St. Joseph's first thought as she stared in disgust at the broken wagon wheel. Her second: that she should never have let her brother, Lucas, talk her into accompanying him on his journey to California. She should have stayed safe and secure in Boston in front of a roaring fire, where she would not have had to worry about the wildlife of New Mexico devouring her while she slept.

Strange noises echoed in the distance, and she shuddered to think of what might be out there.

Of course, it had been her idea to leave Las Vegas, New Mexico, one of the seamier, meaner frontier towns they had visited, for the impulsive sightseeing trip to the Sangre de Cristo Mountains. With the train delayed for repairs, and the children growing more restless by the minute, she'd foolishly thought that her charges, all Bostonian orphans, would benefit from a little adventure. And her brother, who was somewhat of a rock collector, and who had even less experience with children than she did, had jumped at the chance for a little exploration.

There were five orphans altogether, ranging in age from eighteen months to twelve years, and all were staring at her as if she held the answer to their present predicament. She and her brother were escorting them to Sacramento to the newly constructed orphanage Lucas had commissioned and would direct.

A philanthropist of some prominence, it had been Lucas St. Joseph's dream to establish a home in the open spaces of the West, where eastern orphans might more easily be adopted than in the crowded cities of the East.

The St. Joseph Home for Foundlings and Orphans was to be a temporary residence for these children until farm and ranch families could be found to adopt them.

But at the moment, Lucas's dream had to wait. After a rigorous climb up the mountain path, he'd become incapacitated with chest pains and was sitting on a boulder looking paler than Emmaline had ever before seen him. Sweating profusely—something Lucas never allowed himself to do because he thought it unseemly—he looked to be in a great deal of pain. She realized now that she should never have allowed him to climb up the mountain to inspect rock formations. But hindsight always being better than foresight, she hadn't voiced her objection.

Frau Muehler, the nurse they'd hired before leaving Boston, and a most disagreeable woman in Emmaline's opinion, stared at her as if this whole wretched affair had been Emmaline's doing. Which it had. But the old German battle-ax didn't have to look so damned accusing.

"Vat are ve going to do, miss? Da wagon is broke. Ve have no food for da little ones to eat. I am hungry." She crossed arms the size of tree trunks over an equally large bosom and heaved an indignant sigh.

Through slightly narrowed eyes, the Boston socialite stared at the three-hundred-pound nursemaid and thought ungraciously that she could probably live off her fat for the next hundred years if she needed to. She was certainly not in any danger of starvation.

"I'm not feeling too well, Emma my dear." Lucas clasped his chest again. "I think I shall lie down for a bit."

Emmaline rushed forward to help her older brother to recline on the blanket she'd spread out. Lucas's health had always been a bit precarious, and she'd warned him about the vigor of this trek, but he'd been adamant in his plan to open the home on time.

"Careful, Lucas. You've overdone things a bit, that's all. Remember the time you tried to haul that giant fir tree into the parlor for our Christmas party all by yourself and developed a severe asthma attack? Why, Mama was beside herself with worry, thinking you were going to wheeze yourself to death. I'm sure this is nothing more than that."

Emmaline wasn't quite certain whom she was reassuring—Lucas or herself—but she couldn't bear the fear haunting her brother's eyes. "Just rest while I try to figure out what to do."

He patted her hand, and there was a wealth of regret in his voice when he spoke. "I'm sorry to be such a burden, Emma. We were having a delightful time until I had to spoil it."

The love she felt for her brother shone in her eyes and gentled her voice. "It's not your fault you took ill, Lucas." She brushed the damp hairs from his forehead. "Nor is it anyone's fault that our conveyance has a broken wheel."

Just wait until she got her hands on the unscrupulous man at the livery, who had assured them that the rickety buckboard was "as sound as a dollar." No doubt he'd been referring to Confederate money.

Her explanation seemed to comfort him, and he closed his eyes against the pain that continued to plague him.

Unfortunately, Frau Muehler was not buying the young woman's explanation as readily. "You should not have made us come out here in da woods. Vat vill ve do now? The sun vill go down and it vill be cold. And da animals vill come and eat us. *Ja*. Dey vill eat us."

Though Emmaline had had similar thoughts herself, she could see that the foolish woman had frightened the children. The toddler, Theodora, whom everyone called Pansy because she was so sweet-natured and possessed big, brown velvety eyes, started crying, as did the two sisters, Miriam and Miranda Stiles.

"There's still some food in the picnic hamper, Miss Emmaline," Danny offered. "And I think we've got a couple of canteens of water left."

She smiled gratefully at the oldest boy. At twelve, Daniel Forbes was wise beyond his years. She supposed that living on the streets and having to take care of his younger brother, David, was the cause for his maturity.

David, who mimicked everything his older brother did and said, nodded sagely. "It's true." His blond head bobbed up and down. "I seen the canteens myself."

She smiled at the child, but couldn't resist correcting his grammar. "It's 'saw,' David. You 'saw' the canteens."

"Yes, ma'am. That's what I said. I seen them in the wagon."

Emmaline sighed deeply. "Frau Muehler, perhaps you could divide what food is left in the hamper between the children and yourself, while I attempt to get a fire going."

"Vat does a city woman know of such things? Ve vill all be dead by morning," the nurse predicted.

Emmaline hoped that if any of them had to die by morning, Frau Muehler would be the first one to go.

Later that evening, Emmaline stared into the flames of the pitiful fire she had managed to start with some twigs and the phosphorus matches she'd found in Lucas's coat pocket.

That nasty habit of smoking cigars was probably what had landed Lucas flat on his back, as he was now, she thought, gazing at her brother with concern. He was sleeping, but it wasn't a restful sleep, judging by the anguished sounds he'd been making off and on for most of the evening.

Frau Muehler and the children were asleep, too. The buckboard was serving as their hotel room, while Emmaline opted to lie by the fire to keep a watchful eye on her brother, in the event that he worsened during the night.

Lucas was such a dear man. A bit absentminded at times, boring to a fault in his quest for knowledge and things cerebral, but he possessed a heart as wide as this vast country in which they were now stranded.

They had inherited great wealth. But even before their parents' untimely drowning while on a yachting holiday, they'd been taught that privilege had a price—that it was their Christian duty to help those less fortunate than themselves and to be civic-minded and caring of others. And whether it was funding a new wing for Boston Memorial Hospital or an endowment for the arts, the St. Joseph family took their responsibilities seriously.

Lucas, as head of the family, was determined to live up to his parents' expectations and carry on the family tradition of service and goodwill to their fellow man, which is how the St. Joseph Home had come about.

Frau Muehler's stentorian snores, as big as the woman herself, interrupted Emmaline's thoughts. They seemed to drown out the nocturnal sounds surrounding them. Except for the coyotes. Their howls were persistent, and they were giving the nursemaid's foghorn concerto some definite competition.

Why Lucas had hired such a difficult woman to accompany them on their trek west was still a mystery to Emmaline. She supposed the German woman possessed impeccable references—Lucas was a stickler for such things—but her domineering attitude was tiresome.

Emmaline shivered and tossed another branch onto the fire. If it had been left up to her, she would have dismissed Frau Muehler long ago. It hadn't taken Emmaline long to weary of the woman's unending complaints.

Of course, Emmaline would be the first to admit that she needed the woman. She didn't know the first thing about caring for young children, and she didn't particularly want to learn. She had no intention of marrying and was quite content to live out the remainder of her life as a spinster, in charge of her own money and her own destiny.

Emmaline had decided long ago that she didn't need some foolish man telling her what to do. She was far too independent, opinionated, and set in her ways to take orders from a man, who would no doubt be far less sensible and considerably less intelligent than she.

The men she'd had occasion to keep company with had been shallow, fawning, and quite boring for the most part. Emmaline was smart enough to know that most of the men of her acquaintance found her money much more appealing than her person.

She had never considered herself particularly attractive. In fact, some men probably thought her homely. Her brown eyes were nondescript, her red hair too curly and unruly to be considered fashionable, and she was skinny by the day's standards.

But she was strong. Her daily calisthenics, which she performed without fail, had given muscles to her arms and legs.

She squeezed her firm bicep and smiled ruefully. Unfortunately, muscles on a woman weren't all that pleasing to a man's eye.

Men, it seemed, were interested in the false flutter of eyelashes, the shape of a well-turned ankle, the size of a generous bosom—and she was sadly lacking in that department. They were vain creatures, more interested in beauty than brains. Well, she had more of the latter than the former, and she wasn't about to lose sleep over it this night.

Chapter Three

EMMALINE AWOKE THE NEXT MORNING TO FIND Frau Muehler gone. The children's nurse had sneaked away during the night after they were asleep and had taken one of the horses with her.

To compound her problems, Lucas's condition had deteriorated, and it didn't look as if he would survive another night in the wilderness. The chilly air made it more difficult for him to breathe, and the pains in his chest had grown more frequent and severe.

To make matters even worse, the younger children were crying from whatever it was that made young children cry. Emmaline hadn't a clue. Theodora's nappies needed changing. She hadn't a clue about that, either. And there wasn't a morsel of food left to eat.

All in all, things didn't look hopeful at the moment.

"What are you gonna do about Pansy, Miss Emmaline?" Danny wanted to know. "She don't smell too good."

"Has she made a . . . a doodle in her pants?" Emmaline inquired, doing her best not to blush—an impossibility with her red hair and fair coloring.

"She's crapped a pound, Miss Emmaline. And after she's sat in it all night . . ."

"I understand, Danny. Thank you for bringing it to my attention. I don't suppose you could . . ."

The boy shook his head vehemently. "No, ma'am. I ain't changing no shitty diapers. That's woman's work."

"Yes. Well, I suppose under ordinary circumstances it is, but the woman who's supposed to do it has left, and—"

"You're a woman, Miss Emmaline," David pointed out. "You could do it, couldn't ya?"

Emmaline wanted to ask why it was always "women's work" when the task was dirty or disagreeable. She'd never understood the concept of men's work versus women's work. She supposed it was just another convenient way for men to get out of doing tasks they didn't like, and no doubt had been conceived by a man for that very purpose.

But instead of asking, she merely stared at the pitiful child whom Miriam and Miranda held aloft between them, and who was now screaming at the top of her lungs, and replied, "I suppose I'll have to."

Taking the baby in her arms, Emmaline wrinkled her nose at the dreadful odor—the child smelled nothing like her namesake at the moment—ignored the laughter and teasing comments the other children made, and proceeded to the buckboard, where she hoped to find some of Pansy's clean clothing and diapers.

Though she hated using what was left of their precious water, there was no help for it. Pansy stank to high heaven and needed a thorough washing. Just because they were stuck out in the wilds of New Mexico Territory was no reason they had to behave like animals.

Pansy giggled throughout most of her sponge bath, so Emmaline decided that she was doing an okay job. The diapers weren't as snug as the previous ones the child had worn, but they were clean and pinned as tight as Emmaline could get them and would do for now.

Her first crisis mastered, Emmaline cast a worried look at her brother, who slept fitfully, then called the youngsters to her. "Children, we are having a bit of a problem. As you are well aware, Frau Muehler has decided to leave us."

"She wasn't no fun anyway," Danny said, his upper lip curling in obvious dislike of the nurse.

Miranda nodded. "She smelled funny."

"Yes, well, all that aside"—Emmaline wondered if they thought she smelled funny, too—"we are going to have to make the best of our present predicament."

"What's a predicament, Miss Emmaline?" David wanted to know, and Emmaline sighed at the young boy's inquisitiveness. David always had a multitude of questions to fit any situation. And though she encouraged an inquiring mind, there were times when it all got a bit much to deal with. This was one of those times.

"I should have said our present circumstances. You know—the way things are at the moment."

The children nodded in unison, then Danny asked, "Like Mr. Lucas being sick, and us not having any food to eat? Stuff like that?"

Just like that. "I'm not sure we'll be able to procure foodstuffs . . . find something to eat, and I'm perfectly aware that all of you are hungry, because I am, too."

"Shall I check the wagon again, Miss Emmaline? Maybe Frau Muehler missed some of the food. She sure ate a lot."

Emmaline decided that was an excellent idea and told Daniel so, praying that the obese nurse had missed a morsel of food the children could share.

While the children went to search the wagon, Emmaline crossed to where her brother lay and knelt beside him. His color had turned from ash white to sickly gray, and every breath he took seemed a herculean effort. She stroked his cheek gently, and his eyes opened.

"Emma my dear, I'm so sorry to leave you like this."

His words alarmed her, and her hand faltered momentarily. "Hush, Lucas. You mustn't talk so. You're not going anywhere."

"I'm afraid I am, my dear." He clutched her hand. "I've never been a man of strong constitution, but I was so hoping that I could endure this journey and fulfill my mission to open the St. Joseph Home. It's so important to me."

"Don't talk nonsense. Of course you're going to open the home."

With feeble fingers he squeezed her hand. "I will not survive another night, Emma. You must face the facts as I have. I am dying."

She choked back a sob and shook her head in denial. "No. I will not allow it."

"You're a strong, determined woman, sister, but even

you cannot hold back the hand of the Almighty. He is coming for me, my dear, and I must go to meet him."

"Lucas . . ." Emmaline's tears fell freely, splashing onto her brother's hand and hers. She wanted to repudiate Lucas's dire prediction, but in her heart she knew it to be true.

"I need you to promise me something, Emma."

"Anything, Lucas. You know you have only to ask."

He breathed deeply, and she could see that the effort pained him. "You must see that the children arrive safely in Sacramento. You must take it upon yourself to act as guardian and go in my stead. Will you do that for me?"

Her brother's look was so earnest, Emmaline didn't have the heart to tell him that they would soon be following him to the Great Beyond. There was no way she'd be able to prevent their demise, with her limited knowledge of outdoor survival. If the weather didn't get them, the animals surely would. She'd read in one of the guidebooks Lucas had purchased that bears could climb trees. It was a discomforting thought.

"I'll do my best to fulfill your wishes, Lucas. I know how important the orphans and the orphanage are to you."

He closed his eyes, and his labored breathing eased a bit. "I knew I could count on you, Emma. I'm so sorry that I have to leave you on your own. You will be all right, won't you, my dear?"

She nodded, biting her lower lip so she wouldn't blurt out the truth, and forced a small smile. "Of course, Lucas. We'll be fine. I'll see to it."

"When you get to Sacramento, you will need to find a

new director for the home. There's a list of prospects in my travel bag, as well as a package of pemmican jerky and hardtack. I purchased them before setting out on our trip. The guidebooks caution travelers to be prepared, but I didn't have the heart to worry you."

The delighted cries of the children alerted Emmaline to the fact that they had already found Lucas's hoard of goods. "You've always been so well prepared for any eventuality, Lucas. I wish I were more like you."

"I'm as dull as tarnished silver, and you know it. You are the one who possesses the spirit to survive out here in the West, and I have no doubt you will."

Feeling void of anything resembling spirit, all Emmaline could do was nod.

"Please bid my farewells to the children, Emma. I don't want them to see me like this. It might frighten them." His voice faded to a whisper, and she bent her head down to hear him. "I've cherished our time together."

"I love you, Lucas. And someday we will meet again."

"But not too soon, my dear. Not too soo . . ."

He was gone. Emmaline stared down at her brother's still chest, then laid her head across it and wept. She would have given all her worldly possessions to have him back—her own life, if need be. But she suspected that God in his wisdom had another destiny for her.

Perhaps it was getting the children safely to California, or perhaps something else she couldn't quite fathom at the moment. Emmaline just didn't understand why God thought it necessary to take everyone she loved from her—first her parents, now Lucas.

She was truly alone for the first time in her life, and she didn't know how she would cope.

Pushing aside her morbid thoughts and her grief, she covered Lucas with a blanket. The children would have to be told of his demise, and that would be difficult.

In the short time they'd been together, the orphans had formed an unlikely attachment to her stodgy older brother. Lucas's kindness and generosity had drawn them like a beacon of warmth. Now he was gone, and they were stuck with her. Emmaline pitied the poor little tykes, and heaved a dispirited sigh.

She had managed to survive the second crisis. But could she survive another?

Survival was something Rafe Bodine had gotten very good at during his lifetime, and he wasn't about to let the vagaries of nature get to him. Or the fact that Buck had thrown a shoe and he'd lost a day because of it.

Forced to spend the night in Las Vegas, New Mexico, Rafe had been able to gather some additional information about the Slaughters while there, so it hadn't been a total waste of time, which was something he couldn't afford to waste.

Rafe knew without a doubt that Ethan would be coming after him. And once the Ranger learned of Bobby Slaughter's death, he would know who had done the deed, and Rafe would be a wanted man, not only by the Texas authorities but by bounty hunters out to collect the price that would be put on his head.

It was doubtful that Bobby's whore would admit that Rafe had fired and killed her lover in self-defense. She had an ax to grind, as big an ax as Rafe had. She'd been in love with Slaughter, no matter that he was a thief and a murderer. Love blinded people to others' shortcomings.

It blinded Ellie to mine.

Rafe couldn't fault Ethan's sense of justice in coming after him. It was what made him such a great Texas Ranger. He possessed all the traits of leadership: intelligence, unerring judgment, and absence of fear. He was a man who didn't direct his men, but led them to victory.

A Ranger was a man who stood between society and its enemies, and Rafe was now one of its enemies.

Pulling his Stetson low on his head to ward off the heavy rain, he wrapped his long canvas duster securely about him and rode with the knowledge that Hank and the others were heading north toward Colorado and eventually Wyoming.

Bobby's whore hadn't sent him on a wild goose chase after all. Luther's tongue had loosened after a few drinks at the local saloon, and he'd bragged about what he and the others had done to Ellie; he'd also revealed the fact that they were heading to their hideout. Apparently, Luther had been showing off a long braid of blond hair, and Rafe knew he would take great satisfaction in strangling the ruthless outlaw with it.

A couple of the cowboys Rafe questioned had been only too happy to spill their guts about what they had overheard. Killing a woman was tantamount to stealing a horse in their opinion, going against the code they lived by. They'd told him as much.

Too bad men like Hank Slaughter had no code, no decency, no morals. Like rabid dogs that infected everyone they came in contact with, they were violent, furious individuals who cared not for human life, male or female.

There was only one way to handle a rabid animal, and that was to shoot it dead. And there was nothing that would keep Rafe from that goal.

Emmaline had never been an overly religious woman, but she was praying with all her heart and soul at the moment, and she had instructed the children to do the same. They needed a miracle, a savior to help them, and the only way she knew how to accomplish that feat was good old-fashioned down-on-your-knees prayer.

Rafe spotted the buckboard as soon as he rode into the clearing. A group of children were huddled beneath it, all screaming and chanting in some kind of strange prayer ritual, and he wondered if he'd happened across one of those weird religious sects he was always hearing about—"fanatics," Ethan called them.

He rode into their camp, noting the vultures circling overhead and the inert body lying beside the drowned campfire. Dismounting, he squatted before the buckboard to get a better look at what he was up against. Six frightened children stared back at him through the veil of rain. The oldest, the one with the strange red hair, crossed herself and prayed silently.

"Where're your parents?" he demanded in a voice used

to command. "How'd you get stuck out here in the middle of nowhere all by yourselves, little lady?"

The two dark-haired girls giggled, seeming to find Rafe's questions amusing.

Emmaline's jaw slackened, and she rose in indignation, knocking her head against the underside of the wagon, and stared at the stranger as if he were addled.

As if by divine providence, the rain stopped as quickly as it had started, and the sun peeked cautiously through the clouds, stealing Emmaline's words and making her wonder if the man before her had some kind of heavenly influence on his surroundings.

Rafe rose to his feet. "You'd best come on out from beneath that wagon now. Can't believe anyone would be stupid enough to travel the mountains in a buckboard. Didn't your parents have a lick of sense about them?" He shook his head in disgust. "Can't believe—"

Pansy started screaming loud enough to wake the dead and held out her arms to be picked up. The other children followed suit and began shouting all at once, save for Danny, who had a wary look on his face and remained still. Emmaline, too, kept silent, unsure whether to trust the unkempt man before her.

Rafe stared at the bunch in disbelief, then at the red-headed girl, who appeared to be simpleminded, mute, or both. "You'd best tell your brothers and sisters to shut up," he said. When there was no response from her, he shouted to be heard above the din, "Shut up! All of you, shut your mouths and get out from beneath that wagon on the double."

Maybe it was the harsh tone of his voice, or the fact that he was a rather large man, but one by one they quieted and emerged to stand before him. A more bedraggled-looking group he'd yet to meet.

"You," he pointed at Emmaline. "Take charge of that baby. She looks half froze. Then tell me what happened to your parents."

Emmaline picked up Pansy to quiet her and faced the stranger with a look of pure outrage. "Stop shouting, sir. We are not deaf, merely stranded. And I'd appreciate it if you would not refer to me as if I were a child. I am twenty-eight years old, and I happen to be in charge of this group."

Emmaline and Rafe stared, as if seeing each other for the very first time, sizing each other up, neither overly impressed by what they saw.

Rafe clamped his mouth shut, looked into the woman's cocoa-colored eyes, and saw the maturity there, though her face was youthful for a woman of twenty-eight, as was her body. She was as skinny as the young boy standing next to her, no bosoms to speak of, and that curly red hair, flying every which way about her head, appeared to be as unruly as her mouth, now that she'd finally found her voice. But she had spunk, he'd give her that.

Some savior, Emmaline thought. The man had a few years on him, as evidenced by the crinkly lines around his eyes and mouth—not laugh lines, she was sure—and by the leathery texture of his tanned complexion. He was a good five or six inches taller than she, and Emmaline had never been considered a short woman. She hated the fact that she had to look up to him to speak; it put her at a definite disadvantage.

Dressed like many other men she'd seen since coming west, he wore his clothing, like his gun, with casual indifference, as if it had always been part of him, as if he had better, more important things to think about than his appearance.

In a word, he was *virile*.

Emmaline shuddered at the thought. She absolutely despised virile, conceited men who thought a woman's place was at home and in bed—men like her father, who had treated women as ornaments and helpless creatures instead of intelligent helpmates. Though she had loved her father and missed him still, he had not been an easy man to live with. His attitude toward women was archaic, his principles were unbending, and he'd never had the time or the inclination to indulge his children in whimsy or childish things. She and Lucas had been treated like adults from the time Emmaline could remember.

Rafe noticed the way the woman's body shook and asked, "You're not comin' down sick, are you? Because I don't have time to be tending sick folks. I've got business to take care of."

"As do I, Mister . . ."

"Bodine's the name. Rafe Bodine."

"I'm Emmaline St. Joseph, of the Boston St. Josephs. My brother," she cast a saddened look at the body by the campfire, "Lucas and I were escorting this group of children to California. They're orphans, you see, and Lucas has established a home for them there."

"Are you planning on adopting all these kids?" His incredulous look said clearly that he thought she was out of her mind.

"The home I'm referring to, Mr. Bodine, is the St. Joseph Home for Foundlings and Orphans. Lucas was to be the director of it, before his heart failed and he succumbed to his illness. I will have to find a new director, but first I need to get these children settled in Sacramento—"

Suddenly Miranda tugged on the skirt of Emmaline's sodden velvet gown. "Miss Emmaline, Miriam has to go . . ." she rolled her eyes, "you know . . . or she's going to wet her drawers."

"Well, take her into the trees, Miranda, and help her."

The child's blue eyes filled with tears. "But there might be a bear who'll eat us. Frau Muehler said that the animals would eat us all."

"There's no bear around here, little girl," Rafe assured the child, though he didn't know for certain. Black bears inhabited this mountain range and had been known to attack humans when provoked, but he suspected that most were hibernating by now.

"See that your sister gets her business done before she pees her pants," he ordered.

"Mr. Bodine!" Emmaline shot him a censorious look. "That is hardly the proper way for a gentleman to speak to a young lady."

Uncertain that he had heard her correctly, Rafe asked, "You mean that kid? Listen, ma'am, I'm a far cry from a gentleman, but I'm smart enough to know that kids who have to answer nature's call don't usually have time to ponder things."

Pansy, who thought the whole discussion pretty amusing, began to laugh and clap her hands. She bestowed upon Rafe the widest, cutest smile he had seen in a long, long time, and he chucked the baby under the chin. "You're a heartbreaker, ain't ya?"

"The child's name is Theodora, Mr. Bodine. But we call her Pansy. Usually she smells better than she does at the moment." Apparently the toddler had made another deposit in her diaper.

"I'll take her, Miss Emmaline," Danny offered, clutching the small girl to him. "But just this once. I ain't no nursemaid." He stared belligerently at Rafe, daring the man to deny it.

But Rafe, who had brothers, was smarter than that. "That's right good of you, boy. I was beginning to get a bit lightheaded from the smell of that little flowerpot. The kid smells worse than hell on housecleaning day."

Danny couldn't help the grin that split his face, and Rafe answered in kind, watching the boy walk away.

"It appears you've got your hands full, Miss St. Joseph." A hoity name for a hoity woman, he deduced. Emmaline St. Joseph had money. He could smell it on her, sense it in her bossy, independent demeanor, see it in the richness of her city-bought gown, and he loathed her for it. Rich folks always bought their way out of trouble, and he had no doubt that this one wouldn't be any different.

She directed him to the campfire, out of earshot of the

children, and seated herself on a boulder, while he straddled a rotting, downed tree trunk.

Emmaline St. Joseph looked rather regal sitting there in her velvets, dripping wet though they were, like a princess holding court for her subjects. Rafe figured she'd had a lot of practice, being obviously well bred and prominent in society. She was pretty, in an unusual sort of way. Not beautiful by any stretch of the imagination, but attractive just the same. Her eyes were large and doelike, her skin as smooth and white as churned cream, with just a sprinkling of freckles across the bridge of her pert nose. The word *impish* came to mind.

"I can't deny that I'm in a bit of a predicament, Mr. Bodine. Though I'm a capable individual, I confess that when it comes to children I'm a bit out of my element."

His eyebrow shot up. "You're a woman."

It was the kind of statement she had expected from a man of his ilk, and her eyes narrowed. "How kind of you to notice. But that doesn't make me a mother or a nursemaid. We hired a woman to care for the children, but Frau Muehler absconded with one of the horses and disappeared to parts unknown."

"I guess I could help you get back to Las Vegas, though I don't relish wasting the time. I've got business to tend to." He removed his hat and scratched his head, and Emmaline noted that his hair was the color of obsidian and just as shiny; it hung down to just brush the collar of his shirt. He was a handsome man, despite his unkempt appearance. His eyes were the same color as her mother's Wedgwood dishes. His shoulders were broad and well developed, as were his legs, which fit snugly into his trousers, giving evidence to the fact that he was solidly muscled. If one were interested in that sort of thing.

She drew a deep breath. "So you said, Mr. Bodine."

"Why would a bunch of city folk stay in a town like Las Vegas anyway? The place is full of lawless vermin." Vigilantes had hanged so many outlaws from the windmill in the plaza that the owner of it had been forced to dismantle it. "And whose bright idea was it to leave town and journey to the mountains unprotected? Didn't you give any thought to mountain lions or outlaws?" He said the last word haltingly, realizing he was speaking of himself now.

"We discovered, Mr. Bodine, that the guidebooks we purchased weren't entirely truthful about various locales. I think your description of the place is too kind. And we had little choice of towns, as the train broke down and we were stranded and left to our own devices."

"Thought you'd have a little adventure, right?" City folk, especially easterners and foreigners, weren't known for their smarts. One had only to think of the English aristocrats who'd hunted the buffalo from the trains to realize that.

She blushed but said nothing, and he almost smiled. "I don't know what else to suggest, ma'am, besides taking you back to Las Vegas."

Emmaline had already made up her mind that she couldn't take the children back to that lawless town. "I have a suggestion, Mr. Bodine, if you'll permit me to make it." She saw the thinning of his lips, the narrowing of his eyes, and knew that Rafe Bodine was as put off with her as she was with him. But she was a good judge of character, and he seemed an honest, caring individual—when he'd looked at Pansy, there'd been something in his eyes that had moved her—and she wasn't in a position to be too particular at the moment. She needed help, and he was it.

"I ain't looking for work," he said, as if he could read her mind, and she gritted her teeth. Actually, she was sorely tempted to sink her teeth into his thick hide.

There were times when Emmaline absolutely detested being a woman, and this was one of them. She hated having to ask this self-assured cowboy for help, but she had responsibilities to the children, to Lucas's dream of establishing a haven for orphans, and so she swallowed her pride. "Mr. Bodine, I am appealing to the goodness of your heart and asking you to help me get these poor, unfortunate children to California."

She might as well have asked him to lasso the moon, the way he stared at her: as if she'd lost her mind.

"Are you deaf? Hell no, I ain't taking you and this bunch to California. I'd rather be skinned alive and boiled in oil. And I've got important business to attend to."

Emmaline counted silently to ten, then counted to ten again, trying to keep her temper in check. Having been told on numerous occasions that she was as tenacious as a Boston bulldog, she wasn't about to take no for an answer. She couldn't. Her life and the lives of the children depended on this man's help.

"Mr. Bodine, I am willing to pay you the very generous sum of five thousand dollars to escort me and the children to Sacramento." There wasn't a man alive who could refuse such a large sum of money.

But Rafe Bodine did, without batting so much as an eyelash. "Goddammit, woman!" He shook his head. "Do you rich folks think you can buy every damn thing on the face of this earth? I told you, and I'm telling you again, I ain't for hire."

Tears filled her eyes, and she hated herself for using womanly wiles. They were as alien to her as this creature who didn't want her money. In her experience, all men wanted her money.

"Mr. Bodine, if you don't help us, I don't know what I'll do. I promised my dying brother that I would get the children to California. I—" Emmaline covered her face and wept, not for Rafe Bodine's benefit this time, but for everything she'd had to face the last few days.

He sighed, rose, and began to pace back and forth, kicking up mud in his wake. He'd never been a lick of good with a weeping woman. And this woman's tears seemed genuine. And then there was the matter of the children, who had come forward and were staring at him with huge, watery eyes that begged for his help.

It was on the tip of his tongue to deny the woman and ride away, when she looked up at him with those big, tear-filled eyes and said, "I'm sorry, Mr. Bodine. It wasn't fair of me to put you in such an awkward position. I'm sure the older children and I will be just fine on our own. It's Pansy I'm worried about. Perhaps if you could see your way to take her with you, find her a warm, safe place to stay—"

"Shit! God damn! Son of a bitch!" He faced Emmaline again, ignoring the sudden stiffness of her posture. "There ain't no way I'm taking you all the way to California. But since I can't be leaving a bunch of little kids and *young lady* out here in the wilderness, I'll help you get to the next town."

The children let loose with a cheer, and Emmaline swallowed with relief, feeling just a tiny bit triumphant.

"The next *large* town, Mr. Bodine. We'll need to find a train heading west, and we'll need to purchase additional supplies." Her sweet smile only irritated Rafe further.

"Don't press your luck, little lady. I'm a man with a short temper and a long memory."

"I'll try to remember that, Mr. Bodine."

"See that you do."

"Oh, Mr. Bodine?" she called as he walked toward his horse.

He stopped, turned, and glared at her. "What now? I've got to unsaddle Buck."

"Thank you. I forgot to say thank you."

"Son of a bitch," was all he replied.

Chapter Four

THE LIGHT OF DAY FOUND RAFE BENT OVER LUCAS St. Joseph's freshly dug grave. The previous day's rain had cleansed the air and rendered the ground soft, making it relatively easy to churn up the earth with the small spade he always carried behind his saddle.

Emmaline watched as he fashioned a small cross from two bent twigs and secured them with a length of rawhide, and her heart softened a bit to know that this hard-edged man had gone to the trouble of giving her brother a proper burial.

She crossed the short distance to where he stood and handed him a tin cup filled with hot coffee, which he had prepared upon arising. Since her cooking skills left a lot to be desired, she'd been grateful for that.

"Thank you, Mr. Bodine. I wouldn't have been able to do such a fine job by myself." She stared at the soft mound of earth and choked back the lump in her throat.

"The man needed buryin', that's all there is to it. You can't leave a man to be picked over by vultures. It just wouldn't be right."

"I'm saddened by the fact that Lucas never got to accomplish his life's work."

"The only place some folks make a name for themselves is on a tombstone. I guess that was his destiny."

Emmaline found the words harsh, but instead of arguing with Rafe Bodine, which she'd found produced little results, she opted for another tack. "I believe you said that you wanted to leave at first light, Mr. Bodine. The children are dressed and ready, and their tummies are full, thanks to those three delicious jackrabbits you prepared last evening."

Emmaline had never eaten wild game before, but she thought she would have eaten boiled shoe leather, she had been so hungry. And the fact that Rafe Bodine could not only hunt but cook as well had been quite a pleasant surprise.

"You're not like most men, are you, Mr. Bodine?"

He shrugged and cast her a quizzical look. "I don't know what most men are supposed to be like, ma'am."

"Where I come from, men don't perform menial tasks and fend for themselves." Actually, from what Emmaline had observed, men in her social class did little except go to their private clubs, indulge in frivolous activities, and attend to their investments.

Even her socially responsible father had never stooped to perform tasks that he could hire someone to do for a day's wages. He'd always thought labor of any type beneath him.

Being raised a St. Joseph had come with a stringent set of rules and regulations. Like her father, Emmaline had come from wealth and been a product of a privileged environment. But, unlike her father, she sought to make a difference with what God, her parents, and great-grand-father Ezekiel St. Joseph had bequeathed her.

Donating money wasn't enough. One had to give of one's self, too. Lucas had known that, and she was just beginning to realize how benevolent and unselfish her brother had been. He had set the example; now it was up to her to follow it.

Rafe's dark brow shot up. "That so? Well, out here, ma'am, if a man doesn't work, he doesn't eat. And if he doesn't eat, he dies.

"I'll expect you and the children to pull your weight on this trek, Miss St. Joseph. There won't be no mollycod-dling or excuses for things not getting done. And I'll expect my orders to be followed without question. Is that understood?"

His imperious tone raised her hackles. "Perfectly, Mr. Bodine. I wouldn't presume to think that I knew more about living in the outdoors than you. If there's one thing I am not, Mr. Bodine, it's stupid."

"No need to get your feathers ruffled, little lady. I'm just telling it like it is. I'm in charge and that's that."

He turned away from her then to saddle his horse, and Emmaline had a sudden urge to run after him and pummel his arrogant backside. She hadn't taken two steps toward the buckboard when he stated in his annoyingly authorita-tive manner, "We won't be taking that buckboard, so take what you need out of it and leave the rest behind."

"But . . ." She stared at the dilapidated conveyance, then at him. "But how will we travel? And what of our extra clothing? I packed a few things when we left Las

Vegas, in case the children or I soiled our clothing while on our outing." Dear Lucas wasn't the only one who had come prepared.

"We've got two horses for seven people. You can do the arithmetic yourself, Miss St. Joseph. The horses don't need to be carrying any unnecessary weight. And you did say that you'd be buying supplies when you reached town."

She couldn't fault his logic, and that made her all the more irritated.

"You ever ride astride, Miss St. Joseph? Because it's going to be hell riding in that dress you're wearing."

Glancing down at the once-lovely green velvet gown made her wince. It was ruined. Velvet wasn't made to withstand even the slightest bit of moisture, let alone horrendous downpours.

"I have another gown, but it's similar to this one." Yellow trimmed with green grosgrain ribbon. But she doubted he'd be interested in hearing that.

Disgust evident on his face, he said, "Why would anyone come out West and not bring proper clothing with them? It doesn't make much sense. Western women are practical, if nothing else, ma'am. You'd be better off riding in your drawers than in that getup."

She gasped, then turned beet red as the children started laughing at Rafe's comments. "Really, Mr. Bodine! I hardly think I'll be playing the role of Lady Godiva for you."

His forehead wrinkled in confusion. "Who?"

"I will wear what I have on. And there will be no further discussion on the subject," she cast a warning look at the children, adding, "from anyone." They quieted immediately.

"Besides, as poorly as I ride, my attire won't matter all that much."

"Are you telling me, Miss St. Joseph, that you don't know how to ride a horse?"

"Of . . . of course not." The lie made her cheeks blotch bright red again. "Don't be silly. Of course I can ride a horse." Not well. And probably not without killing herself. But she could ride if she had to. She could do anything if she had to.

"Good. Then Pansy will ride with you. I'll put Miranda and Miriam on Buck and lead him myself, so he doesn't get spooked."

Emmaline's heart sank as she stared at the small child now entrusted to her care. It was one thing killing herself, but poor Pansy . . .

"What about us, Mr. Bodine?" Hope shone brightly in David's eyes. "Are Danny and I going to ride horses too?"

Rafe placed his hand on the boy's shoulder. "'Fraid not, son. You and your brother will have to walk with me. It's what men do for their womenfolk."

Emmaline felt pretty certain she was going to be sick, but she couldn't decide if it was because she was now seated atop a large animal or because Rafe's braggadocio made her stomach churn with repressed anger. *Womenfolk, indeed!*

The boys' chests puffed out so far, Rafe was tempted to smile. But his humor died quickly when he thought of the son he'd never have because of Hank Slaughter, and the woman he'd vowed to love and protect, who was by now buried beneath six feet of cold dirt.

"Let's get a move on," he said, his tone harsher than he'd intended. "I don't have all day to dawdle."

Ethan glanced at the Wanted poster he'd been handed, then frowned in disgust at Elmo Scruggs. "You know Rafe would never have shot Bobby Slaughter in cold blood, sheriff. Why the hell did you have to have these printed up? Every bounty hunter between Mexico and the Canadian border is going to be hot on his trail."

"Your brother killed a man, Captain. I'm sorry, but I can't change the facts. I've got a sworn statement from the DeBerry woman saying that Rafe shot Bobby in cold blood. Said they was in the middle of"—his bushy eyebrows shot up—"*things* when it happened."

"She's a whore, for chrissake, Elmo! You can't believe the word of a whore against a Texas Ranger's."

The lawman leaned back in his swivel chair, and though there was something akin to regret on his face, he shrugged. "There ain't nothing I can do, Captain. Your brother is a wanted man. I expect he knew the law well enough when he decided to take it into his own hands."

Ethan couldn't dispute the old codger's words, for they were similar to what Ethan himself had told his father. But damn if they didn't go down hard.

He studied the likeness of Rafe's face on the poster, cursed, then shook his head. "I can't believe I'm having to hunt down my own brother like a criminal. Not after all we've been through together."

"'Tis a sorry thing, Captain, and that's a fact. And there ain't gonna be many places a man like Rafe Bodine can hide. Word of his being wanted's spread faster than a Kansas prairie fire. Man like that's got hisself a lot of enemies."

"I'll find him first," Ethan declared, wadding the poster into a tight ball and tossing it onto Sheriff Scruggs's desk.

The wooden chair squeaked in protest as Elmo shifted his weight. "And when you do, Captain, what then?"

"I'll bring him back to Misery to stand trial. Judge Barkley's already signed a writ of habeas corpus, giving me that right."

The sheriff looked offended. "But he done the deed right here in Justiceburg. Don't seem right, him standing trial somewheres else."

Ethan leaned over the desk, his eyes as cold as the rain pelting the glass outside. "I wouldn't worry about the legalities, Elmo. It ain't healthy to worry over what don't concern you."

Knowing a threat when he heard one, the sheriff leaned back in his chair and nodded, deciding that Captain Bodine was probably right: it wasn't none of his concern. Let the Rangers handle it. Rafe Bodine was one of their own, after all.

They'd been riding nonstop for four hours, and Emmaline's backside felt as if it were on fire. To make matters worse, the baby seated in Emmaline's lap had wet herself again, and the moisture had soaked right through the skirt of Emmaline's gown, making it dreadfully uncomfortable, not to mention odoriferous.

"Mr. Bodine, we really should stop for a while. I'm sure the children are hungry and thirsty"—she'd die if she didn't get something to drink soon—"and we all could use a rest." She rubbed her backside to ease the pain.

Rafe glanced back over his shoulder and frowned, wondering why he'd let a city woman talk him into such a foolhardy trek. Like most women of her station, Emmaline St. Joseph was more ornamental than useful, didn't have enough wind to blow out a candle, and would no doubt take exception to everything he said or did. And though he didn't mind a glimpse of that beautiful smile of hers every once in a while, it wasn't worth the trouble she was causing him.

"We'll stop when I say so, Miss St. Joseph, and not a moment sooner. Don't forget who's ramrodding this outfit." Ignoring her angry glare, Rafe continued walking.

The pace they kept was slow, and he couldn't risk letting Slaughter and his men get too far ahead of them. Although now that he knew where Hank was headed, the time element wasn't as crucial as before. It was likely the gang would stay put once they landed at their hideout in Wyoming, never suspecting that Rafe was trailing them.

Hank Slaughter's overconfidence in himself and underestimation of Rafe was what was going to get him killed.

Just then a horse appeared from out of the brush, stealing Rafe's attention, and he went forward to grasp the reins, which were dragging on the ground. Harnessed for a wagon, Rafe suspected that this was the horse that Emmaline's former nursemaid had stolen.

"Oh look!" Emmaline pointed. "That looks just like the horse Frau Muehler stole from us."

"It sure does," David concurred with a grin. "And now that we have an extra horse, Mr. Rafe can teach me and Danny how to ride."

Rafe held up his hand to forestall the excitement of the children's plan. "Whoa! First of all, the addition of this horse means that we now have three. That still leaves us a mount short, even riding double. Which means, I'm afraid, that you boys will have to continue walking."

At their crestfallen looks, he added, "But I guess you can still learn to ride. As soon as we get some spare time, I'll make it a point to teach you."

Their squeals of delight were interrupted by Miriam, still seated atop Buck, who announced, "I'm awful thirsty, Mr. Rafe. And I have to go to the bathroom."

Rafe glanced quickly at Emmaline, whose innocent visage made him wonder if she was behind Miriam's sudden attack of thirst, but he didn't voice his suspicion. "We'll take a ten-minute break," he announced. "Anyone who needs to do his or her business better get to it. That goes for you too, Miss St. Joseph." Slapping both of the the horses' reins into Danny's hands, he helped the two girls down, then reached up to gather Theodora into his arms and handed the soaking child off to Miranda.

"Do you need help getting down off that horse, Miss St. Joseph?" Her waist was so small he could span it easily with his large hands, he found himself thinking, then chided himself silently for the unwelcome thought.

She did indeed need his help, but Emmaline wasn't about to let this arrogant cowboy know it. "I can dismount by myself, Mr. Bodine. And I can also determine whether or not I need to use the . . . the facilities."

Despite all her drawbacks, Rafe had to admire her stubborn independence. He grinned, and the change in his usually dour appearance was remarkable. His teeth flashed white against his tanned face, and his startling blue eyes sparkled brightly.

Emmaline forcibly shut her mouth, so it wouldn't hang open in awe. Rafe Bodine was even more handsome when he smiled, which was about as often as he said something civil.

"About the only *facilities* in these parts, ma'am, is yonder bush or tree." He pointed to a nearby piñon. "I suggest you make the most of it, *ma'am*."

About to make a scathing retort, the sound of the children's excited pleas robbed her voice. Concerned, Emmaline hurried to them to see what was wrong.

"We heard noises coming from the bushes over there, Miss Emmaline," David said, pointing warily at the sagebrush. "What if it's a wild animal?"

Rafe came to investigate, drawing his gun as he stepped toward the moaning sound. He didn't recognize it as any animal he'd ever heard before, and almost tripped over the obese woman sprawled on the ground. Her blond-braided crown was slightly askew, and her serviceable, dull gray gown was littered with leaves and debris. She was rubbing her ankle, which appeared to be swollen.

"Frau Muehler!" Emmaline made her way through the bushes and stared at the disheveled woman in astonishment.

Holstering his gun, Rafe turned to Emma. "Is this the woman who ran off with your horse? The one you hired to care for the children?" Rafe's gaze swung from the nurse to Emmaline, who stared daggers at the older woman.

The German woman didn't give Emmaline a chance to respond. "*Ja.* I'm Frau Muehler." Rafe helped her to her feet and she leaned against him for support. "I vas hired by Mr. St. Joseph to care for da children, but he said nothing about living in da wilderness. I borrowed da horse, but it did not vant me upon its back." She brushed off her dress before shooting the bay a scathing look. "I have been sitting here for days vid nothing to eat, thanks to dat horse."

Rafe's eyebrows rose as he stared first at the rotund woman, thinking that her forced starvation hadn't hurt her a bit, then at the horse. He decided that the horse had made a wise decision. No doubt Frau Muehler had bounced when she landed, but her backside was padded well enough to prevent injury.

"Horse stealing's a hanging offense in these parts, ma'am. If Miss St. Joseph decides to press charges, you could be in some serious trouble." He glanced at Emmaline, who seemed at first shocked, then contemplative of his suggestion.

"I won't be as uncharitable as Frau Muehler was in stealing our horse and press charges, Mr. Bodine, providing she agrees to resume her duties as nursemaid to these children." It was a far more sensible solution, Emmaline decided, than to put the woman in jail or, worse, hang her.

"How does that sound to you, ma'am?" Rafe asked the matronly woman.

Flashing Emmaline a look of pure disgust, Frau Muehler replied, "I vill stay for now, Miss St. Joseph, because I have no other choice." She reached for the baby and assumed a stoic posture.

"Come, Theodora. Aaah, you are vet." She cast Emmaline a censorious look, as if the child's condition was all her fault. "Come. Frau Muehler is here to take good care of you." Without another word, she waddled away, carrying the child with her.

"Well, of all the nerve!" Emmaline said as she watched the woman's retreating backside.

"Seems to me that foreign woman's got nerve enough for two." Rafe scratched his chin, pondering the newest addition to the group.

"I should warn you, Mr. Bodine, Frau Muehler is extremely disagreeable." And that was putting it mildly.

Rafe didn't appear too concerned. "She'll follow orders, the same as the rest of you. There ain't a soul on the face of this earth, man nor beast, that I can't handle."

Emmaline looked skeptical, and Rafe was soon to eat his words.

"I vill not carry da firewood, Mr. Bodine. I am hired to look after da children, not to root around on da ground like an animal." Frau Muehler crossed her arms over her ample chest, dug in her heels, and prepared to do battle. Her ankle was still slightly swollen but apparently gave her no pain.

She did give Rafe quite a bit, however.

"Look here, Frau . . . whatever . . ." Rafe pushed his Stetson back on his head, a sure sign of his annoyance. "You're going to pull your weight around here, the same as the rest of us. Now get going and pick up some wood, or you'll be staying behind when we head out in the morning."

The stubborn woman jutted out both chins, which shook when she wagged her head. "No, I vill not do such vork. It is not in my contract."

"You have a contract?" He looked at Emmaline for confirmation.

Her nod was almost apologetic. "Lucas was very meticulous about such things."

"Well, Lucas is dead. And so is that damned contract, as far as I'm concerned. Now get moving, ma'am, or I'll hogtie you to the back of my horse and drag you to those cedar trees myself."

Emmaline sucked in her breath at the vicious look Rafe directed at the nursemaid, but she had to give Frau Muehler credit for stubbornness—the woman didn't budge an inch.

"No!" She dropped her plump proportions to the ground and shook her head defiantly. "I vill stay put until da children come back. Dey are my job, Mr. Bodine, not da firewood."

"Son of a bitch!" Rafe took a deep breath and swallowed whatever else he was about to say to the woman. Never in his entire career as a Texas Ranger had he met such open defiance . . . and from a woman!

"I don't believe Frau Muehler is going to follow your orders, Mr. Bodine. And I doubt that shouting at her is going to accomplish much."

The impossible woman had pushed Rafe's temper nearly to the limit. He didn't need Emmaline's interference. "When I want your advice, little lady, I'll ask for it. Now why don't you go help the kids gather some wood. One of you women might as well be of some help."

Emmaline stiffened. "I have been trying to pull my weight, Mr. Bodine, and do my share of the work."

The smirk he sent her was just a step above nasty. "Your weight—and your effort—are downright puny. You can't cook, you don't know how to saddle a horse, you ride like a pilgrim, you're as comfortable with the children as a chicken with a rattlesnake, and you sure as hell aren't the one to be giving orders around here, Miss St. Joseph."

She felt her face heat up and cursed her fair complexion. "You, Mr. Bodine, are a bully!"

"*Ja*," Frau Muehler agreed with a firm nod. "A bully."

Rafe shot both women menacing looks. "I've got work to do. If I'm not back before nightfall, I trust you'll be able to start a campfire." His expression was nothing short of gloating. "There's a saying that the hottest fire is made by wood you chop yourself."

Emmaline swallowed. "You're leaving? But . . ."

He got minuscule satisfaction from the fear clouding her eyes. "I'm going to hunt us up something to eat. Unless you feel more qualified."

"When will you return, Mr. Bodine?" The thought of remaining alone in the wilderness surrounded by bobcats, coyotes, and other assorted creatures set Emmaline's nerves to tingling.

He wanted to shout, *Never!* but the way she was tugging her lower lip with her teeth, like a small child would do, took the sting out of his words. "Don't worry, little lady. I'll be back in time to fix supper."

When he was out of earshot, Emmaline turned to the obstinate woman, who was attempting to rise to her feet. "I can't afford to have you defying Mr. Bodine at every turn, Frau Muehler. Without his help we will all perish."

"He vill not come back. And I say good riddance to him." She brushed her hands together, as if to rid them of a pesky insect. "I do not like Mr. Bodine."

"Whether you like him or not, he's all we have at the moment."

"No onc vill ever have dat man. He is alone. And he vill not be back, I tell you."

"I refuse to stand here and listen to any more of your rude comments, Frau Muehler. If you will not help with the firewood, then I insist that you fetch Pansy and put her down for a nap."

"I vill go and attend to da child. You are too foolish and stupid to know of such things yourself."

Emmaline gasped, but held her tongue, refusing to be baited by the ill-mannered woman. As soon as they reached a large town, she intended to hire another nurse and send Frau Muehler packing.

Dragging the toe of her shoe through the reddish dirt, Emmaline tried not to let the woman's opinions and Rafe's earlier comments affect her. But it was difficult. She prided herself on being an intelligent, self-reliant human being, and it galled her that they thought her so stupid and inept.

Maybe she didn't know how to cook, care for babies, or saddle a horse, but she wasn't stupid. She knew how to organize a charity dinner for three hundred people, how to sail a boat on the open seas, and she could write splendid bits of poetry when the spirit moved her.

She was quite an accomplished woman.

The sun went quickly behind the clouds and the wind picked up, chilling the air and forcing Emmaline to wrap her coat more tightly about her. She stared at the cold campfire, knowing she'd have to start another or they'd all freeze to death before Rafe got back.

Suddenly her accomplishments didn't seem quite as impressive to Emmaline as before, and she sighed dispiritedly.

The aspens were in full autumn splendor, creating a canopy of gold over Rafe's head as Buck picked his way through the forest, but the ex-Ranger was too caught up in his foul mood to give the scenery much notice.

Damn that fat German cow and her obstinate ways! Damn Emmaline St. Josephine for using womanly wiles against him. And damn himself for agreeing to escort her and that motley crew to the nearest town. He'd been with them for only three days and already it seemed like an eternity.

He should have had his head examined before agreeing to such a thing. Wouldn't Ethan be laughing down his sleeve if he knew how easily Rafe had been duped?

Of course, Ethan had no doubt figured out by now how quickly Rafe had tricked him over Ellie's funeral and would be furious. Ethan wasn't a man who liked getting bested by anyone, including, and especially, his younger brother.

The two had had a friendly rivalry for years. Rafe guessed the closeness in their age had something to do with it. And Ben wasn't above adding to the competitive nature of the brothers' relationship by issuing challenges, such as who could chop the most firewood or gather the most strays in an hour.

Though Rafe always enjoyed a good competition, he wasn't ruled by a competitive nature the way his brother was. Ethan possessed an inherent desire to be first, best, and right about everything.

Well, he sure as hell hadn't been right about talking Rafe into joining the Rangers.

Nor had life turned out the way Rafe had expected after retiring. He'd only wanted a bit of peace and contentment. It seemed now that that had been too much to ask of the Almighty.

All his life he'd tried to do what was just and right. Tried to take the higher ground, meting out justice and ridding society of vermin like the Slaughters. And what had been his reward: his wife and unborn child murdered and a life as a fugitive on the run from the law.

And now, to make matters worse, he was leading a group of women and children—a totally inept group—through the wilds of New Mexico Territory.

Though Emmaline obviously possessed intelligence and a great deal of kindness, which was evidenced by her treatment of the children, and though she had a smile he found completely enchanting, she was totally unsuited to the task of escorting five orphans through the rugged country to California. Refinement and money didn't mean squat on the trail, and she sure as hell didn't know the first thing about outdoor survival, though she talked a good game about pulling her own weight.

She'd looked wounded when he'd pointed out her insufficiencies. He felt bad about being so hard on her, but that couldn't be helped. He had a short temper, which she knew just how to ignite, and he'd decided that she might as well learn which way the wind blew from the onset. No use calling a mule a Thoroughbred, and letting her think she was doing right when she wasn't. Lying never did accomplish much, in his opinion.

The orphans, being easterners, were equally incompetent, but they couldn't be blamed for that. Life had already dealt them a harsh blow, especially that little flowerpot Pansy, who wasn't even out of diapers yet and had to face a future with no family to love her.

Rafe had to give Danny credit for trying his damnedest. The boy had put his heart and soul into swinging that ax this afternoon, though he'd nearly chopped off his toes in his effort to learn how to cut firewood.

Frau Muehler probably knew more than she let on about doing chores, her being of the serving class. But the damned foreigner was as stubborn as she was fat, and if she cursed at him in that German tongue of hers one more time, he thought he might be tempted to yank it out of her sassy mouth.

Hopefully by tomorrow they'd reach a town and he could rid himself of his entourage. He still had a job to do, and he resented having to shift his focus from the Slaughters to a bunch of greenhorns who wouldn't be able to find their butts if they weren't attached to their bodies. And he didn't like it at all that he was finding Emmaline attractive, despite his best efforts not to, for it made him feel guilty and unfaithful to Ellie's memory.

The wind picked up just then, blowing a low-hanging branch right into the side of Rafe's head. He cursed as he yanked it aside, and wondered fleetingly if it was a sign of some kind, like maybe somebody somewhere was trying to knock some sense into his thick skull, trying to tell him to ride out now while he had the chance and still possessed his sanity, and never turn back to what waited for him at camp.

It was a damn tempting idea.

Chapter Five

"WHAT'S GOING TO HAPPEN TO US ONCE WE GET to Sacramento?" Seated around the campfire that Emmaline had managed to start after six unsuccessful attempts, his belly full of the fried venison steak that Rafe had brought back to camp and cooked, David asked the question that was uppermost on everyone's mind.

The wind blew determinedly, but not as harshly as before, and the children huddled together beneath shared blankets to ward off the chilly night air.

"You'll go live vith strangers."

At the German woman's insensitive statement, Emmaline shot her a warning look, and Frau Muehler clamped her mouth shut tight.

"What I believe Frau Muehler is trying to say, children, is that when we reach California you'll be taken to the St. Joseph Home for Foundlings and Orphans to live. I will then make every effort to find wonderful, kind families who are looking for lovely children, such as yourself, to adopt."

"But what if no one wants us?" Miriam clutched her sister's hand tighter. "And what if they won't let Miranda and me live together?" Tears filled the child's eyes, and her voice quavered. "I won't leave Miranda."

"I won't leave Miriam neither," the older sister announced defiantly, hugging the small child to her protectively. "They got to take us both."

Emmaline sipped her coffee, welcoming the hot liquid into her body. She was chilled, and it wasn't just the cold wind that caused her discomfort. The questions the children raised haunted her thoughts as well. She sounded far more confident about placing them with good families than she actually felt. The orphanage had been Lucas's domain, his brainchild. What did she know about adoption, suitable families, and the like?

Even filled with self-doubt, she tried to sound confident. "I promise you that I will not split up brothers and sisters. You'll go together, or not at all."

"But what about Pansy?" Danny asked, staring at the contented child in Frau Muehler's arms. "She's like one of our family. How can we let her go to strangers? We might never see her again."

At the thought, Miriam began crying in earnest, which prompted Pansy, who didn't have a clue as to what they were talking about, to follow suit.

Rafe cast an eye at Emmaline, waiting for her answer. He was skeptical of Emmaline's optimistic attitude and assurances but had purposely remained silent. This wasn't his affair, and he didn't want to become any more involved than he was already, but he was finding it damn difficult to remain indifferent.

Tearing the baby away from the children she'd grown to love would be nothing short of cruel, in his opinion. Emmaline had told him of Pansy's abandonment by her alcoholic mother. It wouldn't be fair to yank her away from the only security and stability she'd ever known.

"What are you going to do about Pansy, Miss St. Joseph, if you don't mind my asking?"

Emmaline studied the faces before her and sighed deeply. She didn't have all the answers to the questions they posed. And though she might be able to forgive the children for their impetuousness in asking, she didn't have to forgive Rafe Bodine. "Pansy will be placed with a good family, Mr. Bodine. I will see to it myself."

The German woman shook her head. "You should not make promises if you cannot keep dem, miss. It is not right to do dat."

Emmaline was getting sick and tired of everyone second-guessing her. She didn't have all the answers, but she was trying her hardest.

"Please take the children and get them ready for bed, Frau Muehler. We have to rise early, and there's been enough talk for one evening."

A spew of German words followed the order, which fortunately Emmaline couldn't understand. The nursemaid did as instructed, and the children followed her, albeit reluctantly.

"You've taken on a big responsibility, Miss St. Joseph. Are you sure you're up to it?" Rafe tossed another log onto the fire; it sputtered and smoked before bursting into flame. She looked weary, and he felt a large measure of guilt for pushing her and the kids so hard, and taking his hot temper out on them.

"No one knows that better than I, Mr. Bodine, and it doesn't help to have everyone question my plans, which, I admit, are a bit sketchy. I'm doing the best I can for these children, and I will continue to do so upon reaching Sacramento.

"I intend to hire a new director for the orphanage, as my brother instructed, and see to it that the children are placed in good homes. I can do no more than that."

Rafe poured himself a cup of coffee and refilled Emmaline's cup. "What made you come on this trip, Miss St. Joseph? You're hardly cut out for such an arduous journey."

"I'm stronger than you think, Mr. Bodine. And I came because my brother asked me to. We were very close, Lucas and I, and I always found it hard to deny him his requests, for he very rarely asked for himself but always for others."

"Do you mind if I call you Emmaline? I'm getting a bit tired of sloshing that big name of yours off my tongue."

With a slight smile, Emmaline replied, "Not at all, Mr. Bodine."

"And that's another thing. You might as well call me Rafe, 'cause it seems foolish to do otherwise, considering the present circumstances and all." He'd also decided that since they were going to be together for days on end, they might as well try to get along. It would make the trek easier on everyone, and a woman who tried as hard as Emmaline deserved the benefit of the doubt, and a measure of respect for trying to better the lives of those innocent, neglected children.

"All right. Rafe it is. Is that short for something, like Rafael, perhaps?"

"Rafferty, ma'am. My ma liked the name, bless her soul, but she never gave much thought to hanging it on a grown man. It was bad enough having to wear it as a child. Pa always called me Rafe, but not when Ma was in earshot. How about you? Emmaline's a big name for such a little lady."

Biting her tongue, she forced a smile. "It was my grandmother's name. Mother insisted that I be named after her mother, and so I was. Mother always got what she wanted." In fact, Emmaline couldn't remember a time when Kathryn St. Joseph hadn't gotten what she wanted. She'd been spoiled and loved to distraction by Emmaline's father, and it had turned her into a petulant, sometimes childlike woman. Emmaline had found her behavior appalling and had never cared to emulate it.

"And what about you? Do you always get what you want?"

She shrugged. "My needs are simple. I have everything I want."

"Except a husband?"

Though his question took her aback, Emmaline didn't hesitate in answering. "That is something I don't desire, never have, and probably never will. I like being my own woman, running my own life, with no one to answer to but myself."

"Sounds a bit peculiar, if you don't mind me saying. I mean—it's usually expected that a woman will marry and produce children. Guess things are different in Boston."

"They're not, but I am. I don't want to be some man's brood mare, whose only purpose in life is to produce children to continue a line. As you've probably noticed, I'm not cut out for motherhood. And I've more to offer the world than that."

Rafe gazed into his cup and thought of Ellie. She'd been so excited at the prospect of having a child, and would have been quite content to live out her days as a wife and mother. Knowing that, he wondered at the oddity of Emmaline's comments. Having children was the natural order of things for women, as was wanting to get married. Rafe guessed rich women felt they were above such things.

"Do you plan to stay in California after the children are settled, Emma?"

Emma. She liked the way it sounded on his lips—intimate, friendly. No one but Lucas had ever called her that. "No. I'm going to return to Boston once the children are placed. My home is there, as are the family holdings. With Lucas gone, the responsibility of administering my parents' estate falls to me."

His eyebrow arched. "Must be considerable to need administering."

"With wealth comes responsibility, Rafe. My father preached that credo to Lucas and me from the day we were old enough to understand. I try to do good with the money I have."

"Charity." He wasn't fond of do-gooders who tried to

change the world and folks in it, whether or not they wanted changing.

"I donate to charities, yes. And to hospitals, art museums, colleges. Our holdings are vast and so are the donations we make.

"But that's enough about me. What do you intend to do once you're rid of us?" She smiled at his surprised expression. "Don't think I don't know how happy you'll be to relieve yourself of the burden we've placed upon your shoulders. I hope you know how very grateful I am. Most men would have turned their backs and walked the other way."

Something I've thought of doing more than once. Rafe felt his cheeks warm with guilt. "I've got matters to attend to. Personal matters."

"Things you'd rather not discuss?"

"That's right." He threw the dregs of his coffee into the fire, and the coals hissed loudly in response. "Time to turn in. Tomorrow should find us in a town, if we're at all lucky." His sarcasm went right over her head.

"I've always considered myself extremely lucky. How about you?"

His expression tightened and turned glacial. "I used to think I was, but not anymore. Good night." He walked away without a backward glance, leaving Emmaline to ponder his enigmatic words.

Rafe Bodine had been talkative and almost friendly while they were discussing her background, her plans, but when the conversation turned to him, he'd slammed shut like a New England quahog.

Eastern men were difficult to understand, but western men were quite impossible.

"What does the telegram say?" Lavinia squeezed her husband's arm, trying to infuse her strength into him. She was worried. Since Ellie's death and Rafe's departure, Ben had aged dramatically. The lines around his eyes had deepened, and his mouth was etched permanently into a frown. His shoulders, always so strong and erect for a man his age, sagged as if they carried the weight of the world.

Lavinia had married Ben Bodine five years ago, after his first wife's death, and she'd never regretted a moment of their marriage. Ben was stubborn and set in his ways, but she found out early on that his irascible ways could be soothed with a smile, and she had a lot of smiles to give.

She loved Ben with all her heart and soul. And she adored his children as well. If it was in her power, Lavinia would see that this family was soon put back to rights.

Handing his wife the missive, Ben crossed to the stone fireplace to stare into the flames. The large front room was Ben's study and had always been a haven for him. The comfortable brown leather sofa and chairs were welcoming, as was the colorful braided rug on the floor.

Above the fireplace hung a black and white cowhide— the first steer he'd purchased when starting his spread.

Lavinia hated it, calling the hide a "decorator's nightmare," but he wouldn't part with it. The cowhide was a reminder of how long and hard he, Patsy, and the boys had struggled to make a go of the ranch.

The sacrifices he'd made for his family had been worth it, the two-thousand-acre ranch far exceeding his expectations. But Patsy was gone now, his sons were traveling dangerous roads, and the room no longer offered sanctuary from his problems. Only Lavinia, with her generous heart and ready smile, offered respite from his misery.

He sighed deeply before speaking. "It's from Ethan. Rafe's got a price on his head for the murder of Bobby Slaughter."

Gasping, Lavinia read the words that confirmed her husband's statement. "But why would he do such a foolish thing? Even as enraged as he must have been after Ellie's murder, I can't believe Rafe would kill anyone in cold blood. It's just not in him."

Ben shook his head at her naiveté. "For chrissake, Vin! The boy's been killing most of his adult life. Why should this be any different?"

"But it is different. And Rafe never killed indiscriminately. It was his job to—"

"His job." Anger seeped into his words. "Rafe should have followed his heart and my urging to become a rancher, instead of his brother's rash plan to join the Rangers."

Lavinia clutched his arm, but this time it wasn't support she was giving but censure. "You mustn't blame Ethan. Rafe knew what he was about."

Ben's blue eyes, so much like Ethan's, flashed with hurt and disappointment. "Ethan lured Rafe into that miserable life. Mostly to spite me, I suspect. If he hadn't, my boy wouldn't be in the fix he's in now."

The regulator clock on the mantel chimed two. Ben crossed to the overstuffed chair, its leather well worn and supple from continual use, and dropped into it.

"Ben . . ." The animosity between her husband and his eldest son was as viable today as when she'd married Ben. And try as she might to play peacemaker, to ease the strain between them, they were both mule-headed individuals.

He looked up at his wife, and the sorrow on his face made Lavinia wince. "It's true, Vin. Ethan and I have always been at odds with each other. Patsy used to say we were too much alike."

"Well, you should be happy he is who he is. Rafe's life may very well depend on Ethan finding him first."

"Don't you think I know that? Christ, my boy's being hunted by the law like some common criminal. And the bounty hunters . . ." He jumped to his feet and began to pace. "They'll shoot first and ask questions later. The bastards crave the money and nothing else, giving no thought to a man's guilt or innocence. And you've read what the Wanted poster says: DEAD OR ALIVE."

Ben ground to a halt, drawing his wife into his arms and clutching her tightly to his chest. "I just pray that Ethan finds him first."

The front door banged shut and a few moments later Travis entered the room, hanging his coat on the brass stand by the door. He was dressed for travel, and by the determined set to his chin, it didn't take Ben long to figure out what his youngest son was about.

"I hope to God you're not thinking about going after your brothers."

Travis's blue eyes flashed defensively. "I had given it some thought."

"You're not up to the task, son. Leave it to Ethan to bring Rafe back. He's far more experienced in such matters."

Travis masked the pain his father's words caused. Ben Bodine might be at odds with his eldest son, but he was proud of Ethan's accomplishments despite his frequent blustering to the contrary. Rafe, too, held a special place in the old man's heart. It was only Travis—book-smart Travis—who was completely alien to his father.

"I may not be as good as Ethan and Rafe are with a gun, but I can track, and I—"

"Son." Ben squeezed Travis's shoulder. "Even if you were to follow them, they've got too much of a head start. And from what Ethan says in his telegram, he'll be bringing Rafe back to Misery to stand trial."

Travis read the telegram his stepmother proffered. Concern for his brother's welfare furrowed his brow and shone in the depths of his eyes. "Rafe'll be needing a damn good lawyer when that happens."

"Yep. That's just what Vin and I were thinking." Ben winked at his wife in conspiratorial fashion. He knew his youngest son felt that he didn't measure up to his two older brothers, and maybe Ben had been harder on him than necessary when Travis had wanted to leave the ranch to pursue a law career. But he was damn proud of Travis—proud of all his boys.

"You think I'm up for it, Pa? I haven't had a case quite as difficult as this one's bound to be."

"You're a Bodine, aren't you? And Rafe's your brother. You'll be up for it, son. Mark my words. I won't have anyone else defending my boy."

A mixture of pleasure and surprise showed on the young lawyer's face. "I won't let you or Rafe down, Pa."

Travis just hoped and prayed that Rafe wouldn't get himself captured or, worse, killed by bounty hunters or the law. He wanted the chance to defend him, to prove his own worth, not only to his father but to himself. And he wanted to save his brother's life.

Both Rafe and Ethan had sacrificed much for Travis over the years; now it was his turn to give something back.

The town they came to the following day was seedy, even by Rafe's standards. There were two saloons, a brothel, and little else, and Emmaline was only too happy to point out its shortcomings.

"I hope you don't think that bringing us here relieves you of the promise you made, Rafe. This . . . this place can hardly be thought of as a town. And it's most certainly not a *large* town, which is what you agreed to. There's no hotel, no restaurant. . . ."

Rafe pushed back his Stetson and heaved a sigh. "I have eyes, Emma." From his vantage point at the far end of town, Rafe could see that the irritating woman was right. This was no place for a decent woman and children.

But it might serve his purpose quite nicely.

"We'll make camp on the outskirts of town. I'll ride in later and see if I can stock up on some provisions." *And gather news of the Slaughters*, he added silently.

"I vill stay put in dis place," Frau Muehler announced, and Emmaline's mouth dropped open when the woman picked up her carpetbag and made ready to leave. "I vill find vork here."

"But . . . but what about the children, Frau Muehler? You agreed to remain and care for them. And this is not a respectable town."

The large woman smiled spitefully. "I have changed my mind. I vill not go vith you. You vill care for da children yourself . . . if you can." She laughed at the dismay on Emmaline's face and walked purposefully toward the brothel.

Rafe knew he should make some type of protest, call the woman back, but he just couldn't bring himself to do it. She was more trouble than she was worth. If Frau Muehler was set on leaving, who was he to argue?

"Hope she ain't fixin' to get a job at that whorehouse," Rafe said, almost to himself. "No one's gonna want to—"

"Mr. Bodine!" Blushing, Emmaline silenced Rafe with a look of condemnation while nodding toward the children. "Remember to think before you speak."

He glanced at the wide-eyed youngsters. "It's hard to

forget 'em, ma'am, with you reminding me so often."
Gathering Buck's reins, he issued orders for them to ride
out.

They would set up camp far enough away from town so
as not to be detected, but close enough so he could come
back later for a whiskey. Saloons had always been the
best places to gather information.

Rafe had been gone less than an hour, but already
Emmaline's mind was conjuring up the worst possible
scenarios: What if he'd decided, like Frau Muehler, not to
come back? What if she and the children were left
stranded outside that horrible town filled with outlaws
and miscreants? What if animals came into the camp and
devoured all of them?

As if on cue, the hideous roar of a mountain lion
sounded, the hoot of an owl followed, and Emmaline,
shivering from cold and fear, threw another stick onto the
fire and prayed for deliverance.

"When's Mr. Rafe coming back, Miss Emmaline?"
Danny looked over his shoulder into the darkness, his
eyes growing wide with fright. "I'm worried about him."

The young boy had formed an attachment to the cowboy, and Emmaline didn't approve of Danny's reverence.
From what she had discerned during the brief time she
had known Rafe Bodine, he was a man with a mysterious
past, and not one to let others get close to him. And he
was hardly a role model for an impressionable young boy.
His colorful language gave testimony to that fact.

"Worry about us, if you have to worry about someone, Daniel," Emmaline counseled. "Mr. Bodine can take care of himself."

"I'm co-cold, Miss Em . . . Emmaline." Miranda's teeth chattered as she shivered beneath her blanket. "The wind's bl-blowing right through my quilt."

"You children huddle together and stay close to the fire. There are no more blankets, and we're all just going to have to make the best of things until I can purchase additional supplies."

"When are we going to get to a real town?" David asked, scooting closer to his brother for warmth. "I thought we'd be there by now."

So had Emmaline, but she wasn't going to complain or ask a lot of irksome questions, for she knew Rafe wanted to be rid of all of them, as much as they wanted to get where they were going. She was dying to ask him questions about his past, what his urgent business was, and why he was so secretive about it. But she knew that Rafe was not a man given to sharing confidences about himself, and she couldn't risk angering him and having him leave her and the children stranded once again. Curiosity killed the cat, and she planned to stay very much alive.

The object of Emmaline's thoughts was at the moment leaning against the oak bar at the more crowded of the two local drinking establishments and savoring a glass of rye whiskey. He'd had better rotgut in his day, but at the moment he couldn't recall any that had tasted sweeter.

The Red Dog was about the sorriest excuse for a saloon he'd ever encountered. The cracked mirror above the bar—the result, according to the barkeep, of a brawl two years before—had never been fixed. The lace curtains at the windows were faded and tattered and had seen better days, like most everything else, including the bartender, who looked older than Methuselah and had to cup his ear to hear Rafe's questions.

"You know if Hank Slaughter's come through town recently?"

The old man ignored the question and kept cleaning the whiskey glasses with a filthy bar towel until Rafe placed a five-dollar bill atop the bar. "Maybe this will help your memory and hearing, old man."

The barkeep rubbed his white-stubbled chin, the sight of the money miraculously restoring his faculties. "'Pears that I do remember a group of men calling themselves the Slaughter gang. They was a smelly bunch, as I recall."

"That'd be them." Hank and his cousins had never been much for bathing.

"They was here three, maybe four, days ago. Drank a lot of whiskey and whored a bit, then they up and left."

"Did they happen to say where they were headed?"

The old man shook his head. "Nope. Didn't say, and I didn't ask. In this business it's healthier not to be askin' questions about things that don't concern you."

Rafe couldn't fault the old-timer's logic. Inquisitiveness was not a healthy trait for westerners. He made a mental note to tell David that. Too many questions were likely to get a man shot. It was said that a fool could ask more questions in an hour than ten savvy men could answer in a year.

Rafe laid down money for a bottle of whiskey. "Is there any place hereabouts I can purchase some blankets?" The nights were getting colder, and the childrens' bedding was woefully inadequate for sleeping outdoors on the ground.

"Maybe Merry will sell you some. She's the madam over at the whorehouse across the street. She might have some to spare. There ain't no mercantile, if that's what you're askin'.

Thanking the man, Rafe wondered how Emma was going to feel about sleeping beneath a whore's blanket.

He was about to head to the bordello when a tall, burly man at the far end of the bar called out, "Hey, ain't you that Ranger that rode through here a few years back? The one who arrested Tommy Fuller?" The man staggered toward Rafe, obviously drunk, and Rafe cursed the stranger's excellent memory.

"You must be mistaken, friend," Rafe said.

"I ain't. I'd recognize your pretty face anywhere. That mean son of a bitch brother of yours around? He nearly killed Tommy with his bare hands."

Rafe remembered the incident quite clearly. Tommy Fuller had tried to obtain the services of a whore without paying for them. When the woman had refused, he'd taken out his pistol and beaten her with it, nearly killing her. Ethan had nearly killed him.

Patrons of the saloon turned to stare, their curiosity piqued, and their thirst for a fight today unquenched as yet.

"Beat it! I said you got the wrong man." Trying to

appear unfazed by the man's accusation, Rafe poured himself a drink.

The drunk didn't heed the warning in Rafe's voice, but instead grabbed his arm, knocking the whiskey glass out of his hand. "You cowardly, yellow-bellied dog. Ain't you man enough to own up to what you and your brother done to poor Tom? And him only messin' with some two-bit whore."

Rafe had ignored many insults during his life, but being called a coward was not something he could let pass. He pushed hard against the man's chest, knocking him to the floor, and a cheer went up from the men now crowding around to observe. "Go sober up and leave me be," he said, turning back to the bar, but the man wasn't content to let matters lie and tackled his legs, forcing Rafe to the floor.

"Kill him, Dooley!" someone shouted from the rear of the saloon.

"A dollar says the stranger beats the crap out of Mick," another voice hollered.

Rafe was too busy to pay much attention to the shouting and the bets going on around him. The man called Dooley had nearly put his eye out with a well-placed elbow, but Rafe had turned his head just in time to avoid it.

"You asked for it, friend." Rafe hauled the drunk to his feet and landed a jab to his midsection, following the punch with another to his jaw. With a grunt of pain, Dooley fell backward into a poker table, and chips scattered everywhere.

"You want more, friend?" Rafe asked, towering over the inert form, but the drunk was out cold.

Throwing a couple of dollars on the bar to pay for his drink and the damage, Rafe grabbed his hat off the floor, dusted it off against his pant leg, and left quickly. He wasn't about to allow anyone else with as good a memory as Dooley's the time to discover his identity.

Chapter Six

EMMALINE AWAKENED EARLY. THE CAMP WAS still silent, the children nestled under the additional blankets Rafe had procured and brought back during the night.

There'd been whiskey on his breath when he returned, cuts and bruises on his face that hadn't been there before, and the odor of stale perfume on the blankets had been overwhelming, but she hadn't asked any questions. It had taken all of her willpower not to, but she knew that where Rafe spent his nights was none of her concern. He was her guide, her rescuer, and nothing more.

With her head propped on her palm, she stared at Rafe's back while he shaved. Gazing into the mirror he'd placed on the limb of an oak tree, he lathered soap on to his cheeks, chin, and neck with a brush, oblivious to her perusal.

The sight of this masculine ritual and Rafe's partial nudity made her stomach flutter every bit as aggressively as the oak leaves flapping overhead in the wind. She'd never before had such a strange reaction to the sight of a man's back, but then, she'd never seen a man without his shirt, either.

Lucas had always been quite careful to dress himself fully before rising each morning, but she doubted that her brother's frail anatomy would have compared to Rafe's robust one at any rate.

Well-defined muscles rippled as Rafe stroked the razor down his face with swift, sure strokes, and it was all she could do not to sigh at the sight of such sheer male beauty.

Admiring Rafe was like studying an exquisite piece of artwork. And she'd always had an appreciation for the aesthetic qualities of inanimate and animate objects, which no doubt explained her fascination with her subject.

Suddenly much warmer than she'd been moments before, Emmaline fanned herself with the corner of the covering, and credited the phenomenon to the wool blanket. Just then Rafe turned, and her eyes widened as she glimpsed the perfection of his chest—muscular, tanned, and sprinkled with dark hair. Intense heat suffused her all the way down to the tips of her toes, and she feared she would incinerate right on the spot.

Their eyes locked, and she blushed in embarrassment. "Mornin', Emma. Did you sleep well?" His smile was knowing, which caused her to blush an even deeper hue.

She clutched the blanket to her chin, smelled the offensive cologne, and released it immediately. "Quite well, thank you. It was most considerate of you to acquire the additional bedcoverings."

Never before had she had a conversation with a half-naked man. It was most disconcerting, and Emmaline was vastly relieved when Rafe shrugged into his red wool shirt.

There was a twinkle in the depths of his mesmerizing blue eyes. "I had to do quite a bit of haggling to get Merry to part with them."

"Mary?"

"Merry Stahl. She's the madam at the bordello in town. She charged me a pretty penny, I can tell you that."

The blankets of prostitutes covered her and the children, but she was too cold and too practical to be outraged by it. Though Rafe's smug manner did set her teeth on edge.

"I don't doubt it," she finally replied, wondering what else Rafe had purchased at the brothel. He looked awfully pleased with the world this morning, and it bothered her that she cared at all. Still, she couldn't help commenting, "You seem very refreshed today."

He grinned, amused by her seemingly jealous reaction, and decided to tease her a bit. "I'm feeling very refreshed, Emma. Very refreshed indeed." He knew what she was thinking, just by the way her lips pursed together, as if she were sucking a lemon, and he found it interesting and somewhat flattering that it bothered her to think that he'd been with a whore.

However, he hadn't been. His memories of Ellie were still too fresh, too painful, for him to consider bedding another woman. Even one as comely as Merry.

"I figured you and the kids needed some additional blankets, and she came highly recommended."

Wrapping the malodorous item around her, Emmaline rose to her feet. "How considerate of you. But you needn't have gone to the trouble on my account."

"It was no trouble at all. In fact, I kinda enjoyed the challenge of—"

"I'm really not interested in hearing about your exploits, Rafe. Now if you don't mind, I have some personal needs to attend to."

Rafe watched Emmaline march off toward the woods with the blanket trailing behind her, and he shook his head in wonder. Emmaline St. Joseph was about the strangest, most contradictory woman he'd ever met.

She was small. But sometimes you could find a heap of thread on a mighty small spool.

She wasn't beautiful by any stretch of the imagination. But there was something about her pert nose and that wild red hair that made her . . . he thought about it a moment . . . cute. She was cute.

Of course, kittens were cute, and they were a lot less trouble than Emmaline St. Joseph was proving to be.

Emmaline was exhausted. They all were. Rafe had pushed them for hours on end until she wanted to scream out her frustration. But her pride kept her from doing so. As did the challenging gleam in Rafe's eyes that dared her to complain.

So it was with great relief that they halted late that afternoon beside a gurgling mountain stream. It wasn't very deep, and it wasn't very wide, but it would suit her purposes quite nicely. She was going to bathe and wash her hair, and no one, including the imperious cowboy, was going to tell her otherwise.

"You'll have to take care of Pansy while the girls and I bathe and wash some of our clothes."

Rafe was building a campfire, and he paused to stare in disbelief at the small child she dangled toward him. "You want me to care for a baby? I don't know how to do that." He kept stacking the branches crosswise in the ring of stones, hoping she'd go away.

"Well, neither do I, but I'm managing. Just bounce her up and down on your knee, tell her a story, sing to her. I've got to take a bath, Rafe. I stink to high heaven and so do my clothes. And I haven't washed my hair for what seems like forever."

Rafe thought about how her red curls would gleam in the sun after being freshly washed, how the water would cascade over her body in silken sheets, making her nipples pucker, then he quickly forced away the provocative image. Thoughts of Emma naked were something he shouldn't and couldn't deal with right now.

"The water's freezing in that stream. You might catch your death."

"At least I'll die smelling clean. And how do you know it's so cold? You haven't been in it." Which was probably just as well. Seeing Rafe's naked chest and shoulders again would definitely not be good for her equilibrium, which lately was off-kilter whenever she was around him.

"Because mountain streams are fed from higher elevations where there's snow. That's how I know. It doesn't take a genius to figure that out."

"Well, since you're so smart, you can surely figure out a way to amuse Pansy. Look, she's smiling at you and holding out her arms."

"Horsey, horsey."

"Hurry and take her, Mr. Rafe," Miranda urged. "Me and Miriam want to go swimming. Miss Emmaline's going to teach us."

"We want to go swimming, too," David announced, the envy on his face plainly written.

"You can't 'cause you're going to learn to ride the horse, and me and Miriam already know."

Rafe wanted to point out that it was damned difficult learning how to swim in six inches of water, but the girls were so joyful at the prospect that he didn't want to dampen their enthusiasm. Lord knew they hadn't had much joy in their young lives, and they'd find out about the stream soon enough anyway.

"You did promise to teach the boys how to ride, Rafe," Emmaline reminded him. "And Pansy won't be any trouble at all."

Rafe studied the giggling child as if she were an alien creature and heaved a sigh. "All right, give her over." Pushing himself to his feet, he held out his arms. "But she better not mess her drawers, 'cause I'm not changing them if she does."

"Surely you're not going to let a small child best you. Not the great outdoorsman Rafe Bodine, who knows everything about everything."

"I never said I was proficient with children."

"And I never said I was proficient at making campfires and riding horses, but at least I've tried. If you're not up to it . . ."

The gauntlet was laid, and there was no way Rafe wouldn't meet the challenge. Though he had the strongest urge to take the sassy socialite to the river's edge and . . .

"Go take your bath. The boys and I will take charge of Pansy. Won't we, boys?"

Daniel and David exchanged worried glances, then Danny announced, "We're going to gather up some more firewood, Mr. Rafe," and disappeared with his brother into the woods before Rafe could voice a protest.

"It ain't so bad, Mr. Rafe," Miranda assured him. "I've changed Pansy's dirty diapers before. You just gotta hold your nose and splash some water on her bottom."

A horrified look crossed Rafe's face, and Emmaline grabbed the girls' hands and headed for the stream, her high-pitched laughter trailing behind her.

Rafe finished making the fire, then settled the toddler on his lap. "Now you just hold your droppin's till Emma gets back, little flowerpot, and we're going to get along just fine."

Casting her bright eyes upon him, Pansy patted his cheek. "Rafe, Rafe," she said, but his name sounded more like "Ruff, Ruff" when she said it, making him smile.

"You know, kid, you're mighty cute. And when you grow up you're gonna steal some poor fella's heart when he's least expecting it. Especially if you flash those big brown eyes in his direction and give him that sweetheart grin of yours."

Pansy giggled, and Rafe decided that taking care of the child was going to be as easy as throwin' a two-day calf. Women always made more out of something when it wasn't at all necessary.

"Emma's gonna be real surprised that you and I are getting along so well, flowerpot." He bounced the child on his knee, making her laugh again.

"You know, I almost had me a son." His throat thickened with emotion. "But a daughter would've been all right too. Of course, my pa, now, he's always spouting off about a man having sons to carry on his name. But I figure that a daughter who's smart and pretty can make a pa just as proud.

"And little girls sure do grow up to be beautiful women." His thoughts turned to Emmaline. No doubt she'd had curly red hair and plenty of freckles as a child. The smattering still left on the bridge of her nose and cheeks gave her a youthful appearance. "Of course, not all women grow up to be beautiful," he amended. "But then they have other qualities that make up for it."

The sound of Rafe's voice lulled Pansy to sleep, and he cradled the child close to his chest, liking the way her small trusting hand clutched at his shirt. "I think my pa would have liked you real fine, little flowerpot," he whispered, wondering what his family thought of his abrupt departure.

His father would understand his need for revenge, though he doubted that he would agree with the way

Rafe was going about things. Like Ethan, Ben was always in favor of doing things by the book. He'd always been a law-abiding man, but he was still enough Texan to take matters into his own hands when the situation warranted.

Travis would be disappointed in him, and that hurt. His younger brother had always looked up to him and Ethan, had often tried to emulate their actions. Rafe remembered the time when he and Ethan had taken Travis to town to bed his first woman. They'd gotten him drunk first, and by the time he'd reached the whore's room, he'd been so green in the gills that he'd puked all over the outraged woman before passing out. Ethan had ended up paying her double the amount she usually charged, and the memory still made Rafe smile.

Would he ever see his brothers again? he wondered. Travis had turned into a fine man, a respected lawyer in the community, and Rafe was proud of his accomplishments. Ethan, too, had made his mark in the world, earning the townspeople's respect as a fearless lawman, an admired member of the Texas Rangers.

Rafe sighed, wishing things had turned out differently. He'd have liked nothing better than to turn back the clock, have Ellie alive. . . . But that wasn't the way things were meant to be.

He was a man with a price on his head. An outlaw. The hunter had become the hunted. And he had no one to blame but himself—and Hank Slaughter.

His arms tensed at the thought of the man he'd vowed to kill, which caused the baby to stir, so Rafe forced himself to relax. Staring down at the little girl he held reassured him that there was still good in the world, still innocence and purity to overshadow the evil that existed—the evil that would have to be obliterated before he could ever find the kind of peace he saw reflected in the small child's face.

Chapter Seven

RAFE SPOTTED THE SMOKE CURLING UP FROM THE chimney when they were still several hundred yards away from the house. Halting his entourage, he rode ahead to scout out the situation.

If rangering had taught him anything, it was that things, no matter how innocent or benign in appearance, weren't always what they seemed. Having learned that painful lesson well just a short time ago, he had no intention of placing Emmaline and the children in similar danger.

Slaughter and his gang could be anywhere, and he wasn't about to take any unnecessary chances.

The ranch was nestled in a pretty green valley not far from the lake known as Eagle's Nest. There was an old mining town of the same name about five miles north, where he could purchase tack for the horses and foodstuffs, but Rafe thought it wiser to buy what they needed from the owners of the ranch and head out.

It would save time. And it would save the possibility of his being recognized from the Wanted posters that were no doubt plastered on the wall outside the territorial marshal's office. And if word had spread of an ex-Texas

Ranger on the run from the law, they'd be looking for a single man, not a man traveling with a woman and five children. He chewed on that fact.

By the time he returned a short time later to where Emmaline and the children were waiting for him, a full-fledged plan had taken shape.

"We'll be stopping at a ranch down yonder," he advised them, "and we're going to have to do some pretending while we're there."

Miranda and Miriam jumped up and down excitedly. "We like pretendin', Mr. Rafe," the younger of the girls informed him.

"Good girls."

Emmaline's forehead wrinkled in confusion. "What exactly are we going to pretend, Rafe? And why is it necessary for subterfuge?"

"What's sub-fuge, Miss Emmaline?" David looked up at her with those big question marks in his eyes.

She sighed. "Never mind, David. I will explain later. Mr. Rafe wants our attention now."

"There appears to be a family living at the ranch. I spotted a man, woman, and two boys, about the same age as David." The news made the boy grin.

"I want us to pretend that we're a family. I'll be your pa and Miss Emmaline will be your ma. Do you understand?"

Emmaline stiffened with outrage. What Rafe wanted them to do wasn't pretending but out-and-out lying. "No, I certainly do not understand. Why is it necessary for us to deceive these people?"

"Because I say it is, Emma. I don't want them askin' a lot of questions about who we are, where we came from, and all that. They'll be more likely to accept us if they think we're a family traveling from one destination to another."

"But what difference does it make if they know who we are and of our circumstances? We have nothing to hide." *Or do we?* She searched Rafe's face, but he gave no indication that anything was other than what he'd said. Still, she had the distinct feeling that he was hiding something.

"Where are we heading, Mr. Rafe?" At David's question, Danny nudged his brother in the side with his elbow.

"Hey! Cut it out," David yelled. "What'd you do that for? I was only asking where we was going."

Rafe patted the boy's head, remembering what it was like to be ten and at the mercy of an older brother. "If asked, we say we're going to Denver."

Grateful that she could at last put a name to their destination, Emmaline forgot her misgivings for the moment. Denver was a large city. She'd be able to purchase clothing and other supplies. And she and the children would be able to board a train heading west. Yes, she decided, Rafe had made an excellent choice, and she made a mental note to ask him how long it would take to get there.

"Most folks keep to themselves in these parts, so I doubt there'll be a whole lot of questions. Just remember to call me Pa and Miss Emma, Ma."

"How long we gonna stay at this place?" Daniel wanted to know, and David returned the poke, prompting

Emmaline to shake her finger in warning at the younger boy.

"Just long enough to buy a couple of saddles and any foodstuffs they're willing to part with, then we'll be on our way."

"We won't be staying the night, will we?" Emmaline swallowed, uncomfortable with the thought of spending the night under the same roof with Rafe. Not after seeing him in his almost altogether and liking it too much. She hadn't had the courage to question her reaction. In fact, she thought it safer not to.

Rafe rubbed his chin as if contemplating the idea, and there was a twinkle of mischief in his eyes. "Well now. I hadn't thought of all the possibilities, but now that you mention it . . ."

Flustered beyond her usual control by Rafe's teasing, Emmaline turned her back on him indignantly. "Don't tempt me to tell those strangers what a miserable *husband* you are, Rafe Bodine. Not to mention a horrible traveling companion."

"Now, Emma. Don't get your drawers all twisted in a knot. You don't want to frighten the children again, do you?"

"Why, you—"

"Mount up, everyone. And mind your manners." He stared straight at Emmaline when he gave that directive, and grinned.

The owners of the ranch, Sam and Gerrie Shepard,

were as hospitable and nice as Emma could have hoped for. Too hospitable, it seemed, for they had insisted that she and Rafe spend the night because of the storm now raging outside, and had even offered the privacy of their bedroom. This, after Rafe had mentioned during dinner that he and Emma had been on the trail with the children for a week and would welcome a little time to themselves.

She could only surmise that the blatant lie was Rafe's attempt to appear like any other happily married couple. But they weren't happily married. Why did he feel the need to make it appear so?

"Well, I hope you're happy, Rafe Bodine. You thought you were being so clever to trap me in this ridiculous set of circumstances, but the joke's on you. I have no intention of sharing that bed with you." Emmaline stared at the narrow brass bedstead and shuddered with trepidation.

Ignoring her pique, Rafe continued unbuttoning his shirt. "Keep your voice down. We don't want to wake the rest of the household."

His calm, collected manner irritated the heck out of her. How dare he be so detached about this wretched state of affairs! She'd practically died of embarrassment at the knowing look the Shepards had flashed her before she and Rafe retreated to the bedroom. And when Gerrie had insisted on keeping Pansy with her . . . Well, Emmaline had been completely mortified by the implication that there'd be something other than sleeping going on in the bedroom.

"You are the most hateful man! First you tell me that

we won't be spending the night here, then you turn around and accept an invitation to do that very same thing. Don't you possess a shred of honesty?"

Rafe's eyes narrowed. "If you'd care to look out the window, you'll see that the sleet is as thick as the venom on your tongue. I couldn't take the chance that you or the children would come down sick.

"And you needn't worry about losing your precious honor with me, Miss St. Joseph, because I'm not interested in what you may or may not be offering." That wasn't entirely true, but he wasn't about to let her know it.

"I'm tired, and I will sleep in that bed—with you. We can't take the chance that the Shepards will notice we aren't sleeping together and become suspicious. Now hop in, before I pick you up bodily and toss you there myself."

Gasping, she felt her face flame red and was grateful that only one kerosene lamp lit the room. Emmaline knew she wasn't the kind of woman men dreamed of bedding, but to have this coarse cowboy throw it in her face was horribly humiliating.

"I never insinuated that you were eager to bed me, Mr. Bodine. But it's hardly proper for us to be sharing a bedroom, let alone a bed, considering the fact that we're not married, and I haven't got anything to wear, and—"

His laughter halted her in midsentence. "We've been sleeping in the same vicinity for days, ma'am, in case it's escaped your notice. Most nights I could stretch out an arm and touch you, so I don't see what's the difference. You didn't mind sleeping near me all them other nights."

He looked her up and down, then added, "Just strip

down to your drawers and sleep in them. That's what I intend to do."

"But you aren't wearing any underwear!" she blurted, and he laughed again.

"Why, how unladylike of you to notice, Emma. But to set your mind at ease, I do have on my long underwear now."

Emmaline wished the floor would just open up and swallow her. How on earth had she gotten into such a horrible predicament in the first place? If only Lucas hadn't died and she hadn't assumed responsibility for all those children . . . If only she hadn't asked Rafe Bodine to help her . . . If only he didn't look so darn appealing. So damn virile!

"I'll just make up a pallet on the floor. It won't be any trouble at—"

"Emma."

The cold finality in his voice sent her into retreat, and she sighed in defeat. "Turn off the lamp and shut your eyes until I climb into bed."

"Your wish is my command, little lady." He extinguished the lamp and crawled into bed. "God damn, these sheets are cold!"

"You use far too much profanity, Rafe, and you should learn to curb your tongue in front of the children. You are not setting a good example for them. Young children are impressionable, and it's up to us . . ." Emmaline rambled on for several more minutes about his many shortcomings while she continued to undress.

"Are you done?"

"With what?"

"Biting into my backside while you strip? I'm getting tired of listening to those jaws of yours flappin'. You could talk the ears off a rabbit if you set your mind to it. I need to get some sleep, and I can't do it while you're jawin' me to death."

Slipping beneath the comforter, she shivered as the cold fabric touched her bare skin. Rafe was right—the sheets were colder than the ice pelting the window.

Lying as stiff as a board, with the covers pulled up to her chin, Emmaline listened to Rafe's even breathing. The heat of his body reached out, warming every part of her, except her toes, which remained frozen. The inky blackness of the room shrouded them in a cozy haven. Too cozy, in her opinion.

"Good night, Emma. Sleep tight. We'll have another long day ahead of us tomorrow. I'll be needing to make up some time."

"Good . . . good night." Rafe's head was so close to hers that his warm breath brushed her cheek when he spoke. If she turned only the slightest bit, their bodies would touch. The thought made her mouth go dry.

He chuckled, as if he knew what she was thinking. "This your first time sleeping with a man?"

She resented the cowboy's astuteness. "Yes. And hopefully it will be my last."

He grinned into the darkness. "With a sassy tongue like yours, you'll probably get your wish, darlin'. Most men like a bit more sweetness in a woman." He felt her stiffen beside him.

"I'm not at all interested in what men like or don't like. They're shallow creatures intent on their own pleasures."

"Sounds to me like you just ain't met the right one yet, Emma." His tone grew serious. "Not all men are like that. A man worth his salt always puts a woman's pleasure before his own."

Her toes tingled, and it didn't have a thing to do with the cold. Rafe had misunderstood her words. She meant to say that men were selfish, interested only in . . . Oh, for heaven's sake! She couldn't very well explain that to him now.

Emmaline had no doubt that someone as masculine as Rafe would be very good at giving pleasure. What would it be like, she wondered, to be held close in his arms, to be kissed and caressed, to lie naked and feel his hands on her flesh?

The erotic musings made her squirm restlessly, and she swallowed with great difficulty, knowing that this could very well be the longest night of her life.

"Emma . . . Emma, darlin' . . ." Rafe reached out to the warm body beside him, drawing her close to him and nuzzling her neck with his lips and tongue. "*Mmmm.* You smell so good." His hands moved over warm hills and valleys while his lips covered her mouth in a delicious caress.

Emmaline jolted awake to find Rafe's mouth pressed to hers in an ardent kiss. His tongue sought entry, insinuating itself between her lips; his hands fondled her breasts, then dipped low to seek out the area between her legs, which throbbed painfully, despite the fact that she had drawn her knees together against the onslaught.

Heat curled low in her abdomen, and passion she had never experienced before mingled with panic. Twisting her head from side to side, she pushed hard against his chest, which was plastered to hers.

"Mr. Bodine! Rafe!" She looked into his eyes to plead for her release, but they were closed, and he appeared to be sound asleep.

"Emma," he said again before his fingers continued their torturous assault, teasing her nipples into taut peaks, tampering with her self-control, and she nearly screamed in frustration.

"Rafe . . . Rafe, wake up!" She shoved him again, harder this time, and when there was still no response, she yanked his hair with all her might. That got his attention and he came fully awake.

"*Yeow!* What the hell?" He cradled his head in both hands and looked around in confusion. "What's going on?"

"You . . . you . . ." She shook her head, unable to talk, her cheeks crimson, and pulled the covers to her chin.

There were tears pooled in her eyes, and it only took a moment for Rafe to realize what had happened. "God damn!"

"You were having a dream," she said at his horrified expression, finally finding her voice, though it was small and shaky.

"Son of a bitch!" He cursed himself for losing control, even in his sleep, then bolted from the bed as if springs were attached to his bottom. "Shut your eyes."

Emmaline did, and waited while he put on his pants and shirt, waited for the apology she knew would be forthcoming, and wondered what she would say in response.

But none came.

And when the bedroom door slammed shut and she opened her eyes to see what had happened, she found herself quite alone.

Chapter Eight

Rafe rushed out of the ranch house like a man possessed. God, to think he had been dreaming about Emma . . . Guilt and frustration punched him between the eyes, and he plowed agitated fingers through his dark hair, breathing deep of the frigid morning air. It seared his lungs, cleared his head; he only wished it had the power to erase what had happened.

The sleet had subsided during the night, leaving the ground a muddy sponge. He knew the going would be slow and difficult under such circumstances, but he wasn't going to stay another night in the bedroom with Emma.

She'd been right: the joke was on him. Only what had happened between them was no laughing matter. He hadn't realized until now just how attracted he was to her, how much he desired her, wanted to make love to her. And that just couldn't be. Ellie hadn't been dead that long. It was indecent for him to be having thoughts about bedding another woman. But dammit! How did one turn off desire?

He headed toward the barn, where he knew the

rancher would be waiting. They'd arranged to meet at first light to finish the transaction for the saddles and tack.

Sam stood just inside the doorway of the weathered building, smoking a cigarette, and he offered a pouch of Bull Durham to Rafe. "No, thanks. I've got enough vices," he replied, and Sam nodded in understanding.

"Gerrie's been after me to quit. She says I stink up the place, but I figure a man's got to have some release from his daily problems. And I find that a good smoke relaxes me. With Gerrie in the family way again . . ." His face reddened.

"We'll be heading out this morning, Sam, so I thought I'd take those saddles off your hands, if you're still willing to part with 'em."

"Sure. Take them. The price you offered was fair. And I told Gerrie to pack up whatever flour, salt, and other staples she could spare. There'll be no charge for those."

"That's mighty generous of you."

The rancher's tone grew serious. "I think it'd be better if you don't have to stop off in town."

Rafe shifted his feet, wondering what the man was getting at, and did his best to act nonchalant. "That so? Has there been trouble?"

"A woman was killed about ten days ago—a whore who worked at the local saloon. Still, whore or not, what they did to her made my skin crawl."

Uneasiness prickled Rafe's skin. "What happened?"

"Butchered. Whoever did it practically scalped the poor woman. Cut her bad all over. It was right nasty.

Heard tell some outlaws had ridden through. Figured it was them."

The description was all too familiar, and Rafe's eyes gleamed with hatred and suspicion. "Did you happen to hear the name of these outlaws?"

"Nope. And hope I never do. Pray those scum never set foot in Eagle's Nest again."

"Didn't the marshal do anything?"

"Brett Bixler was out of town at the time, testifying at some horse thief's trial. All hell had broken loose by the time he got back."

Rafe didn't need any more information to know who had brutalized the whore. Coincidences like that just didn't happen. "Just as well, then, that we stay clear of the area."

"You'd best watch yourself on the trail. I didn't want to worry your missus, but if those men are still around . . ."

Rafe patted Sam on the back. He liked the rancher. And he thought that in another time, under other circumstances, they could be friends.

"I appreciate the warning, and the fact that you kept this to yourself. Emma tends to scare easy, and I wouldn't want her worrying for nothing."

"You've got a mighty fine family, Rafe. Hope you'll stop by and visit if you ever pass this way again. Me and Gerrie sure did enjoy your company."

Rafe wondered if Sam would feel the same way if he knew Rafe was wanted for murder. He thought not. "We'll do that, if we're ever by here again."

"Come on," the rancher said, tossing his cigarette butt

to the ground and stomping it beneath his boot heel. "Let's get that tack. I'm sure you're anxious to be on your way."

Emmaline couldn't wait to get out of there. But how she would face Rafe after what had happened this morning, she hadn't a clue. Just the memory of his lips on her mouth and his hands kneading her breasts made her quiver anew.

"Damn!" She slapped Gerrie's borrowed hairbrush down on the dresser. *Get a grip on yourself, Emmaline St. Joseph. The man couldn't have been making love to you. He as much as admitted that he didn't find you desirable. Obviously, he must have thought you were someone else. You should feel humiliated, not giddy.*

"Well, it sure as heck felt like me," she retorted, sticking out her tongue at the person in the mirror who dared to take her to task. "And I sure as heck liked it." But she'd be damned before ever admitting that to anyone, especially Rafe Bodine.

She had enough complications in her life at present— five, to be exact. She didn't need to muddy the waters by fostering an unwelcome attraction to a wandering cowboy. No matter how handsome he was.

Getting the children safely to California had to remain her first priority, her main concern. She had no time for frivolous pursuits such as romance. If there was such a thing.

Not that he was offering romance. Rafe had made it

clear as crystal that he wasn't interested in her in *that* way. The fact that he had called out her name while caressing her didn't mean a thing. She was just handy. His actions had been reflexive, not amorous. She could have been anyone.

She knew that she should be glad that he had no designs upon her person. Overjoyed, deliriously happy. Relieved.

So why was she experiencing a sense of loss? Why, in the deepest, darkest recesses of her heart, did she wish that she was the one he desired?

"Foolishness just isn't your style, Emmaline," she admonished herself. "There is no room in your well-ordered existence for a man. Any man.

"Besides, you have your charities. . . ."

But they're a cold substitute for a pair of warm lips.

"You have responsibilities to your wealth. . . ."

But money doesn't buy happiness.

"You have independence, intelligence. . . ."

But no one to share a life with. Or a bed.

"You have a flair for stupidity and recklessness. . . ."

Now, that's the first sensible thing I've said all morning. The very first thing.

"Bobby's dead!" Hank burst through the door of the seedy hotel room he shared with his cousins and tossed the telegram at them. It fluttered on a wave of cigarette smoke to the floor. "I shouldn'ta let him split off like that. We should have stayed together. There's safety in numbers. But he was upset over that goddamn woman. . . ." Anguish choked his words.

Roy Lee picked up the paper and read it, shaking his head in disbelief. "It's from Bobby's whore. Judy says Bodine shot Bobby down in cold blood. And that he's coming after us."

Paling under several weeks' growth of beard, Luther dropped the boot he was tugging on; it thudded loudly against the pine-plank floor. "The Ranger's on our trail, Hank."

Crossing to the window, Hank looked out, but he didn't focus on any one thing. There were folks milling in the street outside the Denver hotel where they were holed up for the night. Flatbed wagons carrying beer kegs and crates of whiskey rumbled by, and in nearby opium dens cowboys and gamblers gave themselves over to smoking the addictive substance.

Hank wished he had some now, so he could forget. As much as he'd thought his brother was a chickenshit and a poor excuse for a man, he'd loved the little bastard. And now Bobby was dead. Because Hank hadn't been there to save him, like all those other times he'd saved him from their father's drunken rages.

He'd killed the old man for beating Bobby. Killed him with his own two hands, until there was no life left in the drunken bastard. And now he would kill Rafe Bodine for murdering Bobby. A slow, painful death, much worse than what Hank had given Bodine's wife.

"Pack up. We're riding out. I want to put distance between us and that murder back in Eagle's Nest."

Luther look chagrined. "That whore shouldn't have laughed at me, Hank. Not while I was screwin' her and fixin' to come. It ain't right to treat a man like that."

"Well, you fixed her real good, didn't you, Luther?" Roy Lee didn't bother to hide his disgust. "And now we got more to worry about than just the Ranger coming to kill us. That marshal's gonna be hot on our trail, too. And all because you had to diddle some goddamn whore and lift her scalp."

"She was dead anyway. I didn't think it would matter. And I liked the idea of having me another souvenir—like the other one I got."

"Bodine's gonna shoot off your balls when he finds you, Luther." The big man's eyes widened, and his brother laughed. "You won't be diddling no more whores when that happens."

"Shut up, Roy Lee. Bodine ain't going to be killing anyone. He's the one who's gonna end up dead. Now pack up."

"But it's late, boss, and you said we could have us a poke with one of them whores across the street. I ain't had me a woman in a long time." Roy Lee's look was accusatory. "Thanks to Luther killing that woman, I didn't have time to get me any. My dick's hard as a branding iron." He rubbed his crotch to prove his point.

"Stay, then, and end up like that poor bastard Bobby. It don't matter to me. It's your funeral."

Roy Lee and Luther exchanged worried glances, then decided that a poke just wasn't worth dying for. Poor Bobby had already found that out the hard way.

* * *

Rafe knew he should apologize to Emmaline for what had happened back at the house, but he couldn't find the words, so he said nothing. Emmaline, on the other hand, hadn't stopped talking since they'd left the Shepards' ranch.

"How far do you think it is to Denver, Rafe?" She shifted in the saddle Rafe had purchased from Sam, and the worn leather creaked in protest. Pansy, cradled against Emmaline's chest in a papoose-style contraption that Rafe had devised from a blanket, didn't awaken. In fact, the child had been sleeping a good deal of the time since they'd departed early this morning, and that had Emmaline worried.

Glancing over, Rafe shrugged. "Hard to say at the slow pace we're keeping. I'd say we have less than forty miles till we reach the Colorado border, but if we don't step it up, we're never going to get there."

She heard the impatience in his voice, saw the frustration on his face, but still she had to tell him of her concerns. "I was just going to suggest that we stop. I think there's something wrong with Pansy. She looks flushed, and she's been coughing. I don't like the sound of it."

Moving his mount closer to Emma's, he studied the child for a moment but could discern nothing wrong with her. Pansy looked to be sleeping quite contentedly, her little hands gripping Emma's breasts. And though he knew little of children or their illnesses, he did know a lot about the female anatomy, and Emma was far more adequately equipped than he'd originally given her credit for.

Heat crept up his neck at where his thoughts and recent memories were taking him. "We'll make camp up yonder," he announced in a voice that sounded strained even to his ears. "I saw a clearing up ahead with plenty of trees for shelter, in case it rains again." Fortunately, the sun had shone for most of the day, warming the air and melting the frozen ground.

Emmaline couldn't contain her relief. She was weary, hungry, and the incessant chatter she'd been forced to uphold to lessen the strain of this morning's encounter had taken its toll. Rafe no doubt thought her an addle-brained harpy.

Not that she cared what he thought of her, she reminded herself.

While Emmaline tended to the baby, whose cough had worsened during the course of the day, Rafe took the opportunity to clean his gun. Since the day he held his first firearm, his father had drilled into him that a man's weapon had to be as clean as his conscience.

Daniel and David, absorbed in the workings of an ant hill, stopped and came to sit by the campfire to watch Rafe, and David exhibited his usual inquisitiveness. "That sure is a big gun, Mr. Rafe. What kind is it?"

"This here's a Colt .45. Standard issue for most of the Texas Ra—" he stopped himself just in time, "ranchers."

Both boys' eyes widened in awe. "Do you think I could hold it?" Daniel asked hopefully. "I've always wanted to hold a gun."

"A gun's not a toy, son. It's for killing and for defending oneself. If you understand that, then I guess you're old enough to hold it."

"Yes, sir!"

Making sure the chamber was empty of bullets, Rafe passed the revolver to Daniel, who weighed it in his hands. "It's heavy, but that's good. A man needs a good-sized weapon to aim true and hit his mark," Rafe explained.

"You ever killed anyone, Mr. Rafe?" David asked, staring wide-eyed at the weapon, wishing he were as lucky as Daniel to be holding a real gun.

"There've been times when I found it necessary to defend myself. But killing's never easy. When it gets to be easy, then a man's got a lot to account for, to God and to himself."

The brothers nodded at the wisdom he imparted, and Rafe hoped like hell that they really understood what he was saying. There was nothing romantic or glamorous about the taking of a life, and he wanted the boys to learn that lesson well. Too often, young men idolized outlaws and lawmen for all the wrong reasons. The harsh reality of life in the West was nothing like the glorified depictions in those dime novels eastern folks wrote and read.

Emmaline approached the campfire, carrying Pansy, whose fitful cries had taken their toll on her composure. "I can't get her to settle down, Rafe. She wouldn't eat any of the broth I tried to give her."

He held out his arms. "Give her to me. And fetch that can of evaporated milk from my saddlebag. She might not object to that. My mama swore by the stuff." Rafe cradled the child to his chest and spoke to her in a low, soothing voice that quieted her at once.

Danny punched a hole in the top of the Carnation can with Rafe's knife, and Emmaline poured a small portion of the milk into a tin cup and handed it to Rafe. She watched in astonishment as the child began to drink greedily, something Pansy had not done for Emmaline.

"You've got a way with children."

The compliment pleased him, though he didn't let it show. "I figure a baby's about the same as any small animal. You just got to speak their language."

"Mr. Rafe's talking baby talk." David grinned mischievously.

"Where are the girls?" Rafe asked, still worried over what Sam had confided. He couldn't take the chance that the Slaughters were still in the area. As ruthless as they were, he doubted they'd be particular about their victims' ages. "I don't want them wandering off."

"They're playing with the dolls Gerrie gave them. They've spread out one of the blankets and turned the base of an oak tree into their private domain." The sisters had been playing contentedly since they'd finished dinner.

Emmaline had many things to be grateful to Gerrie Shepard for—the jar of chicken broth, their supply of staples, the shelter she'd graciously provided—but she was most grateful for the dolls. Miriam and Miranda had been speechless with excitement at the gift, and Emmaline suspected that the rag dolls were the very first dolls they'd ever owned.

Seating herself next to Rafe on the log, Emmaline watched in awe as he coaxed more milk into the baby and thought that if a small child could be charmed and won over by the gruff cowboy, an adult woman didn't stand a chance. A discomforting thought.

"Don't know what we can do about her cough. It sounds like the croup."

Concern etched deep lines around his mouth and across his brow. "I remember when my brother had it. He gave my mother fits."

"Do you remember what she did for him?"

Rafe thought back to the incident, then grimaced. "I do. But I doubt you'll like the remedy. It's rather unconventional. My mother got it from a Dutch woman in town who swore by it."

"Tell me. Perhaps we can improvise the ingredients. I'm no doctor, but the baby feels feverish to me." Pansy started coughing, that horrible metallic-sounding cough, and Emmaline winced, feeling helpless. "We have to do something."

"Mrs. Vanderhook told my ma to take equal parts of goose grease and . . . urine, and give it to my brother a teaspoonful at a time to make him vomit. She claimed it would clear up the congestion in his chest."

Emmaline's expression conveyed her horror. She would certainly not give this small baby such a vile concoction. "That's out of the question."

He shrugged. "It worked. My brother got well in a few days. At any rate, we don't have a goose."

Praise the Lord for that!

"You could use lard," Daniel suggested. "Mrs. Shepard gave us some."

"Yeah. And I've got plenty of—"

"That will be quite enough, David. Thank you both for your help, but I don't think—"

"We'll do whatever's necessary to get this little flowerpot well," Rafe stated, "even if it offends your ladylike sensibilities."

"It isn't my sensibilities I'm worried about, but this child's health." Emmaline rose to her feet. "I'm going to consult Lucas's guidebook. Perhaps it contains a remedy more palatable than the one your Dutch woman used."

In the end, they agreed to a mixture of lard, sugar, and some of Emmaline's smelling salts, which contained ammonia. The recipe she'd found in the guidebook called for alum, but they didn't have any of that, so Emmaline decided to improvise as best she could.

By the time the concoction was ready, Pansy's cough and breathing had worsened. Filled with self-doubt, but with no other alternative, Emmaline administered the unorthodox remedy to the child, hoping it wouldn't do more harm than good.

They waited for what seemed like forever, then finally the treatment produced the desired effect: Pansy started to vomit. Once she started, Emmaline didn't think she would ever stop. "Oh no! I think I've made her worse." Tears filled her eyes.

Rafe studied the child, whose breathing seemed a bit relieved. "I think it's working." He laid his ear on Pansy's chest and listened. "I think the congestion near her wind-pipe has lessened. She's breathing easier."

Thanking the Almighty, Emmaline ripped one of her flannel petticoats into strips and dipped them into hot water, as she had seen her mother do countless times for Lucas when he'd been afflicted with his asthma, and laid them across the baby's narrow chest. She repeated the process over and over, until Pansy's wheezing stopped and she fell into a natural sleep in Rafe's arms.

Filled with relief at the child's improvement, Rafe couldn't help but be impressed by Emmaline's efforts. She'd kept her wits about her, had used common sense to doctor Pansy, and he appreciated and respected that. "You did good, Emma. Real good."

She smiled gratefully. "We both did. We make a good pair."

Their eyes locked and an awkward silence fell between them, which made the crackling of the fire and the wind whistling through the trees seem louder than before.

Though neither mentioned what had happened between them that morning, it was there as a reminder: passion had passed between them, been ignited, and allowed to burn only briefly before reality reared its head.

But it remained there, beneath all the denials, the excuses, the disdain. Like a banked fire, it was just waiting for the next spark.

Chapter Nine

Emmaline stared with nothing short of revulsion at the gun Rafe proffered and shook her head adamantly. "I don't want to learn."

"That's too bad, because you're going to. I've got to leave you and the kids alone for a while, and I want to be sure that you'll be able to defend yourself." Rafe placed the weapon in the palm of her hand. "Feel the weight of it. Let it become part of you. Think of it as an extension of yourself."

Why Rafe had suddenly decided that she had to become proficient in the use of a gun was still a mystery to her, but ever since crossing the border into Colorado he had insisted that she learn. And nothing she'd said had made him change his mind. But then, she suspected that perversity was an integral part of the cowboy's nature.

"We haven't seen a soul since leaving the Shepards' ranch three days ago, and it's doubtful that we're going to out here in the middle of nowhere. And I sincerely doubt that I'd be able to shoot anyone even if we did." The idea of killing another human being was abhorrent to her.

"There're mountain lions in these parts and other wild animals that could cause you and the children harm."

"Bears, Mr. Rafe?" Miranda's lower lip started trembling, and she clutched her sister's hand.

"No, not bears, darlin'. They're hibernating. Every year, usually in autumn, they find a cave and hole up for the winter. Since it's now October, I expect they're fast asleep." Having placated the child, he turned back to Emmaline.

"I know that if anything or anyone threatens those kids, Emma, you're going to shoot first and ask questions later. That's just human nature. Animal or human, it's a female's instinct to protect her young."

Knowing she would soon be giving the children up, Emmaline had made every attempt to remain detached, but thus far she hadn't succeeded. Rafe was right. She did feel motherly toward them, protective, loving, but that didn't mean she'd be capable of defending them if the need arose. His confidence in her abilities was woefully misplaced, she feared.

Five sets of eyes stared at her, waiting, wondering what she would do next. Rafe stared too, but he had that cold, uncompromising look that said clearly she wouldn't be given a choice. Sighing in defeat, she wrapped her hand about the butt of the gun. "All right. I'll try. But don't expect miracles."

"You've finally learned to saddle your horse, and that was nothing short of a miracle. So I guess you can learn this too."

"How kind of you not to mention that I fell off three

times during those attempts. Maybe if I'm lucky I can shoot myself to please you."

"You wouldn't have fallen off if you'd cinched the horse proper to begin with. I told you to slap his belly, so you could get the cinch strap tighter, but you didn't want to 'hurt the poor creature.' I believe those were your exact words."

Her cheeks filled with color as her naiveté was thrown back in her face. "How was I supposed to know that you were telling the truth about that stupid horse blowing himself up with air. I thought you were making it up."

"Maybe this time you'll listen carefully to *everything* I say. Your life could very well depend on it."

She stared at the tin can resting on the log and knew that he asked the impossible. "You expect me to hit that little can from way back here? Can't I move closer?" She attempted to, but he yanked her back, and the children giggled.

"From here, Emma. Now aim the gun at the can, sight down the barrel, and squeeze the trigger real slow."

Emmaline held out her arm, but the weight of the gun had it bobbing up and down like a cork. "The gun's too heavy."

"I thought you were so proud of your muscles. I saw you showing them off to the kids when you thought I wasn't looking."

She aimed again, this time determined to shoot the damn gun even if her arm fell off, and was sorry she had ever allowed Rafe the opportunity to observe her morning calisthenics.

Following his instruction, she fired.

And landed smack dab on her butt, much to the delight of Rafe and the children, who howled at her antics.

She pushed to her feet, dusting herself off. "That's it. I'm not doing this."

"You don't want the children to think you're a quitter, do you? What kind of example would you be setting for them?"

Eyes flashing fire, she motioned him closer and whispered, "You'd better hope that I don't get proficient with this firearm, Rafe Bodine, because I'm likely to aim it at your arrogant backside."

He grinned and ignored the threat. "Shall we try to hit the tin again?"

"I don't know why you think it's necessary to go off on some hunting expedition by yourself. We still have plenty of beans left."

"I want meat, woman. That's why. And I'm sure the children would welcome fresh rabbit or venison over beans."

"We would," Daniel and David shouted, nodding in unison.

"Traitors!" Emmaline flashed them a look of pure annoyance and fired her weapon again.

At the end of her first lesson, which lasted close to three hours, Emmaline's right shoulder and arm felt as if they were on fire. She ached in places she hadn't known existed, and wondered how someone as physically fit as she considered herself could be so darn decrepit.

Leaning against the base of an oak, she watched in relief as the children fetched firewood, grateful that she hadn't been asked to participate. Closing her eyes, she wished it were bedtime so she could crawl beneath a blanket and go to sleep.

"You look plumb wore out, Emma."

She opened her eyes to find Rafe straddling her outstretched legs. Her gaze traveled up the long length of him to find the most aggravating grin on his face. "I *am* 'plumb wore out,' thanks to you and your sadistic instruction."

He squatted before her. "You can hit the can now."

"Tell that to my shoulder. It'll make it feel so much better." Rubbing the inflamed joint to prove her point, she winced in pain.

"Lean forward. I'll rub it for you."

Her eyebrow arched. "More torture?"

"Consider it reward for a job well done."

His words pleased her more than she cared to admit, and she turned her back toward him, nearly groaning as his hands began to knead the soreness out of her knotted muscles. The word *ecstasy* came to mind.

"I should have realized that despite all those daily exercises you're still a tenderfoot. Guess I pushed you too hard today."

"Well, if I'm not dead by morning, then I guess no harm's been done," she replied with no small amount of sarcasm.

He bit back a grin. "You're a spunky little thing, aren't you?"

"So I've been told. *Mmmm*. Do that some more. It feels so wonderful." She practically purred.

Emma's croons of enjoyment drove Rafe wild. Every *oooh* and *aaah* made his gut tighten in unwelcome awareness. Every *mmmm* tingled his spine, among other things.

Lifting her curtain of hair, he dug his thumbs into her neck muscles, detecting the evocative whisper of the lilac water she'd doused herself with that morning. The scent played havoc with his composure. His mouth went dry, and he forced himself to concentrate on what he was doing, but without much success.

"How's that feel?" His voice sounded strangely pained.

"Absolutely decadent. Scrumptious. I think I've died and gone to Heaven."

His hands moved down her back, the heels of his palms circling slowly. "How about now?"

She sighed again in pure contentment, and the sound registered way below Rafe's ears, somewhere in the region of his crotch. He stepped back as if he'd been burned.

"That should do it."

She showered him with a smile of unadulterated gratitude. "That was wonderful. Thank you."

"You're welcome."

"Perhaps one day I can return the favor."

Emmaline had never seen a man move so fast in her entire life, and she wondered what she'd said to provoke such a reaction.

Two days later, the horses plodded slowly down the

trail. The steady clip-clop, clip-clop of their hooves soothed the baby in Rafe's arm into a contented slumber, while the four other children trudged behind them on foot, keeping up a constant chatter to rival the magpies in the branches overhead. Having three horses at their disposal afforded the two older girls a mount, though they often walked alongside Danny and David to keep them company.

Thick clouds covered the sun, making the afternoon dark and dreary, and Emmaline worried that rain would put in an unwelcome appearance before the day was through.

"I don't like the look of that sky," Rafe commented, echoing Emma's thoughts as he gazed up. "We need to find better shelter for tonight."

"That would be wise. But I haven't seen signs of human habitation for the last couple of days."

His eyebrow arched, and the corners of his mouth twitched in amusement. "You reading sign now? Maybe I should let you ride ahead and scout the area."

Emmaline's cheeks filled with color. "I've been trying to pay attention, Rafe. Isn't that what you're always suggesting?"

"It is. And I wasn't just talking off the top of my head when I told Miranda that bears hibernate in these parts. So there's bound to be caves in these hills. We'll just have to hunt for them."

"How did you learn about wildlife, tracking, and the like? You know so much about living outdoors."

He shifted his weight, uncomfortable with the question,

lest he be forced to reveal things better off kept to himself. "It's part of growing up out here. You have to learn to live off the land, read sign, whether it's weather or animal. Survival depends on it."

"Where are you from? I don't believe you ever said."

"Well now, ma'am, I don't recall you ever asked."

"I'm asking now."

She was. But how much was he willing to reveal? "Texas. Born and raised outside a little town known as Misery."

"Do you have family there?"

"My pa and his wife own a cattle ranch."

"Oh, so you're a rancher?" Funny, he didn't seem like a man who tended cattle for a living.

Rafe thought of the ranch he'd been forced to leave behind, the new life he'd made for himself with Ellie and now would never have, and animosity filled him anew. In the space of a heartbeat, his world had crumbled. But at least there was solace in the knowledge that before he'd left, Ellie had been taken care of properly. Of that, he had no doubt. Of the ranch, he wasn't as certain.

"So to speak," he finally replied. "I've done my share of wrangling and cow punching."

"Any brothers or sisters other than the one you mentioned had the croup?" Emmaline missed her own brother so much her heart ached every time she thought of Lucas buried in the middle of nowhere with nothing but a makeshift marker to indicate the spot. He had always been a man with a mission, determined to do great things and leave his mark on the world.

Well, she wouldn't allow Lucas's death to be in vain. There was still the orphanage, and she would rename it the Lucas St. Joseph Home for Foundlings and Orphans in his honor. It was his dream, his right.

"You sure do ask a lot of questions."

She smiled ruefully, for in truth, she was every bit as inquisitive as David. And there was so much she wanted to know about him, but dared not ask. The mystery surrounding Rafe intrigued her, but she feared that the truth might be something she couldn't handle or dismiss. And ignorance was said to be bliss, though she wasn't certain how much longer she could keep the nagging questions to herself.

"It's just that—I miss my brother so much," she answered finally. "I guess talking about family, even someone else's, makes it easier to bear that I've got no one left."

He took one look at her kitten eyes, so lost and sad, and knew he was defeated. "Two brothers—Ethan and Travis. One's older, one's younger."

"Do you get along with them? Lucas and I were very close, best friends really."

"Ethan and I were like that. Travis, being younger, got left out sometimes. He probably resented us for that."

"Are they ranchers, too?"

He shook his head. "Travis is a lawyer. Has his own practice in Misery." And a shingle outside the tonsorial parlor that read TRAVIS BODINE, ESQUIRE, with an arrow pointing to the top floor.

"That's wonderful! You must be so proud of him." Her

voice and expression grew wistful. "I wanted to study the law at one time. I thought it would be a wonderful way to help those less fortunate than myself. But my father wouldn't hear of it. Said it was unseemly for a woman to have a profession. He said no St. Joseph had ever aspired to work for a living. It just wasn't considered suitable by his standards."

Her eyes filled with pain as she remembered the screaming match they'd had the day she announced her plans to attend Radcliffe. As was always the case, her mother, ever conscious of what others would think, had sided with her father. And even Lucas, her staunch supporter, had chided Emmaline for her impetuousness in wanting to do such an unorthodox thing as study law. His betrayal was the one that had hurt the most.

"You could still do it, if you wanted to," Rafe said. "You've got no one to tell you any different this time."

"I guess that's true. But my life's taken another direction. Sometimes having a great deal of money is as cumbersome and suffocating as having none at all. It restricts what you can and cannot do."

"Well, if I had my druthers, guess I'd take the money." His smile was teasing, but she didn't find her present circumstances amusing.

"It's not all it's made out to be. Oh, I'm not complaining. I have a wonderful life filled with every advantage imaginable. It's just that—I'm not free to just leave it all behind. I have responsibilities that ultimately draw me back, whether or not I want to go."

"What you're saying is that you're tethered on a short

rope." Better than hanging from one by the neck, which would be his fate if a bounty hunter or Ethan found him.

Realizing that the conversation had strayed, Emmaline smiled apologetically. "Here I am talking about myself again when we're supposed to be talking about you. Now tell me about the other brother, Ethan, is it?"

Ethan was the one he wanted to avoid discussing, but Rafe could see there was no way around it, unless he lied. And he couldn't bring himself to do that. He'd lied enough to Emma already. Or at least, hadn't told her the truth.

"Ethan's a Texas Ranger."

Her eyes widened, and she was impressed in spite of herself. She'd always heard that Texas Rangers were incredibly strong and brave men. "Really! I've read about how fearless they are. How they always get their man. Goodness! Your family sounds so exciting compared to mine."

He laughed, and knew that Ethan would have done the same if he'd heard her.

"What is it? Did I say something funny?"

"I guess it's that old adage about the grass always being greener. . . . I doubt you'd find many folks in Misery who think their lives exciting." His and Ethan's had been for a time, but he wasn't going to share that with her.

"Well, at least you're not restricted to attending tedious social functions and entertaining people who you think are utterly boring, and who only like you for your money. And you're not forced to wear corsets so tight that you can hardly draw a breath.

"Men have it so much easier than women." Funny, until this very moment, she hadn't really thought about how unfulfilled her life was. Being on the trail with Rafe, having somewhat of an adventure, experiencing new and exciting things, had painfully pointed out just how mundane her existence had been.

"I've never worn a corset, ma'am, but that don't mean my life's a bed of roses. Men got it tough. It's just different from what a woman's got to contend with.

"It's the differences between men and women that make them interesting to each other, I guess."

"I guess you're right."

He grinned. "Usually am." At that moment the first drop of rain hit Emmaline squarely on the tip of her nose, and Rafe laughed. "See. What'd I tell you?"

There was no time to respond, for just then the heavens opened up, giving credence to Rafe's overinflated ego, which Emmaline was planning to puncture at the first possible opportunity.

Ethan was having a miserable day. Twice he had picked up Rafe's trail after rain had obliterated it, and twice he had lost it. He'd arrived too late in Justiceburg to prevent Bobby Slaughter's murder, and now heavy rain had delayed his departure once again.

The whore who'd accused Rafe of murder had taken sick and he'd been forced to cool his heels in town while waiting to interrogate her. To make matters worse, he'd been accosted by a couple of old ladies concerned about their errant niece, who had taken it in her head to go after Rafe for the reward money. They had begged him to ride out after her and bring her back, as if he had nothing better to do than to play nursemaid to some headstrong woman who fancied herself a damn bounty hunter.

Ethan worried that if he didn't get back on the trail soon, he was never going to find his brother. Rafe had a two-week head start on him to begin with, and now with Ethan hamstrung by the weather and uncooperative witnesses—and old ladies, to boot—even more time and distance were now between him and his brother.

"Dammit, Rafe!" Ethan threw his cigar down into the street and smashed it into the mud with his boot. *Why couldn't you have trusted me to help you?*

With a disgusted sigh, the Ranger headed to the saloon, hoping the whore would be willing to see him today.

The cave Rafe found was warm and cozy in comparison to sleeping outside in the elements, and there was an underground spring bubbling beneath, which would provide an adequate amount of drinking water. Emmaline silently blessed the skills Rafe possessed that had brought them to their new haven.

Children were forever adaptable, and the orphans proved no different. It hadn't taken them long at all to accustom themselves to their new surroundings; they were already entrenched in a fantasy game of pirates and fair maidens, and Pansy was being forced to toddle the imaginary plank.

The rain poured down in earnest now, and it didn't look like it was going to abate anytime soon. So it took Emmaline by surprise when Rafe casually announced that he was going to leave to hunt game.

"But when will you return? I'll be . . ." she didn't want to use the term *frightened*, "worried until you get back." And why was he leaving them again so soon, when they still had plenty of meat left from his last hunting trip? Unless he was hunting a different type of game, like a woman, perhaps. That thought sent pain stabbing into her heart.

"This cave is well hidden, which is why I chose it. You shouldn't have any unexpected visitors. And if you do, then use the gun. That's what it's for."

She swallowed with some difficulty and tried to be brave for the children's sake, knowing that they had less than total confidence in her abilities. "You'll be careful? You won't be gone too long?"

The fear on her face gave him pause, but only for a moment. His mission had to be completed. The snail's pace they traveled had afforded the Slaughters a substantial lead. And though he'd been told they were heading to their hideout in Wyoming, there was still the possibility that they would change their minds, and there was no guarantee that he would actually find them there.

With that in mind, Rafe needed to gather information at the nearest town. There was always a chance that someone had heard or seen something that could point him in the right direction. Trinidad was a half day's ride if he pushed it, and that's where he was headed.

He rubbed his chin, grateful that the beard and mustache he'd grown this past week would prove useful for just such a purpose. The hair would disguise his appearance to a point, making it easier for him to come and go as he pleased. Emma hated the facial hair, and had told him so on several occasions, and he found solace in that too. But he didn't ask himself why.

Rafe's trip into the town of Trinidad proved a waste of time. No one he asked had seen or heard of the Slaughters, or so they said.

There were times when that unspoken code of silence that westerners embraced drove him wild. And now, camped out in the rain with only a spindly stand of piñon pines for shelter, was one of them. He hated wasting time, hated being away from Emma and the children for too long.

It was one of the reasons he'd fled. The woman and children were becoming far too important to him. He needed to keep his distance, maintain a certain objectivity, so that he wouldn't lose sight of what was important.

Avenging Ellie and his unborn child's death had to be his only focus. He could have no life beyond killing the Slaughters, find no rest, no solace in another woman's arms, until that was done.

And even then, he would still be a man wanted for murder. An outlaw on the run from the law. A man with a past but no future.

There was little he could offer a woman, if he was so

inclined. A woman needed a man who would always be there for her, who could be a proper role model for their children, a man who could devote all his energy and love to only them.

A man whose insides were eaten with cancerous revenge was good to no one, including himself. But even as those rational thoughts consumed him, the stick he held began forming letters, and the letters inscribed in the soft mud made his eyes widen in horror, for it wasn't Ellie's name he'd sketched, and it wasn't Ellie's name that was deeply entrenched in his mind.

EMMA, they spelled. Emma, not Ellie. And the guilt of it, the realization of how attached he'd become to the Boston socialite and her brood of orphans, scared the hell out of the fearless ex-Ranger.

"You'd never know that child was near death's door just a few days ago," Emmaline commented to Rafe, who'd returned to camp looking like the weight of the world rested on his broad shoulders, and who now bounced Pansy gently on his knee.

His bright blue eyes were sparked with red threads, as if he hadn't had much sleep. His disposition, though far from cheerful on the best of days, was surlier than usual. He was withdrawn and sullen to be exact, and though she hadn't thought it her business to ask what had made him that way, she was sorely tempted to question him now. His answering grunts and nods at her attempts at conversation were beginning to wear.

He smiled in genuine affection at the small child he held on his lap, and was rewarded with a wet kiss to his cheek. "Ruff," she said, squealing with delight until Rafe's heart twisted inside his chest.

"That's right, flowerpot. Rafe."

"How come you're so talkative with Pansy? You've hardly spoken two words to me since you returned." She hated sounding petulant, but she'd been worried and lonely while he'd been gone. His absence had only confirmed the old adage that the heart really does grow fonder. Though she'd rather have had her tongue pulled out before admitting it, and despised the weakness that made her care.

He'd returned without the promised game, giving the excuse that he'd come up empty-handed. But he hadn't looked her in the eye when he'd said it, and that had made her wonder if he'd spent his time away in the arms of a woman. Rafe was an excellent shot, after all.

He shrugged, setting Pansy down on the blanket to play. "Haven't had much to say, I reckon. That never seems to be a problem with you, Emma."

She stiffened at the rebuke. "I was raised to converse on a multitude of interesting topics. It's called polite conversation."

"Is it now? Well—"

Emmaline's piercing scream had Rafe reaching for his gun and brought the children running.

"Pansy . . . Pansy." Emmaline pointed at the child, her eyes wide with fright. "She's got something horrible in her hand."

Oblivious to the commotion, the toddler held up a huge bug, beaming in delight at her find, and Rafe blanched at the sight of the scorpion. More sensitive than most to the hideous creatures, he'd been bitten once as a child and had nearly died from the venomous sting. His mother had stressed time and again to keep his distance from them. But that wasn't possible now.

If only he'd been smart enough to realize that the damn things would be around. Usually nocturnal—just his luck to get one wide awake during the day—they frequently lived under stones or burrowed beneath the ground, but found their way to the surface when the rains came.

"Keep still. And for heaven's sake shut up! I'll coax it out of her hand, so it doesn't sting her."

"What is it?" Emmaline demanded, shivering in revulsion at the clawlike pincers and elongated tail. It looked like some prehistoric creature she'd seen once in the Natural History Museum in Boston.

"Scorpion! Quiet." He bent forward slowly, hoping he wouldn't startle the bug. Pansy opened her palm, allowing the curious creature to crawl over her hand, and that's when Rafe sprang forward, swiping at it with his hand.

In the space of a heartbeat, the scorpion raised its long upturned tail above its abdomen and struck at Rafe's hand, injecting him with venom. Knocking it to the ground, Rafe grabbed a rock and crushed the creature with a single blow.

Emmaline and the children watched in horror as Rafe grabbed his hand, which had started to swell. "I'm extremely sensitive to the venom," he said. "Don't know how long it'll take . . ." His throat tightened, making it impossible for him to complete his sentence, and his body began to twitch spasmodically, before he dropped to the ground.

Emmaline screamed and rushed forward. Rafe appeared unconscious. His eyes had rolled back in his head, and his skin had taken on a deathly pallor. Listening to his chest, she felt relieved to hear his heart beating, and placed her hand on his forehead, which was clammy to the touch. It was similar to how Lucas had felt before he . . . She bit off the gruesome thought with a strangled cry.

"Daniel, help me get Rafe into the cave. David, go find my guidebook. Perhaps there's something about scorpions in there. Miranda, take care of Pansy."

"Is Mr. Rafe going to die?" the child asked, staring at the unconscious man, and the other girls began to cry.

"No. No, of course not. We'll just get him into the cave where it's warm, and I'm sure he'll be fine."

But Emmaline was to eat those words many times in the next few days.

Chapter Ten

Emmaline's limited survival skills were put to the test during Rafe's paralyzing illness. The everyday necessities of living outdoors—food, firewood, and water—had to be secured. And it was up to her.

The children, realizing the enormity of what had happened, had been on their best behavior since Rafe had fallen ill. Daniel and David, in charge of gathering firewood, performed their duties diligently and with a surprising amount of maturity. Miranda and Miriam fetched water from the spring every day with a minimum amount of complaint. And Emmaline felt fortunate that these children, who'd had so much to bear in their short lifetimes, had risen once again to face adversity.

Pansy stuck pretty close to Rafe's side most of the time, seeming to sense that her new friend was in serious trouble. Emmaline had caught the child patting his cheek and calling his name on numerous occasions, and her heart had ached at the tragic picture they presented.

Wringing out the flannel strips she had once used on Pansy, Emmaline mopped Rafe's fevered brow, hoping the cooling applications would bring down his fever. Her mother had always insisted on administering chamomile tea when she was fevered, but Emmaline had none to make.

She was at a loss as to what to do about the apparent strangulation of his throat and the frequent sneezing spasms that afflicted him. The guidebook had offered little instruction in the doctoring of poisonous stings, and even less comfort that the infected person would survive.

Rafe's mention of his intense response to the scorpion's sting made Emmaline aware that his reaction would be far more severe than most people's, and she hoped with all her might that the fact that he had lived through this once before meant he'd been imbued with some sort of partial immunity to the venom.

"Miss Emma," Daniel said, dropping to his knees and looking extremely serious for a child of twelve, "we're out of food. The last of the dried venison is gone. What are we going to eat tonight?"

Emmaline swallowed, glanced at Rafe's gun, and forced a brave smile to her lips. "I'll just have to hunt us up something, I guess."

The boy's eyes widened in disbelief. "You! Why, you could hardly hit those tin cans. How you going to kill us a deer?"

"I didn't say it would be a deer, Daniel. But I might be able to find something else for us to eat." Daniel didn't look at all convinced.

After instructing the boy in caring for Rafe, Emmaline removed the gun from the holster, checked to make sure it was fully loaded, then went in search of her prey.

Please, God, don't let me run into a mountain lion, she prayed as she walked. *I just need something small, something not too dangerous that I can kill for dinner.*

When she reached the clearing, she spotted the rabbit almost immediately. It was sitting in the meadow, chewing on a nut, looking all brown, furry, and helpless, and she was consumed with guilt at what she was about to do.

Holding her breath, she prayed for thanks and forgiveness all at once, took aim, and fired. When she opened her eyes, it was to find that her bullet had hit its mark. The rabbit was dead, and though she knew she should feel elated at her first successful kill, all she felt was sorrow at the murder of the poor defenseless creature.

Wiping the tears from her cheeks before anyone could see how foolish she was being, she realized that Rafe had been right: she would do anything to protect the children, including killing a defenseless animal.

"That rabbit was pretty good," David remarked later that day, rubbing his tummy contentedly. "There was hardly any hair left on it. Mr. Rafe would be proud that you shot him all by yourself, Miss Emmaline. I can't wait to tell him."

She ruffled the boy's hair. "I guess it gets easier the more you do it, but I don't really like shooting guns." And skinning the poor creature with Rafe's knife had been hideous. When she'd felt that soft hair beneath her fingers . . . She shivered, unable to think about it. The poor thing had hardly resembled anything remotely familiar when she'd gotten done with it.

Rafe's anguished cry brought Emmaline to her feet, and she counseled the children to stay by the mouth of the cave and continue their play until she returned.

"Ellie! Ellie! I'm sorry, Ellie. I should have been there for you. So much blood. So much blood. The baby . . . the baby's dead, Ellie. I'm sorry . . . so sorry."

Emmaline's face blanched as she listened to the ravings of the feverish man, listened to the tortured tale of what she could only assume were his dead wife and child.

But how did they die?

The pain in his voice was heartrending, bringing tears to her eyes, for she knew what it was like to lose family. "*Sssh*," she crooned, and patted his cheek, realizing that the beard he wore was much softer than it looked. "It's Emma, and you're safe with me now, Rafe. Just rest. Let the fever run its course." If it ever would.

He quieted under her touch, and she was left to wonder about Rafe's dead wife and her mysterious demise.

All through the night and into the next morning, Rafe continued to thrash, calling out his dead wife's name, and Emma tended to him as best she could, bathing his fevered brow with damp cloths, changing his sweat-soaked clothing so he wouldn't catch a chill. The children huddled together during this time, trying to block out the hideous cries of the man they had grown to love and admire, refusing to believe that such a kind man could be capable of such violent emotion.

Emmaline wanted to comfort them, tell them that Rafe

would soon be well, that his nightmares would cease, but she had a feeling that Rafe's entire life had become a nightmare since the day he'd lost his family.

Rafe's despair and heartbreak over the woman and child showed a human side to the dictatorial cowboy she hadn't witnessed before. The ruthless, no-nonsense man had revealed a part of himself, a part she'd glimpsed on rare occasions with Pansy, but even at those times he'd been guarded, not wanting to get too close to anyone.

As she watched him sleep a tortured sleep, her heart went out to him. Though she'd tried her damnedest not to become attracted to his dimpled smiles, which were rare, to the easy way he communicated and handled the children, to the smell and feel of his masculinity, Emmaline felt herself weakening.

Years of hardboiled, unflattering opinions about the male sex were beginning to crumble because of Rafe Bodine. He was a man with a heart—a wounded heart that needed to heal. She was a woman with the capacity to care, if only he'd let her. If only he lived long enough to let her.

Rafe lived. But Emmaline wasn't certain that she wouldn't murder him. The man was impossible, ungrateful, and totally back to his dictatorial self, despite the fact he was still lying flat on his back.

"I don't want any more of that putrid water you call soup. Give me some meat, so I can get my strength back." Though his voice was weak and raspy, he had no difficulty getting his opinion across, much to Emmaline's disgust.

Crossing her arms over her chest, she stared down at him, all the while tapping her foot in a no-nonsense manner. "You will get meat when I say you're ready and not a moment sooner." The shoe was on the other foot now. She was in control, and she let Rafe know it. "Because of your incapacitation, I have taken charge."

His face reddening, he tried to rise, but he was too weak and fell back down. "Goddammit, woman!" Though he knew he should be grateful—she had saved his life—it went against Rafe's grain to be incapacitated or to have a woman doing for him. Especially when that woman was supposed to be helpless. But Emma had been far from helpless, tending him and the children quite capably, and it was obvious that his preconceived opinions of her had been wrong.

"Don't you be talking to Miss Emmaline like that, Mr. Rafe." Daniel stepped closer until he was shoulder to shoulder with Emmaline. "If it wasn't for her, you'd be dead. She saved your life."

"If it wasn't for her, I'd have been about my business and wouldn't have gotten stung in the first place," Rafe tossed back, unwilling to concede the point.

The boy didn't back down, despite the fact that he was trembling. He respected Rafe, wanted to grow up and be just like him, but he cared for Miss Emmaline too much to let anyone, including the man he idolized, speak disrespectfully to her. "My father didn't teach me much, but he did say that it wasn't polite to swear at women."

"You should say you're sorry to Miss Emmaline, Mr. Rafe," Miranda said, dragging Miriam forward. "She's been awfully worried about you. We all have."

Rafe's face reddened at the child's rebuke, and it wasn't from the fever this time. He actually looked embarrassed. Emmaline wanted to reach out and hug both children for taking her side, but she wouldn't. Rafe's authority would be reestablished when he was well, and she didn't want them to question it. Not after everything he'd done for them. But that didn't mean she couldn't savor the moment.

"I guess my temper's gotten the best of my mouth." He wasn't a man given to saying he was sorry, and it was the best apology he could muster at the moment. She could take it or leave it.

She decided to leave it.

"Come along, children. There's work to be done. And Mr. Rafe needs his rest. It might help to alleviate his surly disposition." Without a backward glance, Emmaline herded the children outside, leaving Rafe to ponder the twists of fate, the cruelties of life, and the contrariness of some women.

"This is just like one of them Indian powwows Mr. Rafe told us about, isn't it?" David asked.

Daniel tossed pebbles one at a time into a tin cup and didn't bother to look up. "Guess so."

"Me and Miriam don't want to be squaws. We want to be Indian braves like you and David," she told Daniel, crossing her arms over her chest and doing a good imitation of Emmaline at her most obstinate.

Picking up a handful of dirt, Pansy tasted it, made a

face, then toddled over to Daniel and dropped it into the cup, smiling triumphantly at her accomplishment. "Dirt."

Daniel sighed and lifted the baby into his arms. Since beginning this trek to their new home, he'd tried to be brave for his brother's sake, tried to act like everything was going to be all right once they reached Sacramento, but now he wasn't so sure. Sacramento was still a long way off, and pretty soon Rafe would be leaving them. That thought made his stomach ache.

Since his father disappeared, Rafe was the first man who had shown any real interest in him and David. Rafe was smart. He knew everything there was to know about hunting and tracking, and he'd let him handle his gun, trusting Daniel to be responsible and not treating him like a baby, like they'd done at the orphanage.

And Daniel never tired of listening to the stories Rafe told around the campfire. They were usually about Indians or Texas Rangers, or about outlaws like Jesse James. And he never left the gory stuff out, even though some of the stories made Miss Emmaline cringe in horror.

Sometimes at night when he was wrapped up his blanket by the fire, Daniel would pretend that he was Rafe's son. It was a dumb thing to do, he knew, but it made him feel safer just the same.

He cleared his throat. "I called this powwow so we could talk about our going to Sacramento." Rafe had told them about powwows, about how Indians gathered together to discuss real important things, and he guessed what he had on his mind was important enough to warrant such a meeting.

"What's there to talk about? Miss Emmaline already told us the plan. She's in charge of us now that Mr. St. Joseph is dead," David wisely pointed out.

Though he felt traitorous for saying so, because he thought the world of Miss Emmaline, Daniel thought it wise to put the facts before the others. They were all in this together and would need to decide what to do as a group. "Miss Emmaline's not too good at handling things on her own. I know she tries hard, but how do we know we won't be left stranded out in the middle of nowhere once Mr. Rafe decides to leave, like we were once before."

Miranda came to her guardian's defense. "Miss Emmaline's doing better. She knows how to shoot the gun. And she hardly ever burns the biscuits anymore."

"But she doesn't know about reading trail signs, the way Mr. Rafe does, and she doesn't know about hunting large animals."

"And she's scared sometimes when it's dark," David added. "I heard her pacing one night when Mr. Rafe left us alone to go hunting. I'm not sure she likes being alone."

"I don't want Mr. Rafe to leave," Miriam announced, her lower lip trembling, her pudgy hands wringing in distress. "I love him, and I want him to stay with us forever and ever."

"Ruff . . . Ruff!" Pansy squealed her delight at the mention of Rafe's name and smiled to reveal a new tooth.

Daniel nuzzled the little girl's cheek. "I know little flowerpot's going to be upset when Mr. Rafe leaves," he said, coining the nickname Rafe always used for the child. "Probably her new ma and pa will call her Theodora." He grimaced at the thought, and even Pansy looked dismayed at the prospect.

"Far as I can see, there's only one answer to our problem." David kicked at the dirt with the toe of his brogan, feeling wise at the conclusion he'd drawn and very important to have gotten everyone's attention.

"We've got to make Mr. Rafe stay."

Daniel shook his head. "Quit being stupid, Davey. How we gonna do that? He's bigger and smarter than us. If he wants to leave, we can't stop him."

"But what if he didn't want to leave?" Miranda asked, smiling mischievously as she warmed to the idea and let her childish imagination get the better of her. "What if he wanted to stay because of Miss Emmaline?"

"What are you getting at, squirt? That don't make no sense. Why would he want to stay because of her?"

She looked at the older boy with the wisdom of the female mind and replied, as if the solution were really quite simple, "If Mr. Rafe married Miss Emmaline then he would never leave her. He's not mean like my papa and wouldn't beat her. And they could live happily ever after, just like in the books my mama used to read us."

Daniel pondered the suggestion, then scratched his head. "That don't seem likely. Mr. Rafe don't seem fond of Miss Emmaline, like she was his sweetheart or nothin'." Sweethearts talked mushy and sometimes they kissed, but he'd never seen Rafe and Miss Emmaline do anything like that; he blushed at the notion.

"Yeah," David said, his eyes brightening. "But it's still a long ways to Denver. And maybe if we told Mr. Rafe how smart Miss Emmaline was, about how she shot that rabbit and skunk," he held his nose and laughed, "maybe we could make him like her better."

"We could tell him how pretty she is. I think Miss Emmaline's pretty as a fairy princess," Miranda stated, twirling about.

"But what if she don't like him?" Miriam toyed with the hem of her soiled dress. "I heard Miss Emmaline say he's *onnoree*, whatever that means. But it don't sound good."

"What if we talked to her about how he's helped us and how much he knows about hunting and tracking and even cooking? Wouldn't she like him better?" Miranda suggested.

Daniel nodded. "It wouldn't hurt to try. But we can't let on what we're doing, 'cause then they'd be mad and wouldn't like each other just to punish us."

"We could swear an oath," David said, holding out his hand to the others. "Mr. Rafe says sometimes Indians do that. We all got to touch hands and shake on it. And once that's done, we can never tell our plan. Even if we're tortured or burned at the stake."

Miriam's eyes rounded, and she clutched her older sister's skirt with one hand and held out the other toward the hands already joined.

Absorbed in their activity, none of the children heard Emmaline's approach until she was right up next to them.

"What are you children doing? Are you playing some

type of game? It's time to get your chores done before dinner."

They broke apart quickly, making Emmaline wonder at the guilty, secretive looks on their faces, but she discounted it as children's behavior and left to cook the possum she had caught, never realizing that she was to be the target of a newly hatched plan.

It didn't take long for the children to put their scheme into motion. That evening David plopped down next to Rafe, who sipped thoughtfully at his coffee as he watched Emmaline prepare the girls for bed.

"Miss Emmaline sure is nice, isn't she, Mr. Rafe?" He smiled guilelessly and studied the older man intently for some sign of agreement.

Nice and stubborn, Rafe thought, but he nodded at the boy, wondering if David had a crush on his guardian and surprised by the child's elated expression. "I guess she's nice enough."

"She's learned a lot since we started out. She can shoot a gun now, and you should have seen the way she skinned that rabbit the other day. The skunk was a mistake, but—"

Rafe clutched the boy's arm, stopping him in midsentence. "Emma caught a skunk?" He would have liked to see that.

The boy nodded and wrinkled up his nose. "Well, not quite. She tried to catch it, but it let her have it with that smelly stuff it sprays. Miss Emmaline sure smelled bad. I never seen no one scrub themselves with soap as hard as she did that day."

Rafe grinned at the image. "Emma has learned a lot." And he was proud of her for it, though not likely to admit it to anyone, especially Emma. The Boston socialite knew a hard day's work now, and a bit about surviving in the wilderness. She had gumption. And far more intelligence and courage than he'd originally given her credit for.

"She's pretty, too. I'm not sure if I've ever seen a prettier woman, 'cept for my ma, that is. Men liked my ma. They used to hang around our place a lot. And sometimes they'd stay the night."

The child's innocent recital touched Rafe in a way he hadn't been affected before, and it made him want to draw David into his arms and offer comfort. But he didn't, afraid that the boy would cry or become embarrassed. "What about your pa?"

David's eyes took on a faraway look. "Pa was away at sea most of the time. He worked on a whaling ship. We hardly ever saw him. When he didn't come back, Ma said he drowned."

"And your mother? What happened to her?"

"She got some disease that ate up her brain. Daniel said it was the pox." He shrugged, but Rafe could see that the effort to be brave and appear unaffected cost him. "Like the chicken pox, I guess."

Rafe surmised that David's mother had earned her living as a whore and had died from syphilis. He pitied the youngsters for the harshness they'd had to endure. It couldn't have been easy, living the kind of life they'd led, before and after their parents' death.

Eager to change the subject, for distraught children made Rafe as uncomfortable as distraught women, he asked, "You boys anxious to get to California?"

The small boy scrunched up his face and shook his head. "Nope. We don't know what to expect. It's kinda scary going to live with strangers, even though Miss Emmaline will try to find me and Danny a good home. And I'm going to miss the other kids. And you and Miss Emmaline."

No one was more surprised than Rafe when David leaned over and hugged him around the neck in genuine affection, nuzzling his cold nose against Rafe's warm flesh. Rafe felt the oddest strangulation in his throat, and it had nothing to do with scorpion venom.

These kids had wormed their way into his heart; the thought of abandoning them to strangers was a bitter pill to swallow. But he knew that Emma's plan to have them adopted was the wisest course. Children needed the stability of a normal home life, and that had been sadly lacking in their lives up till now.

Little boys needed a father to teach them how to shoot and to wrestle, like his pa had shown him. And little girls—he glanced across the campfire at Miranda and Emmaline—definitely needed a mother's love.

"Do you think Mr. Rafe's handsome, Miss Emmaline?"

Emmaline scrubbed Miranda's face with lye soap and a strip of flannel and wondered how such a small child could accumulate so much dirt in such a short time.

Glancing over to where Rafe sat talking with David, she considered the question, thinking that Rafe did look rather rakish in his beard, despite the fact that she despised chin whiskers. "I guess he is. Why? Do you think so?"

"Oh yes!" Miranda's eyes lit as she warmed to the topic. "We, Miriam and me, think he's the handsomest, most nicest man in the whole wide world. And he sure does know a lot about stuff."

She continued scrubbing, behind the child's ears this time. "I believe you're right about that. Rafe is very skilled at living outdoors."

"Mama always said that a man who worked with his hands would make a good husband."

Staring at the hands in question, Emmaline remembered where they'd once been and blushed as red as Miranda's now clean earlobes. "I suppose your mama was right."

"Don't you want to get married and have children someday, Miss Emmaline? Me and Miriam think you'd make a very good mama."

At the compliment, Emmaline's heart warmed with pleasure. She smiled at the child and kissed her cheek. "You're very sweet, Miranda. But I haven't had much experience with children, except for these past two weeks with you and the others, since Frau Muehler left."

"You've done real good, Miss Emmaline. Much better than that nasty Frau Muehler. She wasn't nice at all."

Emmaline wasn't about to argue that point. There

wasn't anything about the German nursemaid that she missed. "I guess she was an unhappy woman. Perhaps she missed her home and just took it out on the rest of us."

"I don't miss Boston much. It was dirty. And there were so many people. I like it here much better."

"That's good, sweetie. There," she put the finishing touches to Miranda's long braids, "that should do it. You're ready for bed now."

"Are you going to sleep near Mr. Rafe again to make sure he doesn't cry out anymore? I felt real sad when Mr. Rafe cried."

"I . . . I don't know. He's much better now. And doesn't need as much care."

"I think you should. Mr. Rafe told Daniel that he feels much better when you're close by." The child did her best to look innocent despite the obvious lie. "I think he's still scared."

"Really?" Rafe didn't seem the type of man to be scared by anything. But then, he hadn't seemed the type of man who would cry out over a wife and child, either.

"Cross my heart and hope my tongue falls out."

Emmaline bit the inside of her cheek. "Go on now. It's getting late." With a kiss, Miranda skipped off, looking back over her shoulder to wave farewell.

As Emmaline watched the child's antics, she felt a strange tightening around her heart. One day soon, Miranda and the others would be waving farewell for good, and she would never again see their grubby faces and sweet smiles. Never smell Pansy's peculiar baby scent. Never listen to Daniel make that strange buzzing noise as he explained to David about how bees pollinate flowers to make honey.

She swallowed the lump in her throat and willed back the tears. One day soon, she would have to say goodbye to the children and Rafe.

Chapter Eleven

RAFE LAY QUIETLY IN HIS BEDROLL, WATCHING Emmaline through slitted eyes as she attempted to untangle the mass of red curls with her fingertips. She knelt near the campfire, a canteen of water and bar of soap resting nearby, and the light from the flames played over her, casting a burnished hue on the coppery curls, making them appear as if they were on fire.

The nightly ritual had become almost more than he could bear. Emmaline thought everyone was asleep when she washed up each evening, and Rafe, though he felt lower than a Peeping Tom, was content to let her think so.

She turned just then, as if sensing his eyes on her, but he knew she couldn't see him in the darkness. He lay in shadows, while the flickering fire illuminated her slender body.

When she turned back and began to unbutton her gown, Rafe sucked in his breath. He'd never seen Emma undress before, but he guessed she felt safe now because the children were sleeping so quietly—and he seemed to be, too. Pushing her gown down to her waist, she grasped the canteen, soaped the cloth, and began to wash the grime from her neck, chest, and arms.

Her skin shone milky white, like newly churned cream, soft and rich, as the firelight danced over her. Her back was smooth, the flesh on her arms firm, and he smiled to himself, remembering the calisthenics she insisted on doing each morning. Emma had some decent-size muscles for a woman. And that wasn't the only thing decently sized, he recalled, squirming restlessly in his bedroll.

Though he'd tried not to notice, for it made his guilt over Ellie's death more intense, Emma was a damn attractive woman. He'd thought her cute once, but now he could see she was so much more. He had felt her warm flesh in his hands, cupped those firm breasts that pushed insistently against her camisole, remembered the taste of her on his mouth, the satiny texture of her skin beneath his hands.

The memories stirred a longing deep inside, made him hard, as he watched her pull up her dress, though she didn't button it. He closed his eyes, knowing she would now come over to check on him, as she'd done every night since he'd fallen ill, and his heart pounded loudly in his ears, like an untried youth waiting for his turn at making love for the first time.

Quietly, so she wouldn't awaken the children or Rafe, Emmaline padded on bare feet across the short distance to where Rafe lay. She couldn't fall asleep without reassuring herself that his fever had abated and that he'd soon be well enough to travel. He'd been ill only a few days, but it seemed an entire lifetime had passed.

Kneeling by his side, she listened to his even breathing, and though his sleep appeared restful, sweat beaded his forehead. Fearing the fever had returned, she felt his face and was relieved to find it cool.

Rafe was cool, but she was not. For touching him, even in this innocent manner, made her skin hot, her stomach churn with suppressed longing. She often studied Rafe while he slept and had memorized every angle, plane, and line of his face, picturing him as he looked without the beard, remembering how his lips felt pressed to hers.

Sighing at memories best forgotten, she started to turn away.

"Don't go." Rafe clutched her wrist, pulling her down onto his chest. Before she could utter a word, before she could protest that the children might awaken, before she could let him know that she wasn't a woman of easy virtue, he drew her mouth to his.

Like a famished man at a banquet, he covered her mouth with his, hungrily, stealing away her breath and what was left of her composure, and she gave in to the wondrous sensations—the dizzying heights, the swirling in the pit of her stomach, the heat pulsing through her veins.

Just when she thought she couldn't take any more of the glorious torture, he thrust his tongue into her mouth, exploring, conquering, tasting her in the most elemental way. Sliding anxious fingers through his hair, she attempted to meld herself to him, become one with him, lose herself within the heat.

Mindless with need and an uncontrollable yearning,

Rafe pushed down her gown, untying the ribbons of her chemise, needing to feel, to taste, to possess. He explored her breasts with his hands and mouth, teasing the taut nipples into rigid peaks.

"Rafe," Emma whispered in a voice touched with awe, and her cry of surrender was as effective as a bucket of cold water, dousing Rafe's ardor immediately. His senses returned, and he froze, then his hands fell away from her tempting flesh as he tried desperately to regain what was left of his sanity, to remember what his goal, his main purpose, in life was now.

Setting her from him, he stared into eyes fraught with confusion, then embarrassment, and cursed himself inwardly for having lost control. "I'm sorry, Emma. I shouldn't have taken such liberties."

Guilt masked his face, sorrow clouded his eyes, and Emmaline suspected that Rafe suffered far more than she did at the moment. "And I shouldn't have let you, but I guess that's neither here nor there." Her fingers shook as she attempted to button her dress.

Her wounded look seared his soul, and Rafe sighed deeply in regret for what had happened and what could never be. "We'll break camp at first light. It's high time we got back on the trail."

She nodded, unable to find words, too upset at her own stupidity at what she'd allowed to happen. Rafe's heart belonged to another. Though Ellie was dead, his memory of her, of their life together, was still very much alive. That was as painfully obvious as the anguish lighting his eyes.

"This won't happen again. You have my word on it."

That, Emmaline realized, was her greatest fear.

Rafe announced quite unexpectedly the next morning that they would be stopping off in the next town to purchase supplies and clothing and to sleep in a real bed for a night.

The children were ecstatic at the news, and there was a decided spring to their step as they trudged along the trail, chatting excitedly. Emmaline, though grateful for the change of plans—for she wanted nothing more than to soak in a steaming bath—received the news with a heavy heart. It was an act of contrition, an apology on Rafe's part, for what had happened between them the night before.

Emmaline had had plenty of time during her sleepless night to search her feelings, and what she'd discovered made her all the more depressed: She had fallen in love with Rafe Bodine. Fallen head-over-heels for a man who remained buried in his past with his wife, a man with whom she had no future. A man who had promised to leave her in Denver.

So when they finally reached their destination a day later, Emmaline entered the town of Jansen with something akin to regret, knowing that she was another step closer to saying her final goodbye.

The town appeared like many of the rough-and-tumble towns of the West that she had visited. False-fronted buildings lined the muddy main street, as did an excess of saloons and houses of ill repute.

The one decent hotel to be had was a study in disrepair and neglect. Like an elderly horse that has seen better days and been put out to pasture, the Occidental was as tired and unkempt as Emmaline felt at the moment.

Gathering the children to her with an admonishment that they be on their best behavior, they followed Rafe into the shabby edifice. At his insistence, they were to pretend once again to be a family, and she was quite curious to know the reason for this pretense.

It was quite obvious that he was hiding something. But what? Doubts and questions about Rafe's need for subterfuge began to multiply in Emmaline's mind.

Waiting near the entrance while Rafe secured the rooms, Emmaline observed her surroundings. The lobby sported a once colorful, threadbare oriental rug, faded red velvet draperies at the grimy windows, and the most ostentatious chandelier Emmaline had ever seen. Bits of green and red glass glittered beneath the gas globes, making her wonder if the owner had bought it from one of the many bordellos she'd observed.

"Pretty," Pansy declared, pointing at the colorful fixture. And to a small child, who hadn't had much prettiness in her life, Emmaline supposed it was.

Rafe returned, accompanied by the balding proprietor, who handed Emmaline a large brass key. "Welcome to the Occidental, Mrs. St. Joseph. Your husband here tells me you've done quite a bit of traveling and will welcome a hot bath and clean sheets. Let me assure you . . ."

He droned on, but the rest of what he said faded beneath the realization that he was referring to Rafe as

Mr. St. Joseph and she as his missus. Why didn't Rafe want to use his own name?

Before she could ponder the matter further, Rafe clasped her elbow and escorted her up the wide staircase.

Her look held confusion, but Rafe refused any explanation and merely shook his head. "Don't be asking too many questions, Emma. I've got my own reasons for what I do, and I don't want you questioning them." With that, he led her to the first room they'd been assigned and opened the door.

"The three girls will stay in here. I thought the children would welcome a little space and some privacy for at least one night. The boys will be right across the hall." He nodded toward the door and Daniel pushed it open. "And you and I, *Mrs.* St. Joseph, will be staying right down the hall."

Her mouth fell open, and she failed to notice the grins the children sported. Tugging Rafe out of earshot, her words came out in a hiss: "We can't stay in a room by ourselves. That wouldn't be seemly."

"We've done it before, Emma. And I couldn't very well request separate rooms since we're supposed to be married."

"I don't think—"

"You think too much," he said, opening the door and shoving her gently into the room. *Their* room. "I told you there wouldn't be a repeat of last night, and there won't. I'm a man of my word."

She groped desperately for some sort of excuse, unwilling to spend the night with a man she found entirely irresistible. Especially with the preceding night's activity still burning fresh in her mind. "The children . . . They're not used to staying by themselves. They might be afraid."

"I doubt it. They're going to look on this as an adventure. I'm having meals brought up to all the rooms, and after we've had a bite to eat, we'll take them on a little shopping expedition. You're all starting to look like a bunch of rag pickers. And none of you smells all that great either."

She blushed hotly, for she knew what he said was true. "Well, you're hardly one to talk, Rafe Bodine. Just because you got to loll around and be tended to while I cooked your meals and fetched and carried water, hunted for food, and took care of you, and sweated up a storm in the process, is no reason you should be throwing it back in my face now."

He led her to the bed and sat her down on it, then took the space next to her, and his tone grew serious. "I never thanked you for saving my life, Emma." Holding her hand between his palms, he began rubbing circles with his thumb. Darts of pleasure scurried up her arm.

"It's not necessary to thank me. You were injured. You would have done the same for me had I been the one who fell ill."

"You handled yourself real well."

The compliment made her smile. "Thank you. That's high praise coming from you. But don't forget that I had a good teacher." His gaze zeroed in on her mouth, and she licked her lips self-consciously.

"There's still a lot to learn."

Swallowing hard, her heart pounding loudly in her ears was the only sound she heard. "And will you be the one to teach me?"

His gaze flicked over her in an assessing manner, and there was regret on his face when he dropped her hand and pushed himself to his feet. "There are far more skilled teachers than me, Emma. Far better men who know how to teach a woman like you all she needs to know."

"What if I don't want anyone else to teach me, only you?"

Rafe shrugged. "Then I guess you'll just have to remain un . . ." *untouched*, he wanted to say, but said instead, "untutored. I'm going to check on the children and the meals. There's a bathing room down at the end of the hall. Go ahead and use it while I'm gone. And be sure to lock the door. This isn't a hotel of refinement, in case you hadn't noticed."

She'd have to have been blind not to, but Emmaline didn't reply and just watched him walk away.

Rafe was a man with a lot on his mind as he hurried downstairs. The attraction he felt for Emma was too real, too uncomfortable, and much more intense than he wanted to admit.

And it wasn't a one-sided attraction, either. He had felt Emma's response when he'd kissed her last night, had reveled in her surrender to him, and it had hurt both physically and emotionally not to give in to his desire. He'd wanted nothing more than to strip her naked, plunge himself into her waiting warmth, and make mad, passionate love to her.

But he knew that he couldn't. He wasn't free to enter into a relationship with a woman. Especially a decent woman like Emmaline St. Joseph.

And not just because of Ellie and the guilt and grief he carried. The problems and considerations he had to face at present prevented him from pursuing anything other than the Slaughter gang.

They were and would have to remain his first consideration. His one and only passion.

"It surely is good to be back at the hideout, boss." Luther tipped back his chair and stared contentedly into the crackling fire, his hands entwined over his corpulent belly. The smell of burning oak drifted into the room, but Luther was feeling too comfortable to do anything about the fact that the old fireplace didn't draw as well as it should.

The abandoned ranch had been converted into the Slaughter gang's hideout some years back, when a widow and her two young girls had foolishly offered hospitality to the motley strangers. They'd been dispatched, like so many others, after first being raped and tortured.

"That Ranger ain't never going to be able to find us way up here in Wyoming."

Roy Lee snorted in disbelief as he continued to split open the mound of walnuts stacked in front of him and pop the meat into his mouth. "I ain't gonna rest easy until that murdering bastard's dead. We can't take no chances, Luther. Not after what he done to Bobby. Ain't that right, Hank?"

Slaughter kicked at the loose plank in the floor with the toe of his boot, his eyes silvery slits of hatred. No amount of time would lessen the pain of his brother's death or the malice he felt for Bodine. If anything, it was growing worse with every day that passed, festering like a cancer and spreading into every part of him.

The Ranger would die. Hank knew that just as surely as he knew that Bodine would find them. That's why Hank intended to find him first. The lawman wasn't aware that Hank knew he was coming for him. But thanks to the whore's telegram, the element of surprise would be on their side, if they planned carefully enough.

Hank kicked Luther's chair forward, and the big man nearly fell to the floor. A disgruntled look crossed his face. "What'd you do that for, Hank? I'm just sitting here minding my own business, not doing a damn thing."

"Let's ride into Laramie and see if we can learn something about Bodine. We don't know how far behind us he is, and I want to set my plans in motion."

Roy Lee swept the pile of shells to the floor and stared in confusion at his cousin. "What plans? You never told us about no plans."

"I don't much want to ride out again, boss," Luther complained. "We just got here last night, and I'm finally warming up. It's cold outside."

"Get up, you goddamn pussy, and saddle the horses. I'm bossing this outfit and you'll do what I tell you, or I'll shoot you between your eyes. You got that, you fat son of a bitch?"

Swallowing hard, Luther nodded and bolted from his

chair. "I'll get them horses right away, boss. No need to get riled." Grabbing his jacket, he hurried out the door, and a cold blast of air replaced him, making the kerosene lantern in the center of the table flicker.

But Hank was past riled, and his mottled skin and flaring nostrils told how much. "You'd better keep your brother in line, Roy Lee. I won't tolerate much more of his whining. There's nothing I hate worse than whining and complaining. I'm the one who spent years behind bars because of Bodine, not you and that chickenshit brother of yours. Just remember that. I did the time, while you were out carousing and drinking and having yourself a hell of a good time."

"We ain't forgot, Hank. Truly we ain't. You know how Luther gets sometimes. He's lazy. He don't mean nothing by it."

"Bobby's dead 'cause he didn't follow my orders. And you and Luther will be too. And it won't be Bodine doing the killing this time. You get the picture?" Fear lit Roy Lee's eyes and he nodded, his face pale.

Hank was damn pleased with the reaction. There were leaders and there were followers. He'd always been a natural-born leader. He was smart, cunning, and tough. And someday soon he would have to cut his losses and find others more willing to heed his advice. One thing he'd learned while fighting the blue bellies during the war: The man in charge never tolerated dissension in the ranks.

Hank figured himself to be a general, with Luther and Roy Lee his privates. They weren't smart like him.

Weren't as brave, neither. And it took smarts and fear-lessness to lead men to victory.

It was what had set him apart from Bobby. His brother had been too soft, had a conscience and a weakness for women. Bobby hadn't had the guts to kill Bodine's wife, so it had been left up to Hank do the job. Not that he was complaining. Killing had become second nature to him now. A real pleasure, so to speak.

And he wasn't going to bat an eyelash, or feel a lick of remorse, when he murdered his two feeble-minded cousins. Bobby had been right about one thing: He should never have allowed the stupid bastards to join them. They were an embarrassment to the Slaughter name.

"Don't I know you, mister?"

Rafe's face paled beneath his beard; the badge on the lawman's chest glittered ominously in the sunlight. Halting before the mercantile, he shook his head, trying to keep his voice void of emotion. He'd been on the other side of the coin enough times to know when a man was lying, and he couldn't afford to let on to the deputy that everything wasn't as it should be.

He wrapped a proprietary arm about Emmaline's shoulder and pasted an innocent look on his face. "Don't think so. Me and the missus was just heading into the mercantile to replenish our supplies and purchase some new duds for the kids. You know how they grow. Ain't that right, darlin'?"

Emmaline smiled at the stoic, unfriendly sheriff's

deputy, and wondered why Rafe was suddenly so nervous. But loyalty to the man who had saved her and the children won out over other concerns. "That's right, officer. Mr. St. Joseph and I were just about to make our purchases. Is there something wrong?"

The man shook his head and smiled apologetically. It was a handsome face, though not as handsome as Rafe's, but pleasing to the eye just the same. "Nope. My mistake." But he gave Rafe another searching look before heading down the boardwalk.

"You must have one of those faces," Emmaline said after the deputy had gone. "Not that anyone could see it beneath all that hair." Though her eyes held a smile, she was seething with curiosity. Questions almost too hideous to consider came to mind—the most prominent: What was Rafe hiding from the law? And if he wasn't hiding anything, then why had he lied?

"What did that man want, Mr. Rafe?" Miranda asked, tugging on the hem of his coat.

Kneeling down before the child, Rafe held her shoulders firmly between his hands. "Call me Papa. Remember what we talked about earlier, Miranda?" She bit her lip and nodded reluctantly, seeds of distress starting to form in her eyes. He chucked her beneath the chin. "Are you ready for some licorice candy?"

Her upset was gone instantly. "Yes . . . Papa!" she said enthusiastically. The other children shouted in agreement, and they headed into the store, the incident all but forgotten, except by Rafe, who realized he'd come close to being caught today. Damn close. And by

Emma, too, who suspected that there was more to him than met the eye.

The episode with the lawman had been a revelation, of sorts. Once they purchased the supplies they needed, he'd herd everyone back to the hotel and they'd stay there for the remainder of the day.

It had been foolish to chance being recognized in a town the size of Jansen. Foolish and foolhardy. Two things Rafe had been taught never to be.

Emmaline had just set the last of her new clothing into the valise she had purchased when a soft, tentative knock sounded at the door.

Rafe looked up from the newspaper he was reading. "I'll get it. You finish your packing." If the deputy had returned, Rafe wanted to handle it himself. Emmaline might get flustered into revealing something she shouldn't.

If only he were able to leave them in Jansen instead of taking them on to Denver, he thought. But the train heading west didn't come through the town, and he'd already promised Emma he'd deliver them all safely to the larger city.

And though the practical part of him wanted to be free to pursue the Slaughters, to detach himself from the responsibility he'd assumed, the other part didn't want to break that bond just yet.

He opened the door to find Miriam standing there dressed in her new flannel nightgown and robe. Pink, it matched the shiny satin ribbons in her long dark braids. The child's face lit when she saw him, and a strange warmth washed through Rafe.

"Hi!" she said, peeking around Rafe's legs and waving at Emmaline.

Emmaline smiled. "Hi, sweetie. Is something wrong?"

Biting her fingernail, Miriam shook her head. "We just wondered if Mr. Rafe would come and say prayers with us before we went to sleep."

He shot Emmaline a panicked look, and she swallowed a smile. "Well, I don't know, sweetie. I guess you'd better ask him yourself."

"Would you, Mr. Rafe?" Wrapping herself around his legs like a vine, she added, "We want you to come."

His sigh of surrender made Emmaline's heart constrict painfully. There was something truly wonderful about a man who loved children the way Rafe loved these orphans. Though she doubted that he realized the extent of his attachment, he was hooked, just as she, and they were reeling the rough, tough cowboy in an inch at a time.

Rafe and the three little girls knelt beside the bed the children would share for the night, hands clasped in front of them, heads bowed. Outside, the wind blew, rattling the panes of glass, but the atmosphere inside the room was filled with warmth.

"What prayers shall we say, Mr. Rafe? Do you know any for children?" Miriam asked, speaking into her hands.

Pansy snuggled next to Rafe's side, and he patted the top of her head absently before replying, "My mama taught me and my brothers one." Patsy Bodine had been adamant that her children would not grow up to be heathens and had dragged them to prayer service every Sunday. Misery didn't have a fine church back then, so the townsfolk would gather once a week in Murph Roger's livery and recite their prayers together there.

Miranda tugged his sleeve. "Would you teach us, Mr. Rafe? We'd really like to learn."

He nodded. "Now I lay me down to sleep. I pray the Lord my soul to keep. If I should die . . ."

Miriam glanced up at Rafe with panic-filled eyes. "You're not gonna die, are you, Mr. Rafe?"

"Everyone dies someday, darlin', but I've got no plans right now. That's just part of the prayer."

"We love you, Mr. Rafe," Miranda confessed, throwing her short arms around Rafe's middle and hugging him fiercely.

Miriam followed suit, saying, "We love you a whole bunch and wish you were our papa."

"Papa." Pansy flung her arms wide, indicating that she wanted to be picked up, and Rafe acquiesced. "Papa."

Emmaline entered just in time to hear the exchange and witness the touching scene, and a lump formed in her throat. Rafe was at a loss for words, and his face had the most peculiar look on it: love, confusion, desperation, and heartache mixed together as one. And she could certainly empathize with that, for it mirrored her feelings exactly.

Chapter Twelve

WHEN THEY LEFT TOWN THE FOLLOWING MORN-
ing, the children were piled into the rear of an old farm
wagon that Rafe had purchased with Emmaline's funds.
Buck was tethered to the back. It seemed stupid for the
boys to walk when they could just as easily ride, and the
wagon allowed Rafe to set a faster pace to Denver.

It was far more dangerous traveling by wagon, for it
required him to stay on the main roads, and the possibility
of his being recognized became greater, but he was willing to take that risk for the children's comfort, and his
own, to reach Denver quickly.

And Rafe realized now that getting to Denver as
quickly as possible would be his only salvation. From the
children. From Emma. And from himself.

Lying next to Emma last night had been the worst torture he'd ever experienced. He wasn't sure the Comanche
could have devised a worse punishment than making a
wanting man sleep next to a willing woman and do nothing. There had been times when the temptation to reach
out and pull her to him had been so intense that he'd
bitten down hard on his lip to keep his passions in check.

Emmaline had gravitated toward him once or twice during the night, in her sleep, seeking warmth, and God knows what else, and Rafe thought hell, hanging, or both would have been a damn sight preferable to going through that misery again.

"It certainly was wonderful to sleep in a real bed last night, don't you agree, Rafe? I feel so much better now that I'm rested and clean."

Seated next to him on the wagon bench, Emmaline flashed him a smile that gave the brilliance of the sun some serious competition. The sky was unblemished by clouds, and a magpie trilled a cheery tune, but none of it made Rafe feel the least bit enthusiastic. He hadn't slept a wink last night, and he wasn't sure how to respond to Emma's comment. At least one of them was happy with the world this morning. Too bad it wasn't him.

"I guess," he said finally, eyeing with pleasure the blue cotton skirt and white shirtwaist she wore. Emma's new garb was quite an improvement over her other, unsuitable attire. "You look fresh as a Texas bluebonnet."

The unexpected compliment filled her cheeks with color. Rafe didn't hand out praise often, and she hugged his words close to her heart. "Thank you. You look very nice yourself, except for that awful beard you insist on wearing. Any chance you're going to shave it off soon?"

He rubbed the chin whiskers with one hand, hanging on to the reins with the other. "You don't like it?"

She studied him for a moment. "I think you're much handsomer without it."

His eyebrow cocked, and his heart thumped hard. *She*

thinks I'm handsome. It was usually Ethan whom the ladies swooned over, not that it did them much good. Ethan didn't care for women. Unless they were lying naked beneath him—then he tolerated them somewhat. "Most women find my brother Ethan to be the handsome one."

"Really? Well, I guess I'll have to meet this handsome brother of yours sometime."

Though he knew she was teasing, Rafe didn't find her comment the least bit funny, and a scowl crossed his face. Women flocked to Ethan like bees to honey, and he didn't like the idea of Emma buzzing anywhere near his brother. "He wouldn't like you. Ethan doesn't like women, as a rule."

"And you do?" There'd been times when she hadn't thought so.

Much too much for my own good, Rafe decided without commenting, suddenly taking great interest in the mass of humanity huddled beneath the blankets in the back of the wagon.

The children listened with rapt interest to the exchange between the two adults.

"She thinks he's handsome," David said, jabbing an elbow into his brother's side and grinning proudly. "We're making progress."

"That don't mean nothing. But it's sort of a good sign."

"He likes her. I can tell," Miriam whispered, giggling, then covering her mouth when Miranda shook her head in warning.

"They slept in the same room last night, like my mama

and papa used to." The older girl, wearing a worldly look, dared Daniel to dispute the importance of that fact. "Except, Mr. Rafe didn't look all that happy this morning," she added.

"We'll just have to keep after them, that's all," David said. "It's your turn to talk to Mr. Rafe, Danny. I already said my piece."

"You kids doing all right back there? I hear a lot of jabbering going on."

The children quieted immediately as Rafe's voice roared down through the blanket. Danny popped his head up, his expression full of innocence. "Yes, sir. We're doing just fine. Thanks for asking."

"You've got to have your talk with Mr. Rafe tonight, Danny," Miranda insisted in a whisper. "We'll be in Denver soon, and then it'll be too late. They'll send us to live with strangers. We'll never see each other again."

All eyes turned to Daniel, who got a sick look on his face before nodding gravely. He'd never played cupid before, had never a girlfriend of his own, and he wasn't quite sure how he was supposed to persuade Mr. Rafe to fall in love with Miss Emmaline. But he'd try his hardest. Their futures depended on it.

Daniel's opportunity came later that day.

The campfire blazed brightly, but the heat radiating from it had nothing on the warmth Daniel felt on his cheeks and neck as he sat next to Rafe, wondering how to broach such a delicate subject as matrimony.

"You're awfully quiet tonight, Danny. You got something on your mind?" Rafe sipped at his coffee, staring toward the wagon where Emma was just bedding down the girls and David for the night. "There's nothing wrong with your brother, is there? He seemed a bit jumpy at supper."

"No, sir!" Danny's gaze slid toward David before shaking his head. "It's . . . it's just that I've had a lot on my mind lately, that's all. You know, I'm not getting any younger, and . . . and I've never had me a real girlfriend."

At the boy's earnest but embarrassed expression, Rafe swallowed his smile. Puberty was a difficult thing. He remembered quite clearly the awkward, tongue-tied conversations he had with members of the opposite sex, the way his member hardened at the most inconvenient times, like when his ma invited Reverend Potter and his busty daughter, Cora Jeanne, for dinner, and Cora, who was older by three years, kept her hand on his thigh throughout the meal, creating havoc with his privates.

"You're kinda young to be worrying about girls, Danny. You got time before . . ." Rafe rubbed the back of his neck, suddenly uncomfortable with the topic of conversation. He wasn't qualified to give this boy advice about the birds and the bees. And he was hardly one to talk about not being old enough, since he'd had his first woman at the age of fourteen, though it hadn't been Cora Jeanne. And Danny was almost thirteen now.

Of course, Danny wouldn't be led astray by an older brother who got his enjoyment dragging an innocent young boy to a whorehouse, either.

"How come you never got married, Mr. Rafe? Don't you want to have kids someday?"

The pain caused by the innocent question took Rafe by surprise, and his hand jerked, spilling the hot coffee and burning his flesh. "Damn!" he said, flinging off the coffee and the sting at the same time. "What makes you think I've never been married, son? It don't show on a man's person, you know, whether or not he's been married."

Embarrassed but determined, Danny plowed on. "It don't seem that you like women much. Take Miss Emmaline for example. You hardly ever talk to her, and she's about as pretty a lady as I've ever seen."

Rafe's gazed over at Emma. Holding Pansy close to her breast, she was humming softly as she tried to get the small child to sleep. An unwelcome feeling of protectiveness and caring surged over him.

"Emma's pretty. There ain't no denying that, son."

"Miss Emmaline knows a lot about all kinds of different things. Maybe not horses and outdoor stuff, like you, but she's traveled around quite a bit. And she knows how to sail a boat. I thought that was pretty darn impressive for a woman. And she's been to museums and libraries, too. Miss Emmaline knows more about famous paintings than anyone I've ever met."

Rafe didn't want to point out to the boy that the circles they traveled in were far different from those of the Boston socialite and that they weren't likely to visit such places anytime soon. Art, like social graces, was an accoutrement of wealth, and it was just another example of how worlds apart he and Emma were.

"Miss Emma's been raised different, Danny. She comes from what's called polite society," he explained.

Danny nodded, but, unlike Rafe, he saw that as an advantage, not a detriment. "Miss Emmaline sure does have good manners. She never wipes her hands on her clothes, or picks her nose, and she has a real nice way of talking."

Like most New Englanders—Danny included—Emma's words were clipped, precise, and to the point. There was no lazy Texas drawl to be found in her speech pattern.

"I think Miss Emmaline's going to make some man a real good wife."

Rafe nudged the boy playfully and grinned. "You ain't thinking of getting hitched anytime soon, are you, son?"

Daniel turned beet red. "No, sir! But . . . but if I was, I'd sure pick someone like Miss Emmaline. She's pretty, sweet, and smart. And I think that's a real good combination for a wife. Don't you, Mr. Rafe?"

Rafe considered the boy's comments for a moment. "I've had horses with the same temperament, and they've still bucked me off, son. Miss Emma might be all those things, but she's still got a sassy tongue and a stubborn streak a mile wide down her back. The man who tries to tame that filly is going to be in for the ride of his life." And he wasn't sure that it could be done at all.

"Good thing you're so good with horses, Mr. Rafe. I bet you could tame just about anything that came your way."

At Rafe's startled look, Danny jumped up. "Guess I'll be turning in now. Thanks for the talk."

In the blink of an eye, Daniel disappeared, leaving Rafe

to wonder exactly what it was the boy had been getting at, and why he suddenly felt so damned uncomfortable.

Nothing eventful occurred during the next few days. There was no more talk of Emma's glorious attributes, and other than Miriam's scraping her knee on a rock and David's being stung by an angry hornet—curiosity having gotten the better of him once again—life on the trail was pretty routine.

So when a barrage of rifle shots rang out that morning, no one was prepared, not even Rafe, who came dangerously close to being struck by one of the flying bullets. They hit the wagon instead, splintering off bits of woods, causing Emmaline and the children to scream and Rafe to shout out orders as he pulled his Winchester from its scabbard and began to return fire.

"Get down! Take cover!" He swung Buck around toward the wagon, needing to make certain that Emma and the kids were unharmed.

Frightened out of her wits, Emmaline pulled hard on the reins, jerking the horses and the wagon to a halt. The children were screaming and crying—something she wanted very much to do but didn't dare for fear of upsetting them further.

"Are you hit?" Rafe shouted, scanning the outcropping of rocks in the distance for their attacker but sighting no one.

"No. We're fine," Emmaline replied with far more confidence than she felt. "Just scared."

"Get under the wagon. I'll ride ahead and draw their fire. You stay put until I get back."

Emmaline nodded and did as Rafe instructed, herding the children beneath the wagon, and all the while trying to remain composed, but fear, stark and vivid, rushed through her at the thought of Rafe's coming to harm. She wanted to go after him, the urge to defend and aid him strong, but she knew that her first responsibility was the safety of the children, and Rafe knew it, too.

"Who's shooting at us, Miss Emmaline?"

"Will Mr. Rafe be all right?"

"How come someone wants to kill us?"

The questions and tears kept coming, but Emmaline had no answers to give the youngsters, for she was as surprised by the attack as they were. She could only speculate that whoever was shooting at them was after money or valuables. Brigands were common on the trail, and they were fortunate not to have encountered any before now.

"Mr. Rafe will be just fine, children. You'll see." She repeated that over and over again to herself, silently, willing herself to believe it, needing to believe it with all her heart and soul as Rafe disappeared in the distance.

The attacker kept firing. Rafe took cover behind a granite boulder and decided that it wasn't the law cowering behind the rifle. A lawman wouldn't shoot at innocent women and children.

Sweat beaded his brow at the realization of how close Emma and the kids had just come to being shot, and he wiped at it with the back of his hand. His heart pounded fast, not out of fear for himself, but those who had wormed their way into his heart and affections.

Jesus! What kind of animal was after him, not to give thought to a woman and children?

"Come on out, Bodine. You can't hide forever. I've got a Wanted poster in my pocket that says your hide's worth five hundred, dead or alive. I'd just as soon turn you in alive as not, but it's up to you."

Bounty hunter. Bitter bile rose in Rafe's throat, and his lips thinned in disgust. He knew their type very well. They were mercenaries, giving no thought to anything but making money off the misfortunes of others. As a Ranger, he'd seen many outlaws apprehended by the ruthless guns for hire; most often, they were turned in to the authorities more dead than alive.

Rafe pinpointed the man's location by the sound of his gravelly voice, then slowly made his way up and over the rocks, intending to sneak up behind him. There were few men who could move as silently and stealthily as he, except perhaps Ethan, so Rafe knew that the element of surprise would be on his side.

A vulture hovered overhead, as if waiting for the outcome of the fight. Someone had to die. Rafe just prayed he wouldn't be the one.

The bounty hunter was lying on his stomach looking out over the rim of the rocks he used as cover when Rafe found him. "Put down your rifle nice and slow, and you won't get hurt."

The man turned quickly, and Rafe recognized him as Red Wolf McCade, a mean son of a bitch by anybody's standards. His red beard and evil eyes reminded Rafe too much of Hank Slaughter, and his finger started itching on the Winchester's trigger.

McCade smiled, seeming unconcerned about his predicament. "Can't do that, Bodine. I'm fixin' to take you in and claim the reward. It's how I make my living. And you're worth a pretty penny."

"You won't be living long, McCade, if you don't drop that rifle and get to your feet. You'll be jumping coals in hell, if you don't do as I say."

"You won't shoot me, Bodine. You've been a Texas Ranger too long to kill a man in cold blood."

"Haven't you heard? I gave up rangering. Now drop the shooter and get to your feet."

"Your brother's after you, Bodine. You know that, don't you? I saw him down in New Mexico Territory. He had a run-in with some cowboys over a woman. Heard he came out on the short end of the stick and won't be going anywhere for a while. Guess that just leaves you and me, Bodine."

News of Ethan came as no surprise to Rafe, except the part about the fight. Ethan very rarely came out the loser in any disagreement. But if he'd been laid low because of a dispute, at least that would explain why he hadn't caught up to Rafe yet.

He turned his attention back to the bounty hunter. "You almost killed an innocent woman and children today, McCade, so ridding the world of vermin like you won't be too hard on my conscience."

Derisive laughter echoed off the boulders. "Any man

running from the law who's traveling with a woman and kids has gone soft, Bodine. I say you don't have the balls to shoot." The bounty hunter raised his weapon just as the ominous sound of a rattle rang out. Fear clouded McCade's eyes, and he turned to look. Just then, the rattler sprang from its hiding place between the rocks McCade had been leaning against and sank his venomous fangs into the bounty hunter.

McCade screamed, then dropped to the ground, clutching his chest where the viper had bitten him. "You gotta help me, Bodine. You gotta get this venom outta me."

The unusually large rattler had bitten McCade close to his heart. The man didn't stand a chance of surviving. "I figure you've just been handed down your sentence, McCade. Now it's up to God whether you live or die. Hope you atoned for your sins. Hell ain't a pleasant place to visit."

"Shoot me, then. Help me die. Have some mercy."

The snake's venom did its job quicker than Rafe had thought possible. Sweat broke out over the bounty hunter's face, and he started to scream in agony. Removing McCade's only weapon, Rafe backed away from the hideous sight.

There was nothing he could do to help the man. Nothing he would have done even if he could. McCade had sealed his fate when he chose to fire at Emma and the children. Rafe hadn't killed him, but he would die just the same. And Rafe didn't feel the least bit sorry about it.

With one last look at the dying man, he headed back to Emma and the children.

Jubilant shouts greeted Rafe's return to the wagon. There were tears in Emma's eyes, and Pansy grabbed hold of his leg as soon as he dismounted.

"Rafe, thank goodness you're all right! You were gone so long and were too far away for us to know what was happening. I could only imagine the worst, and I was so worried!" Emmaline threw her arms around his neck. "*We* were so worried about you," she amended quickly, her cheeks flushed.

The sweet scent of her drowned out the stench of death still clinging to his nostrils, and he welcomed it, and her, into his arms. "I'm fine, Emma. There's no need to worry." Patting her back, he tried to offer comfort, and winked at Danny, who was grinning from ear to ear.

"What happened? Who fired at us? Are they dead?" Her questions spewed forth like a geyser, and the color of her cheeks heightened.

"Did you plant 'em in the ground, Mr. Rafe?" Danny's eyes widened at the prospect. "Did you fill 'em with lead?"

"Daniel Forbes!" Emmaline shook her head at the child's ghoulish questions.

"There was only one, and I didn't shoot him. He was snakebit and didn't survive."

"Though it's unkind to speak ill of the dead, I can't say that I'm sorry about that. Did the man say what he wanted of us? Most likely money. Thieves and brigands are always after other people's money."

"You're right, Emma," Rafe said, grateful for the plausible explanation she provided. "He was out to rob us."

"I just knew it. The guidebook warned of desperadoes on the trail. I guess we were lucky up until now. I was so terrified that the children would be hurt. And you riding off to who knows where . . ." She took a deep breath and clutched her sides. "I guess I'm not cut out for the Wild West."

David and Miranda shot Daniel pleading looks.

"Of course you are, Miss Emmaline," the boy reassured her. "You can shoot and ride as well as any western woman. Isn't that right, Mr. Rafe? Miss Emmaline makes a real good western woman, doesn't she?"

"Why, thank you, Danny. That's very sweet of you to say." Emmaline patted the boy's cheek, causing him to blush fiercely, then she turned her eyes on Rafe, who looked decidedly uncomfortable with the question.

Rafe rubbed the back of his neck, wishing the boy wouldn't keep putting such awkward questions to him all the time. "I don't think she's going to have a chance to find that out, son. We should be getting into Denver the day after tomorrow, so I guess Miss Emma will go back to her citified ways once we're there."

Though Rafe's answer was disappointing, for Emmaline felt she'd performed as adequately as any westerner, the real sting came with his mention of Denver. The end of the trail was two days away, and her association with Rafe would then come to an end.

He seemed not at all disturbed by the prospect.

She, on the other hand, was devastated.

Chapter Thirteen

DENVER WAS A METROPOLIS COMPARED TO THE other cities of the West that Emmaline had visited. Long, wide streets, brilliantly lighted by gas lamps and shaded by tall cottonwood trees, were lined with attractive and substantial-looking houses with lovely gardens fronting them.

And even used to the better things in life as she was, Emmaline had a difficult time keeping her mouth closed as she gazed wide-eyed at her surroundings, and at the snow-covered peaks of the Rocky Mountains in the distance.

"It's so refined, so cosmopolitan. I can hardly believe my eyes. It's like being back in Boston."

"There ain't no river smell here, Miss Emmaline," Daniel pointed out from the rear of the wagon.

Rafe reined the horses to a halt, allowing a streetcar to rumble past. "At any rate, we won't be staying in the downtown area, Emma. I know of a boardinghouse a few blocks from here. A widow by the name of Mrs. Goodman owns it. We'll stay there until arrangements can be made for your travel to California."

Loretta Goodman was a friend from his rangering days. A former madam turned respectable, she'd keep his counsel and not offer any judgment as to what he'd been accused of. She absolutely adored children, never having had any herself, and would welcome them with open arms.

And though he'd feel safer staying on Holladay Street, the center of the red-light district, he couldn't very well bring Emma and the children there.

Emma's face fell at the news that they wouldn't be staying at one of the elegant hotels they'd passed. One particularly impressive structure, the five-story, three-hundred-room Windsor Hotel, was still under construction, and she could just imagine how very elegant it would be upon completion.

The Boston papers had been all agog over the plans for the interior. The taproom floor was to be studded with three thousand silver dollars, and the ballroom floor suspended from cables to provide bounce for its dancing patrons.

Horace Tabor, the silver baron, or H.A.W, as his friends called him, had struck it rich at the Little Pittsburgh Mine in Leadville and had funded the hotel's construction. Tabor was said to be wealthy to the point of being gauche and loved creating monuments to his wealth. Not unlike many who had grown rich overnight. Denver had grown from a dream of gold, but silver had turned that dream into reality.

Loretta Goodman dashed down the front steps of the

boardinghouse like a whirlwind when she spotted Rafe. "Well, as I live and breathe, Rafe Bodine! I never thought to see you again." She hugged him as fiercely as her diminutive five feet would allow.

Rafe grinned, bussing the woman's cheek. "You're looking good, Loretta. But then, you always did."

"Oh, go on with you. And what's all this?" Shading her eyes from the glare of the sun, she stared at the wagon, noticing Emmaline and the children for the first time. "You went and got hitched, had a passel of young'ns, and broke an old gal's heart. For shame, Rafe. And here all along I thought you was going to marry me."

She smiled at Emmaline, who'd been rendered speechless by the exuberant greeting of the small woman. "Welcome, Mrs. Bodine. You are one lucky woman to have snagged such a devilishly handsome man as Rafe. I bet hearts were breaking all over Texas the day you up and wed. Why, I could tell you stories—"

"Emma's not my wife, Loretta." Rafe interrupted what could very well have been an embarrassing revelation, deciding to clear up Loretta's misunderstanding before the pink blush on Emmaline's face turned crimson. "And these are not my kids. Though they are a fine bunch of youngsters."

Daniel and David exchanged a look that said, *Not yet, anyway*.

Loretta had the grace to look chagrined. "Well, shoot me for a fool. Excuse me, ma'am. I tend to run off at the mouth, as Rafe can attest to. I'm Loretta Goodman, in case this big bad cowboy ain't told you as much."

Rafe helped Emma down from the wagon, wondering if Loretta was going to stop jabbering long enough to take a breath of air. It didn't seem likely. Once she had a full head of steam she could rattle on for hours.

It was obvious to Emmaline that Rafe and Mrs. Goodman had a history between them, but just what that entailed was a mystery. "I'm pleased to meet you, Mrs. Goodman," Emmaline said, completing the introductions. She decided to explain her present circumstances and why she and the children were traveling with Rafe, just in case Loretta Goodman had a prior claim on him.

Unprepared for the sudden spurt of jealousy that that notion created, Emmaline tamped it down before continuing. "Rafe said you might have room at your boarding establishment to put us up for a few days, until I can secure passage to California."

A blond eyebrow arched. "California! Ain't you the lucky ones. I've always had a hankerin' to go to San Francisco. Of course, that was in my younger days, when I was . . ." She paused. "I've got the room and the experience to handle just about anyone's needs, honey," she said, winking at Rafe, who nearly blushed at the woman's audaciousness. He'd nearly forgotten how earthy she could be, despite her newly found respectability. "Ain't that right, Rafe?"

"Loretta's a very astute businesswoman," Rafe said as he herded the children together and led everyone up to the clapboard house before the woman could comment further.

The two-story structure was painted yellow, the same

color as Loretta Goodman's hair and dress, which just happened to be her favorite color. Colors held various meanings for Loretta: yellow was sunshine, bright and warm; red, like the shutters and trim, a subtle reminder of the profession she'd given up to marry Cal Goodman, who'd been dead these past three years.

She brushed absently at the stray hairs threatening to escape her lopsided chignon. "Come on into the parlor and set. You must be tired after such a long journey. I'll fetch lemonade for everyone."

Her gaze fell on Miriam and Miranda and her eyes lit with pleasure. "Would you girls like to help? My back just ain't what it used to be, and . . ." Like eager pups on a leash, they trailed after Loretta while she continued to talk, disappearing through the swinging door that led to the rear of the house and the kitchen.

"Goodness!" Emmaline seated herself on the horsehair sofa, feeling just a little bit breathless. "I feel like I've just ridden on the tail end of a tornado."

An apt description as any for Loretta, Rafe decided with a grin. "Loretta's a good friend. And she'll be a big help with the children. She never had any of her own."

The parlor was attractively furnished, though a bit colorful for Emmaline's more subdued taste. Like the exterior of the house, red and yellow dominated the color scheme, from the paint on the walls to the red velvet draperies at the windows. A red, green, and yellow braided rug covered the floor, and Emmaline wondered if Mrs. Goodman had sewn it herself. Though she thought it doubtful that the woman could sit still long enough for such an enterprising project, as energetic as she was.

A few minutes later, Mrs. Goodman and the girls returned with a frosty pitcher of lemonade and a plate full of sugar cookies. Judging from the sugar coating the girls' mouths, it was obvious that they'd eaten their fair share before leaving the kitchen. Spying the confections, Daniel and David licked their lips, and Pansy, who had occupied herself by tracing the pattern in the brightly colored rug with her pudgy finger, cried out at the sight.

"Cookie! Cookie!"

"Well, ain't she the most precious little thing." Loretta's face softened as she handed the baby a cookie. Responding to the attention, Pansy thrust her arms out to be picked up and was not disappointed.

"Why, look at that. She's letting me hold her." Nothing could have pleased the woman more, and the joy showed on her face.

"Pansy's a very affectionate child, Mrs. Goodman. She's especially fond of Rafe."

"I ain't a'tall surprised. All women like Rafe. Why should this one be any different?" She kissed the baby's cheek and was rewarded with a handful of smashed cookie in her hair.

Rafe and Emmaline locked eyes for a moment, then Rafe grew uncomfortable and looked away. "I'm sure you're right, Mrs. Goodman," Emmaline said. She'd fallen hard under Rafe's spell, just as she believed had the rest of the women he'd come in contact with. And from the way Mrs. Goodman talked, that had been a substantial number.

"Call me Loretta, honey. Cal's been dead for years, and only the folks who don't know me well call me Mrs. Goodman. If you don't mind me asking, ma'am, are you married?"

"Emmaline's a woman of independent means, Loretta," Rafe answered, leveling an enigmatic look at the socialite. "She doesn't want a man running her life. She has no use for a husband, never has, never will, under any circumstances."

All eyes stared at Emmaline, who grew hot under the scrutiny. Had she really said that once? Had she really declared that she had no use for a husband under any circumstances? Because if she had, she certainly didn't feel that way now. Unfortunately, the only man she would ever consider taking for a husband didn't want her. And even if he did, Rafe would definitely not fit in to her way of life. The confining structure of Boston society would strangle the life out of him, just as it had nearly done to her.

Swallowing with some difficulty, she cleared her throat. "I may have been a bit hasty in my vehemence."

Rafe's eyebrow shot up. Loretta nodded knowingly. All five of the children heaved a deep sigh of relief.

"I can't believe you're on the run from the law, Rafe. But from the sound of it, that bastard Bobby Slaughter got what was coming to him." Loretta shook her head, handing him a glass of whiskey from the bottle she kept in her parlor for use on special occasions. "I'm sorry about your wife being murdered."

"*Sssh*. Keep your voice down." He glanced toward the stairs, relieved that Emma and the children had retired early. It afforded him the chance to speak to Loretta privately. "I haven't told Emma about the trouble I'm in."

Loretta looked aghast. "You mean after traveling with you for nearly a month, that gal still don't know? Mercy, you do know how to keep a secret."

"I've kept yours all these years, haven't I?"

A worried look creased her brow. "And I've appreciated that, and the help you've given me to break free of my other life. But I'm afraid there's some not as generous or kind as you."

He welcomed the amber liquid down his throat, then asked, "What do you mean? Has there been trouble?"

Her eyes misted, which was highly out of character for the worldly woman. "I've had trouble with one of the saloon owners—Simon DuMonde, a Frenchman from New Orleans. I worked for him once, years back when I was just starting out. About three months ago he moved to Denver and opened up a real fancy place on Holladay Street. He paid me a visit a few weeks back, said he wanted me to come to work for him, offered me a percentage of the profits if I'd take charge of his girls."

She sighed. "I'm out of that business now, Rafe. Cal saw the good in me, and gave me respectability by marrying me. I'll not tarnish his name by going back to a profession he hated. He was a God-fearing man, my Cal was."

"So, just tell DuMonde no. He can't force you to work for him. I don't see the problem."

"He's blackmailing me. Says if I don't reconsider, he's going to spread it all over town that I was a prostitute. I won't be able to earn a respectable living in Denver if he does that. You know how narrow-minded folks are. I get a lot of referrals from Reverend Baxter, and he ain't likely to continue sending people here if he knows I used to whore for a living."

Rafe's eyes narrowed. "Maybe I should pay this DuMonde a visit before I head out after Slaughter. It's probably going to take Emma a few days to make the arrangements for California anyway."

"First off, I don't want you getting involved in my troubles. Simon wouldn't think twice about turning you in to the law if he finds out you're wanted. He makes his money any way he can. And second, how can you even think about leaving that kind woman and those wonderful children? You can see just by looking at them that they're crazy in love with you."

Heat shot up his neck that had nothing to do with the whiskey or with the fire burning brightly in the hearth. "I don't have room in my life for anyone right now, Loretta. I can't lose sight of avenging Ellie's death. She was my wife, for chrissake! And she was carrying my child when that filthy bastard killed her."

Loretta gasped, covered her mouth, then picked up her glass of whiskey and downed it in one gulp. "Rafe, I'm so sorry. I had no idea."

"He's got to pay, Loretta. Hank Slaughter's got to pay

for what he did to Ellie." And no matter how much he wished things could be different for him and Emma, they never would. She had her plans; he had his.

"Hate can eat a body up, Rafe, until there's nothing left inside. That gal loves you. I can see it every time she looks at you. And unless I miss my guess, you're sweet on her, too. You got another shot at happiness. Don't throw it away. Ellie wouldn't have wanted that, no matter what."

"You've been drinking too much whiskey, woman. Emmaline St. Joseph doesn't want a man in her life. She told me so herself. She's afraid of losing control of all that money she's got. Sure, she might be attracted to me, like I'm attracted to her. But love . . ." He shook his head. "That's just not possible. And even if it was, as soon as she found out about my past, about Bobby's murder, she'd hightail it in the other direction." And who could blame her? Certainly not he. What kind of life could he offer a woman like Emma? She was a free and independent woman, used to the finest money could buy. He had nothing to give her.

Loretta didn't look at all convinced. "I don't know Emma well, having just made her acquaintance, but I'm a damn good judge of character, and I say that woman's got grit. You told me yourself that she could barely sit a horse when you met her. And look how far she's come. A woman with that much determination shouldn't be short changed and prejudged. She just might surprise you."

"I hate to admit it, Loretta, but Ethan was right. I should have stayed with the Rangers instead of settling down.

I've brought nothing but grief by my actions, by my self-ish decision to marry Ellie. I knew I didn't love her like a man should love a woman he wants to wed, but I married her anyway because I wanted to get hitched and put down roots."

"There's nothing wrong with wanting that, Rafe. And love grows. Just look at me and Cal. I didn't love him when I met him, but love came, in time. I'll bet deep in her heart Ellie knew your true feelings. A woman knows those kinds of things."

"All she ever wanted was me, Loretta. She loved me from the first time I can remember. And I caused her and that innocent babe to be murdered. Because of my past life as a Ranger, some sadistic, murdering fool took out his revenge on her—a young woman still in the prime of her life."

He poured himself another whiskey and gulped it down. "I can't bring grief to Emma and those kids, like I did to Ellie. They were almost killed by a bounty hunter's bullet. I'll not put them in danger again. It's best that we go our separate ways. It'll be safer for them that way. No one will get hurt."

Having seen the love shining brightly in Emma's eyes when she gazed at Rafe, Loretta knew that he couldn't be more wrong. Someone was going to get hurt, and that someone was Emmaline St. Joseph.

Kneeling by the side of the shiny copper tub, Emmaline scrubbed Miranda's hair until her fingers ached, trying to get out all the dirt accumulated during the long weeks on the trail. She'd done her best to keep herself and the children clean while traveling, but there was no substitute for a long, hot bath.

"Yeow!" the child cried out, and Emmaline paused in her ministrations. "You're pulling my hair, Miss Emmaline. Pretty soon there won't be none left to wash."

"I'm sorry, sweetie. But we need to scrub hard if we're going to get it clean."

"Miriam said you made her head hurt."

"Well, it can't be hurting too much. She's fast asleep, and so is Pansy." Though Loretta had offered separate rooms to all the children, Miriam and Miranda had opted to stay together and insisted that Pansy stay with them. David and Daniel shared a room down the hall, having turned down the friendly proprietress's offer as well.

Emmaline knew just how difficult it was going to be to separate the children when the time came for them to say their goodbyes. She tried very hard not to think about it.

"Mrs. Goodman is nice. I wish we could just stay here in her pretty house and not go to California."

Helping the child from the tub, Emmaline wrapped Miranda in a large, fluffy white towel and proceeded to dry her off. "We can't stay with Mrs. Goodman, sweetie. She's got a business to run, and we're just paying customers. Though her house is nice, it's the same as if we were guests staying at a hotel."

"How come Mr. Rafe decided to stay at a hotel instead of staying here with us? I thought he was friends with Mrs. Goodman. How come he didn't want to be with us?"

Allowing the child's flannel nightgown to float down
over her head, Emmaline seated herself on the stool near
the door and lifted Miranda onto her lap, unsure of exactly
what she should say. Rafe's decision to stay at a hotel had
come as a complete surprise to her as well, but she
guessed he was already trying to distance himself so that
their parting would be that much easier.

"He's got business to take care of, Miranda. I bet he
thought it'd be easier if he was right downtown."

"Maybe when Mr. Rafe finishes with his business he'll
want to come with us to California."

The hope in the child's eyes, and the love in her voice,
made Emmaline's throat tighten; the innocent suggestion
was one she had silently considered countless times.
"Rafe's got family in Texas, sweetie. I think he'll probably go back there when he finishes up whatever it is he's
got to do." She'd never found out what his immediate
plans were. Rafe's obvious reluctance to discuss his business had made her hesitant to ask questions. And she was
fearful of what his answers might be.

"You could ask him, Miss Emmaline. Until you ask,
you won't really know for sure if he wants to come or
not."

"It's a bit more complicated than that, Miranda. I won't
be staying in California either, after I get you and the
other children settled. I have to return to Boston. And it
wouldn't be fair to ask Rafe to accompany us, knowing
that we'll all be going our separate ways."

The tears came then, and Miranda laid her head on
Emmaline's shoulder and sobbed. "Please don't leave us

with strangers, Miss Emmaline. We love you. And we don't want to split up." Wrapping her thin arms about Emmaline's neck, the child hugged her fiercely, as if sheer will and wanting could somehow make her hopes come true.

Emmaline's eyes misted, but she tried very hard not to cry, for she knew it would only make matters worse. As much as she might want to keep the children with her, she knew that a woman alone—a woman with little or no mothering experience—could not provide a proper home. Children needed a suitable environment and a nurturing mother and father, not a socialite whose only recommendations were a large bank account and a mansion.

She could kid herself into thinking that Miranda and the others would be well off with her, that her money would make an appropriate substitute for a family life, but she knew that would be selfish and wrong. They needed real families and stable homes, and she would do her damnedest to find them.

She tried to explain. "If things were different, sweetie, I would keep all of you in a heartbeat. But I'm not married, and I'm not the kind of person who would make a very good mother. I'd probably make all kinds of mistakes when it came to making the best decisions for your upbringing. And, well . . . I'm not married, and children need a father. I'm adamant on that point."

Miranda looked up, wiping the tears from her eyes and cheeks with the back of her hand. "You could get married, Miss Emmaline. Then we could stay with you."

Sighing, Emmaline realized that she'd done a poor job

of explaining things. Instead of giving a suitable answer, she'd offered hope. "At my age, women are considered spinsters, Miranda. And to be perfectly honest, I never really had much interest in marriage. It always seemed quite stifling to me."

"But you said earlier that you'd changed your mind."

"Sweetie, sometimes even adults don't always get what they wish for. And even if I wanted to get married, there's no one asking me to be his wife. I can't just go out in the street and grab a man and haul him to the altar, now can I?"

The child nodded enthusiastically, and Emmaline's eyes widened as Miranda's next words came out in a rush. "You could if it was Mr. Rafe. I know he'd marry you if you wanted him to. He told David you were pretty. And if he knew how much you liked him—"

"I do not! And you mustn't say such things." Emmaline's cheeks crimsoned, and she was glad no one else was there to witness her humiliation. "You haven't told Mr. Rafe such things, have you, Miranda?"

The child's silence spoke volumes, and Emmaline shut her eyes against it. Dear Lord! These children had been playing matchmaker for her. Rafe probably thought she was desperate to marry him. No wonder he'd decided to stay at a hotel. He likely feared she would throw herself at him, begging and pleading.

"Miranda, you must promise me that you and the others will not speak of this again to Rafe. As much as you might want it to happen, Rafe and I don't love each other, and we're not going to get married."

Rather than shatter the child's will, Emmaline's words seemed to strengthen her resolve. "You are too, Miss Emmaline. You are too! You and Mr. Rafe *are* going to get married." She rushed out of the bathing room, slamming the door behind her before Emmaline could contradict her.

The child's vehemence surprised Emmaline. Miranda had always been such a levelheaded, soft-spoken child. But the impending separation and changes she faced had no doubt caused a whirlpool of emotion to stir up all sorts of crazy ideas in her head.

Imagine Miranda thinking that Emmaline would marry Rafe Bodine. It was preposterous, unthinkable, totally out of the realm of possibility.

But if wishing could make it so, perhaps . . .

But wishes were fairy tales, and Emmaline was too grounded in reality to believe that just because you wished for something it would come true.

And though her head told her it was the most ridiculous idea, that she and Rafe were as different as night and day, and that he'd never given her any inkling—aside from those few wonderful kisses—that he was even remotely interested in her in a romantic way, her heart had her shutting her eyes, crossing her fingers, and chanting over and over in a hushed whisper, "I wish I may, I wish I might, have this wish come true tonight. . . ."

Chapter Fourteen

LA PETITE CHATTE WAS A FANCY NAME FOR A whorehouse. Rafe supposed it was somehow fitting, considering that most brothels were referred to as "cathouses" by those who frequented the establishments.

DuMonde's place was nicer than most. Crystal chandeliers hung from ceiling beams and expensive oriental carpets covered the wide-plank floor. But then, a man who made his living off women's misfortuncs could afford the lavish things in life.

Rafe remembered the first time he'd laid eyes on Loretta. She was Loretta Whitby then. Young and green, the way pimps liked to find them, she was plying her wares at a saloon in Fort Worth, and he was ashamed to admit that he'd taken advantage of her youth and her body and purchased her favors for the night.

They had been together only that one time, for by morning Loretta had revealed how her father had sold his youngest daughter to the highest bidder in order to buy a bottle of rye whiskey. Rafe had gazed at a face unmarred by time, into eyes that had lived longer than most, and had vowed from that moment on that he and Loretta would be friends and nothing more.

When she wanted to quit the profession, some years back, he had helped her to settle in Denver and purchase the boardinghouse with her ill-gotten gains. Calvin Goodman, a traveling shoe salesman, had rented a room for a week and had never left, and Loretta had won her chance at respectability and a new life.

And Rafe would be damned if he would let Simon DuMonde ruin it for her with his blackmail scheme.

Searching the gambling parlor that fronted the three-story building, Rafe spotted a nattily dressed man leaning against the bar. Rigged out in doodads, his dark hair greased back, his mustache dressed with wax, Rafe didn't need an introduction to know that he was a fancy man. He'd already heard that DuMonde had a fetish about his clothes and appearance, and no one else in the place fit the description of being "slicker than snot on a doorknob."

Rangering had taught Rafe to size up his enemies. And anyone fixing to hurt someone as sweet and kind as Loretta, Rafe considered an enemy. He strolled casually to the long mahogany bar, ignoring the tinkling of the honky-tonk piano and the scraping of coins against the felt card tables.

"Howdy," he said with a nod, sidling up next to DuMonde and ordering a whiskey. "Don't short the pour," he told the barkeep.

DuMonde looked affronted. "I run a respectable place, monsieur. I would never cheat my patrons." His French accent was as dandified as his appearance, his words as slick.

"You run this place?" Rafe tipped back his drink, noting that the whiskey had indeed been watered down. He wasn't at all surprised—it was a common enough practice—but it always got his dander up.

His lip curling in disgust, he spit the contents on the floor. "This tastes like piss. What kind of liquor are you pouring, anyway?"

The owner glanced around, grateful that most of his regulars had missed the man's tirade. "Pour the gentleman a shot of the good stuff, Maurice. He's obviously a man of impeccable taste." DuMonde sized Rafe up and down. From the gleam in his eyes, he obviously liked what he saw, and that gave Rafe pause.

"I like your style, monsieur. Are you perhaps looking for work? I'm in need of someone to keep things under control here, and I like your commanding nature. I see from the size of your gun that you surely know how to use such a weapon."

"It's no wonder you got trouble in this place, if you're serving your customers that swill I just sampled."

"Most of my clientele come for the gambling, or the other delights we offer abovestairs. The liquor is secondary."

"Whores, huh?" Rafe sipped at the new glass of whiskey, noting with satisfaction how smoothly it went down. "Women are nothing but trouble in a saloon. Mixing men, women, alcohol, and money is just plain stupid, in my opinion."

DuMonde smiled smoothly. "I have ways of keeping my girls in line, Mister . . . ?"

"Rafferty. Just Rafferty."

"Well, Rafferty, let me assure you that the women in my employ never cause trouble. They are under my spell, so to speak."

"Really?" Rafe snorted in disbelief. "You some sort of magician?"

"I've had a number of women tell me so after I bedded them."

The pimp looked so pleased with himself that Rafe couldn't decide whether to laugh or to puke. DuMonde was a conceited ass, that was for certain. "Men who brag about their prowess in bed are usually a couple of inches short, or so it's said."

Rather than take the insult for what it was, the fancy man smiled. "I like your style, Rafferty. Are you interested in coming to work here? I pay well. And there are other compensations." He glanced toward the curved staircase that led to the whores' rooms upstairs.

"I'm picky about who I bed, DuMonde. And my gun don't come cheap."

"An enterprising man can make a lot of money in this business. Are you daring and resourceful enough to make your fortune?"

Rafe's eyes narrowed slightly. *Yeah*, he answered silently. *And determined enough to put a crimp in your dirty dealings, DuMonde.*

"Merciful heavens! Look at all those packages. You must have bought out the whole of Denver, Miss St. Joseph."

Dropping several brown-paper-wrapped parcels onto

the sofa, Emmaline removed her new bonnet and smiled at the proprietress. "It's 'Emmaline.' And yes, the children and I had a splendid time shopping." The only thing that would have made the excursion better would have been Rafe's presence. But Rafe would be leaving them soon, she reminded herself, and couldn't be relied on to provide companionship or entertainment.

"Take your packages upstairs, children, and put them on the beds," she told the weary youngsters. "I'll be up shortly to help sort everything out before we begin our packing." She thought of the train tickets in her reticule and sighed dispiritedly. The time to depart was at hand.

As the children dragged themselves upstairs to do her bidding, Emmaline glanced about the room, a questioning look on her face when there was no sign of the baby. "Was Pansy any problem?"

"Lord, no." Loretta beamed as proudly as a mother hen. "That doll baby is as sweet as molasses. I put her down for a nap about an hour ago. She was a bit fretful, and I guessed she might be tired."

"I can't thank you enough for offering to care for her her, Loretta. As sweet as she is, Pansy's a bit more demanding than the other children because of her age."

"Would you care to join me for a cup of tea? I was about to fix some when I heard you come in."

"That would be lovely," she replied, following the older woman into the kitchen. She was feeling a bit under the weather and thought a cup of tea might prove restorative. And tea in a real kitchen with another woman was just the ticket to lift her spirits. Not since her visit with Gerrie

Shepard had she realized how much she had missed female companionship and talk of mundane matters.

The last two days had been wonderful. No horses to saddle, no cooking over a campfire, no relieving oneself in the bushes. There was a lot to be said about town life, and Emmaline didn't feel the least bit sad about saying goodbye to life on the trail.

And the shopping! She had missed that most of all, and had gotten a bit carried away with all her purchases. She had even bought Rafe a couple of new shirts to say thank you for all he had done—blue, to match his eyes.

"Did Rafe say when he would return?" Emmaline tried to sound only mildly interested, lest she give Loretta ideas.

But the woman pinned her with a knowing look anyway. "Nope. And I don't know why he wanted to stay in a hotel when he could be living here among friends. Maybe there's too much temptation under this roof." She smiled, and Emmaline's cheeks crimsoned.

"I'm sure he thought it would be ill advised for us to live together under the same roof since we're not married. You know how people like to talk."

"I know it very well, honey. It's one of life's more difficult lessons. Cal, bless his soul, always said that people talked just to hear themselves speak."

"You must miss your husband very much. Has he been dead long?"

"Nearly three years. Died of consumption. Cal wasn't a strong man to begin with, and the disease took its toll. I nursed him as best I could, but it wasn't enough."

Seeing the sadness that clouded the woman's eyes, Emmaline patted her hand in a comforting gesture. "At least you had someone to love, if only for a short time. They say it's better to have loved and lost than never . . ."

"Ain't you ever been in love, Emma? It's hard for me to imagine you not having a man to share your life with."

"Men are mostly interested in my money, not my person. I'm not a beauty, and men set great store by things like that."

"Not Rafe. He judges people on their own merits."

Emmaline's heart thumped at the mention of his name. "Have you known him long?"

Loretta nodded, then sipped thoughtfully at her tea. "We've shared some times, both good and bad. He's a good friend to have in a pinch." Even now Rafe was putting himself on the line for her by taking that job at DuMonde's and risking his neck. Though he'd assured her that he would only be working a few hours a night in an attempt to find out more about DuMonde's operation, Loretta was worried. DuMonde was a dangerous man to cross, and Rafe was already riding on the edge of ruin.

"He's been wonderful. We would have perished if Rafe hadn't come to our rescue." Her voice grew wistful. "I can still picture him sitting tall in the saddle, the rain pouring down. . . ."

"You're in love with him, ain't ya?" At Emmaline's stunned look, Loretta smiled in understanding. "It's written all over your face, honey. Rafe must be a fool for not seeing it himself."

Resigned to her fate, Emmaline sighed. "I never meant for it to happen. It just did."

"That's usually the way of it, honey. Love just sort of smacks you alongside the head and renders you unconscious. I remember the morning I woke up and stared at my husband lying beside me and suddenly realized how much I loved him.

"*Boom!* It was like an explosion inside my chest, in my head, and it scared the living bejesus outta me. I'd never loved anyone before, never thought I could."

"Did your mouth get all dry and your palms start to sweat?"

"Exactly. I felt just like I'd come down with the influenza. Only I didn't have to throw up." She grinned.

"Well, I'm practical enough to know that nothing much will come of my loving Rafe. I'll be leaving soon for California and he'll be riding off to who knows where. He's never really said where he's going. Perhaps you know?"

"It ain't my place to tell you Rafe's business, but I can tell you that he's got good reason to go. I'm sure if things were different . . ."

Emmaline shook her head to dismiss that notion and along with it any possibilities of a future with Rafe. "We're nothing alike, Loretta. As different as night and day. There's not much we have in common."

"How about them five young'ns? You've got them in common. And even if they're not yours or Rafe's, you've been caring for them together. You're like a family."

Emmaline pushed herself to her feet. "If I didn't know

better, I'd say Miranda and the others have been bending your ear."

"There's no denying that those kids want to stay with you and Rafe. Their little faces light up whenever you or he comes into a room." Loretta dabbed at her eyes with her apron. "It's touching, that's what it is. And a damn shame to boot."

"Do you really think it would be possible for me and Rafe to . . ." Emmaline paused. "I'm just wishing for the impossible, Loretta. Though I may be in love with Rafe, I know he doesn't feel the same way about me."

The blonde shook her head. "You don't know that for a fact. Some men are just harder to read than others when it comes to matters of the heart. And wishing for something to happen between you ain't gonna make it happen. What you need is action. There ain't no way you can wish a man into your bed; you got to drag him there, whether or not that's the place he wants to be."

Emmaline turned three different shades of red. "Good heavens, Loretta! You forget yourself."

The woman stood, and her tone grew as serious as her expression. "Wishing's for little girls, honey. Women have to go about things in a whole different way. If you want Rafe, then go after him."

Emmaline stared up at the ceiling and pondered Loretta's words of advice: "If you want Rafe, then go after him." She had been on the verge of doing just that, had come very close to ripping up the train tickets she'd purchased, when fate had stepped in, in the form of chicken pox, to bring her to her senses.

What had started out during her shopping expedition three days ago as a couple of small red blisters on her chest was now spreading like the plague over her entire body. Loretta, who had examined the strange rash at Emmaline's request, had announced with a great deal of certainty for a woman who'd never had any children that Emmaline had contracted the disease from one of the children, though none had yet fallen ill with the malady.

Being quarantined in her bedroom, with visits from the children prohibited, Emmaline had had plenty of time to think about the situation between her and Rafe, and had come to the conclusion that as soon as she was well, she would leave for California with the children. However, the illness would delay her departure for at least two weeks, maybe more. At Loretta's insistence, the doctor had come to confirm the proprietress's diagnosis, issued a list of instructions to be followed to the letter, and hastily departed with an apologetic smile, as if fearing infection himself.

Emmaline had been feverish off and on, the rash itched like the devil, and no amount of witch hazel or the special oatmeal baths Loretta gave her made her feel the least bit better.

Lucas had had chicken pox as a child, and everyone, including Emmaline's mother, had thought how glorious it was at the time that Emmaline had been spared the illness. But Emmaline knew that it would have been far easier to suffer through it at age ten than it was at twenty-eight, and she wondered fleetingly if Rafe had ever had the disease, knowing he'd be immune to it if he had.

Rafe hadn't visited her or the children since their arrival in Denver and wasn't aware of her illness. And though Loretta had supplied a list of excuses as long as her arm as to why he hadn't seen fit to come, Emmaline decided that his absence was probably a blessing in disguise. And not just because of vanity, for she looked godawful and smelled as if she were rotting from the inside out.

She and the children had grown too reliant on Rafe's company and his counsel, and it was time they weaned themselves from him. It would be for the best in the long run.

A soft knock sounded, then Loretta entered the shuttered room and set an enameled tray on the marble-topped nightstand. "I've brewed up some boneset tea. It'll help bring on the sweats and break your fever."

"Thanks, Loretta. But I don't feel much like drinking tea. My throat hurts, and I itch something awful. Do you suppose I could have another bath?" Bathing seemed the only way to relieve the constant urge to scratch.

The woman nodded. "I'll run you one just as soon as you're through drinking this tea."

"Thank you," Emmaline said, still sounding miserable.

"Honey, you're dispirited and worried about the children, which you shouldn't be. We're having a grand time. I've been baking Halloween cookies with the older girls, and the two boys have been a big help with the chores. I'm not sure David knew that eggs actually came from chickens and not from the grocer until he started gathering them. And little Pansy and I have just had the best time playing with her rag doll."

The glow on Loretta's face and the enthusiasm in her voice made Emmaline realize just how much the woman missed having a family of her own. "I don't know how I'll ever be able to repay you, Loretta. We're practically strangers and yet you've treated me with so much kindness and generosity. I—"

"Hush now. You're a friend of Rafe's, and in my book that's good enough. And I'm enjoying the heck out of myself with those young'ns. The biggest disappointment in my life was not having children, so don't you worry yourself that they're a bother, because they're not. I'm sorry you're sick, but I'm not sorry that I get to play at mothering them for a few more days."

"Have you heard from Rafe?" Emmaline couldn't help asking. With nothing else to occupy her mind, she'd thought of little else but him.

"No." At Emmaline's disappointed expression, she added quickly, "But that don't mean a thing. That man's got business to deal with. And you know how men forget about time and everything else when they're busy. Why, there were times when my Cal would get so preoccupied with one thing or another that he'd have forgotten to eat if I hadn't been there to remind him."

Loretta had no sooner risen to her feet than she heard the banging of the front door and the children's excited screams. "Well, speak of the devil. I do believe Rafe Bodine has returned."

Emmaline's hands flew to her cheeks, a look of alarm crossing her face. "Don't let him come up, Loretta. I look terrible!"

Chuckling, the older woman patted her shoulder. "You're entitled to look awful, honey. You've got the pox. And be glad it's just the chicken pox. The other is a lot more fatal."

Discerning the woman's meaning, Emmaline nodded and watched her depart.

A few minutes later, Rafe appeared in the open doorway. He looked handsome, and Emmaline's heart beat a tatoo in her chest. The stunned expression on his face when he saw how frightful she looked made Emmaline wince and feel ten times worse than she already did.

Emma looked small and miserable huddled beneath the covers, and Rafe's heart constricted. He wanted to wrap his arms about her, draw her close to his chest, and offer comfort. But of course he couldn't. She might misconstrue his concern as more than comfort, and at the moment comfort was all he could give.

"Loretta said you were ill."

She pulled the covers up to her chin. "Don't come any closer. I've got chicken pox."

Despite the warning, he strode right up to the bed and sat down on it. "I've had them. Once Ethan got 'em, we all got 'em. So don't worry that I might catch them again. You can only get 'em once."

"You must think I look hideous."

He smiled to himself, wondering how a woman could concern herself with vanity at a time like this. "I've seen you lookin' better, Emma. There's no denying that. But hideous?" He shook his head. "Not by a long shot. You're still as pretty as a Texas bluebonnet."

He gave her a rakish wink that made her want to cry, she was so grateful for the comment. But she knew that tears would only blotch her face and make her look even worse. "The children have missed you. They ask for you every day."

Staying away from Emma and the kids had been the hardest part of Rafe's subterfuge at La Petite Chatte, but he couldn't afford to let DuMonde become suspicious of him, so he'd remained at the saloon most days and evenings, trying to ferret out information from those who worked there.

He hoped that by securing the right information, he could gain leverage against DuMonde that would allow Loretta to get free of his hold on her. So far nothing concrete had surfaced—other than a rumor that DuMonde liked to dabble in opium—but he hoped something substantial would present itself soon. He needed to be on his way. The Slaughters were never far from his mind. Though the inevitable may have been postponed briefly, sooner or later justice would be meted out.

"And have you missed me too, Emma?" he finally asked.

She could lie, Emmaline thought, but there seemed no purpose in doing so. "I guess I've gotten used to your being around."

"I've had business to take care of that's kept me pretty busy. I wasn't trying to ignore you or the children."

At his guilty expression, she said, "You don't owe us anything, Rafe. You did as you promised and brought us to Denver. And for that I'll be eternally grateful. You shouldn't feel obligated beyond that. That was never my intention."

It had never been his, either, but he felt obligated just the same. Obligated. Needed. Wanted. And he liked feeling all those things, though he knew nothing could ever come of it or of his feelings for Emma and the children.

His life had been mapped out for him by the senseless murder of his wife and unborn child. Because of one man's need for revenge, Rafe would never be free to experience the joys of marriage and family. He would live out his life alone.

Alone. The word conjured up years of bleakness, emptiness, unfulfillment. It was such a contrast to how he felt whenever he was with Emma and the children.

Alive. Like the passion pumping through the pretty socialite's veins—passion she was only dimly aware of. Like the warmth of her smile, which brightened even the gloomiest days. Like her enthusiasm for living, which consumed her every waking moment.

"I'd be lying if I said that I didn't feel some responsibility for your welfare and the children's."

" 'Responsibility' is another word for *burden*. I never wanted to be any man's burden. I can take care of myself. I—"

Out of nowhere the tears began, surprising Emmaline as much as they surprised Rafe. She felt too sick to care whether she was humiliating herself. She knew only that if she didn't die from the chicken pox, the ache in her heart would surely kill her.

Rafe felt her forehead and was relieved to find her burning up. He didn't want to think that those tears streaming down her face were for him. It was easier to believe that they were caused by the fever.

"You've got a fever." He reached for a washcloth and the bottle of witch hazel on the nightstand, wrinkling his nose at the smell. "This'll help some." Gently, he bathed her face and forehead and wiped away her tears with his thumb.

"Thank you," she whispered. "I'm usually not a weepy woman, but I'm not feeling my best right now."

"You're a strong woman, Emmaline St. Joseph. And I'm proud to have made your acquaintance and happy we've gotten to know each other. I'll miss you."

His words brought new tears, and she looked away, unable to face him or the reality of her imminent departure. "I'm tired. I want to sleep now." She closed her eyes, willing sleep to overcome her and block out the pain of his words.

I'll miss you . . . I'll miss you . . . I'll miss you.

Like a mantra, they played over and over in her mind until finally she succumbed to exhaustion.

Rafe crossed to the door and then looked back, knowing that his days with Emma were numbered, and he wondered how he would exist without her.

* * *

"I told you, Loretta, your time's running out. I'm not a patient man, and I can't wait much longer for you to give me an answer. You either come to work for me or I'll blow this respectable facade of yours clean out of the water."

Rafe paused at the top step of Loretta's boardinghouse and shrank back into the shadows. DuMonde's threat filled him with rage, as did Loretta's plea, which seemed to fall on deaf ears. A few moments later, the front door slammed shut, and Rafe heard the woman's quiet sobs as she tried to cope with the problems facing her.

"I'm going to have to kill the bastard, Loretta. There's just no getting around it."

She looked up, wiping her face hastily on her apron as Rafe descended the stairs. "You'll do no such thing. I'd rather live a life of humiliation than have your death on my conscience."

He led her from the door into the kitchen, where they could talk. From the window he watched the children playing outside in the yard. They remained untouched by the ugliness of the pimp's words, and Rafe was grateful for that. "I'm already wanted for murder, Loretta. Might as well make the charges against me accurate." He filled two mugs with coffee and handed her one.

"You're no killer, and anyone with a lick of sense knows that. I can't believe your brother is actually coming after you. I thought Ethan had more smarts than that."

"It's his job. I don't fault Ethan for doing it. If the shoe was on the other foot, I'd be riding him down just the same." Rafe wondered why Ethan hadn't caught up with him yet. Only another criminal pursuit, illness, or death would delay the determined Ranger, and Rafe, though grateful for the reprieve, was worried that Ethan's problems in New Mexico had been more extensive than the bounty hunter had led him to believe.

"Why not wait for him, then—let him help you with the Slaughters? You could arrest them, let them stand trial for—"

"No! Much as I hate saying it, the court system can't be trusted. The Slaughters could escape, or serve time and be released. Or they might not be found guilty at all. I can't take that chance. And it's my spoken vow to mete out their justice."

"Well, it's not your vow to lose your life over my problem, Rafe. I won't hear of it. Do you hear me? If you can find something we can use against DuMonde, so be it. But I'll not have you doing anything rash on my behalf. Do you understand what I'm telling you?"

He grinned. "You're starting to sound like a mother, Loretta. I think these children are a bad influence on you."

"God love 'em, but it's going to be difficult letting them go. But you already know that, don't you, Rafe?"

The pain in his eyes shuttered, until he gave no further glimpse as to his feelings. Loretta always could read him like a book, and he found it disconcerting. "Of course I'll miss them. Just like I miss you every time I ride out of here."

She could see Rafe retreating from her, and she decided not to pursue the subject further. But she wouldn't let up on it, either. Rafe and Emma belonged together. Those orphans deserved a home. And Loretta wouldn't rest until she'd done her best to make it happen.

"Have you learned anything about our mutual acquaintance? Other than the fact that he's a slimy pig and a dirty rotten bastard?"

Rafe smiled at her vehemence. Loretta could swear like a drunken sailor when she put her mind to it. "He's a frequent visitor at some of the hop houses in Chinatown. I hear he likes the hookah pipe and the opium that goes with it."

"I wondered how he kept those girls under control. Now I guess we know."

The light of understanding entered Rafe's eyes. "You know, you could be right. I hadn't thought of it before, but it's possible they've been drugged."

"It's a common enough practice. You get the girls addicted so that they become so dependent on you and the drug that they never refuse anything you ask of them. It's the ultimate form of control." Her face twisted in disgust. "I'll never go back to that kind of life. I'd rather die first."

He wrapped a comforting arm about her shoulders and squeezed. "I'll think of something. I promise you won't ever have to go back to that kind of life again."

"You give me your word that you won't do nothing foolish?"

"A man lives and dies by his word, Loretta. It's all he's got to take with him to the great beyond."

"But that don't answer my question, Rafe Bodine."

His only answer was a smile.

Chapter Fifteen

"MR. RAFE, I GOT ME A SERIOUS PROBLEM."

Leaning against his shovel, Rafe mopped the sweat from his brow with his shirt sleeve and stared questioningly at Daniel, the tulip bulbs at his feet forgotten for the moment.

"This ain't about women again, is it? 'Cause I'm probably not the best person to ask about that." And he had no desire to get into another birds-and-bees discussion. When the boy shook his head, Rafe almost sighed in relief.

"It's about Miss Emmaline. Tomorrow's her birthday, and I don't have the money to get her a present. Mrs. Goodman said she'd give me a dollar for planting these flower bulbs, but I don't get it until I'm finished, and at the rate we're going I might not ever get paid."

"Are you sure tomorrow is Emma's birthday? How'd you find out?" Knowing women as he did, he seriously doubted that Emma would confide her age or her birthdate.

"I heard her telling Mrs. Goodman that it was stupid for a grown woman who was about to be twenty-nine years old to have the chicken pox, and that being sick was surely a horrible way to spend her birthday.

"After Mrs. Goodman found out it was tomorrow, she decided we should do something nice for Miss Emmaline, like make her a party."

Rafe scratched his head, feeling mildly irritated that Loretta hadn't mentioned a thing about it to him. "I wonder why she didn't tell me."

Daniel shrugged, grateful that he and Mrs. Goodman had joined forces to get Mr. Rafe and Miss Emmaline together. Like Mrs. Goodman said: Two heads were better than one. "Guess she figured you wouldn't be interested."

"Really?" Rafe fought to keep his annoyance under control. Loretta always was one to hold a grudge. And he supposed her not telling him about Emma's birthday was his punishment for denying his feelings for Emma and the children. *Opinionated, interfering woman*, he thought, shaking his head.

"Guess we should finish the planting," Danny said, bending over to pick up another tulip bulb.

Rafe glanced down at the ground and sighed. He'd always hated gardening—he and plants just never did see eye to eye, and he was more likely to kill them than not—but he'd promised Loretta to help Daniel with the chore, and so he would, albeit reluctantly. They'd only gotten five bulbs into the ground, and there were at least fifty more to go.

Sensing an opportunity for a reprieve, he said, "Let's hitch up the wagon and go downtown and buy Miss Emma some birthday presents. I'll advance you the money, and when Mrs. Goodman pays you for planting the bulbs, you can pay me back."

"But what about the others? I know Miranda and Miriam will want to buy presents. And Davey, too."

"Gather everyone up, then. Loretta can take care of Pansy and Emma while we go on a little shopping expedition."

"Does that mean that you'll be coming to Miss Emmaline's party tomorrow night?" Hope sprang eternal, lighting the boy's eyes, but Rafe only shrugged.

"Maybe, maybe not. Don't know if I can get away." There was DuMonde to consider, and each meeting with Emma and the children kept him wishing for the impossible.

Emmaline didn't think volcanic eruptions had a thing on her chicken pox. She stared into the mirror, horrified, and was tempted to throw her hairbrush at the reflection staring back. Tears filled her eyes.

If she'd ever felt more ugly or miserable, she couldn't remember when. Even living on the trail with dirt, insects, and snakes for company was preferable to having the pox, as Loretta called them.

"Happy birthday, Emmaline! You look every bit your twenty-nine years today. Actually, you look more like forty-nine," she told herself, sticking out her tongue at the mirror. The unsightly eruptions on the tip of it made her feel uglier than a bullfrog.

Loretta, bless her heart, had purchased a new nightgown and robe for her, saying that a woman should have something pretty to wear on her birthday, and that if Emmaline would wash her hair and fix herself up, she'd look and feel ten times better for it.

But Emmaline was a long way from looking ten times better, even with the pretty violet-flowered flannel gown and robe and her hair clean and mildly presentable for a change instead of the mass of orange hay it usually was. At least her face wasn't glowing red like a kerosene lantern now that the fever had subsided. Of course, it was difficult to see her complexion at all, what with the unsightly scabs covering every inch of it.

The knock on the door interrupted her self-criticism. Daniel stood on the other side, holding a small bouquet of chrysanthemums and looking ill at ease. "Happy birthday, Miss Emmaline."

"Why, Daniel! How thoughtful of you. Are these flowers for me?"

His face reddening, he nodded. "Mrs. Goodman said I was to escort you downstairs. You're to join us in the dining room for dinner."

She could tell he had practiced what to say, and she wanted to kiss him for it. He sounded so grown-up. "Are you sure she wants me to come downstairs? I'm still awfully itchy."

"Mrs. Goodman says that if we ain't caught the pox by now, we're not going to, and that you're to come down straight away 'cause her dinner's getting cold."

"Just let me get my slippers on and I'll be right with you."

Daniel glanced down at the bare toes peeking out beneath Emmaline's nightgown and blushed furiously. It wasn't seemly for a gentleman to view a lady's bare feet. Mrs. Goodman had told him so during her lectures to him and David on proper gentlemanly comportment.

And Mrs. Goodman knew what she was about. She'd also counseled them on their mother's fall from grace, as she put it, saying that sometimes no matter how good a woman's heart was, or how much she might love her two little boys, circumstances could lead her onto a path she wouldn't have otherwise taken.

Daniel had felt comforted by that notion. And by the fact that Rafe had promised to attend Emma's birthday celebration.

Rafe paused before the boardinghouse and sucked in a breath of cold November night air. Stars glittered against the canopy of black velvet. In the distance, thunder rumbled off the snow-capped mountain peaks, and a dog's insistent barking ripped the silence.

He shouldn't have come. No matter how much the children had begged and cajoled, he still shouldn't have come. He had a job to do here in Denver and an obligation to fulfill once that job was done. He didn't have time for birthdays and frivolity, didn't have time to waste socializing.

Staying in one place too long was bound to get him caught, get him killed. Ethan would find him, as would bounty hunters like McCade, and he had to leave before that happened.

But he couldn't bring himself to go. Not yet.

He had promised Loretta to help with DuMonde. But the real reason he stayed was Emma. He couldn't leave while she was ill, couldn't ride away without a second glance, always to worry, to wonder if she fully recovered.

These were the excuses he gave himself, the ones that kept him rooted. But they were flimsy excuses at best. Emma was on the mend and would recover.

The real reason he hadn't left was that he loved her. Though he had no right to think of Emma in those terms, he couldn't help himself. He'd probably fallen in love with her that first day he saw her squatting beneath the wagon, looking like a bedraggled, drowned kitten.

Clutching the present he'd purchased close to his chest, Rafe wondered if she would like it, if after they'd gone their separate ways she would look at it sometimes and think of him.

"Damn you for a lovesick fool, Bodine!" he chided himself, and made his way to the door, hoping that Loretta wouldn't be in a snit because he was so late.

"I guess he's not coming." Daniel looked at the empty seat at the head of the long walnut table and couldn't hide his disappointment. "I thought for sure he'd be here. We all asked him to come."

Emmaline's heart ached at the distress on the boy's face, and she reached out a hand to him. "It's all right, Danny. It's still a lovely party. And I'm sure Mr. Rafe had more important things to do than attend my birthday celebration."

"Damn the man!" Loretta groused, stuffing her face with a forkful of mashed potatoes.

"The dinner was absolutely delicious, Loretta. Thank you for going to so much trouble on my behalf." Rafe's absence stuck in her throat like the overbaked chicken, and she washed both down with a large drink of water.

"Are we going to open presents now, Miss Emmaline?" Miriam's eyes glowed with excitement. "I can't wait for you to see what I got you."

Pansy squealed, banging her hand on the table to show her support of the idea and nearly knocking over her glass of milk.

Emmaline looked to Loretta for guidance. "Whatever Mrs. Goodman decides is fine by me. But you children shouldn't have purchased presents. Goodness knows, I never expected any."

"It wasn't us that bought them, Miss Emmaline," Davey explained. "It was Mr. Rafe. He took us downtown shopping while you was sleeping yesterday and let us pick out whatever we wanted to buy you."

"Really?" The generous, considerate gesture sent spirals of warmth rushing through her. "That was very nice of him."

Daniel nodded in agreement. "He likes you a lot, Miss Emmaline. He told us so."

"Yes, he does," Miranda concurred with a nod. "He said you was pretty and kind and that you smelled real nice too."

Emmaline smiled at their matchmaking efforts. "My, my. I doubt he'd feel that way now if he could see me looking so awful." And she didn't exactly smell like a bed of roses, despite her frequent baths and the lavender-scented toilet water she'd doused herself with before coming down.

All the children stared at her and were unable to hide their reaction: they winced.

"Let's go into the parlor," Loretta instructed. "We'll have cake and open presents there."

Just then the front door opened, and for the briefest of instances Emmaline's heart stopped. *He's come. Rafe's come to my party after all.*

"Hope I'm not too late for the festivities." He removed his Stetson and sheepskin-lined leather coat, hanging them on the brass rack by the door.

"You've missed dinner, Rafe Bodine, but you're in time for birthday cake," Loretta replied with a look of censure, obviously annoyed by his behavior.

The sight of Emmaline out of her sickbed and looking a tad bit healthier brought a smile to Rafe's face. "Happy birthday, Emma." He crossed the room to where she sat on the sofa and bussed the top of her head, then took a seat in the chair opposite her.

Emma could hardly blame him for not wanting to kiss her cheek, though she would have welcomed it. "Thank you, Rafe. I'm glad you were able to come."

Like an awkward schoolboy handing an apple to his favorite teacher, he thrust his present at her. "Me and the kids thought you might like to have this."

Miranda and Miriam smiled widely, then Miranda said, "Do hurry and open it, Miss Emmaline. It's a special surprise."

Her hands shaking with excitement, Emmaline carefully unwrapped the white tissue paper surrounding her gift. For Rafe to have gone to so much trouble. . . . The color of rose petals filled her cheeks at what that might imply.

Studying the silver-framed photograph of Rafe and the four older children, her heart thundered in her ears. "It's wonderful," she said softly. The gesture touched her more than words could possibly say. Now she would always have a reminder of the man she loved. Not that she needed one. Rafe's face, his teasing grin, the kindness in his eyes, would be permanently etched in her mind and heart.

"We did it just for you, Miss Emmaline," David said, staring up at Rafe with a proud smile. "It was Mr. Rafe's idea."

Tears brimmed in Emmaline's eyes and a lump formed in Rafe's throat. "I thought maybe you'd like a remembrance of our time together."

"Will you look at that?" Loretta peered over Emmaline's shoulder at the photograph. "And it's such a good likeness, too."

Swallowing with great difficulty, Emmaline replied, "Yes. Yes it is."

"My Cal always said that a picture was worth a thousand words. And by the looks of them faces in that one, there's a whole lot of love showing."

Emmaline stared intently at the photograph, hoping to see what Loretta saw when she looked at it. But Rafe's expression was diffident, offering no telltale signs of undying love and devotion, as much as she wished to see them.

Rafe cleared his throat, clearly uncomfortable with Loretta's comment. "How about a piece of birthday cake? It's been a good while since I've sampled any, but I can already taste the sweetness of it."

Though his words were aimed at Loretta, Rafe's eyes were trained on Emmaline's lips, and the hunger inside him was evident for all to see. Except Emmaline, who was staring down at the photograph, unaware of the heartfelt emotion on his face that said clearly that he loved her.

Chapter Sixteen

Rafe set down one crate of liquor atop another, then paused as angry voices floated into the storeroom from the adjacent saloon. One was unmistakably DuMonde's. A person would have to be deaf and dumb not to recognize that frenchified accent. But the other, Chinese by his estimation, he hadn't heard before.

The voices grew louder as they drew near, and Rafe squeezed into the narrow space between the wall and the tall shelving to conceal his presence and listened, hoping to gain some small bit of information that might prove useful to Loretta.

"You owe me a great deal of money, DuMonde," the Chinaman said. "The opium you devour does not come cheap, and I cannot afford to extend you any more credit. It will be very unpleasant for you if you do not pay what is owed."

"You know I'm good for it, Lee Poon. I just need a little more time."

Lee Poon. Rafe knew the name. The man owned a restaurant called the Peking Duck, which was located not far from the saloon in the drug-infested area known as

Hop Alley. It was said that Lee Poon served more opium than food in his establishment, and it was obvious that Simon DuMonde had a very big appetite.

The wizened little man shook his head. "I wonder what your partner would say if he knew how much money you spent each month on the opium. You have a very expensive habit, monsieur."

"I promise, Lee Poon, you will be paid, but you must not mention my debt to anyone, including the judge."

Rafe's ears honed in on the word *judge*. No wonder DuMonde was seldom bothered by the law for the illegal practices Rafe had observed in the short time he'd been working at the saloon. The gambling games were rigged, the dice obviously loaded, and the liquor was watered down. But DuMonde's greatest affront to human decency, which no honest law-enforcement official would condone, was his use of drugs to keep his whores in virtual bondage.

Lee Poon smiled, looking very much like an apple that had been left out in the sun too long. "You have picked two very dangerous men to cheat, DuMonde. Either way, you will die if you do not pay what is owed. I want the three thousand dollars by tonight, or my emissary will be forced to pay a visit. And Wang Ho is not a gentle man."

Shivering at the mention of the celestial giant, DuMonde nodded. "You'll have your money by tonight."

Nodding, the Chinaman tucked his hands into his black silk robes and disappeared out the door, leaving the Frenchman pale and shaken.

Rafe watched as he sank down into a chair, grasped the sides of his head, and rocked back and forth as if in pain. He remained that way for several moments, then stood, straightened his clothing, and walked back to the wall on the opposite side of the room from where Rafe stood.

Once there, he ran his hand over the wooden panels, pushing against one until it sprang open to reveal a hidden safe. Paying close attention to the twists and turns of the dial as DuMonde performed the intricate maneuver, Rafe sucked in his breath as the door to the safe opened and DuMonde removed a stack of bills from within.

Rafe would have placed a hefty wager that the judge knew nothing of this special safe and the hidden cache of money. Obviously, DuMonde was skimming the profits and stealing from his partner at the same time. It was an interesting, helpful bit of information that Rafe would put to good use in a very short time.

"You're not thinkin' of leaving *now*, are you?" Wringing her hands nervously, Loretta stared at the open valise on Emmaline's bed and panicked at the thought of never seeing those five darling children again. She'd grown so attached to them in the three weeks they'd been living in her house, she just had to think of a way to prevent Emma from leaving.

Turning to look over her shoulder, Emmaline's smile held a touch of sadness. No one was more distressed by her leaving than she was herself. "It's time we made our arrangements to depart, Loretta. Putting it off won't make it any easier. And we've got many miles to travel before the children are finally settled."

"But you've been ill! You shouldn't be traipsing over the countryside with all those children in tow. What if something were to happen? What if you had a relapse? Who would take care of you? Of the children?"

Emmaline set aside her folded clothing and turned to face the woman, whose anguish showed clearly on her face. Emmaline knew that Loretta couldn't stand the thought of being parted from the children, and vice versa, but there was no help for it. Neither she nor Loretta would make a suitable parent. Children needed the love and attention of *both* a mother and a father.

They had to go sooner or later, and sooner was better, in Emmaline's opinion. The children's welfare had to be considered above all else, including her own selfish wants and needs. And she wanted very much to stay with Rafe Bodine. Unfortunately, that wasn't going to happen.

"I defy you to find one ugly pockmark on my person," she said with a grateful smile. "Thanks to your good care, Loretta, I'm completely free of them. And I've got no reason to stay any longer."

"But Rafe hasn't left yet! There's no sense leaving before he does."

Gently, she clasped the other woman's hand. "It'll only make it harder on both of us if I don't leave now, Loretta. Rafe's got his own plans to consider, and I know he's been putting them off because of me. It's not fair of me to linger unnecessarily. It's time we both got on with our lives. Besides, I can't remain a burden to your generosity any longer."

"You and those darling children are welcome to stay here as long as you like. I've got no one else to share this big house with." And it was going to seem awfully empty without the laughter of the five little ones running about.

"You know perfectly well that you've turned down other paying boarders to accommodate us. Pretty soon folks will stop coming here because they'll think you're not open for business. I can't allow you to ruin your livelihood."

"But Thanksgiving is only a few days away. And . . . well . . . it's a family holiday—and since I have no family I thought I'd be able to share it with you, Rafe, and the children."

Emmaline sighed. "Loretta . . ."

Though she hated to use guilt, Loretta decided that drastic measures were called for. "You'd think, after everything I've done for you, Emma, that you'd stay and help me with the preparations for the holiday. There are pies to bake, a turkey to truss. . . . Why, I'm not sure I can manage it all by my lonesome." She covered her face with her hands, doing a fairly good impersonation of a woman in great distress—good enough to fool Emmaline, at any rate.

Cheeks pinkened in embarrassment, Emmaline wrapped a comforting arm about her friend's shoulder. "Of course I'll help you. I didn't realize that you were counting on me to such a degree. We can delay our departure until after the holiday. A few more days one way or the other shouldn't make any difference."

"You're sure? I wouldn't want to interfere in your plans, Emma," Loretta said, sniffing for good measure, all the while thinking that she'd missed a true calling for the stage. Of course, whoring had its acting moments as well. She'd certainly faked pleasure enough times, being of the opinion that the customer should get what he paid for.

Emmaline waved off her objection with a flick of her wrist. "Don't be silly. After all you've done for me, this is the least I can do. And you know how much the children will enjoy celebrating the holiday. I doubt that any of them have had the experience of a real family holiday with all the trimmings."

Loretta's face brightened instantly, and her smile beamed with so much satisfaction that Emmaline immediately grew suspicious.

"Well then, it's all settled." Loretta crossed to the bed and snapped shut the valise with a great deal of finality. "There'll be no more talk of leaving until after Thanksgiving. And who knows . . . You might just change your mind by then. Women have been known to change their minds a time or two."

"Why do I suddenly think that I've been outsmarted and outmaneuvered?" Crossing her arms over her chest, Emmaline leveled an accusing look at the woman.

"Because you have." With a grin, she added, "Better hurry on down, honey. We've got a mess of pies to bake and only a few days to do it." Whistling a cheery tune, she departed the room, leaving Emmaline secretly grateful for the excuse to stay, if only for a few more days.

Rafe knocked twice on DuMonde's office door, then strode in, ignoring the surprised expressions of the bartender and his employer.

"Rafferty!" DuMonde slammed shut the leather ledger on his desk, and his lips narrowed in annoyance. "This is a private meeting. You'll have to wait until I am finished with Maurice."

"I don't have time to wait. I've got an appointment with Judge Hobbs in about thirty minutes, but I thought I'd come speak to you first. That is, if you have the time to spare, DuMonde. And I surely hope you do."

At the mention of the judge's name, Simon cast his bartender a meaningful look, then instructed him to leave and close the door behind him. Motioning Rafe forward, he said, "How odd that you should know Judge Hobbs, Rafferty. I thought you were fairly new in town."

Rafe shrugged, taking a seat in the slat-backed chair in front of DuMonde's desk. "We haven't really met, but I hear the judge is a man always interested in information. And like you advised the day we met: 'An enterprising man can make a lot of money.'"

DuMonde nervously swiveled about in his chair and fidgeted with his collar, which had suddenly become two sizes too small for his neck. "I can't imagine what kind of information you could offer Hobbs. He doesn't usually mingle with men of your ilk."

"I guess if a man was being cheated, he'd want to know. I know I would. And I wouldn't care what kind of man it was giving me the information."

"Cheated?" The word came out like a croak.

"Don't play innocent with me, DuMonde. I know about the stash of money you keep hidden, and I'm figuring that your partner doesn't."

Outraged by the threat, and by his own poor judge of character, the Frenchman bolted up from his chair. "What do you want? I thought you could be trusted."

Rafe smiled smoothly, rubbing his whiskered chin. "A man who cheats his partner, drugs his whores, and blackmails an old acquaintance shouldn't speak to me of trust."

Comprehension came instantly, and DuMonde dropped back into his chair. "I only offered a whore a position—a chance to make some money. I see nothing wrong with that."

Rafe leaned forward, his eyes darkening ominously as his hands flattened on the desktop. "Loretta Goodman's a friend of mine, DuMonde. I'd hate to think that you were trying to force her to work here against her will, especially since I went to a lot of trouble to get her out of the whoring business some years back. It sure wouldn't set well with me if I thought that was the case."

"Loretta must have misunderstood," he said quickly. "I never meant to imply that she was being forced to come work for me."

"I overheard the discussion you had with her, DuMonde, so spare me your explanations. I also heard the one you had with the Chinaman. I'm sure Judge Hobbs would be interested to learn of your opium addiction, as well as the fact that you've been stealing him blind all these months."

Paling as white as his shirt, the pimp shouted, "You can't prove a thing!"

"Do you want to take the chance? Do you think the judge will doubt my story when I show him your secret safe? It would be an easy matter to persuade Lee Poon to explain how you regularly purchase large quantities of opium from him. And I'm sure some of your whores could be persuaded to—"

"What do you want? I have no money to spare, as you already know, if blackmail is your motive."

Rafe sneered. "That's your area of expertise, DuMonde. I just want you to leave Loretta Goodman alone. I don't want you threatening her, and I don't want you breathing her name to a soul. And if I ever hear that you've spread the word about her past association with you, I will make sure everyone learns your secrets as well. Do I make myself clear?"

DuMonde swallowed, then nodded. "I will agree since I have no choice. But answer me this: Why is this woman so important to you? Why would you go to so much trouble to help her? She's only a whore."

Rafe's lips thinned, and he had to forcibly restrain himself from beating the daylights out of the frenchified son of a bitch before him. He sucked in a calming breath and said, "Because she's a friend. And friends are few and far between these days."

* * *

"That was a mighty fine meal, Loretta." Rafe leaned back in his chair, his hands folded over his stomach, a smile of pure contentment on his face. "When I'm back on the trail eating beef jerky I'll think of it fondly."

Emmaline almost winced at Rafe's mention of leaving, and though she'd be doing the same soon enough, it saddened her to think about it.

"Why, thank you, Rafe!" Loretta beamed proudly. "Emma helped with the pies. And the children all took a turn at basting the bird. And for the first time in a very long time, I've got something to be truly grateful for this Thanksgiving holiday, what with you, Emma, and the kids here to share it with me."

There was also the matter of DuMonde. Upon his arrival, Rafe had revealed to her DuMonde's dirty dealings with Judge Hobbs and the way he'd been cheating him. Loretta didn't feel sorry for the judge—he was as crooked a fella as ever she'd met—but she was damned grateful that he'd provided a roundabout way for Rafe to get the goods on DuMonde and free her from his grimy clutches.

Now, all she had to do was find a way to prevent Rafe and Emma from carrying through with their plans to leave. Then she'd really have something for which to be thankful to the Almighty.

Emmaline pushed aside her own maudlin thoughts, unwilling to dampen the kind woman's spirits or ruin the holiday. "The dinner was utterly delicious, Loretta. And I feel every bit as stuffed as that poor old Tom. I don't think any French chef could have prepared a better

Thanksgiving meal. Thank you for going to so much trouble for us."

"I never had a drumstick before, Mrs. Goodman," Daniel confessed with a grin, licking his lips. "It sure was tasty."

Loretta winked at the boy, then said, "Rafe, why don't you take Emma outside for a little stroll? Since she's been cooped up with her illness and hasn't had much of a chance to get any exercise, the fresh air would do her good."

She turned to Emmaline. "I'm not counting those crazy movements you're so fond of doing with your arms and legs, either." She shook her head. "I never heard of grown people jumping up and down like you do and calling it exercise. Seems to me a walk would accomplish the same thing, and you'd get a bit of air at the same time."

Rafe grinned at Emmaline, whose face was fast turning red. "Come on, Emma. Loretta's suggestion has merit, and I could use the benefit of a walk myself."

"But it's so cold out, and . . ." And though she relished a romantic walk in the moonlight with the man she loved, she didn't think her heart could take another disappointment. Noting the matchmaking gleam in Loretta's and the children's eyes, she sighed, thinking that in the overall scheme of things one more letdown wouldn't matter.

Freezing was the word that came to mind when Emmaline stepped onto the front porch. Even through her wool coat she shivered, feeling chilled to the bone.

Rafe, who didn't seem at all bothered by the temperature, gazed down in concern before wrapping his arm about her shoulders. "Are you cold? Perhaps this wasn't such a good idea. You haven't been out of your sickbed long."

Now that she had his arm wrapped tightly around her, Emmaline wasn't about to give in to the elements. Besides, she was rapidly heating up. "I'm fine. Once we start walking I'll warm up quickly enough."

They proceeded down the front walk to the street. The blackness enveloped them in frigid silence. The holiday, coupled with the cold weather, kept everyone indoors, and Emmaline felt as if she and Rafe were the last two people on the face of the earth.

"It's so quiet," she commented, looking up at the sky. "And there are so many stars out tonight. They seem so close, as if I could reach out and touch them."

"Would you like me to get you one?" He reached his hand heavenward and pretended to pluck one out of the sky and give it to her. "Careful, it's hot and might burn your fingers."

She laughed. "I've never been gifted with a star before. Have you?"

His expression sobered as his thoughts turned to the one he used to wear on his chest. "It's been a long time."

"I don't think I've ever enjoyed a Thanksgiving more. I'm so glad I let Loretta talk me into delaying my departure."

"So am I." He stopped suddenly and turned her to face him, and Emma's heart thudded in anticipation of what was about to happen.

"I've missed you, Emma. Missed kissing you, holding you, being with you on the trail."

"I've missed you, too."

Her confession was all Rafe needed. Down his lips traveled gently to capture hers in a searing caress. The thrilling surge of his tongue as it entered her mouth sent her senses soaring in a million different directions.

She gave herself freely to the passion of his kiss, wrapping her arms about him, nestling close to share in his warmth. There were no thoughts of the cold, of her leaving, of his lack of avowal. All her energy, her love, and her sense of awareness were centered on this man, this moment, this kiss that she wished would go on forever.

But too soon it was over.

"I could go on kissing you, Emma, but you might catch your death if I keep you out here any longer."

"You won't hear me complain," she replied boldly.

"No?" His brow lifted and he smiled ruefully. "But Loretta would have my hide if I allowed you to get sick again."

It was an excuse, and they both knew it. There could be no commitment between them. Rather, would not. Because of Rafe's promise to his dead wife and unborn child, and Emmaline's commitment to her dying brother's request.

"Will you be leaving soon?" Though she needed to know, the words felt raw in her throat.

He nodded. "Day after tomorrow. How about you?"

"The same. It's time we let Loretta have her house back and get on our way. We still have many miles to travel before we reach California."

They talked of mundane things as they walked back to the house. When they reached the front walkway they paused.

"I'll say good night now, Emma, else I may be tempted not to."

She caressed his cheek. "I understand. And though I know I should be grateful, for propriety's sake and a million other reasons, I can't honestly say that I am."

The pain of knowing that she wanted him as badly as he wanted her plunged like a dull knife straight into his heart. He kissed her again, hard, almost punishing, trying to absorb every inch of her being into himself. When she grew pliant in his arms, he set her from him, cursing himself for a fool. "Good night, darlin' Emma. Sweet dreams."

Her gaze lingered on his broad back as she watched him walk away. Then, after staring up at the sky glittering with so many unfulfilled wishes, she shut her eyes tightly and made one herself.

Chapter Seventeen

IT WAS A SOLEMN GROUP THAT GATHERED IN THE front parlor of Loretta Goodman's boardinghouse the following evening. The bags were packed and lined up in the foyer by the door, while the children sat on the sofa, silent and somber as church mice. Even little Pansy seemed to comprehend that something dire was about to happen and was not her usual ebullient self.

Loretta had spent most of the day hugging the children and crying, while Emmaline wallowed in guilt at the pain she'd caused the older woman, who had been nothing but kind to her.

"I guess there ain't nothing I can do or say to change your mind, Emma. If there was, I'd surely try." Loretta dabbed at her eyes with the edge of her apron.

Emmaline felt herself weakening and fought against it. "We've been through this before, Loretta. I'm so sorry for the pain we're causing you by leaving, but it can't be helped. These children deserve a better life than either you or I can offer them."

Loretta was unable to find fault with that reasoning, though she desperately wanted to, and she nodded reluctantly.

"Mr. Rafe'll be here in a few minutes, Miss Emmaline," Miranda said quite matter-of-factly. "Then you'll see that we won't have to leave. He'll want to marry you, and we can all stay together."

The look of hope on each child's face filled Emmaline with despair and made her want to cry. They were so sure of being rescued from a fate they feared and despised, but there was nothing Emmaline could do. Rafe was not coming to offer marriage. He was coming to say goodbye.

"You'll all be very disappointed if you keep thinking along those lines. I know you love Mr. Rafe. But he is coming here tonight to say his goodbyes. And I don't think it would be fair to make him feel guilty for not offering what you think he should.

"If it weren't for him, we might all have perished on the trail. I think we owe him a fond farewell, don't you?"

Reluctantly, each child nodded, and Emmaline was overwhelmed with relief that she would be spared a difficult scene and the humiliation of public rejection.

Loretta wiped her eyes for what seemed like the hundredth time that day and sniffed loudly. "The man is an absolute fool! I can't believe he's going off on some crazy mission and not—" Realizing she'd said too much, Loretta snapped her mouth shut.

Before Emmaline could question her, the front door slammed open and Rafe entered the room. Dark circles shadowed his eyes, as if he hadn't slept much the night before.

Which was the absolute truth. Rafe had spent most of

the night tossing and turning in his bed, dreaming of Emmaline and trying to envision just what it would be like to make love to her.

Emmaline took one look at his haggard appearance and guessed that the parting was as hard on him as it was on her. They both loved the children so much.

Pansy eased herself off the couch and toddled toward Rafe, her arms outstretched. "Papa . . . Papa," she cried out, and Emmaline's heart wrenched. By the look on Rafe's face, he was hurting, too.

"How's my little flowerpot?" His voice was thick with emotion, and he swept her up into his arms and tickled her under her chubby chin and kissed her, rubbing his beard against the smooth skin of her cheek, inhaling her baby scent, and memorizing every detail.

"Hurt." She pulled hard on his beard and made a face, and Rafe laughed, though he died a thousand deaths inside. "Ouch! That's attached, you know."

Rafe's gaze drifted to the children on the sofa, and his gut tightened at the pleading looks they wore. He knew what they wanted. But if he remained in Denver any longer, someone was bound to recognize him. He'd done his best to confine himself to the seamier parts of town, where folks had their own secrets to hide and were not likely to ask questions. And he'd been lucky so far. But he wouldn't push his luck any further. He'd almost been recognized once in Jansen by that curious deputy. If he stayed now, no doubt some astute citizen would turn him in to the law.

"How are you all doing? I see your bags are packed

and ready to go. Are you excited about riding the train tomorrow?"

Daniel shrugged, doing his best to maintain his composure, as Miss Emmaline had instructed him. "It should be okay. We've ridden one before."

"That's right. I forgot."

An awkward silence ensued, then Emmaline prompted, "Don't you children have something to say to Mr. Rafe?" She looked expectantly at them, crossing her arms over her chest as she waited.

"Thank you for helping us on the trail," Miriam recited by memory. "We're all going to miss you." Covering her face, she suddenly burst into tears.

"Don't go, Mr. Rafe," Miranda pleaded, jumping off the sofa and wrapping herself around his legs. "Please don't go away and leave us. We don't want to go to California. We want to stay with you."

Rafe stared in helpless frustration at Emma, who sighed deeply and stepped forward to comfort the crying little girl by drawing her into her arms. "Hush now, Miranda. You're only making this harder on everyone. I was counting on you to set an example for the others." The admonishment served to subdue her heartrending sobs.

Rafe thought the hardest thing he'd ever witnessed or had to deal with was the murder of his wife and unborn child. But now, confronted with these children and his impending departure, he wasn't so sure. There were different kinds of suffering, he was finding out. And the pain of leaving these children, whom he had grown to love, was nearly as heartbreaking as losing his real family had been.

"I know it won't be easy going our separate ways," he said, hugging the child in his arms tighter without even realizing that he was doing so until she squirmed. "But you're all going to find wonderful families to live with and in time you'll forget all about me."

No, we won't! Emmaline shouted silently, but then maturity won out. "Mr. Rafe is right. Time heals all wounds. I know it's difficult to believe that right now, but it's true." Her eyes locked with Rafe's, and she could see that he knew her words for the lies they were. Neither of them was going to forget the other. Not in ten years or twenty.

Rafe cleared his throat and handed Pansy off to Loretta, who was misty-eyed over the exchange she'd just witnessed.

"Emma, I was wondering if I could have a private word with you."

Miranda sucked in her breath, and Emmaline shot her a warning look. "Of course." She turned to her friend. "Loretta, perhaps the children would like some of that leftover pumpkin pie you've been saving."

The proprietress shook her head at the stupidity of the whole situation. "Come into the kitchen, children, so the grown-ups can talk themselves to death. Looks like that's all they're ever going to do," she muttered, leaving the room, the children trailing after her like she was the Pied Piper.

Rafe rubbed the back of his neck. "That woman is . . ."

"Loretta might be a pain in your neck, but she's wonderful. I love her, and I'm going to miss her."

His somber eyes reflected the truth of her words. "Listen. I know this is rather late notice, but I was wondering if you'd like to join me at my hotel for a late-night supper? I don't want to say goodbye to you in front of an audience."

Emmaline's heart lurched, and she swallowed, knowing the proposal for what it was: indecent. Nice women, unmarried nice women, didn't go to a man's hotel room for supper or anything else unless they were planning to . . .

Before she could help herself, she nodded. "I'd like that very much." And it wasn't as if she were likely to get a better offer in her lifetime. And memories of their night together could be a comfort and something to hold close to her heart in the lonely years ahead. The decision really hadn't been difficult to make.

"Are you sure?" He searched her face for signs of regret but could find none, and it filled him with relief. Coming here tonight to say his goodbyes to the children had been damned difficult, but summoning the nerve to suggest to Emma what he'd just suggested had been near to impossible.

Smiling shyly, she placed her hand on his. "I'll need time to change and make myself presentable."

"But you look just fine. Pretty as a picture, even." And he would take the memory of that picture-perfect face to his grave.

Her heart swelled. "There are some things in life a woman wants to look perfect for, and I think this is going to be one of them."

* * *

Emmaline wasn't certain if the strange sound she heard was her knees knocking together or her heart beating out a staccato rhythm.

But one thing was certain: she was nervous.

Rafe had asked her at least ten times since entering the hotel if she wanted to change her mind and return to the boardinghouse, and each time she'd shaken her head and said no. Nervous or not, she was going through with this evening's encounter. The consequences be damned!

She had only herself to answer to now. There'd be no disappointed looks from her mother, no outraged demands for satisfaction from her father, or Lucas's fretful admonitions of caution. If she made a mess of her life, she only had herself to account to.

Money bought many things, including respectability and husbands. If she had need of either after tonight, she would use her inheritance to get it. One evening of happiness and fulfillment with Rafe was worth her entire fortune.

"Are you cold?" Rafe asked as they reached the door to his room, noting how she trembled. "You're shaking like a cottonwood in a heavy wind."

Emmaline doubted that she'd ever be cold again, with all the hot blood rushing through her veins. "I'm fine. Just . . . just hungry, I guess."

His look was predatory. "You're not the only one, darlin'. I'm mighty famished myself." Removing the brass key from his coat pocket, he unlocked the door and pushed it open, then stepped back for her to enter.

Emmaline was vastly relieved to find that Rafe's hotel

room looked fairly respectable. "It's very nice," she said finally, trying to keep her eyes averted from the huge four-poster. The crackling logs in the marble-fronted fireplace looked much more benign than the bed, so she gazed at those instead.

"From your relieved expression, I assume you thought I was staying in a bordello over on Holladay Street."

She shook her head, but crimson cheeks belied the denial. "No. I . . . I wasn't quite sure what to expect. I've never been to a man's room before."

His look was measuring. "Hand me your coat and I'll hang it up."

Her hand flew to the shiny brass buttons as she suddenly remembered the borrowed dress she wore beneath—one of Loretta's, which the woman had insisted she wear after hearing of Rafe's offer of a late-night supper.

"It's much too small for me now, Emma," she'd said. "But it's just the thing for making a man's eyeballs pop out of his head. I credit this dress with bringing my Cal to his knees."

Emmaline recalled Loretta's words and naughty smile as she now removed the outer garment to reveal the deep burgundy velvet dress. The décolletage was much lower than anything Emmaline had ever worn before, and she felt naked under Rafe's scrutiny as his eyes feasted on her breasts in surprise and pleasure. Unless Emmaline was very much mistaken, some eyeball popping was going on at this very moment.

"Well now, darlin'! Ain't you a sight."

"I'm taking that as a compliment." Nervously, she

smoothed the folds of the dress. "I didn't have anything appropriate to wear for supper so Loretta insisted that I wear one of her dresses."

His eyebrow arched, then he smiled. *Good for Loretta.* "This must be the infamous 'Salivating Cal' dress she told me about. I can see why the man started foaming at the mouth. I kinda feel like howling at the moon myself."

Cal, the poor bastard, hadn't stood a chance. Not if Loretta had looked half as good as Emma did in the gown. There was no shortage of bosom to admire, and though he'd had occasion to fondle the delicate globes, he couldn't recall them looking quite as sumptuous or as tantalizing as they did right now.

Unable to remember when she'd felt more embarrassed or admired, Emmaline hid her feelings behind a sharp rejoinder. "You are making me feel quite naked, Rafe Bodine. I'd appreciate it if you didn't look like a hungry mountain lion ready to pounce."

He stepped forward, and a low growl emanated from deep in his chest. "You bring out the animal in me, Emma." He nuzzled her neck, heard her sharp intake of breath. "I could eat you up, you look that good. And God knows you smell good, too." He inhaled deeply of the lilac scent she wore, and it went straight between his legs.

"You're scaring me!" she said in a choked voice.

"You should feel scared, little lady. I won't be content with just a few kisses and caresses this time. I want it all. I want you, Emma."

She swallowed, trying to think of some witty rejoinder

to lighten the moment while she recaptured her equilibrium, and was vastly relieved when an insistent knock sounded at the door.

Rafe cursed under his breath, then said, "Hell of a time for the supper I ordered to come. And you needn't look so damn pleased about it."

The banging continued, and she tried not to smile too widely. "You'd better hurry to the door before whoever's on the other side kicks it in."

A waiter dressed in dark jacket and pants hurried into the room carrying a large silver tray, and he looked like he was about to collapse beneath the weight of it. "Where do you want it?"

Rafe pointed to the mahogany table in front of the fireplace. "Your timing stinks. I'm tempted not to give you a tip because of it."

Noting the menacing-looking gun slung at Rafe's hip, the wiry little man opted not to comment and backed toward the door. When Rafe stuck his hand into his pocket to pull out a coin, his eyes grew wide with fright and he paled, fairly running out the door to escape.

"What the hell do you suppose was his problem? The fool didn't even wait for his tip."

Emmaline hid her smile and stepped toward the covered dishes. "I can't imagine."

Though the fare was plain—steak, fried potatoes, and green beans—Emmaline was too famished to care. And too caught up in watching Rafe consume the food in front of him. He had a large appetite, and she wondered if he was going to devour her the same way he was devouring the steak. The thought sent butterfly wings flapping wildly inside her stomach.

"Why'd you come here tonight, Emma? Surely you knew my invitation wasn't just for supper?"

She took a large swallow of wine, and felt her face flush. "It wasn't?"

He smiled indulgently at her attempt at coyness. "Can I assume that you want to be with me as much as I want to be with you?"

"It's not gentlemanly of you to ask such a question." Especially since she couldn't bring herself to admit the truth to him.

"You're not only beautiful, Emma, but a very interesting woman, and full of contradictions," he said between bites of potato. "I'm not sure I've met a more complex one. You've got all this money, yet you risked your life to fulfill your brother's dream of bringing those kids to California." His eyes filled with admiration. "You're one of a kind."

"What about you? You had your own itinerary, yet you stopped to help a bunch of misfits. Guess your actions were pretty contradictory, too."

"Not really. I just did what any man would have done in similar circumstances."

"But you're not just any man, are you? I've got the feeling that there's more to Rafe Bodine than just a wandering cowboy."

"Women are always trying to see more in a man than there is." Ellie had done that, and look where she'd ended up. "If you take someone at face value, you'll be a lot better off. What you see is what you get. No more, no less."

She sipped her wine thoughtfully and wondered just what it was he was hiding. It was time she posed the question she should have asked long ago. "Where are you going when you leave here tomorrow?"

"I've got urgent business in Wyoming. And that's all you need to know." It was a dismissal, plain and simple.

"Why won't you tell me? Maybe I can help."

His jaw tightened and set, and she knew she would get no answers from him this night. "Well then, what shall we talk about?"

He set down his fork and knife, pushed his plate forward, and backed up his chair. "I'm tired of talking, aren't you?"

The predatory look was back. "I . . ." She shrugged. "I was taught that conversation after a heavy meal was stimulating."

He grinned, reached for her hand, and pulled her out of the chair and into his arms. "Darlin', I'm going to show you something that's a hell of a lot more stimulating than talking."

The kiss he used to demonstrate his point fairly melted her toes. Currents of desire shot through her until she couldn't form a coherent thought, let alone a protest. Her knees became like gelatin, her arms leaden, and her stomach roiled as if she were sailing her skiff on turbulent seas.

Rafe broke the contact and stared into eyes filled with desire and uncertainty. "I want you, Emma. There's no denying that. I've wanted you for the longest time, and now I aim to have you. But only if you want me to. I won't take you against your will, or take advantage of your inexperience."

Her heart raced so fast, it took her a moment to catch her breath. "Does it show? My inexperience, I mean?" She blushed at his tender smile.

"No, darlin'. It doesn't show at all. And that's the hell of it."

"I'm new at this, so you'll have to show me what to do."

"With pleasure. Turn around so I can unfasten your gown and feast upon that delectable little body of yours."

"Aren't we going to turn off the lamps?" The idea of Rafe seeing her unclothed body in the dark was one thing, but . . .

"You've got a beautiful body, Emma. And I want to memorize every detail of it, every hill and valley." He smoothed her breasts and hips with sure strokes as he drew down her gown.

Standing before him in her chemise and drawers, Emmaline felt terribly vulnerable. All her life she'd protected the one thing that many had coveted but no man had ever won: her virginity. And now she was about to give it to a man who was leaving tomorrow. A man she would never see again. A man she loved, but who didn't love her back.

"Unfasten my shirt," he coaxed, and Emmaline's hands trembled as she reached for the bone buttons.

What if he asks me to undo his pants?

Caught up in her dilemma, she didn't realize that Rafe had untied the ribbons of her chemise, unfastened the tapes of her drawers, and was removing the last of her clothing.

Rafe backed toward the bed, bringing Emmaline with him. He sat on the edge of the mattress, holding her between his thighs, then explored her soft breasts. "You're truly beautiful. Sweet as a spun sugar." His voice was filled with awe.

Palming her buttocks, he drew her forward until his mouth reached her succulent nipples, then he began to tongue the hardened nubs.

Emmaline lost all her inhibitions and worries as Rafe continued his pleasurable pursuit. She grasped his head, holding his mouth to her breast as he suckled, reveling in the exquisite feelings.

Lifting her onto the bed, Rafe continued to love Emmaline with his mouth and hands, trailing exploring fingers down her breasts and stomach, until he reached her woman's mound.

"Open for me," he urged, gently sliding his finger deep inside to ready her for their joining. She was hot, wet, tight, and wanting. And she was his.

Rafe wasted little time in shedding the remainder of his clothing. As he gazed in worshipful adoration at the woman beside him, his chest tightened. "God, Emma. You make me feel things I shouldn't."

His confession bolstered her courage, and she wrapped her arms about him, kissing him with pent-up longing and desire. "Show me. Show me how you feel. Make me yours."

If he'd had any doubts, they were swept away now on the tide of passion her words produced. He covered her body with his, settling his weight between her thighs and urging them apart with his knee. "You're tight, Emma. And this may hurt a bit."

"I don't care. I want you."

He covered her plea with his lips, driving his tongue into her mouth. Slowly, until the agony of holding back made sweat form on his brow, he eased into her.

Emmaline knew a brief moment of pain as she took him fully within her, and then there was only pleasure. Sweet, exquisite pleasure. Pleasure so intense, so magical, so overwhelming, she wanted it never to end.

She lifted toward him, trying to meld her body to his, trying to find the fulfillment she knew awaited her.

Faster he pumped, taking her higher, until the heat grew unbearable, the excitement too intense, and she shattered like an explosion of fragile crystal as she reached her climax.

"Rafe . . . Rafe, I love you!" Emmaline cried out.

Kissing her lips to silence her vow, Rafe's heart twisted like a knot in his chest. *Emmaline loves me.* The reality of that was humbling, shattering, inconceivable. For the truth of it was, he loved her, too. With his heart, his soul, with every breath he drew.

And the hell of it was, there wasn't a damn thing he could do about any of it.

Chapter Eighteen

EMMALINE AWOKE THE FOLLOWING MORNING TO find Rafe gone. The only sign that he'd been there at all was the indentation on the pillow next to her, and the perfect red rose that lay against the white of the slip.

Her eyes filled with tears as pain stabbed her chest. "Rafe," she whispered, feeling more bereft than betrayed. She'd known before coming, before lying in his arms, that he would leave this morning. He'd never lied to her.

Holding the rose, she inhaled its sweet scent, and she knew that she would never be able to look at another without thinking of Rafe and what had occurred between them during the night.

The dull ache between her legs would heal, but the pain in her heart would not. She had loved. And lost. And the searing, devastating agony of that loss could never be assuaged. It might lessen with time, the memory tarnish with age, but the burning love she felt for Rafe Bodine would live on forever.

It was that knowledge that propelled her out of bed.

She had to see him again, if only once more. Had to kiss

him goodbye, feel his face beneath her palm, look into the blue of his eyes before letting him go.

Emmaline dressed quickly, giving little thought to the mass of red curls framing her face in riotous confusion and the horrendous wrinkles in Loretta's gown, which she knew would gain her a tongue-lashing from the older woman.

"Well, it can't be helped, Loretta," she muttered, trying to fasten the tiny row of buttons down her back by performing feats of contortion only circus performers were known to do.

Splashing cold water on her face, she inspected herself in the mirror, grimaced, then grabbed her coat. With a longing look at the bed, she tucked the rose into her pocket and made to depart the hotel as quickly and stealthily as possible.

If luck was with her, Rafe would still be at the livery stable. She remembered his mentioning that Buck needed to be reshod and that he planned to have it done before departing Denver.

The lobby was empty save for an elderly couple who shot her a censorious look, as if she were a woman of the evening. She might be tarnished goods now, Emmaline thought, but she was hardly a whore. Head held high, she waltzed through the lobby and out the front door, praying that fortune would smile upon her this bright sunny morning and Rafe would still be waiting.

Hurrying down the thoroughfare, she paid scant attention to the hustle and bustle surrounding her. Wagons pulled by mules lumbered down the muddy street, still wet from the preceding night's rain, and young boys stood on street corners hawking papers, fresh fruit, and other wares.

She refused one enterprising young man's offer of a delicious-smelling apple tart. Though ravenously hungry, she had no time to spare.

A commotion in front of the police department forced Emmaline to pause and wait while a feisty, garishly dressed prostitute cursed her fate and the arresting officer's ancestors in a loud, screeching voice as she was hauled into the building.

Embarrassed to have witnessed such a display, Emmaline turned to face the building, and her eye caught the poster nailed there. The likeness of Rafe was unmistakable, the words beneath his picture, unthinkable:

WANTED DEAD OR ALIVE FOR THE MURDER OF BOBBY SLAUGHTER. RAFE BODINE, FORMERLY OF THE TEXAS RANGERS, $500 REWARD. WIRE ELMO SCRUGGS, SHERIFF, JUSTICEBURG, TEXAS.

The breath went out of Emmaline, as if she'd just been kicked in the stomach by a mule, and she had to prop herself up against the building to keep from falling over.

Dead or alive, Wanted, Dead or alive, Wanted, Dead or alive. The words kept replaying over and over again in her head until she wanted to scream out that it couldn't possibly be true.

Not Rafe.

Not the sweet, caring man who had saved her and the five orphaned children from certain death. Not the man who had made such tender love to her only hours before.

She'd had her suspicions that Rafe was in some trouble, but she refused to believe he was capable of murder. When no one was looking, she ripped the hated Wanted poster off the wall and shoved it into her coat pocket along with the rose, grateful that the poster hadn't been displayed elsewhere in town. It was common practice for such notices to be hung in the vicinity of law-enforcement offices rather than in stores and businesses where impressionable women and children could read them and grow frightened.

Suddenly the mystery surrounding Rafe made sense. He had been hiding something. But she had never realized the extent of his secret.

Texas Ranger. Murder. It can't be true.

That thought sustained her, gave wings to her feet, as she hurried to the livery at the far end of town.

The farrier was shoeing a bay gelding when she strode up. "Excuse me, but do you know if a bearded gentleman with a buckskin horse is still here? He said he was coming to have his horse shod."

The burly man paused, hammer in hand, and looked up. "No, ma'am. He left about an hour ago. Seemed in kind of a hurry, so I finished the job as quickly as I could and saw him on his way."

Thanking the man, Emmaline turned to leave, disappointment and worry clawing at her composure and tears welling in her eyes. The split-second decision she made shocked her, but the simplicity of it could not be refuted: She would go after Rafe and have him explain the circumstances surrounding Bobby Slaughter's death.

She had a responsibility to the children, but she knew

that Loretta would keep them for her. She had an equal responsibility to the man who had apparently risked all to help them when they needed it—the man she loved. And if there was something, anything, she could do to help him, she had to try.

The buckskin picked his way through the decaying leaves and rotting timbers that littered the wooded trail. Pines were in profusion at the higher elevation, and Rafe turned his collar up against the chill morning air, which belied the brightness of the sun.

The only thing warm about the day were his memories of the night before.

Emma. He'd been unable to get the sweet, passionate woman out of his mind. He doubted if he ever would. She had wormed her way into his heart—a heart he'd once thought incapable of love.

After everything that had happened—Ellie, the baby— he had closed himself off to that kind of hurt and filled himself instead with vengeance and hatred. And though those were still within, and the Slaughters still had to be dealt with, there was now another side to him—the side Ellie had always known was there, but he had refused to acknowledge.

Leaving Emma while she slept had been difficult and had filled him with guilt. But if he'd stayed to hear the softness of her voice, to see the love shining bright and untarnished in her eyes, he would never have had the will to ride away.

He would miss her. But the memory of her soft lips, the feel of her satiny skin beneath his hands, the warmth that surrounded him when he made her his own, would remain a part of him forever.

They were one now. One entity. Two parts of a whole. And neither time nor distance would ever separate them.

But at that very moment, Loretta Goodman was trying her hardest to do just that.

"Are you crazy, girl! As much as I want you and Rafe to be together, you can't just go traipsing off after him. You might get yourself shot. He is wanted by the law, you know." Loretta crossed her arms over her chest, as if the matter were already settled. "Nope. I can't allow you to go."

The ticking of the Regulator clock on the wall kept time to the agitated beats of Emmaline's heart. She leveled an accusing look at Loretta, and a blush rose to the older woman's cheeks. "Maybe if you'd told me about Rafe's situation to begin with, Loretta, I wouldn't have to ride after him now. I thought we were friends, yet you told me nothing of his difficulties."

"Emma, honey, we are friends. You know how much I care about you and the children. But Rafe's my friend, too. And I had to respect his wishes when he asked me not to say anything to you about his being wanted by the law. I guess he didn't want his difficulties to touch you. It was always obvious to me that he loved you."

Arms akimbo, Emmaline shook her head, disbelief etched clearly on her face. "Well, he has a funny way of showing it, running off as he did. A man who loves a woman doesn't usually run off in the middle of the night after he's—" Heat rushed to her cheeks.

Just a few short hours ago she had credited Rafe with never having lied to her. And maybe he hadn't, technically. But his omission of the circumstances regarding his trouble with the law was as big a deception as ever there had been, and she couldn't help but feel betrayed because he hadn't trusted her enough to confide in her.

"I don't think he had much choice, Emma. If he'd stayed, he would have been caught. It's only a matter of time till his brother catches up to him. Lord only knows what's prevented Ethan from doing that already. The man's as single-minded as they come."

Emmaline's face paled. "His brother? The Texas Ranger who could track a dog through a swamp and come out the other side without getting his pants wet? That brother?"

Loretta nodded. "I've known them both for years, and I've said more than I should. You'll have to ask Rafe if you want to know more. I gave him my word, and I don't break it lightly. But rest assured that Rafe only did what he thought was best for you and the kids."

Sighing, Emmaline wrapped her arms about the woman and hugged her. "I know that, Loretta. But I'm so afraid for him. And I won't be able to rest until I see for myself that he's all right. And maybe there's something I can do to help him. I've got lots of money and . . ."

"Now, Emma honey, you know yourself that you're not so proficient at riding and such. The kids told me how it was with you on the trail."

Chin set mutinously, she replied, "I'll have you know that I learned a great deal from Rafe while riding the trail with him. I can saddle a horse, make a campfire, and I know something about tracking. I paid close attention when Rafe was explaining things to Danny and David."

Loretta knew there was no chance of talking any sense into the stubborn young woman. "When are you fixing to leave? And what about them young'ns? What are you going to tell them? They think you're all going to California today. Why, at this very moment they're out back saying goodbye to the chickens and that damn three-legged dog Davey brought home."

"Trust me." Emmaline smiled. "They won't be the least bit upset about not going to California. When the children hear that they'll be staying here with you awhile longer, they'll be ecstatic.

"Would you call them in now, Loretta? I'm going to need to borrow some of Daniel's clothing." She had already purchased a mount from the livery. The horse she had ridden on the trail had been sold weeks ago, but the farrier had promised her that Matilda, as he called the mare, was as gentle as a spring morning.

Minutes later the children filed in. Emmaline met their confused looks with one of determination and a pasted-on confident smile. "Children, there has been a change in plans. We will not be leaving for California today."

The joyous shouts resulting from that announcement had Loretta covering her ears.

"Please listen carefully." Emmaline clapped her hands

to regain their attention. "I have several important things to tell you."

"Did Mr. Rafe leave, Miss Emmaline?" Miranda asked, her voice filled with sadness. "Is he ever coming back?"

"How come you still got that fancy red dress on, Miss Emmaline?" Daniel wanted to know. "And how come there's a strange horse tied out front?"

"There is?" David ran to the window and looked out. "There sure is. There's a strange horse out front. . . ."

"Maybe it's Mr. Rafe." Miranda ran after David.

Loretta stuck two fingers between her lips and let out a shrill whistle. The room quieted immediately. "Hush, now, and let Emma talk."

"Mr. Rafe is in some trouble, and I am going to ride out after him to see if I can help."

"Trouble? What kinda trouble?" Miriam asked, her brow furrowed with worry.

"Papa! Papa!" Pansy screamed at the top of her lungs.

"All of you be quiet!" Emmaline demanded. "And don't say another word until I'm finished speaking. I can see that I've been remiss in instructing you in your manners, but as soon as I return, that will be rectified."

Wide-eyed, all five children, who'd never before heard Emmaline's voice raised in anger, scrambled to the sofa and sat down, hands folded in their laps, their lips sealed shut.

She nodded in approval and continued. "I'm going after Rafe. I'll be gone a few days, maybe more than a few. I'm not really sure." She had no earthly idea how far it was to Wyoming, where Loretta had said Rafe was headed, and the weather, though not forbidding at the moment, could change suddenly. Winter was only a few weeks away, and it would be colder at the higher elevations where she was headed, but she had no intention of letting a little thing like the weather slow her down.

"While I'm gone I expect you to behave for Mrs. Goodman. She'll be in charge during my absence. Do you understand?" At their solemn nods, Emmaline smiled. "Good."

Explaining to an astonished Daniel that she needed to borrow some of his clothing, she went upstairs to ready herself for the journey. She'd already lost precious time making arrangements to depart and couldn't afford to lose any more.

In less than thirty minutes, dressed in boy's clothing, Emmaline St. Joseph, Boston socialite, heiress, and philanthropist, was riding hell-bent-for-leather in pursuit of outlaw Rafe Bodine.

Chapter Nineteen

"GENTLE AS A SPRING MORNING, MY AUNT Sophie's corset!" Emmaline said in very unladylike fashion, as she bounced atop the back of the ornery mare. She should have learned her lesson about the veracity of liverymen after she'd been cheated over that buckboard that was supposed to have been sound as a dollar.

"If you're gentle, Matilda, then I'm going to sprout wings and fly." No sooner said, than Emmaline was catapulting through the air, landing square on her backside in a pile of autumn leaves, too stunned to scream.

Matilda turned to stare at her with what Emmaline could only call satisfaction, snorted, then began grazing on a clump of grass.

Eyes narrowing, Emmaline was sorely tempted to stick out her tongue at the contrary steed. "You vicious animal!" With nothing injured but her pride, she rose to her feet and dusted off the seat of her denims, which were snug since her body was shaped differently from a twelve-year-old boy's. Though not much, she thought ruefully.

Remembering what Rafe had taught her about showing

your mount who was boss, she grabbed hold of the horse's reins, slapped Matilda soundly on her nose, and said in a voice that brooked no refusal, "Don't ever try that again, Matilda. I'm in no mood for your shenanigans. Now, if you don't behave yourself and help me find Rafe, I'm going to sell you to the glue factory when I get back to Denver. What do you think of that?"

Apparently not much, for the horse suddenly gentled and nuzzled Emmaline's shoulder, as if offering an apology. Touched by the conciliatory gesture, Emmaline kissed the very nose she had so recently slapped and apologized to Matilda for losing her temper, grateful that neither Rafe nor the children were there to witness her "sissy" behavior, as they were wont to call it.

Mounting again, and satisfied that she was now in control, Emmaline resumed her pursuit.

Due to the recent rain, Rafe's trail hadn't been that difficult to find, but he did have a good head start on her; Emmaline wasn't sure she'd be able to find him before nightfall. The idea of camping out alone in the woods caused shivers to run down her spine that had nothing to do with the cold temperature. She shifted restlessly in her saddle, wondering how smart she'd been to attempt such a daring stunt by herself.

Rafe would have been the first to tell her that her impulsive nature would be the death of her. Not a comforting thought, especially considering that she could run smack dab into one of those ruthless bounty hunters Loretta had warned her about. Or Ethan Bodine himself.

Heavens! What a disaster that would be.

From the little Rafe had said of his brother, it was obvious that the man had little use for women. And what made her think that she could find Rafe when an experienced tracker like Texas Ranger Ethan Bodine, who lived by his wits and survived outdoors on a regular basis, hadn't been able to?

Of course, Ethan didn't have nearly the incentive that she did in finding Rafe. She was in love with Rafe. Ethan merely loved him. There was a big difference in that. And how much could Ethan love Rafe if he was hunting him down like a common criminal? That's what she wanted to know. And she intended to ask the woman-hating Ranger just that, if she ever got the opportunity. She had pretty much decided that she and Ethan were not going to get along very well.

Night came early in the mountains, and it wasn't long before Emmaline was forced to make camp for the night. Having unsaddled and tethered her mare, she managed to get a small fire started, remembering to keep the smoke to a minimum, as the Indians did, so as not to alert enemies to her presence.

Sated from the two sandwiches Loretta had packed for her dinner, and sipping on a hot cup of coffee, Emmaline stared into the flames and wondered what Rafe's reaction would be when she found him. No doubt he'd be surprised. Never in a million years would he believe that she was capable of tracking him down all by herself. Most likely he'd be furious with her for risking her neck and interfering in something that was absolutely none of her business.

But she was confident that after everything was said and done, Rafe would be delighted to see her.

If he didn't kill her first.

Rafe was finishing his morning coffee when the hairs on the back of his neck prickled, a sure sign that something was wrong. A twig snapped, leaves rustled, and he reached for his gun, knowing instinctively that someone or something was out there behind the stand of aspens.

When he heard a horse's whinny and the sound of creaking saddle leather, he dropped to his belly and scrambled over an outcropping of rocks to see just who this unexpected visitor was. After Red Wolf McCade, he wasn't taking any chances.

Rafe spotted the stranger at once. He was slightly built, but Rafe knew that bounty hunters came in every shape and size. And there was a gun strapped to his narrow hips, giving credence to his thought that this was no simple tinker or traveling snake-oil salesman.

The man's back was turned, which gave Rafe the element of surprise, and he took it without hesitation. Leaping from behind the rocks, he tackled the intruder and forced him to the ground, pushing his head down into the dirt, and keeping his body prone with a well-placed knee to the small of his back and a gun pointed at his head.

"Gotcha, you sneaky bastard! Now let's see who the hell you are. You sure as hell ain't no professional tracker. Not with the amount of noise you made coming in here." He flipped the man over, and his eyes widened in stunned disbelief.

At the shocked look on Rafe's face, Emmaline was tempted to smile, and would have under ordinary circumstances, but she couldn't catch her breath. She had a mouth full of dirt. And Rafe didn't look the least bit happy to see her.

She'd spent the preceding night debating the wisdom of her decision to go after him, especially after hearing what sounded suspiciously like mountain lions. She'd spent a sleepless night and arisen before dawn. The light of day had bolstered her courage, and his tracks hadn't been that difficult to find, due to the soft mud. But now, seeing how angry he looked, she wasn't sure she had made the wisest choice after all.

"Son of a bitch! What the hell are you doing here? Are you crazy? Son of a bitch!" He holstered his .45. "I almost shot your fool head off, woman." He released her then, yanking her to her feet.

Spitting the dirt from her mouth, Emmaline took a deep breath and forced a smile. "Your vocabulary is limited, to say the least, Rafe. And you needn't have tackled me quite so roughly. I didn't come here to do you any harm."

He stared at her as if she were crazed. "And how the hell was I supposed to know that—to know who you were? Do you want to answer me that? And why are you dressed in boy's clothing?" He studied her from head to toe, thinking that a pair of denims on a woman looked pretty damned indecent. And pretty darn arousing! "You've got a lot to answer for, Emmaline St. Joseph."

But God, he was glad to see her. Even though he'd come close to killing her. To look upon that beautiful, dirty face—something he'd never thought to do again—filled him with joy. But he wasn't about to let her know that. The foolish, impetuous woman had almost gotten herself killed.

And what the hell was she doing there anyway? And how the hell had she found him? His own brother hadn't been able to, and Rafe had serious concerns about Ethan's welfare. His brother was either sick, injured, or dead; otherwise, Ethan would have found him by now. And if something had happened to his brother because of him . . . Well, Rafe wasn't sure he'd be able to live with that.

He led her to a small campfire by the edge of a gurgling stream. An owl hooted, and the wind whistled shrilly through the trees.

"You'd better tell me everything, Emma."

Arms crossed over her chest, she fought to keep her temper under control. "I think it's you, Rafe Bodine, who has some explaining to do."

His look was incredulous. "You mean to tell me that you came after me because I slipped out of your bed during the night and—" At her gasp of outrage, and the furious look on her face, he stopped in midsentence. Her complexion was nearly the same color as the flames dancing in the fire.

"My being here has nothing to do with your ungentlemanly behavior. Though now that you mention it, leaving like a thief in the night was a pretty ungentlemanly thing to do, considering the circumstances."

Now it was his turn to crimson; he rubbed the back of his neck, clearly embarrassed by his previous behavior. "I . . . I'm sorry for leaving, Emma, but I had no choice. If I hadn't left when I did, I never would have gone."

His words filled her with pleasure, but she didn't let it show. Let him stew in his own juices, she thought. He deserved to. "Your behavior of the other night is not why I'm here." Before he could question her further, she pulled the Wanted poster out of her back hip pocket and presented it to him. "But this is."

Unfolding it, he stared at the ragged sheet with something akin to regret, and heaved a dispirited sigh. "I was hoping to spare you this. I never wanted you to know."

"And why not? After all we've been through together, did you really think that I would believe you murdered someone in cold blood? Do you really think so little of me, Rafe? You must, since you didn't bother to tell me of your trouble."

He handed her a cup of hot coffee and sat next to her on the log. "I didn't want my problems to rub off on you, Emma. Murder is a sordid business. And I'm a wanted man. It's not safe for you to be around me any longer." It was never safe, though it had been necessary for a time.

"I think I should be the judge of that. I'm a grown woman, in case you've forgotten, and capable of making my own decisions about whom I travel with and whom I sleep with. They just happen to be one and the same person."

Her explanation far from comforted him. "I guess I should have told you the truth. But what good would it have done? I don't intend to stop my pursuit of the Slaughters."

"Tell me everything. Tell me why you're accused of shooting this Bobby Slaughter, and why you're so determined to reach Wyoming."

He sucked in his breath, reluctant to revisit the sordid details.

"I already know that you've lost a wife and child. At least, I assume they were your wife and child. You spoke about them when you were in a feverish delirium after the scorpion bit you. But I never questioned you about it, because I figured it was your private business.

"Now, however, I'm asking. And I think you owe me an explanation. If for no other reason than the fact that we're friends." *And lovers.*

Slowly, and with a great deal of patience and exacting detail, he recounted his years with the Texas Rangers and his ultimate desire to quit and settle down. He told her of his lifelong friendship with Ellie Masters, of their short-lived marriage and the impending birth of their child. Then he recounted the scene he had stumbled upon: Ellie's vicious murder, the death of the baby, his vow to exact vengeance on the Slaughters.

Through it all, Emmaline listened. Though she had tears in her eyes, and bile filled her throat at the gruesome details he recounted, she didn't interrupt. Rafe needed to expunge his soul, as much as she needed to hear and understand what motivated a man like Rafe to want to commit murder.

"And Bobby Slaughter? Did you murder him like

they're claiming?" In her heart she knew he hadn't, but she needed to hear it from his lips.

"I went there to kill him. I won't deny that. But he drew on me first. If I hadn't defended myself, I would have been the one to die."

"Then why are they hunting you down like a common criminal? I don't understand."

"Bobby's whore lied. Said I killed Bobby in cold blood. They believed her."

"And your brother Ethan? Does he think you murdered in cold blood?"

Rafe's expression softened, and he shook his head. "Ethan's only doing his job. He's sworn to uphold the law, and that's what he's doing. I think his coming after me is done out of love and concern for my welfare. But also duty. You've got to know the kind of man Ethan is to know why finding me is so important to him."

Rafe's idolatry of his brother was clearly evident, but Emmaline still could not understand why a brother would do what Ethan Bodine was doing to Rafe, and her disgust and anger with the man registered on her face. "If your brother loves you, he shouldn't be hunting you down like an animal."

"I'd have done the same if the shoe had been on the other foot, Emma. Rangers are a special breed. We take our oath very seriously. Ethan, being a captain, took his to heart more than most."

"Blood is thicker than water, and family ties should come first."

Rafe's smile was rueful. "That might be the case in

most families, but not in ours. Ethan's a Ranger first and a brother second."

"I don't understand that kind of thinking, and I don't believe I like him at all."

"Ethan won't care. He's not partial to women."

"So you said. It's probably the reason he's so sour and callous."

"Ethan prides himself on those traits." Noting how Emmaline shivered, Rafe tossed a few more branches onto the fire, uncertain whether she was cold or merely expressing her distaste for his brother.

"Don't judge him too hard, Emma. He's a good man."

"So are you, Rafe. And you had every right to defend yourself against some vicious killer who was trying to shoot you." Though Emmaline had been sheltered from the cruelties of life, and murder was as inconceivable to her as being without money, she couldn't condemn Rafe for what had happened to Bobby Slaughter. He would have been justified in shooting the man down in cold blood, after what Slaughter had done to Ellie, but Emmaline was grateful that he hadn't. Rafe was no cold-blooded killer. He had too much love and compassion in him to be anything but the brave, honest man she knew him to be.

But Rafe's innocence might not be easy to prove in a court of law. The only witness to the crime was a hostile, bitter woman who was not likely to tell the truth. Self-defense or not, Rafe wasn't likely to get a fair trial, considering that he had run away and was still bent on killing the rest of the Slaughter gang.

Never having had a problem she couldn't solve, Emmaline put her thoughts and energies into finding a solution to Rafe's dilemma, unwilling to risk his incarceration or his life. When the answer came, it was so simple that she almost smiled. It was the perfect resolution to Rafe's predicament. Now all she had to do was convince Rafe of that.

"I don't think you should wait around for your brother to find you," she said. "After everything you've told me, I'm not sure the law is going to treat you kindly."

He grinned, liking that she felt so protective of him. "I'm not planning for the law to find me, darlin'. I took risks to help you and the children, but luck's been with me, and I've managed up till now."

"I have a very simple solution to all your problems. And I think after you hear it, you'll have to agree that it's the best—the only—recourse for you to take."

His eyebrow shot up. "You sound pretty darn sure of yourself. Pardon me for being skeptical by nature, but I don't see any way out of this for me."

"You can go with me to California."

The words, so simply said, took him totally by surprise. "California? You want me to go to California with you and the kids? Is that what you're suggesting?" The idea was totally irrational, unthinkable. But it fit Emma's way of thinking to perfection.

She clasped his hand. "It's so simple it scares me. No one would think to look for you there. Why, even Ethan will be at a loss as to where to find you."

Ethan wouldn't rest until he'd accomplished his mission, but to try to explain a Ranger's sense of justice and dedication wasn't an easy thing to do, especially to someone like Emma, who wasn't versed in matters of the West, and who'd never had dealings with the Texas Rangers, a breed unto themselves. If Ethan was still alive—and Rafe prayed that he was—he'd be coming after him.

Emma thought it would be so easy; he knew it would be anything but.

"It's a nice thought, Emma. But let me assure you that my brother will not be diverted by my leaving with you. It might slow Ethan down for a while, throw him off the scent, but like an old coon hound he'll pick it up soon enough."

"The more I hear about this brother of yours, the more I dislike him." She pursed her lips. "Fine, then, we'll go to Europe. I have plenty of money. We can . . ."

"Emma!" Rafe shook his head at her stubborn refusal to listen. "Ethan's not the only reason I can't go to California or Europe with you. Are you forgetting the Slaughters? Because I haven't. Not for one minute. I'm going to exact my pound of flesh. I owe that much to Ellie and the baby." Though he loved Emma with all his heart and soul, he couldn't forget where his first loyalty lay.

Fear and anger masked her face. And pain. For to go to such lengths, take unreasonable risks, he must have loved his wife a great deal, and Emmaline couldn't help the unreasonable stab of jealousy she felt as she realized that.

"That's just plain foolishness, Rafe Bodine. You have a chance to leave all of this ugliness behind and start anew. California is the land of opportunity."

"Emma, I appreciate your effort in trying to protect me, but I'll not change my mind about this. My mama always said that I was as obstinate as a cow with a sucking calf. And that's pretty darn stubborn."

"I'm not expecting a commitment from you, Rafe, if that's what's keeping you from taking me up on my offer."

He squeezed her hand. "It's not. And I don't expect a woman like you to understand what motivates a man like me. But finding the Slaughters and killing them is something I have to do. I won't be able to live with myself otherwise."

"But you're not a murderer, Rafe. And if you hunt them down and kill them, you'll be no better than they are. Don't you see that? Two wrongs don't make a right, no matter how much you may want them to." The fact that he was still contemplating murder scared her almost as much as the threat to his safety.

"It's pointless arguing, Emma. I'm going and that's final. Tomorrow you'll return to Denver, and I'll continue on to Wyoming. It's the way it's got to be."

"I don't think so."

"Now, Emma, don't be meddling in things you—"

"I'm not going back to Denver tomorrow, Rafe. If you're going after the Slaughters, then I'm going with you." Maybe she could save him from the Slaughters, and from himself.

He jumped to his feet, his face bright with rage. "The hell you are!"

"Just try and stop me." She stood and faced him, and

the mutinous set to her chin told Rafe clearly that he was in for a real fight.

"I'll tie you to that damned tree to keep you from coming with me if I have to."

"What good will that do? I'll just freeze to death or the mountain lions will get me."

Better a cat than a Slaughter. Emma didn't know what she was asking by wanting to ride with him. He couldn't risk her life, couldn't take the chance that Hank and the others would do to Emma what they'd done to Ellie.

He shook his head in firm denial, and his voice was harsh as he said, "No! I won't risk your life. You don't know what kind of men we're dealing with. I've told you, they're brutal animals, vicious killers who rape and mutilate." He shook his head. "No. And that's final."

His words filled her with fear, but she wasn't about to show it. Fear of the Slaughters was one thing, but fear of living without Rafe in her life, without knowing if he lived or died at the hand of these ruthless people, was something she couldn't cope with. She had to go with him, and she had to make him understand that she wouldn't take no for an answer.

"I can be of help to you, Rafe. I know how to shoot a gun, and my presence will offer you a cover of sorts—an element of surprise. They won't expect you to be with a woman."

"That's because I won't be."

Frustrated, she wanted to lash out, to kick him right in his male ego. "Your mother was right. You are obstinate. But so am I. And I'm not taking no for an answer. You don't own me, can't tell me what to do. If I want to follow you, I will. This is a free country. I'm a free woman. I can go where I want, when I want, and you can't tell me—"

He grabbed her suddenly and hauled her to his chest, kissing her senseless and effectively halting her diatribe. When he felt her compliant response, heard the soft whimper in her voice, he broke contact and stared into eyes filled with passion and promise.

"If kissing you is the only way I can silence you, then this is going to be a pretty pleasurable trip."

A cry of relief escaped her. "Then you'll let me go with you?"

"Do I have a choice? You'll talk me to death otherwise."

She grinned impishly. "You won't be sorry."

"But you might be. We're not dealing with horse thieves and cattle rustlers, Emma. These men are dangerous. Your life will be in danger, and it's going to be very important that you heed every word I say."

She wrapped her arms about his waist. "Now who's talking too much?"

Pressing his palms to her buttocks, he pulled her close. "I am."

Chapter Twenty

"HAVE YOU EVER MADE LOVE OUTSIDE ON THE ground before, darlin'?"

The provocative question and the huskiness of Rafe's voice sent Emmaline's imagination soaring, and her pulse pounded loudly in her ears. "If it's half as good as it was in a bed, I'm willing to try," she said almost shyly, then added, "and you know very well that I haven't, Rafe, because you were the first, and—"

He smothered her words, his tongue caressing her lips before plunging into the recesses of her mouth. "I think I'm going to like shutting you up, darlin'." He unfastened her wool jacket, running featherlike kisses down her neck as he worked the bone buttons free from their holes.

The temperature was near freezing, but Emmaline didn't feel the least bit cold when her jacket dropped to the ground. They moved nearer to the fire for additional warmth, but Rafe's hands fondling her breasts provided Emmaline with all the heat she needed.

"Your breasts are so perfect, darlin'." He teased the taut buds with his fingertips, fondling the small globes, and shots of desire raced through her.

In a voice so feathery she hardly recognized it as her own, she sighed, "I always thought they were rather small."

"Hmmm. This bears closer examination. A man doesn't like to be accused of lying about something so important." With mock seriousness and swift efficiency, he removed her shirt and chemise until her bare bosoms glowed softly in the firelight. Cupping her mounds, he weighed them in his hands, as if considering her comment. "There's only one true way to find out if a woman's breasts are perfect," he said finally.

Emmaline's mouth suddenly went dry, and she swallowed as his head moved down her chest and his lips captured her swollen nipples. Circling the bead with his tongue, he suckled first one breast and then the other until she thought her knees would buckle beneath her.

"They're perfect," he pronounced, capturing her lips again.

Rafe's assessment filled Emmaline with a warm glow, making her feel truly beautiful for the first time in her life. No man had ever paid her such compliments, and even if they were gross exaggerations and lies, she loved hearing them.

"I wonder if the rest of you is as perfect." His hands went to her belt, and her breath caught in her throat. "I was so caught up in the moment the other night, I didn't have time to take a close look. I think I'll rectify that now, darlin'."

Her legs wobbled like a newborn filly's as he unbuttoned her denims, one copper stud at a time. She wore nothing beneath, as her drawers had proven too cumbersome under the tight material. Rafe seemed inordinately pleased by the discovery.

"You are full of surprises tonight, darlin'." Slipping to his knees before her, his lips trailed down her abdomen as he kissed the area he slowly exposed, pushing her pants down the length of her, until they gathered at her feet.

Cupping her buttocks, he drew her toward him, planting his mouth against the soft nest of red curls.

Spirals of pleasure swirled low in her stomach, and Emmaline gasped, clutching Rafe's shoulders like a lifeline as his tongue slid between the cleft of her womanhood and he tasted her. Never had she experienced anything so wonderfully wicked, so excruciatingly pleasurable, and she nearly fainted from the thrill of it.

Slowly Rafe lowered Emmaline onto his bedroll on the ground, then covered her naked body with his own. "You excite me more than any woman I've ever made love to before, Emma."

"I'm glad that I please you," she said softly before his mouth captured hers again and his hands began their magical assault on her flesh. Like a sorcerer, he worked his wicked spell, making her writhe restlessly beneath him, her breasts tingling against his hair-roughened chest, now naked as her own, as she sought the release quickly building within her.

Lifting her hips off the ground, he wrapped her legs about him and plunged into the welcoming warmth of her body. "Oh!" she cried out, pushing hard against him as passion rose in her like the hottest flames, clouding her senses, rendering her incapable of speech or coherent thought.

She was a quivering mass of emotion—hot, wanting, climbing the pinnacle of satisfaction that eluded her. Then it came crashing down on her, stealing her breath, filling her with such wonderful pleasure that she thought she would die from it.

Using every ounce of his self-control, Rafe held back his own release. He wanted to give Emma all, needed to know that he'd given her the ultimate satisfaction before he claimed his own pleasure and exploded into an earth-shattering climax, spilling his seed deep within her.

"I love you, Rafe."

Her declaration was so simple, so full of sweet devotion, that it brought a lump to his throat, and he wanted to respond in kind, wanted to tell her of his deep feelings for her. But he would not.

He was not free to give himself to her as a man unfettered by past or revenge, and he would not offer her false hope and promises that he might not ever be able to fulfill.

And so he kissed her, trying to communicate with his lips, his touch, the words he dared not say.

The going was slow and arduous on the trail. Sleet and snow became prevalent at the higher elevations as they ventured ever closer to Wyoming, and Emmaline wasn't sure that she would ever feel warm again.

In fact, the only times she felt truly warm was when she was snuggled next to Rafe in his bedroll, sharing his body's heat and passionate embrace. At night in his arms, she could forget his quest for revenge, the bitter cold that pervaded them, and concentrate instead on her need for Rafe, their time together, the love she had for him.

What she couldn't forget was his reluctance to commit his heart as he had his body. If she judged his feelings by the urgency of his kisses and caresses, then she knew without a doubt that he loved her. But the physical response just wasn't enough. She needed the reassurance of a spoken vow. Without his affirmation that he loved her, the rest was merely the physical joining of bodies and not hearts. Though clearly she had given him hers.

She gazed at him sitting so tall and erect in the saddle, his eyes fixed on the trail and the surrounding area, a rigid set to his jaw. He'd grown more vigilant the closer they'd drawn to their destination, and she could see the worry in his eyes whenever he looked at her, see the remembrance of his wife's murder reflected in their depths.

What had she been like, this woman he had married? Emmaline had wanted to ask Rafe a thousand times about Ellie, but had always held back, afraid the timbre of his voice, the grief on his face, would reveal a love so great it would overshadow any chance of their being together.

But she had to know. The uncertainty was too great a burden to bear.

"Rafe?" she began, nudging Matilda closer to Buck, who had taken a liking to the contrary mare. "I'd like to know about your wife, if it wouldn't be too painful for you. But I'll understand if you'd rather not discuss her."

Aware of Emmaline's insatiable curiosity, Rafe wasn't

at all surprised by the question. He'd been expecting it a whole lot sooner, in fact. Like right after they'd made love the first time.

"I don't mind talking about it. Sometimes it helps to talk things out. It eases the pain a bit."

"Did you love her a great deal?"

He smiled softly, noting the insecurity she wore as openly as the love shining in her eyes. "Ellie Masters was my best friend. I loved her like I loved my brothers, or like a brother would love a sister. But I never felt about Ellie like a man should when he marries a woman and pledges his heart. And I'll carry that sorrow to my grave."

Her brow furrowed in confusion. "But why did you marry her, if you didn't love her in that way?"

"Because it was always expected that we would. It was all our parents ever talked about. And I had the need to settle down after all those years of rangering, and there was no one else, no special someone, I wanted to share my life with. Ellie had always loved me, always wanted to marry me, so it seemed the easiest solution. And I knew it would make her happy."

"People of the upper classes marry for money and expediency all the time. You shouldn't feel guilty about it, Rafe. At least you loved her in your own way, and she loved you a great deal, I'm sure." *How could she not?*

"If I hadn't been selfish and married her, Ellie would still be alive today. The only reason she was murdered was so Hank Slaughter could get back at me for putting him in prison. I'll bear that guilt on my conscience for the remainder of my days."

"Sometimes when a woman loves a man it doesn't matter what danger she faces, or even that the man doesn't share her love. It's enough just to be with him."

Though Emmaline's heartfelt confession touched him more than words could say, for he knew she was talking about herself, Rafe hardened to her words. If he let his feelings rule his judgment, if he became distracted by a look or a touch, he could get them both killed. And Emma's death on his conscience was something he would never be able to live with.

"Love ain't worth dying for, darlin'. I want you to remember that in the days ahead. And if anything happens to me, I want you to hightail it outta here just as fast as that pitiful nag will carry you."

Matilda jerked her head at the rude comment and snorted, as if she understood Rafe's words and disagreed with them, as did Emmaline. "I may have agreed with that remark at one time in my life, Rafe Bodine, but I know better now. Love is the *only* thing worth dying for."

"You've got the kids to think about, Emma. Don't forget them when you consider doing something foolish or heroic."

"I'm not likely to forget. I think about those dear hearts every hour of the day and wonder what they're doing, if they miss me, and how much Pansy will have grown by the time I get back. But the children merely prove my point, Rafe. I love them, and I would give my life to protect them if need be. Just as I would give it to protect you."

He yanked on the reins, pulling his horse to a halt,

and Emmaline did the same, fearing that she had revealed too much, by the frustrated expression he wore.

"I've never known a woman who had an answer for everything. Your logic doesn't make a lick of sense, and neither do your arguments, but I'll be damned if you haven't given me the biggest damn hard-on by just the mere uttering of them."

Relieved, she smiled and leaned closer to him. "Why, Mr. Bodine! I'm shocked. Does this mean you want to halt our journey for the day and make camp?"

Reaching out, he hauled her out of her saddle and settled her atop his lap. "What it means, little lady, is that I'm going to strip you naked and make love to every inch of your delectable little body until you beg for mercy. That's what it means."

She wrapped her arms about his neck. "And if I don't beg for mercy, what then?"

"Then I'm going to have to teach you the same lesson all over again."

Chewing her lower lip, she contemplated the threat. "I never have been a very good student, I'm afraid."

"But, darlin'," he said, grinning as he tightened his arms around her, "I'm an excellent teacher."

"I need me a woman," Luther grumbled, rubbing his crotch as he paced back and forth in front of the fireplace. "You got us holed up here at the hideout so tight my dick's clean up my ass, and I can't take it anymore. It ain't natural, Hank, not being able to screw. It's makin' me feel poorly."

Slaughter laughed at his cousin, then shuffled the cards in his hand before laying them out on the table in a game of solitaire. "Hanging ain't natural neither, Luther. And if you go parading about, showing your face off, it's your neck that's going to be stretched, not your dick."

Roy Lee came into the cabin at that moment, kicking the door shut behind him with his boot and dropping the load of firewood by the hearth. "*Sheeet!* It's colder than a mother-in-law's kiss out there. My balls have probably turned blue by now. And there's more snow a-comin'. The sky's darker than Luther's expression."

He grinned at his brother. "What's the matter, Luther? You still got a stiff prick? Why, when they bury you, the undertaker ain't gonna be able to close the lid on the coffin."

"It ain't funny, Roy Lee. A man can do hisself harm by not getting rid of them poisonous secretions inside him. A whore down in Tucson told me about it. Said it could damage my brain if I was to take care of unloading it myself. And I ain't partial to hand jobs anyway."

Hank let loose a loud guffaw and slammed the tabletop with the flat of his hand, knowing full well that Luther didn't have much of a brain to damage. "Guess it must be the gospel truth if a whore told ya, Luther. They ain't known to ever lie. Ain't that right, Roy Lee?"

Noting Hank's jovial mood, Roy Lee nodded quickly and grinned, not wishing to aggravate him. Nothing bothered Hank more than someone who didn't agree with him.

And lately he'd been in a piss-poor mood, almost as dour as Luther's. But not for the same reason.

Hank didn't have the diddling urge like most men. It came on him once in a while, but he hated women so much he didn't like the thought of sticking his dick inside 'em. Said he felt dirtied by it or something. Hank always was peculiar, Roy Lee reminded himself, thinking that he wouldn't mind dirtying himself on some whore.

A week ago, he and Luther had ridden into Laramie for a little recreation at Lulu's. Of course, once Hank had gotten wind of what they'd done, there had been hell to pay. They should have known better anyway—Luther had come damn close to getting his balls cut off over that little episode with the redheaded whore.

Roy Lee had tried to explain to his brother that sometimes it was best not to rile Hank when he was in a stew and just to eat crow. But Luther had been drinking and his mouth had gotten the worst of him, and he'd told Hank that he was nuttier than Aunt Tootie's fruitcake.

Roy Lee couldn't remember ever having seen Hank so mad, not even the time they'd cut up that Ranger's wife. Hank had never been partial to Aunt Tootie or her fruitcake, and he sure as hell hated being called crazy. Though it was closer to the truth than not.

"Don't know why we got to lay so low," Roy Lee finally said. "It's been weeks and we ain't seen any sign of that Ranger following us. And no law's come around about that other incident back in Eagle's Nest."

"We lay low because I say we lay low," Hank said, not

bothering to look up from his cards as he put the queen of hearts atop the king of spades and smiled. "When one of you boys think you want to challenge me to a knife fight to take over this gang, just let me know. My blade's always sharp, and I'm happy to oblige."

"No need to get riled, Hank. I didn't mean nothing by it. We was just wondering."

"Well, quit your wondering, Roy Lee. If you boys would think with your brains instead of your dicks, we'd be a lot better off. Now go muck out the privy, Luther. It stunk the last time I used it, and the chore'll take the edge off your urge. Too much screwin' makes a man weak, remember that."

Defiance shone clearly on Luther's face, and his lips twisted in disgust. "I didn't join no gang to shovel shit. Besides, it ain't my turn, it's Roy Lee's."

"Is not," his brother retorted angrily.

Hank silenced the exchange by pulling a long-bladed knife from his scabbard and placing it on the table. "Who wants to go first?"

Luther took one look at the knife, at the meanness on Hank's face, and grabbed his jacket. He'd go clean the shit right now, but sooner or later he was going to get even with Hank. And he was going to find himself a whore.

It had been years since Loretta had had the pleasure of seeing Ethan Bodine, but the Ranger looked as mean and businesslike as ever. And as handsome. If there was ever a man who had flint in his eyes and steel for a spine, it was Ethan, and she shivered as he studied her closely, trying to ferret out whether she was telling the truth about his brother's whereabouts.

"I'm having a hard time believing you, Loretta. I know you and Rafe are friends. But he's wanted by the law, and I'm sworn to bring him in."

She swallowed nervously, clinging to the door frame for support. "I already told you, Ethan, Rafe ain't here. He was for a time, but he took off weeks ago. Said he might be going to Oregon—Portland, I think. Didn't say why, and I didn't ask. A woman like me knows when to keep her mouth shut."

Ethan frowned, puffed on his cigar, and shook his head. "That's what I'm afraid of, Loretta. And protecting Rafe could very well cost him his life. The Slaughters are going to shoot first and ask questions later." If only he'd arrived in Denver sooner, but that damn trouble in New Mexico with the Murray brothers had cost him precious time, not to mention the female bounty hunter who'd been dogging his every movement, and who was still to this day a thorn in his backside.

"I've told you everything I know, Ethan. Sorry I can't be more help."

"Not as sorry as I am." Ethan thanked the woman and turned to leave. It was unlikely that Rafe was in Portland, but Ethan had to follow up every lead, even if it led him on a wild goose chase, as this one was likely to do.

Loretta watched the Ranger ride away and breathed a sigh of relief.

"Is he gone, Mrs. Goodman?" Looking about, Daniel stepped into the hallway from his hiding place in the kitchen.

At the first sign of the Ranger, Loretta had herded all of the children into the other room, admonishing them to be silent. Much to their credit, they hadn't uttered a peep the whole time the Ranger was there.

She nodded. "Yes, praise the saints! I wasn't sure I could keep a straight face for long."

"I thought you said it wasn't good for us to tell lies. Are you saying now that it's okay?"

She blushed, dabbed at her perspiring forehead with a handkerchief, and shook her head. "No, boy, I'm not saying that at all. But there are times when a little white lie is necessary to protect those you care about. I told one to protect Rafe and Emma, and I pray that the good Lord forgives me." But even if He didn't, she wasn't going to feel sorry for what she'd done.

"I wish I could have met Mr. Rafe's brother. He's a real Texas Ranger, isn't he? Did he have a gun, and a star on his chest?"

"Why, I suppose he did, Danny. But I was so nervous and anxious to have him gone from here that I didn't really notice."

"I might become a Ranger someday. Just like Mr. Rafe. I want to be like him."

"He's a good man, Rafe is. You could do a lot worse than to pattern yourself after him. I just pray that he comes out of this with his hide intact. And Emma too." She'd spent many sleepless nights worrying over that foolish, headstrong woman, about whether she'd be able to find Rafe and return home safely.

Daniel reached out and squeezed the older woman's hand, displaying a maturity far beyond his tender years. "You shouldn't be too worried, Mrs. Goodman. I know Mr. Rafe will protect Miss Emmaline. He loves her, even if he don't say so."

She ruffled the boy's hair, and a small smile touched her face. "You're pretty smart for a kid. How 'bout we gather up them young'ns and have us a piece of pecan pie. All this Ranger business has given me a powerful appetite."

"We can have pie if it'll make you feel better, Mrs. Goodman," he said. "But I know that Mr. Rafe and Miss Emmaline will be coming back real soon. Just you wait and see."

If only she had a child's optimism, Loretta thought with a sigh. If only she hadn't seen so much ugliness in her lifetime to doubt the boy's words. If only Rafe and Emma would come home.

Chapter Twenty-one

"Did you find out anything?"

Rafe's gaze zeroed in on the naked woman in the tin tub, and he felt himself harden instantly. Emmaline looked downright appealing fully clothed, but naked she was the personification of Eve—tempting, alluring, impossible to resist.

He fought against the weakness overwhelming him. "I told you to lock the door after I left. What if it hadn't been me coming through the door? I don't relish every man in this town drooling over what's mine."

His possessive tone made her smile widen into a grin. *Maybe he does care after all.* "Why, Rafe Bodine! If I didn't know better, I'd think you were jealous." She continued to scrub her arm, letting the warm water dribble over it, and ignored the chastisement and the sensuous gleam she saw in his eyes.

After days on the trail, a hot bath and a soft bed were luxuries she would never again take for granted, and she wasn't about to let Rafe spoil her enjoyment.

He dropped several wrapped parcels on the bed. "I bought you some decent clothes. I don't want you parad-

ing around town dressed like a boy. You look too ..."
appealing, he wanted to say, "boyish. And if we're going
to use your idea of me traveling with a woman, it'd be
nice if you looked like one."

She rose to her feet, her body wet and glistening in the
lamplight, and made a great pretense of separating her
curls with her fingers. The passionate look in his eyes told
her that he was affected by her nakedness, and she reveled
in that fact. "I doubt I'll be mistaken for a boy, Rafe." She
stared straight at his crotch, which was bulging promi-
nently. "Looks like you can tell the difference."

Before she could utter another word, he stepped forward, scooped her up in his arms, and deposited her in a
heap on the bed. "You're asking for it, little lady. And I'm
only too happy to oblige." He tossed his hat on the chair
and began to unbuckle his gunbelt.

When they were sated, and basking in the glow of their
lovemaking, Emmaline turned on her side and trailed her
finger through Rafe's chest hair and down his flat belly.
"You never answered my question earlier, Rafe."

"Mmmmm. Which one was that, darlin'? I thought I
gave an adequate demonstration of being able to tell the
difference between a boy and a girl." His chuckle was
short-lived as she leaned over and grazed his nipple with
her teeth, a little harder than necessary.

"*Ouch!* What the hell'd you do that for?"

"Because you weren't paying attention to the question.
And you shouldn't be such a big baby. You do that to me
all the time, and you don't hear me complaining, now do
you?"

He stared at her nipples, which hardened instantly under his gaze, and she pulled up the sheet to cover herself. "You said when you left that you were going to try and find information about the Slaughters' hideout. Did you have any luck?"

Mention of his hated enemies deflated his ardor as effectively as a bucket of ice water; he leaned back against the pillow, hands behind his head. "Actually, I did. They're purported to be in or around Laramie. Supposedly they're living at some abandoned ranch a few miles outside of town.

"We'll head for Buford tomorrow. It's about thirty miles south of Laramie, so we should be able to pick up some useful information. If I know Luther and Roy Lee, they've been frequenting the whorehouses, and whores always talk for a price."

Emmaline's heart thudded nervously. Having picked up their pace, they'd been covering close to forty miles a day and had crossed into Wyoming Territory late last evening, and it wouldn't take long for them now to catch up to the Slaughters. The idea of seeing the men face to face who had murdered Rafe's family so viciously sent shivers down her spine.

Sensing her fear, Rafe drew her to him and wrapped his arms around her. "You don't have to come with me, Emma. I'd rather you wait right here, where I know you'll be safe and warm. There's no need to subject yourself to the Slaughters, and to what's eventually going to happen."

Murder. Bloodshed. Emmaline swallowed with difficulty at the gruesome thoughts, wondering if she was truly up to such a task, but knowing she could never let Rafe face those men alone.

Somehow, someway, she had to persuade him to arrest the Slaughters and bring them to justice, not kill them. Rafe might not realize it now, but their deaths would remain on his conscience just as strongly as Ellie's. He wasn't a murderer; she had to make him understand that.

"I'm going with you. We've come this far together, and I'll not abandon you. Not now, when we're so close."

He kissed her then, hard, passionately, needing to convey what was in his heart and soul, wanting to tell her how much he loved her, needed her, and never wanted to let her go. But his sanity returned, as did his common sense.

He and Emma had no future together. He had none alone.

"I bought you a few things. Don't you want to take a look at them? You're the first woman I've met who hasn't been all agog over frills and furbelows."

She spied the packages at the foot of the bed and gathered them to her. "I like presents as much as the next woman." She tore the brown wrapping paper off the first package to reveal a set of woman's undergarments. They were silky and trimmed with lace. And though she was lying naked next to a man with whom she had just made passionate love, Emmaline blushed hotly and quickly wrapped them up again.

"They're lovely."

He chuckled. "Open the next one. I promise it's not the least bit indecent."

She did as he asked and found a pretty green wool dress trimmed with ecru lace collar and cuffs, and her eyes misted at the thought that he'd picked out the dress all by himself. It looked like it would fit, too.

"I know it's not fancy like what you're used to. . . ."

She covered his mouth with her fingertips. "I love it. It's the nicest gown I've ever owned." And she had a closet full of Worth's and other designer dresses back in Boston. But none she would treasure and enjoy wearing more than this one.

He heard the trembling in her voice and sighed. "You're not going to cry, are you? Because if you do, you'll splotch that pretty face of yours."

"No. I'm not going to cry." Because she feared that once she started, she would never stop.

It was snowing hard by the time they reached the town of Buford, and only Emmaline's warm thoughts of the night before, spent in Rafe's arms, kept her from freezing to death.

"Oh look! There's the hotel. Such as it is," she said.

The hotel—the only one in the small town—had an unsavory reputation as a refuge for gunslingers, whores, and the like, which was why Emmaline was garbed in boy's attire, rather than the lovely dress Rafe had purchased, to keep from drawing attention to herself.

"I want you to remain just inside the doorway of the hotel while I go pay for our room," he said, dismounting. "Don't talk to anyone or you'll give your sex away."

"I thought I'd already done that," she quipped, feeling quite frisky despite the snow and the lack of decent lodging.

His eyes narrowed, and his expression said he was anything but amused. "I'm warning you, Emma. This isn't the time for teasing. We've got serious business to attend to, and you've got to promise to pay attention to what I say."

"I'm just trying to make the best of a horrible situation. There's no need to get upset."

"Keep your hat pulled low and your coat buttoned at all times. And try not to walk. You sashay like a woman. I won't be long."

She refrained from pointing out the obvious as she watched him stroll to the bar. He seemed oblivious to the two painted women who immediately sandwiched him between them, but Emmaline was anything but, and felt a surge of pure, unadulterated jealousy.

When the blonde on his right reached down and caressed Rafe's derriere in blatant invitation, Emmaline had to physically restrain herself from marching over and yanking out her bleached hair by its dark roots. And to make matters worse, Rafe was now laughing with the woman, whispering something in her ear that made her face glow. Emmaline wanted to scream.

But she was denied that privilege when a buxom brunette walked over to her and smiled suggestively. "Ain't you kinda young to be in here, sonny?" she asked, and Emmaline wanted to fall through the floorboards. The woman obviously thought she was a young man!

Not daring to speak, she shrugged, hoping the whore would go away. But instead the woman stepped closer, until her large breasts were pushing into Emmaline's shoulder. Her cloying gardenia scent mingling with her unclean body odor made Emmaline nauseated.

"I could teach you a few things, honey. I like 'em young. And I'll give you a reduced rate, seeing as how you look so inexperienced and all."

Emmaline stared helplessly in Rafe's direction, but he was still flirting with the blonde and paid no attention to her. "My brother don't want me messin' with no whore," she said in the deepest voice she could manage, indicating Rafe with a nod of her head.

The whore gave Rafe a practiced once-over, and her eyes filled with lust and admiration that had little to do with her profession. A woman would have to be dead or blind not to appreciate a man like Rafe Bodine, and the brunette seemed to have perfect vision.

"Guess he's saving us for himself. And that's just fine with me, sonny, 'cause he's a real good-lookin' man, your brother is."

Emmaline thought quickly, hoping Rafe wouldn't kill her for what she was about to say. "He's got the clap. Doc said his pecker's gonna fall off one of these days."

The whore's eyes widened in horror, then she shook her head in lamentation. "What a damn shame. Sure I can't interest you in a poke? Yours still works, don't it?"

She laughed when heat rose to Emmaline's cheeks, but fortunately took the hint and walked away. Rafe returned moments later, scratching his head in bewilderment as he stared after the brunette.

"What'd that whore want? She looked at me like I had the plague."

"I'm sure I don't know. You told me not to converse with anyone."

"Follow me," he ordered. "I've got a room for as long as we need it."

"We won't be sharing it with the blonde, will we?" she asked, despite her best intention not to show her pique.

Rafe grinned. "Why, if I didn't know better, I'd say you were jealous."

Annoyed at herself, but mostly irritated by Rafe's knowing smile, she said, "I'm not a bit worried. Not one of these whores is going to pay you the least mind."

His brow furrowed in confusion. "And why is that? My money's as good as the next man's, if I was so inclined to spend it. And the blonde made it clear that I'm more than welcome in her bed."

Emmaline told him to bend down so that she could whisper in his ear. And when he did, she said, "Because I told the brunette with the large breasts that you had the clap, and that your privates were about to fall off. That's why."

His head snapped up. "You told her *what*?"

Before he had time to react further, Emmaline headed for the stairs, with Rafe close on her heels.

"I don't know why I have to stay put in this dirty old

room when you're planning to go downstairs and flirt with that blond woman again." Emmaline crossed her arms over her chest, and defiance shone bright in her eyes.

Rafe sighed. "You've already been propositioned once—guess these whores aren't too particular about who they bed if they're after pretty boys who are still wet behind the ears—so you could run into that problem again if you venture downstairs."

"They're not after diseased men, either."

Rafe's eyes glittered dangerously. "I've a mind to turn you over my knee and give you the spanking you deserve for that little stunt, but I won't, as long as you remain in this room until I get back. I want your word, Emma. It shouldn't take long to find out what I need to know."

"All right, I'll stay put. You have my word. But you must promise not to be gone too long. I'm planning to take another bath, and I might need you to scrub my back." Her look was blatantly suggestive.

"For a proper Bostonian socialite, you've turned into quite the vixen, Miss St. Joseph. Perhaps I've been misinformed about the ladies of the eastern seaboard."

"I suppose you heard that we were cold, unfriendly, and that our corsets were laced too tight."

"Something like that."

"Well, it's no worse than what I heard about Texas cowboys being crude braggarts who'd rather kiss their horse than a woman."

Rafe threw back his head and laughed. "You must be referring to my brother, not me. That description fits

Ethan like a glove." With an admonishment for her to lock the door after him, Rafe departed.

The tinny sound of the honky-tonk piano floated up the stairwell along with raucous laughter, making Emmaline feel lonely and just a bit sorry for herself.

Crossing to the narrow bed, she plopped down on it and closed her eyes, wondering how long Rafe would be gone and wondering when she had grown so dependent on his companionship. Her life felt incomplete when she wasn't with him.

And to think that she used to pride herself on being an independent woman. Lucas would laugh to know that his stubborn, man-hating, dyed-in-the-wool-spinster sister had succumbed to the mysteries of love.

More like the *miseries* of love, she amended.

But Lucas, of all people, would have been happy for her. He'd always said that someday she would find someone, fall in love, and get married.

Two out of three wasn't bad. Too bad marriage would never enter into her relationship with Rafe. He hadn't even said he loved her, even after all the times she'd declared herself a lovesick fool.

What would happen, she wondered, to her and Rafe—and to the children—if they managed to survive the Slaughter gang?

And that was a big *if*.

They were outnumbered three to two. If you counted her as help, which she doubted Rafe did. He still thought of her as useless in the overall scheme of things, and the odds were definitely against them.

If only they could get more help.

But Rafe was prideful to a fault and determined to fight his own battles, even if it killed him. And that was Emmaline's greatest fear.

The second was being at the mercy of the Slaughters.

The frightening thought sent ripples of cold cascading over her until gooseflesh broke out on her arms, and she buried her head beneath the blanket, blocking out the hideous images that had haunted her dreams of late.

"Come on, Ruby honey. Give me another peek at them tits of yours. I ain't had me a woman in a right good while and I'm fixin' to burst." She was sitting on his lap, right on top of the painful erection pressing against his pants, and Luther couldn't think straight.

If Hank found out that he'd ridden to Buford, he'd be a dead man. But it was worth defying Hank if Ruby would let him diddle her tonight. But the bitch was playing hard to get, just like all women did.

The whore shook her head. "Not until you put your money on the table, Luther. I ain't giving it away for free this time. Fool me once, as the saying goes. You stiffed me the last time you was in, in more ways than one."

Licking his lips in anticipation as he stared at the whore's opulent globes and the pink tips of her nipples rising above the low neckline of her satin gown, Luther knew that he didn't have the two dollars it would take to bed the avaricious bitch. But he'd be damned if he'd leave before sliding into that hot little snatch of hers. He had risked his life for a poke, and he'd get one even if he had to drag Ruby kicking and screaming out back and take what he wanted by force.

He'd done it before. And it was always more fun when they resisted anyway. He remembered how the Ranger's wife had pleaded for him to stop. It had made him want her all the more, made him feel important.

Running his hands up Ruby's skirt, Luther felt for the tuft of coarse hair and gently massaged her there. "I know you want me, Ruby. You're wet. I got the proof right here in my hands."

She squirmed restlessly. "Oh, all right. But just this once. Sam'll kick me out on my rear if he finds out I been shelling out for free. You know what a damn tightwad he is."

Sam Mahoney owned the saloon, and Luther had no desire to get on his bad side. He had a temper worse than Hank's and arms the size of tree trunks. It was said that Sam could kill a man with his bare hands without breaking a sweat, and Luther had no desire to find out whether that was true.

"We don't have to tell him, Ruby. It'll be our secret."

They were walking toward the stairs when some sixth sense told Luther to turn and look over his shoulder. What he saw made his blood run cold: the Texas Ranger whose wife they'd murdered was having a drink at the bar.

Chapter Twenty-two

"WHAT'S THE MATTER, LUTHER HONEY? YOU look like you seen a ghost. Why, you're trembling. I guess you really do need some of Ruby's—"

"Shut up!" Luther said between clenched teeth, his eye on the back door. He had to get out of the saloon before Bodine saw him, or he'd be a dead man for sure. The ex-Ranger had a dangerous look about him, like a man who shot first and asked questions later, and Luther wasn't waiting around to find out how good Bodine's aim was. He'd already planted Bobby six feet under.

"Well, you can just go screw yourself, big man. I don't need no nasty, mean-tempered cowboy in my bed." Ruby walked off in a huff, her satin-covered fanny swishing defiantly in her wake, leaving Luther feeling vulnerable in more ways than one.

He had to ride back to the hideout and warn Hank and Roy Lee that Bodine was nearby. That information might buy him a pardon from Hank. But Hank was more likely to nail his hide to the door for defying his orders. Maybe he should just ride away and forget about Bodine and everyone else, Luther thought. He didn't want to die.

He eased his way to the back exit, all the while keeping an eye on Bodine's back and praying that the tall man didn't look in the mirror or turn around. Sweat beaded his neck and forehead, fear knotted his belly, and he almost puked up the whiskey in his stomach.

For Luther, there was a decision to make: face Hank's wrath, or face Bodine's bullet.

In the end, the choice was easy.

In the darkness, Rafe undressed and eased himself into bed, snuggling against Emmaline's warm body. She didn't awaken, and he was grateful for that. He needed the quiet time to think, to plan, to worry.

He'd received confirmation from the blond whore, Alice, that the Slaughters were at their hideout. She'd seen Luther and Roy Lee in town a time or two, and had bedded Roy Lee on occasion. The outlaw had bragged that he'd be coming back soon because he wasn't that far away and was always in need of a good lay.

Rafe figured the ranch to be located about fifteen miles southeast of Laramie, judging from the comments Roy Lee had made to Alice, which would put it about fifteen miles from Buford. It would take them about two hours of hard riding, maybe a bit more with the snow on the ground and the inclement weather, to cover the distance. They would ride out in the morning.

Smoothing back the soft coppery curls from Emmaline's face, Rafe pressed a kiss to her cheek and heard her murmur of contentment. His gut knotted at the thought of what might happen if the Slaughters got their hands on her.

He'd thought about leaving her in Buford, about riding out tonight while she slept, and leaving her a note with instructions to stay put. But he knew without a doubt that she would defy his wishes.

Emmaline was headstrong to a fault. And she was determined to go with him, "come hell or high water," as she'd told him yesterday, much to his amusement at the westernism. He'd decided it would be safer to have her with him than have her trailing after him. Stealth wasn't one of the attributes she'd learned during her brief sojourn west.

If only she'd stayed in Boston instead of accompanying her foolish brother, she would have remained safe and distant from all the ugliness of his world.

But then, he would have never met her, made love to her, fallen in love with her. And that would have been a terrible loss.

Rafe wasn't a praying man, but as he stared down at Emma in repose, he prayed hard that God would see fit to spare this courageous, impulsive, stubborn snip of a woman. One dead woman on his conscience was all his heart could stand in this lifetime.

He didn't know what tomorrow or the next day would bring, but he hoped that he and Emma would live to find out.

It was still snowing hard the next morning, and Rafe questioned himself about the wisdom of leaving Buford behind. But the more time he wasted, the more chance the

Slaughters had of changing their whereabouts, and now that he was so close to catching up with them, the need for revenge was too strong to ignore.

"How do you know they're going to be at their hideout?" Emmaline shouted, wiping the blowing snow out of her face. The wind was so fierce, its howl so loud, it was difficult to be heard above the din. "What makes you so sure? They might be long gone by now." She prayed hard for that eventuality.

Rafe's expression was implacable. "I just know. I can feel it in my gut. I can feel their presence so strongly that it makes the hairs on the back of my neck stand up on end and my stomach tighten."

"Next you're going to tell me that you possess second sight and can see into the future." She wished it were true. Not knowing what was going to happen was the hardest thing to accept.

Rafe reined Buck to a halt, and the horse, whose breath rose up in a clouded mist, seemed grateful for the respite. Having lain awake most of the night, Rafe knew now what had to be said. There was a chance that neither of them would come out of this day's events alive, and he couldn't let Emma go without letting her know of his feelings.

"What's wrong? Why are we stopping?"

Her face was chapped red from the cold, and her eyelashes were caked with snow, but right now Rafe couldn't imagine a more beautiful sight than his Emma. "There's something I've got to tell you."

Her stomach clenched at the possibilities, at the *proba-*

bility that he would send her back, tell her he had no more use for her, that he had to go on alone. She swallowed with difficulty. "What's that? I already told you I'm not leaving, so if that's what's on your mind . . ."

Laughing, he shook his head. "It's a fine thing when a man can't even tell a woman he loves her without her running off at the mouth, accusing him of all kinds of terrible things."

Her heart dropped to her stomach. "You love me?"

He nodded. "Yep. This isn't the most romantic way to tell you, I know, but I decided that it was something that needed saying, and right now."

Her face felt frozen in place, but she attempted a smile anyway. "Well, don't just sit there. Kiss me or something."

Leaning over in his saddle as far as he could, he grasped the back of her head and thawed out her lips most effectively, until the blood rushing through her veins had heated to far beyond the normal level.

"I love you, too. And no matter what happens, I want you to know that I'll never regret the time we've shared. It's meant more to me than you'll ever know."

A sinister laugh came from behind the thick stand of trees, and instinctively Rafe went for his gun, then cursed aloud for letting his guard down, for forgetting that the snow and howling wind would muffle the sounds of the Slaughters' approach. For allowing the love of a woman to interfere with his good judgment.

"I wouldn't try it, Bodine. We've got you covered," Hank Slaughter said. "We would've surprised you sooner, but the little lady's declaration and yours was just so darn touching, me and the boys couldn't bear to butt in."

Roy Lee laughed, and Luther, who'd made his choice and was now sporting a black eye and a red welt on his cheek because of it, said, "I saw you in the saloon, Bodine. You ain't such a smart Ranger after all."

The three men were every bit as disgusting and sinister as Rafe had described them, and Emmaline had to fight the urge to scream. Not that it would have done any good out in the middle of nowhere.

The redheaded man with the graying beard was obviously Hank. Rafe hadn't taken his eyes off the outlaw, and the hatred flowing between the two was palpable. The other two reminded Emmaline of predatory animals. Though she was sure they were as dangerous as their leader, it was Hank with his silver eyes alive with insanity that sent frigid fear rushing through her.

"Tie 'em up," Hank ordered. "I want to have a little fun with them before we dispose of the Ranger and his new lady love. Didn't take long for you to forget about the other one, did it, Bodine?"

Rafe lunged forward, but Roy Lee grabbed hold and held him back, tying his hands with a rope.

Hank laughed. "Hit a nerve, did I?"

The demonic sound echoed off the surrounding hills and trees, reverberating in Emmaline's ears and landing in the pit of her stomach like a leaden weight. But she remained silent, believing it the wisest course for the time being.

"Luther, put the bitch on your horse," Hank ordered. "She'll ride with you back to the hideout."

Fear so palpable she could taste it infused her. She gazed imploringly at Rafe, but he was busy staring daggers at Hank.

Spittle ran down Luther's thick lips, and his eyes lit with excitement at the prospect of riding double with the pretty woman. "I've always been mighty partial to redheads," he said, dragging an unresisting Emmaline off her horse and onto his.

"Leave her be, Hank. Your quarrel's with me, not with Emma. You've had your revenge, so leave her be. She's got nothing to do with any of this."

"Anything that's part of you has to be destroyed, Bodine. That's just the way it is. You should've been smarter than to kill my brother. Poor old Bobby was the least guilty of all of us. It might interest you to know that the fool actually begged us to spare your pretty wife's life."

Rafe blanched at the knowledge that Bobby had told the truth.

"Now shut your mouth or we'll shoot her dead right here and leave the little lady for the vultures to find."

Emmaline paled chalk white, and Rafe cursed himself for a fool. As before, all of this was his fault. And the woman he loved was going to die because of his stupidity.

She hadn't uttered a word, and Rafe supposed she was too frightened to speak. And maybe that was good. Her unruly tongue was bound to get her into trouble if she decided to use it on Slaughter. The mean son of a bitch was just itching for an excuse to kill her.

"We'll cooperate," Rafe said, the words meant more for Emmaline's ears than Slaughter's; he could see by the slight inclination of her head that she understood.

"Well, that's mighty big of you, Ranger. But seeing as how you've got no other choice, I expected no different. Now let's make tracks. I want to make it back to the hideout while there's still daylight. No telling how many others will be coming after you."

His brow arched. "Or is this a solo mission, Bodine? You always were an arrogant fool, just like your brother. You two thought yourselves invincible. Guess now you know you're not. You'll have to concede that I've won the day."

Rafe's eyes glittered hard and unyielding like shards of blue glass. "Day ain't over yet."

"It's the night I'm looking forward to." A sadistic smile twisted the demented man's face as he eased his horse nearer to Emmaline. "This little lady and I are going to get a whole lot better acquainted when we get back to the hideout."

"You touch a hair on her head and I'll kill you, Hank. I swear it."

"Is that so? Why, Luther here touched a lot of hairs on your wife's head and he ain't dead yet. Show the man your trophy, Luther. We wouldn't want the Ranger to think we make idle threats."

Luther reached into his saddlebag, withdrew a braid of golden hair, and held it up before him. Emmaline thought she would faint. Her ears started to ring and bile rose thickly in her throat.

She prayed, *O God! Please deliver us from this evil.*

"You're dead, Luther! You sick son of a bitch. You're dead! Do you hear me?"

The three men glanced at one another, then at Rafe, who struggled in vain against his bonds. Then they laughed. And Emmaline decided that if she and Rafe were going to survive this nightmare, they'd have to do more than count on the aid of the Lord.

The Slaughters' hideout, comprised of a number of dilapidated, weather-weary buildings, including a ramshackle ranch house, a pasture overgrown with weeds, and broken fence rails, seemed in keeping with the sordidness of the Slaughters themselves.

Luther's vile stench had permeated Emmaline's nostrils during the long and arduous trip, his grimy hands violating her person until she wanted to scream out her disgust and revulsion. But, as before, she kept silent and suffered his abuse in silence, knowing that to protest would only inflame his passions further and give him an excuse to use brutality.

Every time he had fondled her breasts, pinching her nipples, and she had thought to cry out in protest, Emmaline had shut her eyes and forced her mouth shut, remembering the golden braid of Ellie Bodine that rested in his saddlebag like a hunter's trophy.

She'd not had an opportunity to talk to Rafe during

the three-hour ride to the ranch. They'd only made eye contact a few times.

"I can't wait to take a peek under them drawers, little lady. You're going to share your pretties with old Luther now, ain't ya?" She jerked her head when he tried to nuzzle her ear, and he laughed. "I like my women feisty, so it don't matter none to me if you fight back. It makes it all the more pleasurable." He dragged her down from the horse and she shot him a lethal look, then spit in his face.

"You pig!"

He raised his hand to slap her, but Hank cried out before he could make contact. "Leave her be for now, Luther. I want the pleasure of maiming her myself. It's going to be fun putting on a little show for Bodine. He deprived me of the pleasure of performing for him in person last time."

"But she spit on me, Hank."

"You dirty bastard, Slaughter! I'm warning you, don't you lay your filthy hands on her."

Hank's eyes glittered with madness. "Bring the Ranger into the house, Roy Lee. I think he needs a lesson in manners before we proceed with the little lady here."

Inside the large room of the cabin, Rafe was shoved to the floor, his feet tied as securely as his hands. Emmaline watched, helpless, knowing that Rafe's survival skills were the only thing that could save them from certain death, but also knowing that the likelihood of his having the opportunity to use them was slim to none.

"All trussed up like a hog for slaughter, Bodine," Roy Lee said with a snicker, then kicked Rafe hard in the side, and smiled wide when Rafe grunted in pain. "Hope I didn't hurt you none." He kicked him again for good measure.

Luther busied himself making a fire, while Roy Lee was set to the task of fixing something to eat. Of the three men, he was the only one who apparently had any culinary skills, though Emmaline wasn't eager to sample the fare, considering the filthiness of the cabin.

Empty whiskey bottles littered the floor, and dirt and debris could be seen in every corner of the room. Cobwebs, not curtains, draped the windows, and the smell of rotting garbage and unwashed bodies filled the air.

Hank pulled his knife from the leather sheath, then circled Emmaline slowly, like a hungry animal on the prowl.

"You don't talk much, do you, lady? The other woman, Bodine's wife, now, she screamed and screamed the whole time we was messin' with her. It's partially what got her cut so bad. The woman started getting on my nerves something fierce. And that ain't a very smart thing to do. I ain't partial to screaming women."

"She sure did scream when I stuck it to her, didn't she, Hank?" Luther grinned and tossed a match onto the logs, watching them burst into flame. "But I liked her screams. They made me feel good." He spit a stream of tobacco juice onto the flames and they hissed in response.

"Shut up, Luther. I don't give a rat's ass what you like. Just keep your mouth shut while I'm talking to this here little lady. Her and I are getting acquainted, ain't that right, Emma? That is your name, isn't it?"

She nodded, mustering up what was left of her courage. Perhaps she could talk to them, reason with them. "Yes, that's right. Emmaline St. Joseph of Boston. And I'm prepared to offer you a great deal of money to let us go free."

Hank's brow shot up. "That so?"

"*Whooeeee.* I knew she was a real lady, boss," Roy Lee said. "I bet she wears real nice silky underwear and bathes in scented water. All real ladies do. I read it in some magazine."

Luther snorted. "You can't read, Roy Lee, and you know it."

"So, I looked at them pictures. I can see what a real lady looks like, can't I?"

Hank shot them a disgusted look. "Shut up, the both of you. I can't hear myself think when you're carrying on like a bunch of old biddies."

Hank placed the tip of his knife on the top button of Emmaline's shirt and flicked it off. "Don't want your money, little lady." It bounced to the floor, landing near Rafe's feet, and he struggled more fiercely against his bonds.

Emmaline thanked the Almighty that she had donned the new undergarments Rafe had purchased along with the dress. If she was going to meet her Maker, she decided, she was going to do it in clean, new underwear. Had she not worn them, Hank's game would be over in a flash.

"Leave her alone, Slaughter. I tell you she's an innocent bystander in all this."

Hank gazed at Rafe, who still fought against his bonds,

and the hatred emanating from him was palpable. "You must care an awful lot for this woman to be protesting her innocence so much, Bodine. It makes a man wonder what lengths you'd go to to save her hide, and vice versa." His gaze flicked over Emmaline in nasty appraisal, the tip of the knife touching the second button, then the third.

"You'd do just about anything to save your lover's life, now wouldn't you? Lady or not, you're still just a goddamn whore at heart, like all women."

Bodine's woman was an added bonus, in Hank's estimation. He would use the woman like he'd used the wife to exact his revenge, before shooting the Ranger dead. But first he was determined to drag out Bodine's torture, knowing it was the fear of what was going to happen that ate at a man's gut. And Hank wanted Bodine to suffer, mentally and physically, the way he had suffered in prison.

He thought he might screw the woman once and discard her, like so much rubbish. Or, he might even be magnanimous and let Roy Lee and Luther diddle the bitch for a while. That'd make them happy, and she'd be a goner once they got their greedy hands on her. Luther wasn't known for his finesse when it came to women.

Time was on their side, and he would savor every moment of it. *Foreplay*, he'd once told the boys. Foreplay was the key to enjoyment, and that's what he intended to have with Bodine and the woman. And when he was done, maybe a taste of whiskey to celebrate his brilliance in succeeding in such perfect revenge.

"Stick a gag in Bodine's mouth, Luther. I'm sick of his

bellyaching. Then teach the bastard how to show a little respect."

The big man took Rafe's red bandanna and tied it tightly around his mouth so that he couldn't talk, then struck him in the face with his fists over and over again, pummeling him until blood dribbled from the corner of his eye.

Emmaline watched in horror as Rafe slumped to the floor. "No! Please! Don't hit him like that."

"We're just warming up, Emma." Hank reached for the ribbons of her chemise. "And you should be worrying about yourself, not your boyfriend. He's a dead man."

She pulled back in revulsion. "Don't. Don't touch me! What kind of animals are you? Have you no decency?"

He grabbed her hands and forced them behind her back. "Not a shred, I'm afraid. I had a little, before going off to prison, but they beat it outta me there. You have lover boy here to thank for that."

Rafe watched in horror and rage as Hank encouraged Roy Lee and Luther to kiss and fondle Emma, then bit the inside of his cheek, feeling every bit of her pain and humiliation.

The buzzing in his ears blocked out their hideous laughter, and his swollen eye mercifully blurred his vision. They wanted him to watch, to witness their mastery over what was his, to lose his self-control and become like them. But Emma had been right: he wasn't like them. He was smarter. And he'd find a way to kill those bastards if it was the last thing he did. And he'd do it soon. Very, very soon.

Tears rolling down her face, Emmaline struggled, to no avail, as they continued to kiss and caress her. She forced herself to think of other things, of happy times. Shutting her eyes against the onslaught, she imagined each of the children's faces, bright with innocence and full of love as they gazed at her, Loretta's impish grin as she told a ribald joke, Rafe's passion-lit eyes when they'd made love this morning.

Then she imagined her revenge. She wouldn't utter a word of protest if Rafe got the opportunity to murder the vicious outlaws. Once, she had thought to dissuade him, make him change his mind about killing them, but now she could see that she'd been wrong.

The Slaughters needed killing. They were the personification of evil, of all things malevolent, and if Rafe missed the opportunity, she would do the deed herself and not think twice about it.

Chapter Twenty-three

EMMALINE HUDDLED IN THE CORNER, FORGOTTEN for the moment by the three outlaws, who were more intent on getting their amusement out of a bottle of rye whiskey than on tormenting her.

She'd been slapped across the face a few times by Hank—more for show than anything else—then tossed into the corner with the rest of the garbage while they concentrated on getting drunk. And from the looks of it, they were doing a good job.

Hank had suddenly felt the need for a drink, and though Emma had thought it odd at the time, the more she observed the sadistic leader of the group, the more she realized what a manipulative bastard he was. Hank needed to savor the moment of his victory over Rafe, and he also needed to keep his overanxious cousins in line. He wasn't as eager to bed her as Luther and Roy Lee were, and she decided that this little victory celebration was a good way to postpone the inevitable. Which was fine with her.

Rafe sat across the room in the opposite corner, his head buried in his arms, and Emmaline suspected he'd given in to his injuries and fatigue. They had beaten him viciously, over and over again. Hank, in particular, had taken great delight in punching Rafe's face black and blue. He kept referring to Rafe as "pretty boy" every time he landed a blow. Emmaline feared that Rafe's ribs had been broken from the many kicks he'd taken to his midsection.

Though she felt ashamed sitting there in her chemise and pants, she hadn't yet been violated totally, and she took some solace in that. But Emmaline knew her time was drawing near.

Roy Lee and Luther had talked of little else but bedding her in the most graphic terms imaginable until her stomach had knotted into a tight ball and she wanted to retch up the bile that continued to rise. Even Hank, who'd confessed an aversion to women, had hunger in his eyes whenever he studied her.

Emmaline could still feel their hands on her breasts, their mouths on her lips, smell their fetid breath in her nostrils, and she wondered whether the ugly memories would fade if she survived the ordeal.

She continued to watch them, and the fear in her belly grew.

"Pass me that damn bottle, Roy Lee," Luther demanded. "You're so shit-faced now it's a shame to waste good whiskey on you."

Roy Lee teetered in his chair and snatched the bottle out of Luther's greedy hands. "I ain't had my fill yet." Tipping back his head, he poured the amber liquid down his throat, slammed the bottle onto the table, then promptly fell off the chair onto the floor in a motionless heap.

"Fool's out cold," Hank remarked with a sneer, shaking his head as he refilled his glass. "Your brother never could hold his liquor worth a damn."

"When we gonna diddle the woman, Hank?" Luther asked, caring little about his brother. "You said after we was done celebrating our victory over Bodine we could screw the bitch."

Hank tossed back another whiskey, then wiped his mouth on his shirt sleeve, casting the disgruntled man an annoyed look. Luther was always pressing for answers Hank didn't want to give. "I said I was going first, Luther. So don't be getting any ideas."

The big man glanced out the window and frowned. "It's gettin' dark out, and you still ain't screwed the bitch. How long we gonna have to wait? Maybe you ain't eager, Hank, seeing as how you ain't partial to women in general, but me and Roy Lee want our share, and we want it now."

His eyes narrowing to slits, Hank toyed with the knife at his belt. "You trying to tell me what to do, Luther? 'Cause that ain't too healthy, if you get my drift. And what do you mean—I ain't partial to women. You trying to infer I ain't a man?" The truth was that Hank got no pleasure from fucking a woman. He didn't have the same need as other men. But he couldn't allow his cousins to think he wasn't capable, or as manly as they were, so he usually went along with them.

Luther swallowed hard as he looked from Hank to the

woman and back, then shook his head in quick denial. "I ain't saying no such thing, boss. No such thing."

Shoving the bottle at him, Hank smiled smoothly, pleased with the control he had over the dimwit. "Have another drink. I ain't done celebrating yet, and the woman ain't goin' nowhere. I promise when I'm finished with her, you'll get your turn. Why, if you play your cards right, Luther, I might even let you keep her for a while. You'd like that, wouldn't you?"

The bleary eyes lit, and Luther nodded like an eager puppy with a bone. "I'd like that real fine, boss. No doubt she'd welcome a real man after having that Ranger between her legs."

They both laughed at Luther's jibe, ignoring Rafe, who seemed to have passed out in the corner but all the while was slowly working to loosen the bonds on his wrists.

Rafe had done his best to pretend he was unconscious. Let the bastards drink themselves into oblivion. It would make doing what he planned a whole lot easier.

He'd been biding his time. And with every drink the Slaughters took from the whiskey bottle, he knew his time for retaliation was drawing near. They had a lot to answer for: Ellie, the baby, their abusive treatment of Emma. And he'd see that they paid, in spades.

The odds were getting better now with Roy Lee passed out, and Rafe knew that if he was going to act, it had to be soon, before the other Slaughter sobered up.

Fifteen minutes later, Luther pushed back his chair and let loose with a belch. "I gotta take a piss." He staggered to his feet. "I'll be back in two shakes of a stick."

Hank stood. "You do that. And while you're gone, I'm gonna have me a little fun with the lady. I'll be done by the time you get back."

Even in his drunken state, Luther could barely contain his excitement, and the prominent bulge in his pants brought a disgusted look from Hank. "You got all your brains in that cock of yours, boy. If you had more upstairs, you'd be a lot better off."

Too befuddled to realize that he'd just been insulted, Luther stumbled to the door and disappeared into the cold night.

Emmaline kept her eyes shut tightly, unwilling to acknowledge the man who now stood before her, hoping that if Hank thought her asleep he might leave her alone.

"Get up, bitch." He kicked at her feet until she opened her eyes and met his gaze. "I gotta take my ease with you now before that drunken fool, Luther, comes back." When there was no response, he reached down, grabbed Emmaline's arm, and hauled her to her feet.

"Leave me alone, you filthy pig! I'd rather die than have you lay a hand on me." She trembled at the insane look on his face.

"That can be arranged, bitch. I can screw you dead or alive. It's all the same to me. But I thought you'd probably enjoy it more alive. It's time you got a taste of what a real man's like."

Emmaline glanced at Rafe, who didn't acknowledge what was happening; his head remained buried in his arms. She assumed he'd passed out from his injuries and thought that that was probably for the best. She couldn't bear to have him watch as she was violated and killed like Ellie.

Hank hauled her to the door leading into the bedroom. "Get in there. I got little time to waste before that asshole Luther comes back."

Emmaline's protests were the last sounds that Rafe heard before the door to the bedroom slammed shut.

With no time to waste, he managed to free his hands of the rope around his wrists and pull down the bandanna covering his mouth. He then reached into his right boot to extract the knife hidden there. With one slice, he released the bonds on his feet, then rose, working loose the soreness in his arms and back from the beatings.

Much as he wanted to rush to Emma's aid, he knew it wouldn't be wise until he had dispatched Luther to hell. Like a cat on the prowl, he silently made his way to the back door and into the night to search for his prey.

"Please don't do this," Emmaline pleaded, though she knew she was wasting her breath. There was indifference in Hank's eyes as he gazed at her body and ran the tip of the knife blade up and down her torso and across the sensitive area of her nipples.

She thought he was more excited about the prospect of murdering her than bedding her. Remembering what he'd said earlier about hating a woman's screams, she had bitten her lip whenever she felt the urge.

"Hank, don't do this! I know somewhere deep inside you there has to be some good. Please! I haven't done you any harm. And there are innocent children who are depending on me for their welfare." Though she knew that Loretta would care for the orphans should anything happen to her; the kind woman had promised as much before Emmaline left.

The outlaw laughed maniacally. "You're Bodine's whore. And in my mind, sweetheart, that's reason enough. Now take off them pants and spread those lily-white legs of yours," he demanded, his hand going to the fastening of his trousers. "It's been a long time, and I aim to do what's expected."

"*Noooooo!*" she screamed.

Rafe heard Emmaline's wail, just as he jumped Luther exiting the privy. With one swift, lethal movement he captured the man's neck in the crook of his right arm and snapped it like a twig, leaving him lying half in and out of the outhouse—a fitting burial place for a piece of offal like Luther.

Moving quickly to the bedroom window, he looked in. What he saw filled him with killing rage: Hank had positioned himself over Emmaline and was about to rape her, just as he'd raped Ellie.

Bursting through the window in a shower of glass, he landed on his side, then rolled to his feet in one fluid movement.

Slaughter's eyes widened at the sight of the Ranger, and he was too stunned to offer anything but token resistance. Rafe pulled Hank off of Emmaline and dragged him to the floor, the knife pointed at his throat.

"I told you I'd kill you if you touched her, Slaughter."

Hank's smile was taunting. "She wasn't nearly as good as your wife, Bodine. I liked fucking the other one a whole lot more." He made a grab for Rafe's knife. That was the last evil act Hank Slaughter made before Rafe cut his throat like the pig that he was.

Emmaline watched the entire episode in horror, unable to believe that there was blood spurting from Hank's neck and that Rafe had come in the nick of time to save her. She stared for several seconds, trying to make sense of everything before her mind finally cleared in acceptance.

"Rafe? Rafe!" She launched herself at him, throwing her arms about his middle to make sure that what she was seeing was real.

He hugged her fiercely. "God, Emma. I died a thousand deaths when I looked through that window and saw that bastard . . ."

She glanced down at the inert body on the floor, feeling no sympathy or remorse for Hank Slaughter. "Is he dead?"

"The bastard's dead. He won't be hurting any more women and children."

"And the others?"

"Luther's dead, too. He's outside by the privy. The only one left to deal with is Roy Lee."

She followed him into the main room of the cabin, mindful of the shards of glass on the floor and her bare feet, and watched as he located his weapon, shivering in anticipation at what he was about to do.

"Don't shoot him, Rafe. He's not worth the effort. And he's passed out cold. He can't harm us now."

But Rafe wasn't listening and kicked Roy Lee in the side. "Wake up, you bastard. It's time to meet your

Maker." There was no response from the drunken outlaw, and Rafe cocked his .45 and pointed it at his head, ready to mete out the final act of justice.

"No, Rafe!" Emmaline moved forward and wrapped her arms around him. "I love you, Rafe. Please don't add this man's death to my conscience and yours. I want to build a life with you. Start over, away from here and all this ugliness. Please don't kill him. Let the law handle his punishment."

The pleading in her voice finally reached Rafe, and he lowered his gun and drew her into his arms. "How can you ask me to spare his life after what he almost did to you?"

"We're not like these men, Rafe. Neither one of us. We have morals and a conscience. They had none. I won't allow myself to become like them. I thought I could, when they were hurting me and beating you. I thought I could kill them and think nothing of it. But it's not within me. I don't want that kind of cancerous hatred festering inside me, and neither do you.

"We have our whole future ahead of us, Rafe. Let's not mar it with another killing."

He weighed her words for several moments. "All right. We'll do it your way. I'll tie the bastard up while you find your shirt and boots. Then we'll ride back to Buford and I'll have someone notify the authorities."

Emmaline could see that the concession cost Rafe. He would never know for certain who of the four men had actually murdered his wife and unborn child, and to leave one alive went against his plan for retribution and his code of honor.

"Thank you." She caressed his cheek, and he turned his head and kissed her palm.

"You were right, Emma, when you said the only thing worth dying for was love. It's because I love you more than life itself that I'm doing this—allowing this animal to live and walk away from the hatred in my soul. It's the only reason."

"Then it will have to be reason enough. And I'll make sure from this day forward that you'll never have cause to regret it."

Chapter Twenty-four

THE KNOCK ON THE FRONT DOOR STARTLED Loretta. Gazing up from the storybook she'd been reading to the children, she glanced toward the hall and heaved a sigh.

It was way past suppertime, and no one she knew would call so late. Unless it was another would-be boarder. She'd turned down several paying guests in the three weeks since Rafe and Emma had been gone. She wanted nothing to interfere with her spending time with the children, and she had money put aside to see her through.

"Do you want me to answer it, Mrs. Goodman?" Danny asked, an eager-to-escape look etched on his face. "I'm not much for *Cinderella* anyway."

"Me neither." David pulled a face. "It's a sissy story."

"You boys could stand to learn a thing or two about becoming Prince Charmings, so just sit yourselves down and wait while I go see who's at the door." It might be Ethan Bodine again, and she didn't want him seeing any of the children and asking questions about whose they were. He sure as heck wouldn't believe they were hers, though she felt very proprietary about them.

The knock grew more insistent. "I'm coming!" she shouted, her annoyance clear as she hurried to answer the summons. "I don't know what's so dang important that you have to come out here in the middle of the night to disturb . . ." she pulled open the door, "decent folks . . ." Then she gasped, and her eyes widened in stunned disbelief.

"Praise the heavens! I never thought to lay eyes on either one of you again. It is you, isn't it, Emma?" Loretta squinted into the darkness at the filthy, dust-covered creature littering her porch, and grinned.

Emmaline rushed forward into Loretta's outstretched arms. "Of course it's me! I've missed you so much." Tears filled her eyes and trickled down her cheeks, making rivulets through the grime.

"Good Lord. You'd better stop that or you'll have me leaking like a sieve all over my carpet."

Rafe cleared his throat. "Aren't you happy to see me, too, Loretta?"

"Well, shoot! Of course I am. Come in outta the cold and give me your duster. You two look like you've been through the gates of hell and back."

That was closer to the truth than Emmaline cared to admit at the moment, but there would be time enough to fill Loretta in on her encounter with the Slaughters. She was just now starting to put it behind her. And she had Rafe to thank for that. His gentleness and caring had saved her sanity and her soul; her love for him had made her strong.

"Where are the children? I'm so anxious to see them."

"They're in the front room huddled in front of the fireplace like darling lambs with a story about Prince Charming." She harrumphed. "As if any actually existed."

A moment later the front hallway was filled with children's excited squeals and shouts of joyous laughter.

"You came back, Mr. Rafe." Miranda latched on to his legs with such a fierce hug that she nearly knocked him over. "And you didn't let anything bad happen to Miss Emma, either."

Painful thoughts clouded Emmaline's eyes for a moment, but she quickly brushed them aside. "Come here and give me a hug, all of you. I've missed you so much." She hadn't realized just how much until this moment. Danny looked as if he'd grown two inches, and Pansy was sporting a new tooth.

"Papa," Pansy cried excitedly, her little face beaming as she lifted her arms up to Rafe. "Papa, Papa!"

"How's my little flowerpot?" He kissed the baby's cheek, his scratchy beard next to her soft skin, and he felt as if he'd come home.

"Your beard ain't as big as it used to be, Mr. Rafe." David gave Rafe a careful once-over. "Looks like you trimmed it some."

Daniel clutched Rafe's arm. "Mrs. Goodman was worried about Miss Emma, but I told her you'd bring her back home safely." The boy's chest puffed up with pride. "I've been taking care of things while you were gone."

Rafe and Emma glanced at each other and exchanged grins filled with contentment, happiness, and gratitude that they'd survived to see these wonderful children again. But their future—all of their futures—had yet to be decided.

"I need to go upstairs and clean up. We kept a pretty grueling pace."

"You look just like a real western cowboy, Miss Emma," Miriam said with an impish grin. "Why, you're even packing iron."

Emmaline's eyes widened, then she turned to stare at Loretta, whose cheeks had turned bright red.

"I only had dime novels to read them at first," she explained. "But I've bought some storybooks since."

"It looks to me like you've taken wonderful care of the children, Loretta. You'll hear no complaints from me. I don't know how I can ever thank you enough or repay you for what you've done."

"I'm sure I'll be able to think of something," Loretta replied, a secretive smile crossing her lips. "Now you run along to your bath. I intend to hog this handsome man's attention for a while. He can clean up when you're done."

The children followed Emmaline up the stairs, eager to hear all about her adventure, while Loretta escorted Rafe into the parlor and poured him a whiskey.

"I don't mind telling you that I was worried sick the whole time you were gone. And from that haunted look in your eyes, I guess I had good reason."

Rafe told her everything that had happened, leaving out

only the intimate details of his relationship with Emma. When he finished, Loretta swallowed her whiskey in one gulp, then grinned.

"So she told that whore you had the clap, huh? I always knew Emma was a woman after my own heart. And yours, I take it?"

"I love her more than anything else in this world."

"So what happens now? Are you going to California with her and the young'ns?"

He sighed. "It's what she wants. But I'm not sure living with an outlaw is the best thing for Emma and the children. I've made no firm commitment as yet."

"Well, it sure as heck ain't safe to stick around here, Rafe." She told him about his brother's visit, how determined Ethan was to find him. "I sent him off on a wild goose chase to Oregon, but he's smart. He'll soon figure out he's been hornswoggled and return here."

Relief filled Rafe at the news that his brother was all right, and he was not at all surprised to hear of Ethan's visit. The Ranger was single-minded in his determination to track him down and bring him back to stand trial. He'd ridden with Ethan too long to think any different. But even imminent danger couldn't force Rafe to make a decision that might be detrimental to the woman he loved.

"I want to do what's best for Emma, not what's best for me."

"That woman dressed up in boy's clothes and rode like a bat outta hell to find you after you left, Rafe Bodine. And if you don't marry her now, why there's just no—"

"Marry Emma?" His face whitened beneath his bearded face, his eyes rounding, as if he'd never actually considered the idea.

"Well, of course you gotta marry her. You can't go off to California and live in sin. Emma deserves better'n that."

Rafe rubbed his chin and contemplated Loretta's suggestion. Marrying Emma would be a dream come true. He loved her, wanted to make a life with her. After everything they had been through together, he couldn't imagine going on without her. But would his love be enough to sustain them through the difficult months ahead? Would his love for her, and hers for him, shield them from the long arm of the law?

He thought long and hard about his options, but in the end he knew what his answer had to be. "Seems a mite peculiar having a prostitute preach to me about sin," he said finally, smiling.

"That's *former* prostitute, *ex*-Ranger. And someone needs to preach some sense into that thick skull of yours. Lord, save me from fools and Texans. I ain't sure there's a difference."

Rafe stood, a determined look on his face. "There is."

"Where you going now? You just got here. Don't tell me you're planning to go back to that hotel and stay with strangers?"

He shook his head. "I'm planning to go upstairs and propose to Emma, if she'll have me. Then I'm planning to . . ."

"Hell, I know what you're planning to do after that. It

ain't been that long, you know. Don't worry—I'll take charge of them young'ns."

He kissed her cheek. "You're a good woman and a smart one, too, Loretta."

She blushed. "And you ain't as dumb as you look, cowboy. Now get outta here. I got me a wedding to plan."

Emmaline spun around at the sound of the closing door and gasped as she saw Rafe standing there.

"You shouldn't be in here. One of the children might see you." She clutched the towel more firmly in front of her, attempting to cover her nakedness, but her protestation produced only a grin from Rafe.

"They might as well get used to it." He walked toward her, prompting her to take a step backward.

"I know we've been together on the trail, but it's different now. I've got the children's moral upbringing to think about, and—"

A firm tug had the towel falling to the floor, then Rafe's mouth covered hers in masterful persuasion. And for a moment, Emmaline forget all about morals and propriety. But only for a moment. She broke the contact. "Stop that! I can't think clearly when you do that."

"I don't want you to think clearly. And how clearly do you believe I can think with you standing there as naked as a jaybird, with those luscious breasts just begging for a little attention." He grinned as her nipples hardened instantly.

"It's not proper for you to be in here, Rafe." She

reached for the wrapper on the bed, but he grabbed it out of her hands, ignoring her shriek of frustration.

"I want you naked, Emma. I want to make love to you. And I don't want anything between us."

She gazed down at the prominent bulge in his pants and thought that that was going to be next to impossible. "We have to consider the children. What would they think if they knew you were in here making love to me?"

"That I love you?"

Her heart warmed, but she shook her head against the melting sensation. "No. They'd think that I was a fallen woman. You know how impressionable children are at this age. Especially Daniel. What kind of example are you setting for him?"

He wrapped his arms about her and pulled her against his chest. "I'm showing him how a man sets about proposing marriage to the woman he loves."

Her head shot up, and her eyes widened. "Marriage? You want to marry me?"

"Loretta said that we couldn't live in sin if I was to go to California with you. And I'm fixing to go to California with you."

Bells started ringing in Emmaline's head; birds started singing, despite the fact it was nearly the end of December. Wrapping her arms about his neck, she kissed him hard, then burst into tears. She'd been doing that a lot lately. "I'm so happy."

He tipped up her chin and kissed the tears from her cheeks. "Will you marry me, Emmaline St. Joseph?

Because if you don't, life just isn't gonna be worth living." At her stunned silence, he added, "I'd get down on my knees, but I might be tempted to attend to matters other than matrimonial."

Discerning his provocative meaning, she blushed to the roots of her hair. "Rafe Bodine!"

His tone grew serious. "Will you marry me, Emma? It won't be easy. I'll still be wanted by the law. But I love you, and I promise I'll do everything in my power to make you happy."

It took her less than a heartbeat to answer. "Yes." She kissed him full on the mouth. "Yes, yes, yes, yes, yes . . ."

He scooped her up in his arms and headed toward the bed. "Darlin', I'm taking that as a yes."

"I just can't imagine where Loretta is." Emmaline scanned the train station one more time, and the worry lines deepened on her forehead. "I told her to meet us here with the children promptly at ten o'clock. It's nearly five after, and the train leaves in fifteen minutes."

"She'll be here. Quit worrying so. She probably thought we just needed a little more time to ourselves. You know, being *newlywedded* and all." He kissed the tip of her nose, and she blushed.

"Last night was wonderful."

"A wedding night should be special."

And it had been. They'd supped on oysters and champagne in front of a blazing fireplace in the sumptuous suite Rafe had procured for the evening. Loretta had kept the children.

"I can't believe I'm actually married." She glanced down at her left hand, now sporting a lovely gold band on her ring finger, and her heartbeat quickened. In the three days since they'd returned from Wyoming, a wedding had been planned and executed, travel arrangements finalized, and now they were finally ready to leave for California.

"A married woman needs a ring, as does a mother of five children."

She squeezed his hand, and her smile brightened the dreary day. "Oh, Rafe! I can hardly wait to tell the children the news. They're going to be so excited that they can all stay together and live with us. After we formally adopt them, we'll truly be a family. One big happy family. I'm so thrilled."

He kissed her lips, ignoring the outraged looks of two elderly matrons standing nearby. "I want you to be happy. And this is only the beginning, Emma. I know it won't be easy, because of the way things are for me right now, but we'll start a new life. No one knows me in California. And no one will be looking for a married man with children."

She kissed his chin, which was finally void of whiskers, and smiled. "I love you."

A loud commotion and shouts of greeting announced Loretta's arrival with the children. They were marching in a straight line behind the older woman, like chicks following a mother hen; Loretta carted a valise under one arm and Pansy in the other.

"Sorry we're late. Pansy messed her diaper and had to be changed." She cast a censorious look at the child. "*Hmph.* Some flowerpot! I told Miranda not to give her those prunes last night, but . . ."

"I'll take her," Rafe said, not caring to discuss the properties of prunes this early in the morning.

Emmaline glanced down at the woman's luggage. "Did you decide to take a trip, too?"

Loretta nodded, looking awfully pleased with herself. "Yep. I've always had a hankering to see California, and since you were headed in that direction I thought I might as well tag along. Hope that's okay."

Emmaline was so startled, she didn't say anything at first, which caused Loretta's face to cloud with uncertainty. "Of course, if you rather I didn't . . ."

Tears filled Emmaline's eyes. "I didn't think I could be any happier, but now, knowing you're coming with us . . . Well, I'm just bursting I'm so pleased." She threw her arms about the older woman and hugged her.

Loretta sighed with relief. "That's good. Because you were going to have a heck of a time getting rid of me. I've grown so attached to you and these kids. You're family now, and I just can't bear to part company."

"But what of your house and all your belongings?"

"I have a friend who's looking to make a career change." She winked at Rafe. "She's going to rent it and run the boardinghouse for me."

"*All aboard!*" the conductor shouted above the train's shrill whistle.

Loretta held out her arms for Pansy. "I'll take the children and get them settled on the train. We'll wait for you there."

"But their tickets . . ."

"Rafe already gave them to me."

She disappeared before Emmaline could question her further. Rafe wasn't so lucky. She turned to him. "You knew? You knew Loretta was coming with us? You let me cry my eyes out last night thinking I would never see her again, and all the time you knew she was coming with us?"

He had the grace to blush. "We'd better hurry. We don't want to miss the train." He tried to grasp her elbow, but she pulled away, and the two elderly ladies, who'd been listening to the entire exchange, nodded their heads in approval.

Crossing her arms over her chest, her chin tilted mutinously, Emmaline said, "I have a good mind to stay rooted to this spot, Rafe Bodine. I am furious. To think you would keep something so important from me. That is no way to start a marriage. Didn't you hear what the minister, Mr. Kentfield, said about trust and communication?"

"It was a surprise, Emma. And you were surprised, weren't you?"

"Of course I was surprised. It's a wonderful surprise. I'm thrilled she's coming with us."

"Then what's the problem?" If he lived to be a hundred, he'd never understand the workings of the female mind.

She clutched his arm imploringly. "I don't want any secrets between us, Rafe. I want everything from here on out to be in the open. We're married—husband and wife. I want you to promise me that no matter what, you'll always tell me everything."

He arched an eyebrow. "Everything?"

She nodded firmly. "Everything."

"And does this honesty rule apply to you as well?"

"Of course it does. I would never think to . . ." Her cheeks crimsoned, and her hand went to cover her abdomen. "You know?"

"A man doesn't make love to a woman countless times and not notice that her body is changing. When did you plan to tell me that you were carrying my child?"

She bit her lower lip. "I wanted to be sure. And I didn't want you marrying me because you had to. I wanted it to be because you truly wanted to. Because you love me."

"All aboard!"

"I do love you, Emma. And if it takes me the rest of my life, I'm going to prove it to you." He scooped her up in his arms. "If you like, I can make love to you right here in front of God and everybody to prove it." There was a definite challenge in his eyes, and Emmaline knew he meant every word.

Mortified as she noticed the interested onlookers, she wanted to melt into the railway platform. "Put me down, Rafe. People are staring. And it's not very wise to draw attention to yourself."

He kissed her long and hard, until she went limp in his arms, then marched her to the waiting train.

"I love you."

"I know."

"I'm happy about the baby."

"I know."

"You talk too much."

She grinned. "I know. I find that it's an excellent way to get you to kiss me."

It was. And he did.

Please read on for a
preview of
Book II in The Lawmen Trilogy

Dangerous

Coming from
Warner Books
in
February 1998

PROLOGUE

Justiceburg, Texas, Autumn, 1879

Slamming the door to the sheriff's office behind him so hard the windows shook, Texas Ranger Ethan Bodine stepped onto the wooden sidewalk, puffing his cigar with agitation. Staring out at the driving rain, he tried to control his fury with Elmo Scruggs.

The man was a fool to think Ethan's brother Rafe Bodine had shot Bobby Slaughter in cold blood. Ethan had let him know in no uncertain terms what he'd thought of both his misguided opinion and that damned WANTED poster Elmo had printed.

Both Ethan and Rafe had ridden with the Texas Rangers for years, but Rafe had resigned a few months back—against Ethan's wishes—to marry their neighbor Ellie Masters, a lovely young woman they'd known most of their lives. Rafe's wife had been brutally murdered by Hank Slaughter's gang, the ruthless criminals who held Rafe responsible for putting Hank in prison five years before for robbing the bank in Misery, Texas.

1

Now Rafe was on the outlaw trail himself seeking revenge against the four men.

Ethan couldn't blame Rafe for wanting to avenge his wife's murder. He might have been tempted to do the same if he'd been married—a situation not likely to happen in his lifetime. But he also couldn't allow Rafe to take the law into his own hands. The day Rafe decided to go after Hank Slaughter was the day he became an outlaw in the eyes of the law. And it was the same day Ethan had been forced to ride down his brother like a common criminal—the saddest day of his career as a Texas Ranger.

He hadn't taken a full step toward the street when two elderly white-haired ladies accosted him. One was as thin as a rail with skin so parchmentlike he could see tiny veins beneath the surface of her cheeks; the other was plump as a peacock and almost as colorful.

"Mister," they called out in unison, waving frantically to gain his attention.

Drawing to a halt, Ethan touched his hat brim in greeting to the two women, flicked the ash off the end of his cigar, and deposited it in the pocket of his sheepskin jacket.

"Afternoon, ladies. What brings you out on such a dreary day?" The rain was pouring down with no end in sight, but Ethan knew he had to leave anyway before his brother Rafe got too far ahead or some crazy bounty hunter caught up with him.

"Something terrible has happened, sir, and we need your immediate assistance," the plump one with the godawful hat explained. Flowers, bows, and feathers in

2

every imaginable color decorated the crown. Ethan tried to keep a safe distance.

"Isn't that right, Birdy?" the peacock asked.

The other lady twittered, fluttering her thin arms in the air, as if she couldn't quite decide what she should do, before nodding, reminding Ethan of a hummingbird. It wasn't difficult for him to understand why she'd earned such a nickname. Birds of a feather and all that.

The last thing Ethan needed right now was to play knight in shining armor to a couple of elderly damsels in distress.

"I ain't the law in these parts, ladies. Afraid you'll have to speak to Elmo Scruggs if you've got a problem." He started to leave, but the next question stopped him midstride, and he turned back.

"Aren't you the Texas Ranger who's following that murderer?"

"Eunice! Don't be so blunt." Birdy smiled apologetically. "Eunice isn't known for her tact, so you'll have to forgive her."

Ethan didn't intend to remain in town long enough to forgive anyone, but he sure as hell didn't like these ladies calling his brother a murderer. "Whether or not a man's found to be a murderer is decided by a jury, ma'am. But yes, to answer your question, I'm going after him."

"We're the Granville sisters. I'm Eunice, and this is Bernadette. But we call her Birdy, Mister . . ."

"Bodine, ma'am."

"Mr. Bodine, we need your help," Eunice Granville

stated. "Our niece has gone and done something rash and we fear for her life."

"Her life," Birdy parroted, nodding in agreement.

"I'm sorry to hear that, ladies, but you'll have to inform the sheriff. I don't—"

"Wilhemina has gone off to hunt down the man you're looking for, Mr. Bodine. She has become a bounty hunter." Both women stared at each other, wringing their gloved hands nervously.

"What?" Incredulity punctuated his words. "You're joking, right?" A woman bounty hunter? He'd never heard of such a thing.

"It's true," Birdy assured him. We've been experiencing some financial difficulty of late, and well . . ."

". . . and our niece decided to take matters into her own hands," Eunice finished, clutching his arm with surprising strength for such an elderly woman. "Wilhemina's always been a bit impulsive, but she's never done anything quite as drastic as this. You've got to help us, Mr. Bodine. Wilhemina could be in grave danger."

"Of all the harebrained, stupid things I've heard of in my lifetime, this takes the cake." Women didn't have a lick of sense about them as far as he was concerned, and this Wilhemina Granville sounded more empty-headed than most. "How experienced is your niece at tracking?"

Eunice swallowed. "Not very. You see, Wilhemina is a horticulturist by profession. And—"

"A what?"

"She studies plants, things like that," Birdy said. "And she's very good at what she does."

4

"Wilhemina has always been a tad bit headstrong. She gets that from me, I'm afraid," Eunice confessed. "And from our brother, her father, God rest his soul. And when that horrible man at the bank, Mr. Bowers, threatened to foreclose on our home . . ."

Birdy dabbed at her eyes with a frilly lace handkerchief. "Well, I'm sure you can understand why she felt compelled to go after this criminal. The price on his head is awfully appealing." Pointing at the WANTED poster of Rafe now hanging in front of the sheriff's office, which offered a reward of five hundred dollars, dead or alive, she dabbed at her eyes once again, as if the sight of him was just too much to bear.

"What if he tries to kill our Wilhemina?" Eunice clutched Ethan's arm tighter. "She's so young, so full of life. I just couldn't bear it if anything happened to her."

Ethan's voice chilled to arctic proportions, and he extricated himself from her hold. "My brother isn't a murderer."

He heaved a frustrated sigh, for he wanted to put Justiceburg behind him and be on his way to find Rafe. He'd been on his brother's trail for over a week. But he'd been stuck in the two-bit town for days. He'd come here to talk to the prostitute who'd sworn that Rafe had shot Bobby Slaughter down in cold blood. Ethan needed to interrogate Judy DeBerry, Bobby Slaughter's former lover, before he could depart, but the woman hadn't been the least bit cooperative in making herself available to him, and her stubbornness had cost him precious time.

And now it seemed these little old ladies would cause more of a delay.

Both women gaped at Ethan, then turned to stare at the likeness on the poster, noticing for the first time the name printed there. "Why, we didn't notice that he has the same name as you do, Mr. Bodine," Birdy pointed out. How silly of us."

Ethan sighed at the understatement. "Yes, ma'am. Rafe is my younger brother."

The woman's blue eyes brightened, even as they reflected and calculated the possibilities. "Why, that's wonderful, Mr. Bodine! Now you and Wilhemina will have a common goal."

His forehead wrinkled at the woman's convoluted logic. "I'm not following your drift, ma'am."

"You obviously want to find your brother and bring him back safely." Eunice took up where Birdy left off, "before someone else does. So it only stands to reason that since our niece is going after your brother to collect the price on his head, it's in your best interest to find her first."

"Wilhemina's not a crack shot," Birdy interjected, piping up for her sister, "but she's proficient enough with a gun to hit what she aims at. And she'll be aiming at your brother, Mr. Bodine. We're sure you'll want to stop her from hitting her mark."

The two women smiled in complete satisfaction, nodding at one another as if they had just solved their very immense problem.

Ethan frowned, wondering if the two women were touched in the head. Because there was no way in hell that he was going after some errant horticulturist when his brother's life was in jeopardy. And he doubted very much that this Wilhemina Granville could sneak up on Rafe and shoot him anyway. He was a Texas Ranger, after all—ex-Texas Ranger, he amended. It wasn't likely that Rafe would allow some fool woman to get the drop on him.

"Sorry to disappoint you, ladies, but I'm going after my brother and no one else. It's my sworn duty to bring him back to Misery to stand trial, and that's just what I intend to do." Judge Barkley had already issued a writ of habeas corpus giving Ethan the right to bring him back to Misery, though the murder took place in Justiceburg. And he wasn't about to get sidetracked by some mindless female.

"It's doubtful your niece will get very far. She'll probably come home this evening. Women don't like being out in inclement weather. It tends to muss their hair."

Eunice's double chins quivered in indignation. "I think you may have misunderstood us, Mr. Bodine. Just because Wilhemina isn't an experienced tracker doesn't mean to say that she isn't the most stubborn young woman on the face of this earth. Once she sets her mind to doing something she does it. And she's an excellent horse woman. Why, she's won several blue ribbons for her equestrian abilities at the county fair."

"Is that a fact? Well, she'll just have to ride back here on her own then, because I don't have the time to find her. Now, if you ladies will excuse me?" He stepped into the street to where his horse was hitched to the post.

"But, Mr. Bodine," Birdy implored with a shake of her head, "what about our niece? Wilhemina is all we have left in this world. If she were to perish . . ."

Tears rolled down both women's cheeks, and Ethan wished to God he had Wilhemina the horticulturist in his clutches so he could strangle the inconsiderate woman.

What kind of person would ride off and leave two old ladies to fend for themselves?

He mounted the large black stallion. "If I come across your niece in my travels, I'll be sure to let her know that you're worried about her."

"And you'll send her straight home?" Birdy looped her arm through Eunice's, and both women smiled bravely.

"You can be sure of it, ladies."

Tipping his hat, Ethan rode away, wondering how many more strange encounters he would have before finding his brother, and thinking that Rafe had a lot more to atone for than just the alleged murder of Bobby Slaughter.